Readers love
KIM FIELDING

Astounding!

"...if you are looking for another sweet story from the very talented Kim Fielding, this could be just what you need."

—My Fiction Nook

"I loved this book! It was quirky and the characters were interesting and fun... And the ending was so damn perfect! The happiest of happy endings, in my book."

—Reviews by Jessewave

"I absolutely love it when Kim Fielding decides to go on yet another genre freestyling endeavour. I get chills when she does this."

—On Top Down Under

Rattlesnake

"*Rattlesnake* is a fantastic read and… very well written."

—Joyfully Jay

"This was… beautiful. Beautiful in the way that hurts. Beautiful in the way that heals. Beautiful in the way that is imperfect. Beautiful in the way that challenges you, treats you, surprises you, fulfills you."

—Boys in our Books

"Kim Fielding is an amazing writer. She has a keen eye for human behavior, and she manages to find ways… to really dig deep through the layers and expose the person underneath in ways that are unique and sometimes startling."

—The Blogger Girls

By KIM FIELDING

Alaska
Animal Magnetism (Dreamspinner Anthology)
Astounding!
The Border
Brute
Don't Try This at Home (Dreamspinner Anthology)
Grateful
A Great Miracle Happened There
Grown-up
Housekeeping
Love Can't Conquer
Men of Steel (Dreamspinner Anthology)
Motel. Pool.
Night Shift
Pilgrimage
The Pillar
Phoenix
Rattlesnake
Saint Martin's Day
Snow on the Roof (Dreamspinner Anthology)
Speechless • The Gig
Steamed Up (Dreamspinner Anthology)
The Tin Box
Venetian Masks
Violet's Present

Published by DREAMSPINNER PRESS
www.dreamspinnerpress.com

By Kɪм Fɪᴇʟᴅɪɴɢ (ᴄᴏɴᴛ.)

BONES
Good Bones
Buried Bones
The Gig
Bone Dry

GOTHIKA
Stitch (Multiple Author Anthology)
Bones (Multiple Author Anthology)
Claw (Multiple Author Anthology)
Spirit (Multiple Author Anthology)

Published by Dʀᴇᴀᴍsᴘɪɴɴᴇʀ Pʀᴇss
www.dreamspinnerpress.com

LOVE CAN'T CONQUER

KIM FIELDING

Published by
DREAMSPINNER PRESS

5032 Capital Circle SW, Suite 2, PMB# 279, Tallahassee, FL 32305-7886 USA
www.dreamspinnerpress.com

This is a work of fiction. Names, characters, places, and incidents either are the product of author imagination or are used fictitiously, and any resemblance to actual persons, living or dead, business establishments, events, or locales is entirely coincidental.

Love Can't Conquer
© 2016 Kim Fielding.

Cover Art
© 2016 Brooke Albrecht.
www.brookealbrechtstudio.com
Cover content is for illustrative purposes only and any person depicted on the cover is a model.

ISBN: 978-1-63477-320-1
Digital ISBN: 978-1-63477-321-8
Library of Congress Control Number: 2016901599
Published June 2016
v. 1.0

Printed in the United States of America
∞
This paper meets the requirements of
ANSI/NISO Z39.48-1992 (Permanence of Paper).

PROLOGUE

JEREMY COX first heard the news about Keith Moore at the Sav-Rite.

Mama had sent Jeremy to fetch some milk and cigarettes, and he took his time along the way, scuffing his tennis shoes over the dusty asphalt and listening to the cicadas shrill. He had his T-shirt balled in his hand, the heat baked him like a biscuit, and the sun turned his hair a shade paler as it birthed another freckle or two on his bare shoulders.

When he was halfway to the store, a car inched up behind him. He stepped onto the dry grass of the shoulder, but the car kept pace until he looked up.

"Hey, Germy!" called a familiar voice from the driver's seat of the beat-up Buick. It was Troy Baker with his usual crew, and Jeremy anticipated the taunts that followed: "Germy Cox, ugly as rocks. Cox-sucker. Pansyass. Faggot!" The last one was accompanied by a tossed can that bounced off Jeremy's shoulder and dribbled its final drops of warm beer onto his arm. Finally Troy sped away, trailing mocking shouts and leaving Jeremy with lungs full of exhaust.

Jeremy had hoped the torture would end when Troy and his friends graduated in May. But they'd all stuck around Bailey Springs, Kansas—Troy working at the gas station and the rest staying on their family farms—and they hadn't yet lost interest in tormenting Jeremy. He realized that the only way out would be graduation and escaping town. *Three more years. Just three more years.* It sounded like forever.

Inside the Sav-Rite, he didn't pay much attention to the little cluster of adults at the checkout. He walked back to the coolers, where he snagged a carton of milk and a glass bottle of Coke, which he'd drink on the way home. But when he went to ask for Mama's Virginia Slims, he overheard the store manager.

"...as if the Moores need any more heartache in their life," Mr. Stoltz was saying.

Mrs. Peasley nodded. "The Lord knows those poor folks have been through so much already." Her purchases lay on the counter in front of her, not yet rung up. Looked as if she was getting ready to make coffee cake for the Wednesday card game at her house. Jeremy's grandmother went every week and always came home complaining that Mildred Peasley couldn't bake worth a darn.

"Are you sure he meant to kill himself?" asked Betty Ostermeyer, reaching for the bag of flour. She'd graduated from Bailey Springs High just a couple of years before. Her husband had run off and left her while she was still pregnant with their little girl, so now Betty kept the toddler home with her mother during the day while she rang up groceries at the Sav-Rite. "Maybe he just wanted to go for a swim. It's been hot."

Mrs. Peasley clucked her tongue. "Not even the Moore boy would be foolish enough to jump from the Memorial Bridge just for a swim. It's too high, too dangerous."

Jeremy's heart was beating so fast he was certain they must hear it, but none of them even glanced his way. The carton and bottle felt heavy in his grip.

"That boy's a delinquent, but he's not stupid," Mr. Stoltz said. "He'd know better than that."

Mrs. Peasley nodded and leaned forward, as if intending to share a secret. But she didn't lower her voice. "And anyway, *I* heard he tied a rope around his neck before he jumped! But the rope broke."

Jeremy must have asked for the cigarettes and paid, although he didn't remember doing so. He was dizzy, his stomach roiling like it had at the county fair when he rode the Fire Ball after eating three corn dogs and a cotton candy. Somewhere between the Sav-Rite and home, Jeremy upchucked into a clump of scraggly weeds. The bile stung his throat, and the hot sun burned the back of his neck.

Eventually he stood, wiped his mouth on his forearm, and continued to his house. He didn't notice the little bungalows as he passed, each with sunflowers and hollyhocks nodding in the yard, some with Big Wheels or chalked hopscotch squares on the walkways.

What he saw was Keith Moore, clothes too baggy on his tall, lean body, dark hair hanging in his face, legs constantly jiggling as he sat. Keith was two grades ahead of him, but they'd shared math and biology classes because Keith had flunked them the previous year and Jeremy had been allowed to skip ahead. Few of their classmates spoke to either of them—Jeremy because he was a freshman and Pansyass Germy Cox, Keith because he was scary. But sometimes Keith would look at Jeremy, and while he never quite smiled, one corner of his mouth would lift a little. If Jeremy blushed, which he usually did, Keith's hazel eyes would sparkle for a moment. He made Jeremy feel funny in a way that both exhilarated and terrified him.

Only now Keith had jumped off the Memorial Bridge.

The rest of the story came to Jeremy in bits and pieces during the following days. His father mentioned it over dinner before Mama glanced significantly at Jeremy and changed the subject. A couple of junior high kids whispered about it loudly in the public library. Jeremy's best friend, Lisa, called to tell him what she'd heard from her older sister. Some of the details were contradictory.

By the time school started two weeks later, Jeremy had the truth, or at least as close as he was going to get. Keith Moore had slipped out of his parents' rambling Victorian one night and walked the mile and a half to the river. He'd crossed to the middle of the bridge, climbed over the concrete railing, and leaped into the dark water far below. He hadn't used a rope; police found one nearby, but it likely had nothing to do with him. Just after dawn, a fisherman had discovered Keith far downstream, caught on a sandbar. Broken and unconscious, but alive.

Nobody in Bailey Springs saw Keith Moore again. Some said he ran away after being released from the hospital, while others insisted that he'd eventually died of his injuries. The most persistent rumor was that he'd been locked up in a loony bin somewhere out of state. Dr. Moore continued to treat his patients, and Mrs. Moore continued to reign over the garden club, the women's club, and the PTA. Neither of them spoke about their son.

Over the next three years, Jeremy thought about him now and then. He wondered if Keith would still be the taller one now that Jeremy had finally had his growth spurt. He remembered the crooked hint of a grin and the way it made Keith look beautiful instead of menacing. And when several make-out sessions—first with Jenny Novak and later with Pam Archer—failed to inspire him, Jeremy grudgingly admitted to himself why Keith's scrutiny had made him blush.

And finally Jeremy was free. He got a scholarship to a small private college in Oregon. Learned to love misty gray skies, the scent of Douglas firs, the sight of a snow-covered mountain on a clear day. He hardly ever thought about Kansas. And almost never remembered a boy named Keith Moore.

CHAPTER ONE

"I'M NOT doing anything wrong," the kid snarled. Sitting on the concrete step, he tugged his dirty backpack closer, as if it might protect him from the tall, muscular man heading his way. The boy was fourteen, maybe fifteen. Hard to tell. A beanie and a hoodie obscured parts of his thin face, and his oversized green jacket covered what appeared to be a scrawny frame.

Jeremy kept his distance and pitched his voice softly. "Nobody said you were, and I'm not a cop."

The kid raised his eyebrows and gave the badge on Jeremy's chest a pointed look.

"Yeah, I know I'm wearing a uniform. But it's green, not blue. I'm a park ranger."

"Like Yogi?" the kid asked incredulously.

Jeremy chuckled. "No, Yogi was the bear. I think the ranger's name was Smith, if I remember my cartoons correctly."

The kid's scowl softened, but he didn't quite smile. "This is downtown Portland, not Jellystone."

"True. But we *are* in a park." Jeremy gestured at the enormous fountain beside them. The water was turned off for repairs, which meant the park was quieter than usual. And that was good. He didn't want to shout at the boy.

"Whatever. I didn't steal any pic-a-nic baskets."

"Actually, I was going to ask if you want to join me for lunch. There's a great burger place a couple blocks from here."

A heavy layer of distrust fell over the kid's face, and he looked away, his jaw working. His muscles tensed, as if he might bolt, but then he clearly thought better of it. Jeremy would catch him before he hit the sidewalk. "What'll it cost me?" the kid finally asked. He kept his gaze fixed on something in the distance.

Jeremy hoped his expression didn't betray his disgust. "Nothing. We'll stay in the public view, and I'm not going to touch you. You just look like you could use a good meal. And I hate eating alone. C'mon.

They have milkshakes too. The really thick kind that come with extra in the metal cup."

The tip of the kid's tongue darted out for a split second, and Jeremy knew he had him. He remained out of arm's reach while the boy stood, shouldered his pack, and nodded. Then Jeremy led the way to the street. A few passersby glanced at him curiously because of the uniform, but no one seemed to notice the skinny kid walking at his side.

"What's your name? I'm Jeremy."

"Shouldn't you be something more official? Ranger Rick, maybe."

"I'm not a raccoon. And sure, you can call me Ranger Cox if you want. Or even Chief Ranger Cox, if you want to be a hundred percent accurate. But if you're gonna laugh at my name, get it out of your system now."

The kid snorted a loud laugh. "Cox? Really?"

"Yep. A surname that has amused countless adolescent males for generations. At least my parents didn't name me Richard."

The boy puzzled over this as they crossed the street, then hooted with laughter. "Yeah, Dick Cox would be really awful. I'm Toad."

Jeremy shot him a quick look, and the kid shrugged. "'S what they call me."

"Why? You're not warty."

"Dunno. It's just a name."

"It's a pretty good one. I like toads. *Anaxyrus boreas*, for instance. Handsome fellows, and they can live in lots of different environments. They make a cute little peeping sound. Their skin secretes a mild toxin, so some predators avoid them. Populations are dropping, though, which is a worry. Road traffic and wetlands decline are probably to blame."

"That's... a lot of toad factoids."

Jeremy grinned and tapped his badge. "Ranger, remember?"

By then they'd reached Perry's Good Eats. Jeremy held the door open for Toad and followed him inside. About three-quarters of the tables were taken, with businesspeople and college kids occupying the orange vinyl seats. Smells of frying food hung thick in the air, loud conversations bounced against one another, and white-apron-clad waitstaff scurried around. Perry's served above-average diner food, but it wasn't too fancy for scruffy homeless youths.

"Hey, Chief," called the hostess from behind the counter. "Sit wherever. Friday specials are on the board."

Jeremy waved his thanks and took Toad to a booth in the corner. "Order whatever you want," Jeremy said as they sat down. He handed Toad one of the laminated menus tucked behind the napkin dispenser. Surrounded by so many people, Toad seemed more subdued; he ducked his head and studied the menu.

Their waiter was a heavily tattooed guy in his twenties who didn't bat an eye at Toad's somewhat unkempt state. He'd seen Jeremy come in with worse. He took their orders, winked at Jeremy, and hurried away.

"I'm gonna wash up," Toad mumbled. He scooted out of the seat and hurried to the bathroom, taking his backpack. Jeremy made an automatic assessment: the kid had been on the streets long enough to distrust everyone and to learn never to abandon his few possessions, but not so long that he'd forgotten basic hygiene.

Toad returned a few minutes later with his face rosy from scrubbing. After sitting, he asked, "So, um, what does a park ranger do?"

"Lots of things. Share information with visitors. Enforce rules. Give people a hand if they need it. We do a lot of educational programs. Work with the foresters and grounds crews and folks like that."

"It's weird."

"I like it. I get to help people and work outdoors. And there's a lot of variety—no two days are the same."

As Toad mulled that over, their waiter arrived. Jeremy cradled the warm coffee mug and watched Toad's eyes widen slightly at the mound of whipped cream and the bright cherry crowning his chocolate shake. He slurped fruitlessly at the straw before shrugging and digging in with a long spoon. He looked almost like a little kid, which made Jeremy smile. *Not lost. Not yet.*

Their burgers arrived promptly, each with a towering pile of fries. Jeremy was going to have to run extra miles the next day; his body couldn't just absorb endless calories as it had when he was younger. Toad, however, had no such qualms. He attacked his food like a starving wolf.

"You look sorta like a cop," he said with his mouth full. "Tough."

"I was one for a while. Decided it wasn't my thing."

"Do you carry a gun and shit?"

"Nope. I'm not a sworn officer anymore. If someone needs to be shot, I call in the bigwigs."

Toad frowned and popped a fry into his mouth. "Cops are assholes."

"Some of 'em, sure. But the world is filled with assholes, you know? I'd rather pay attention to the good guys."

"Yeah, right," Toad said. He took a long pull from his shake, which had melted enough for the straw.

Now came the tricky part. But Toad looked comfortable, and he hadn't completely demolished his lunch yet. Maybe he wouldn't run, as long as Jeremy was careful.

"Where's your family?" he asked softly.

Toad's eyes turned hard and his lips thinned. "Don't have one."

"You just dropped out of the sky—*plop*—right into my park?"

Instead of answering, Toad glared, then took a vicious bite of his burger. Jeremy sipped his coffee and remained silent. Either Toad would open up to him a little or he wouldn't; pushing rarely helped.

When the answer finally came, Toad spoke barely above a whisper. "They kicked me out, okay? Didn't want a faggot for a son." He lifted his chin and raised his voice a bit. "Doesn't matter. I don't need 'em."

Jeremy had anticipated this story, or one fairly like it. He'd heard it plenty of times before. Nonetheless, he tasted bile in the back of his throat and felt his gut clench. He swigged his coffee before responding.

"You're right," he said with a sigh. "You don't need them. But you need someone. Someone who'll care about you the way you deserve."

"Like you?" Toad spat.

"Not me. I told you—I'm not going to touch you. But I can help you out. It's my job, right?"

"If this is the part where you give me that 'it gets better' bullshit, you can save yourself the effort. You don't know what the fuck it's like."

"I kind of do," Jeremy said mildly.

Toad narrowed his eyes. "How?"

"I'm gay. My parents didn't kick me out, but that's only because I didn't have the balls to come out to them until years later. They've had fifteen years to get used to the idea, and they still won't talk about it."

"See? It doesn't get better." Toad pushed his empty plate aside and crossed his arms.

"Yeah it does. 'Cause I have plenty of friends who don't give a shit that I'm gay. I'm out at work and nobody cares. I have a great home, a cool car, all sorts of stuff. I wish I got along better with my parents, but in the end, it's more their loss than mine. And I'm happy. When I was your age, I thought that was impossible, but here I am."

Toad toyed with his straw, trying to draw the last of the melted shake out of his glass. "What about a boyfriend?"

This part was harder—for Jeremy, at least. "I'm single right now. But I've been serious about a couple of men in the past, and they were serious about me. Neither of them worked out in the end, but we loved each other. And I'm hoping that one of these days I'll find someone to love for good." Hoping, but not overly optimistic. Maybe he was one of those people who were destined to remain unpartnered. He was okay with that. Mostly. At least this way he could arrange his life however he wanted.

The waiter came by. "Anything else, gentlemen?"

"You want some pie, Toad? The pie here is awesome."

Toad considered a moment before shaking his head. "Nah, I'm good."

"Enjoy your afternoon," the waiter said as he handed Jeremy the check and then winked again before walking away. Yeah, he was cute, but also way too young. Jeremy had learned the hard way that guys a decade and a half his junior might be fun for a quick hookup, but Jeremy was tired of quick hookups.

Toad gathered the straps of his backpack. "Uh, thanks for lunch, man. I gotta go."

"You're welcome. Thanks for the company. And we both know there's nowhere you have to be. But I can take you somewhere."

Narrowed eyes again. "Where?"

"It's called Patty's Place. It's over on the east side, in a real nice neighborhood. It's safe. They'll give you somewhere to stay, feed you, help you find a job or finish school. They're good people, Toad."

The brief flash of raw hope on Toad's face broke Jeremy's heart—but not as badly as the bleak expression that followed it. "They'll throw me out on my ass if they find out I'm queer."

"Nope. Patty's Place is specifically for kids who are LGBT. Q. Um, P. And whatever the other letters are."

Toad chewed on his lip so viciously that Jeremy was surprised it didn't bleed. Fuck. Toad should be worrying about which video game to play next or an upcoming chemistry test, not this kind of stuff. It wasn't fair that he didn't get to be a kid. "What if I hate it?" he asked quietly.

"Nobody there is going to tie you down. If you hate it, you can book. But I think you should give it a try. I've driven a lot of kids over there, and I've never known one who regretted it." Although not all of them had made it. Some of them ran, some got strung out on drugs. A couple of them found their burdens too heavy and their hope too thin and ended their lives. But at least they'd had a better chance than the streets would have provided. At least for a while, somebody cared for them.

Toad didn't say anything. He just nodded.

BY THE time Jeremy delivered Toad into the hands of the staff at Patty's Place, the streetlights had come on. He called to check in with a few of his rangers, and he stopped off at Laurelhurst Park for a brief chat with representatives of a neighborhood group. They were worried about a string of recent burglaries and believed the culprit was hanging out in the park. He promised to have his rangers keep an eye out, which seemed to satisfy the group, at least for now.

He had some reports to complete and a few spreadsheets to review, but he just wasn't in the mood. Although he was always glad to help kids like Toad, the experience was emotionally draining. What he wanted to do now was work out, have a light dinner, and maybe hang out for a while at the neighborhood coffee place. He didn't think P-Town would have live music tonight, but that was fine. He'd be happy to have other people's conversations wash over him like soothing waves. The paperwork could wait for Monday.

The gym was only a few blocks from home, so he parked the Jeep in his garage and jogged up three flights of stairs to his loft. God, he loved this place. He'd lived here for five years—ever since the train wreck of a breakup with Donny—and although it wasn't likely to feature in any magazine spreads, it was airy and attractive. High ceilings, tall windows to let in as much of Portland's limited sunlight as possible, polished concrete floors, and gleaming stainless countertops. A partial wall shielded his bedroom from the large main living area, and the bathroom was ridiculously enormous. Between the oversized bathtub and huge shower, he could have hosted an aquatic orgy, had he been so inclined. He kept the furnishings comfortable, but few and spare. He didn't like clutter.

The floor below him was office space, which meant no noise on weekends and nobody to complain if he tromped around at night. He shared the underground parking garage with the office staff and with patrons of the spa housed on the first floor. The neighborhood offered him an abundance of restaurants and bars, plus a fancy-schmancy grocery store with prices that would have made Mr. Stoltz from the Sav-Rite stroke out.

It took Jeremy only a few minutes to get ready for the gym, changing from his uniform to sweatpants and a tee and then slipping on a pair of running shoes and his fleece jacket.

He worked out longer than he should have, until his muscles ached in a reminder that he'd passed forty a few years ago. In the gym shower, Jeremy noticed a brunet he'd seen lift well over two hundred pounds. He wasn't as built as Jeremy, but he had a nice ass—round and meaty. Unfortunately Jeremy was too tired to admire it. If the other man paid him any attention, Jeremy didn't notice.

With his short blond hair toweled dry, Jeremy pulled on the clean clothing he'd brought in his gym bag. Just jeans, a white T-shirt, and a comfortable green sweater he'd owned forever. He wasn't exactly a clotheshorse.

By the time he stepped outside, the evening's light mist had coalesced into a steady drizzle. He pulled up the hood on his jacket and smiled, thinking of Toad spending the night in a warm, dry bed. The kid had looked relieved at the welcome he received at Patty's—maybe a little overwhelmed with the friendly new faces, but in a good way. He'd be okay. That thought warmed Jeremy, as did the Thai grilled chicken and noodles he ate for dinner. He considered picking up a few groceries—his cupboards were bare—but shopping felt like too much effort tonight. Instead, he ambled into P-Town Café.

"Regular, Chief?" asked Ptolemy, the gender-fluid barista. Today she wore a low-cut, lacy blouse and striped skirt; the day before he'd been decked out in an approximation of biker gear. Either way, the hair was short and multicolored, and the intellect was sharp as a razor. Ptolemy was midway through a doctorate and was probably capable of taking over the world.

"Yeah. Big."

Ptolemy nodded, rooted behind the counter for an oversized mug, and filled it to the brim. "Here," she said, scooting it across the counter. "Craptastic day, huh?"

"Nothing a little weekend won't cure."

Jeremy took the cup, paid, and found an empty table near a corner. The café was crowded, but not as much as on live music evenings. He liked the heavy scents of coffee and sugar as well as the bright paintings on the walls. The nearest one reminded him of *American Gothic*, only instead of a farm couple, it depicted a handsome shirtless man standing next to a wolf. They both looked happy.

He was still staring up at the artwork when the café's owner pulled out the chair opposite him and sat down. Rhoda was a tall, imposing woman with a prominent chest that reminded Jeremy of a ship's prow. *Bosoms*. That word might have been invented to describe her breasts. Somewhere in the neighborhood of fifty, she wore clothing in bright colors and bold patterns, and she kept her short curly hair dyed an improbable red.

"Ptolemy says you had a rough day," Rhoda said.

"Wasn't really that bad. Picked up a street kid and delivered him to Patty's. I think he'll be all right."

"That sounds pretty fantastic, actually. Most of us don't get to rescue people."

Jeremy lifted his mug in a salute. "Ah, but your coffee is a lifesaver." He slurped greedily.

Rhoda sat back in the chair and lifted her eyebrows. He'd met her midway through the god-awful Donny mess, when her friendly presence was one of his few tethers to normalcy. And he'd sat with her for months when she'd grieved her husband, killed in a car wreck. They knew how to pry the truth from each other.

"I'm tired," he admitted. "Maybe Toad's safe, but tomorrow he'll be replaced by another kid."

"Toad?"

"That's what he said to call him. Anyway, it's not just the kids or the other homeless people. It's… everything." He didn't have words for the hole in the middle of him, the space where something belonged but nothing ever fit.

"So what do you need, Jer? A vacation? You haven't had one in years. A boyfriend? A new hobby?"

He looked down. "Dunno. I think I just need more coffee."

She huffed at him but snatched up the mug and walked away. He let his eyes go unfocused while he listened to the many voices and the *zhoop* of the espresso machine. The noise was like a barrier—to what, he didn't know. Thinking, maybe.

When Rhoda returned with his refill, she looked determined. "I have a plan. Well, a plan for a plan."

"Yeah?"

"Tomorrow night. You and I are going to have dinner at the Bosnian place. We can fill up on chevapi, go out for a few drinks afterward, and *then* we'll get your life in order."

"Sounds like you're asking me on a date," he said, smiling.

"Nah. If it was a date I'd take you somewhere fancier. This is an intervention. You up for it?"

He wasn't optimistic about finding a cure when he had no clue about the disease, but at least he'd have a good meal and good company. "Yeah. Sounds good."

"Perfect. Meet me here at six." She stood and patted his arm. "Maybe you should get together with some of the guys tonight."

"I think I'll just hang here for a while and turn in early."

Rhoda patted him again before leaving to clear some tables.

For a moment Jeremy actually considered her advice—maybe he should call a friend or two. He wasn't really all that close to anyone. He'd had a lot of pals when he'd been with the police bureau, but the mess with Donny had soured most of that. His one remaining cop buddy, Nevin Ng, was a good guy, but he'd been mysteriously busy lately. Jeremy couldn't get too friendly with the other rangers since he was their boss. He spent most of his time working, running, or at the gym, and a good chunk of his free time with his ass parked right where it was now.

Maybe that was his problem. Maybe he should expand his social circle or take up a new hobby. Drums. He'd always thought drummers were cool.

He nursed his coffee until it was too cold to stomach, and then he just sat back, watching the ebb and flow of humanity. His gaze caught for a while on a man at the opposite side of the café, sitting alone with his back to Jeremy. His hair was black, shot through with threads of silver, and it was short enough to reveal a long, vulnerable-looking neck. The man wore a battered leather jacket, and he hunched his shoulders forward over his book. Jeremy wondered what the guy was reading; he certainly looked engrossed.

After Jeremy cracked his jaw on a yawn, he decided he'd had enough Friday. He'd wake up early, have a long run. Do a little grocery shopping. Maybe hit the gym before his not-date with Rhoda. Yeah. That sounded like a decent enough day.

He bussed his own table, earning a grin from Ptolemy, and ventured outside with his gym bag over his shoulder. Light sprinkles fell, causing the damp pavement to reflect the streetlights and neon signs. A bus trundled by, splashing through puddles, and the din from a nearby bar carried out into the street. Sounded like the Trail Blazers were winning. If he'd had a little more energy, he might have ducked in and watched for a while over a beer.

Instead he ambled the three blocks home. Even from the street he could tell that the office workers were gone and the spa was closed; he'd have the building to himself. He could blast his music and watch Internet porn for an hour or two. Take a bath to soak out the kinks from the evening's hard workout. Jack off in his big, comfy bed.

He'd climbed the first flight of stairs and started the second when the smell hit him—the metallic, salty tang of blood and sweat overpowering the stairwell's usual odor of damp concrete. He took the remaining steps two at a time, then turned the corner to the little landing outside his loft.

A man sat slumped against the door. His torn clothing was dark with dirt and blood, and a small red puddle had formed on the tiles beneath him. He raised his head and attempted his patented boyish grin, but he was foiled by the swelling in his face. "Hey, Jer."

Jeremy could manage only a single word: "Donny."

CHAPTER TWO

"REFILLS ARE free."

Qayin Hill looked up from the pages of his book and frowned at the woman in the brightly patterned tunic. "I can pay."

"Doesn't matter. They're still free. Can I get you one?"

His glower faded against the onslaught of her wide smile. "That'd be great. Thanks." He watched her plow through the Friday evening crowd, stopping now and then to lay a hand on a customer's shoulder or greet someone as she sailed by. She must be the owner, he concluded. Her walk had a proprietary set to it.

She returned a moment later with a steaming mug. "I left room for cream," she announced as she set it on the table. "Do you want me to fetch you the creamer?"

By now, his slight offense had shifted to amusement. "I have money *and* I'm capable of walking across the room. I can get my own cream."

"Yeah, but you're snuggled in here with what looks like a good book, and I'm trying to get more steps on my Fitbit. I'll do it." Before he could argue, she was gone again, this time heading to the wooden counter that housed the sugar, cream, stirrers, and other café accoutrements. She snagged a metal pitcher and a couple of packets of sugar, then returned to his table. "Here you go, hon."

"Thanks. Um, I've been here awhile. That doesn't bug you?" All he'd bought was the one cup of coffee, and the place was hopping. Almost all of the tables were occupied.

She laughed as if his question was the funniest thing she'd heard all day. "I'm supposed to be annoyed when a customer finds my shop comfy enough to make himself at home? Darling, if I wanted people to leave quicker, I'd blast annoying music. Dubstep, maybe? My son used to listen to that." She shuddered theatrically.

Qay poured cream into his cup until the liquid almost reached the rim, then dumped in a single packet of sugar. He didn't stir. He liked the flavor better when he didn't; it was layered. "Some places don't like it if you sit too long," he said carefully.

"This isn't one of those places. Plus, I always cultivate patrons who read actual dead-tree books instead of tip-tapping on laptops and phones. It gives my shop a more intellectual air." She grinned at him before taking the cream and gliding away.

His book was a good one—a sort of black comedy set during the gold rush—but he didn't wade back in right away. Instead he took a cautious sip of his coffee and sat back in the comfortable padded chair. He wasn't supposed to be reading the book anyway. He was supposed to be studying for Monday's exam. But who the fuck was he kidding? He wasn't going to pass the fucking class anyway, and he was never going to get his goddamn associate degree. And even if he did get the degree, nobody was going to hire him to do anything but grunt work.

Positive thinking. Don't talk yourself into giving up. Because he knew all too well where that would lead, and it was nowhere good.

Fine. He'd read tonight, work tomorrow, and have all of tomorrow evening and Sunday to make sense of John Stuart Mill.

He opened his book and resumed reading. But a half chapter later, he got that itchy-shoulder-blades feeling of being watched. He hunched his back slightly, trying to ignore the sensation but not succeeding very well. It made him feel like a mouse being eyed by a cat. His leather jacket, which usually felt like a second skin—or perhaps a suit of armor—was too confining; the cheerful din in the café was too loud. Until recently, he probably would have grabbed his book and taken off, but tonight he stayed put. *Grownass man. You won't let anyone hurt you.*

Eventually the sensation eased, and Qay dared to twist his neck around and glance behind him. *Fuck.* The watcher was an enormous guy, tall even when sitting, and rippling with muscle, his pale hair shorn to bristles and his hands dwarfing even his oversized cup. He wore jeans, a plain green sweater, and a jacket, but everything about the way he held himself screamed cop. He was also handsome in a square-jawed way, like a movie superhero. *Captain Caffeine. Here to save the world from weak espresso and underfoamed cappuccinos.*

Well, at least Captain Caffeine wasn't staring at him anymore. The man's gaze shifted aimlessly around the crowd, but Qay sensed that the guy's thoughts were far away. He looked troubled.

Hell, even superheroes got the blues.

QAY'S BASEMENT apartment was dark and damp and always smelled faintly of cat piss, even though he didn't own a cat. The Victorian house perched over his head had seen better decades and looked in danger of collapsing entirely. Qay's larger room held a kitchenette, a scarred table with mismatched chairs, a lumpy couch, and a particleboard entertainment center with an old cathode-ray tube television. The colors were wonky, but the set still worked. The adjoining room had a twin-size mattress and box spring sitting on the floor and an enormous dresser that looked as if it would have been at home in Dracula's castle. In the 1970s, somebody had redone the bathroom, leaving orange vinyl floor tiles, a sparkly Formica countertop, and brass fixtures.

He hadn't lived there long, but already the small rooms were cluttered. Well-thumbed books—paperbacks, mostly—lay everywhere in precarious piles. Little knickknacks, many of them slightly chipped or cracked or otherwise damaged, filled horizontal surfaces. He'd torn photos from magazines and taped them to the walls. Mostly pretty landscapes or cute animals, but there was a liberal sprinkling of nearly naked men from underwear ads.

As always when he first entered, Qay paused to look around and smile a bit. Home sweet home. It was safe and relatively quiet, with bus lines and a laundromat nearby. And he could afford the place, barely. If he didn't mind eating his fair share of ramen. *It's all mine*—as long as he paid the rent on time and remembered to keep the TV volume low.

He hung his leather jacket on the hook next to the door, tossed his book onto the couch, and kicked off his sodden sneakers. He wasn't hungry, he'd finished the book and didn't want to begin another, and the boob tube held little appeal. Although he had to wake up early for work, he wasn't tired either, thanks to the caffeine he'd consumed at P-Town. He felt at loose ends. In the past, that feeling had led him into trouble. God, he didn't want to head down that road again.

He decided he'd be less inclined to head back outside—into Christ knew what predicament—if he had to make the effort to get dressed first. So he stripped off all his clothing and dumped it into the plastic hamper near his bed.

But that left him naked and shivering. Well, there certainly was a way to deal with that issue.

He plodded into the bedroom and lay down on the unmade bed, pulling the blankets up to his waist. The ceiling was low and unevenly textured, with mysterious little lumps and discolorations. Without much effort, he could imagine patterns and pictures, as if they were constellations in the night sky. Or Rorschach tests—but that raised painful associations he pushed away with long practice.

He turned off the bedside light that perched on a plastic milk crate, and he closed his eyes. Then he ran through his mental porn stash. The time in Memphis he'd let two guys pick him up, and the three of them had spent an entire sweaty August weekend in bed, until they were so drained and replete that none of them could move. Or the guy on that California beach who'd led him into the public restroom, dropped his board shorts, and fell to his knees, then jacked himself while apparently attempting to suck Qay's brains out via his dick.

The mental porn stash hadn't been updated lately and contained mostly scenes and images from years past. Not only that, but Qay had ruthlessly censored it, cutting out scenes involving drugs or booze. So, most of them.

Maybe the shortage of decent material was to blame, because Qay found his mind helpfully bringing up images of Captain Caffeine. Pecs straining the cotton of his sweater, big hands curled around his coffee cup, laugh lines at the corners of his pale gray eyes. He probably wore a cape and Spandex under his clothing. Probably had a rumbly voice that rang out when he fought for truth, justice, and fair-trade arabica beans. Probably his biggest problem was whether to work his quads or lats first.

Okay, that last part was unfair. Captain Caffeine had looked genuinely troubled. Qay knew that just because someone was easy on the eyes didn't mean his life was all peachy keen. Every superhero had an evil nemesis or two.

As Qay stroked his hardening cock, he imagined what Captain Caffeine would look like without the fleece and sweater, without that pair of well-worn jeans. His biceps would bulge as he propped himself over Qay, his dick—*oh hell, let's give him nine inches*—would strain and slide against Qay's, and his ass would bunch and flex under Qay's questing hands. Qay thought about the grunting sounds Captain Caffeine would make when he finally thrust into Qay's body, the taste of sweat as Qay licked it off his chest, the musky smell of him filling Qay's little apartment.

Qay's entire body tightened with need, and he moved his hand faster, twisting hard at his peaked nipples with the other. His teeth dug into his lower lip. And then he pictured Captain Caffeine *looking* at him, pale eyes locked with Qay's darker ones and shining with lust and… something more.

Qay came with a muffled sob.

QAY'S JOB was across the river. Getting there required either two buses or one bus plus a sizable hike. Because the buses were running on a weekend schedule today, Qay opted for the walk. A light drizzle started at the halfway point, and by the time he got to work, he was wet and chilled. He spent several minutes standing by the space heater near the front office, waiting to warm up. An apartment closer to work would have been nice, but there wasn't much housing in the industrial zone, and the nearby neighborhoods were out of his price range.

Saturdays were quiet at the window factory. Most of the crew had the day off, leaving just a couple of grunt workers like Qay to clean the equipment and floors, get shipments ready for Monday, and assemble the cardboard packing materials that would protect the completed products. If Qay didn't fuck up, he might eventually move into a more skilled position, measuring, cutting, and glazing windows. Glass finisher wasn't exactly his dream job, but it was a decently high aspiration for a man like him. With it, he'd get a better schedule, and his salary would rise too, which would be nice. Right now he made just a smidge over minimum wage. He had a much greater chance of achieving the job position than getting a goddamn college degree.

"Hill! Move your ass and grab a broom!" Stuart was the shift supervisor, which he seemed to think put him only one step lower than God. He liked to boss people around. That was bad enough, but it especially rankled because he was half Qay's age.

Although Qay would have happily told the little douche bag where to put that broom, he held his tongue because he needed the goddamn job. With one last mournful look at the space heater, he made his way to the supply room, where he collected an armful of cleaning supplies and set to work.

You had to be at least somewhat mindful while cleaning a glass shop, because shards and jagged pebbles bided their time before assailing the unwary. Even with his heavy boots and gloves and the thick safety goggles, Qay had been cut more than once. Today he tried to pay attention as he pushed the broom across the endless concrete floor, but he wasn't very successful. First he imagined all the things he'd like to say to that prick Stuart, and when that got boring, he pondered his upcoming exam and John Stuart Mill. *Over himself, the individual is sovereign.* Yeah, easy for Mill to say.

After he swept the floor, Qay took his fifteen-minute break with the other guys, sitting on plastic chairs just inside the open loading dock and watching the rain fall. "Got a smoke?" asked Barry, addressing the group at large. Nobody did. Sometimes Qay wished he still smoked, but he'd given it up during a stint in a psych ward and never took it up again.

From an open window in the futon factory across the alley, the mournful notes of an acoustic guitar wafted out, slow and bluesy. "How come the weekend crew at the futon place gets live music?" Qay asked.

Barry shrugged. "Probably some kinda hippie-dippy New Age shit to make 'em happier. Hell, they prob'ly sit around on their fancy mattresses smoking weed and making tie-dye during their breaks."

"Or screwing," suggested another man. Rob. Or Rick. Qay could never remember.

Everyone laughed, but Qay's mind drifted to the one place he'd been avoiding all day—memories of last night. Jerking off to fantasies about a muscle-bound cop was stupid and embarrassing. Never mind that the guy was probably straight—and even if he was gay, he'd be way more likely to arrest Qay than fuck him. Not that Qay was currently doing anything illegal, but that hadn't necessarily stood in the way of certain law enforcement personnel in the past. As one police officer had said after cuffing him and while slipping something into Qay's pocket, "Yeah, doesn't really matter if this shit isn't yours. It helps make up for the zillion times you *were* carrying and didn't get caught."

Something else was bothering him too, something that had tickled at the edges of his consciousness the previous evening. It was weird, but something about the big guy was familiar. Sure, Qay had seen men *like* Captain Caffeine before—men who were built, men who had the wary cop look, men who sat in coffee shops with the weight of the world on their shoulders. There had been something specifically recognizable about him, though, and Qay couldn't for the life of him say what.

"Hill! You're back on the clock!" Stuart's strident voice startled Qay from his uneasy thoughts. Qay took a deep breath and hauled himself to his feet.

THE WORKDAY crawled by, interrupted by a brief sack lunch and an even briefer final break. Qay was deeply grateful when Barry gave him a lift downtown to catch a bus home. Usually Qay refused Barry's offers out of pride, but not today. Dinner was—surprise!—ramen noodles, but pan fried with some frozen mixed veggies and some fatty ground beef Qay had stocked up on during a recent sale. He washed the dishes, put them away, and sat down at the table with his textbook and notes.

The small basement noises became oppressive: the upstairs tenants walked around and ran water in the sink, a neighbor's dog barked, Qay's ancient refrigerator hummed. He kept rereading the same sentences and still they didn't make sense. "Fuck this!" he growled, slamming the book shut and shoving it away. Fuck the exam and the class and the entire fucking community college.

Maybe he should just go out. Find a bar. Hook up with someone and screw his brains out. Yeah, that would be... idiotic. He'd only be ten times as miserable in the morning.

Then it occurred to him that he didn't have to stay home and study. He could take his book somewhere else. Like to a café, for example. The owner of P-Town had given every indication that she wouldn't mind if he parked himself there for a few hours to drill utilitarianism into his brain.

Qay threw his school shit into a backpack, shrugged on his leather coat, and headed out into the rain.

CHAPTER THREE

DONNY WAS bleeding all over Jeremy's bathroom. Okay, maybe not *all* over—it was a big space—but red was smeared on the toilet, on the sink, on the floor tiles, and on several towels. Donny sat on the closed toilet, shirtless, his pale skin blooming purple bruises.

"Thanks for not calling 911." He squeezed his eyes shut as Jeremy applied a butterfly bandage to a deep cut over one eyebrow.

"Don't need to call 911. I've got the chief and most of the commanders in my contacts list."

"That's right. I forgot how la-di-da you've become, Chief."

"Shut up." Satisfied that Donny's face wasn't going to peel off, Jeremy took a closer look at the slices on his left forearm. Defensive wounds. The bleeding had stopped, but the flesh gaped. "These need stitches. You need to go to the ER."

Donny attempted to smile, but the facial swelling permitted only a slight stretch of his lips. "You can do it. You're a Boy Scout."

Knowing the futility of arguing with Donny, Jeremy shook his head in resignation and stomped away to gather supplies.

The thing with Donny had been a lavish, explosive mistake, like a Michael Bay movie that lasted six years. They'd met when they worked for the police bureau. Jeremy had been single for some time, and Donny, who claimed to be straight, was in the midst of an ugly divorce. At the time, Jeremy didn't exactly wear a rainbow pin on his uniform, but he didn't take any pains to hide who he was, and most of the people he worked with were quietly aware he was gay. Then he and Donny worked a case together, and what started as friendly colleagues somehow ended up with the two of them in bed, Donny howling like a banshee while Jeremy plowed his ass.

The chemistry between them had been amazing. Mind-blowing. Every time Jeremy came, he was slightly surprised to discover the Earth hadn't actually moved. Formerly hetero Donny took to gay sex like a starving man plonked in front of an all-you-can-eat buffet. Even when they weren't fucking, they had fun together. They went to movies and ball games, took long hikes in the Cascades, spent hours spotting each other at the gym. They moved in together. Too quickly, maybe, but with all good intentions. Jeremy had fallen hard.

But fairly rapidly, Jeremy admitted to himself that Donny drank too much and too often. Donny also tended to stretch regulations at work. They fought about it. A lot. Sometimes Donny denied everything; sometimes he made promises to get treatment—promises he never kept.

Jeremy ended up quitting the bureau rather than let himself be caught between loyalty to his lover and loyalty to his job. Donny resigned soon after, circumventing his inevitable firing.

The arguments got worse. Donny kept promising to clean up his act but then would come home drunk. Finally one afternoon they'd ended up screaming at each other, and Jeremy had come so close to hitting Donny that the fingernails of his clenched fists dug bloody furrows into his palms. He'd stomped out of their shared apartment and gone for a long run, followed by a lengthy heart-to-heart with Rhoda.

He'd come home to find Donny in their bed, fucking some girl he'd picked up at a bar.

Now, Jeremy plunked his supplies onto the edge of the tub. "I'm not a doctor. Not even a medic."

"But you have steady hands and a shitload of first-aid training. C'mon, Jer. Don't make me beg."

Jeremy gritted his teeth, slipped on a pair of latex gloves, and got to work. He gave a small, satisfied grin when Donny winced at the application of antiseptic. "A hospital would numb you up first," Jeremy pointed out as he held the needle in a match flame.

"Just give me some booze and that'll do me fine."

"No."

"Jesus, Jer. You gotta have something around here. Some beer at least. It's medicinal."

For a moment Jeremy wavered. He had a six-pack in the fridge— and a bottle of whiskey and another of rum in a cupboard. But dammit, he'd spent way too long turning the other cheek while Donny trotted out excuses to get wasted. "If you want medicinal, go to the ER."

Donny let out a noisy sigh. "Sadist," he muttered. But then he held remarkably still while Jeremy worked the alcohol-dipped needle in and out of his flesh, tying off the cotton thread after each suture. It wasn't a pretty job. Jeremy's thick fingers weren't well suited to tying delicate knots. But it would probably hold Donny together long enough to heal—albeit with some ugly scars.

Throughout the ordeal, they were both quiet, apart from occasional mumbled expletives. Jeremy wrapped Donny's arm in what was probably too many bandages, then gave a few last swipes of a damp towel at some of the abrasions and dried blood on Donny's face and torso. They looked at each other.

"I fucked up," Donny finally said.

"Figured."

"You're not yelling at me."

A bitter laugh escaped Jeremy. "You're not my boyfriend. Your screwups aren't my problem." He frowned. "Except you showed up at my door. What the hell, Donny?"

Donny couldn't meet his eyes. "I… I needed help from someone I can trust. And the bitch of it is, I don't trust anyone but you."

They hadn't seen each other or spoken in five years. If Donny was telling the truth, his life was even worse than Jeremy had suspected. "You need to get your act together," Jeremy said gruffly. "I don't know who did this to you—"

"You don't want to know. Look. I need to sort of make myself scarce for a while, you know? I'm gonna go stay with my sister. She lives in California."

"I remember." She and Jeremy had met a few times but hadn't much liked each other. He thought she was snooty. And she, well, she was pretty much pissed that her brother's significant other had a dick.

Donny nodded repeatedly and pulled at a frayed thread on the leg of his boxers. "It's kinda late, and I can't really go back to my place. Can I stay here for the night? On the couch," he hastily added. "I'll be out of your hair first thing in the morning, I promise."

"With my clothes on your back and my money in your wallet."

"I'll pay you back."

He wouldn't, and they both knew it. And that wasn't the issue anyway. But if Jeremy was going to turn him away, he should have done it before unlocking his front door. Now he couldn't bring himself to shove Donny back out into the night—and possibly into the hands of whomever attacked him.

"One night. On the couch. Gone before breakfast. And I'm not doing this again, Donny."

Donny closed his eyes for a moment. "Thanks. Thanks, Jer."

Jeremy gave Donny some things to wear since Donny's were ruined. Jeremy was several inches taller than Donny and had always been more muscular, but even so, he was slightly shocked by the way his sweatpants and T-shirt hung on Donny's frame. Whatever Donny had been up to lately, it hadn't been kind to his body. He'd lost a lot of weight and had clearly given up exercising. He looked a lot older than forty.

And speaking of older, Jeremy felt like a hundred—exhausted and just plain weary. He dug bedding out of a closet and tossed it onto the couch. "You can make up your own bed," he growled. Donny nodded and began to unfold the sheets.

Jeremy sighed deeply over the mess in the bathroom—dried blood, dirty towels, discarded wrappers, an open first-aid kit. He cleaned up the worst of it and decided to save the rest for the morning. At least he had tomorrow off.

By the time he retired to his bedroom, the lights in the main room were off, the fridge humming through the quiet. Good. Donny was probably asleep already. He always could drop off almost instantly.

As tired as Jeremy felt, and cozy as his king-size bed was, he tossed and turned for a long time. Even though he didn't want to, he worried about Donny. Had Jeremy done the right thing in not getting the authorities involved? Hell, Jeremy *was* the authorities. But he didn't feel that way tonight. He felt… well, a little lost. Like he really needed someone to pat his shoulder and tell him everything would be okay. He couldn't entirely blame Donny for these feelings, because Jeremy had already been out of sorts before entering his building tonight.

Shit. He probably just needed a decent night's sleep.

HE WAS climbing a tree to rescue a cat, only the cat kept turning into a teenage boy and slipping away from him. The ground was far away and possibly covered in something deadly. Hungry alligators or thousands of knife blades—he wasn't sure which. Then some creature snuck up behind him and started licking his nape, and Jeremy began to fall… and ended with a start in his own bed, thrashing and pushing something away.

"What the fuck?" Jeremy got tangled in the blankets as he struggled off the bed, and he almost knocked over the bedside lamp when he reached to turn it on. He squinted in the sudden bright light.

Donny knelt in the middle of his bed. Naked. Grinning through his swollen face.

"What the fuck?" Jeremy repeated, his voice cracking.

"Your couch isn't all that comfy to sleep on. And you've got this nice bed the size of a football field." Even from several feet away, Jeremy could smell the alcohol on his ex's breath. Donny must have found the cupboard with the booze.

"Get out of my bed."

"Aw, c'mon, Jer. When's the last time you got laid? I'm not saying it's gonna be a thing—I'm still out of here in the morning, like I promised. It's just…. Jesus. Do you remember how good the sex was with us? We used to see *stars*, man. Fucking fireworks. We can do that again. You're single."

Standing in his boxer briefs with a cramp working through his hamstring, Jeremy was cold and hollow. He didn't say another word to Donny. He simply marched into the main room, lay down on the couch, and wrapped himself in a blanket. The couch wasn't quite long enough for him to stretch out his legs, but at least there wasn't room for anyone else.

DONNY WAS subdued in the morning, his facial swelling somewhat reduced but the bruises fully technicolor. He sat quietly on a bar stool while Jeremy brewed coffee. He managed the ghost of a smile when Jeremy passed a steaming mug over the counter. "Thanks." He took a swig and winced. Damned fool burned his tongue every time.

Jeremy poured a splash of milk into his own cup, then added a dash of sugar from the shaker he kept on the counter. He leaned back against the cabinets, cradling the drink in his hands, enjoying the heat and aroma.

"Last night I was—" Donny began.

"Save it. Not in the mood."

"Yeah. Okay." Donny looked down at his bandaged arm. "It's kinda throbbing."

"Infected?"

"Nah. Just… messed up."

Jeremy put down the coffee and padded to the bathroom, which still looked like the aftermath of a disaster. He grabbed a bottle of ibuprofen from under the sink. "Here," he said when he returned to the kitchen, tossing the bottle to Donny.

Donny caught it neatly, even with the stitches and bandage. The lid gave him a little trouble, but he eventually pried it off and shook out a few tablets, which he popped into his mouth. He washed them down with a swallow of coffee, then stared at the bottle as he spoke. "I don't *try* to fuck things up, you know? Shit just sort of happens. It's like I'm cursed."

Jeremy didn't argue with him. "I have about two hundred bucks on me. Will that get you to your sister's?"

"Ought to. Thanks."

Thirty minutes later Donny stood at Jeremy's front door, wearing Jeremy's sweatpants and tee and his favorite pullover hoodie. Donny's front pocket contained most of the contents of Jeremy's wallet as well as the bottle of ibuprofen. "Leaving Portland, that's something I should have done a long time ago. I'm gonna get my act together. I have plans. You'll see."

Jeremy simply nodded. "Good luck, Donny. Be careful."

"Yeah." One more attempt at a cocky grin and Donny was gone, shuffling noisily down the concrete stairs.

A HARD run didn't chase Donny out of Jeremy's mind, nor did a stint at the gym. Aching yet also numb, Jeremy scrubbed the bathroom until every surface gleamed, then continued his cleaning binge throughout the rest of the loft, which wasn't actually dirty. He washed the sheets on his bed and the ones on the couch. He found the bottle of whiskey Donny had gotten into the night before, and he dumped the remaining inch of liquid down the drain. The grocery shopping could be postponed another day.

By five o'clock he knew he wasn't in the mood to go out with Rhoda. He didn't want to just blow her off, though. She didn't deserve that. Besides, she would listen with a sympathetic ear to his recounting of the previous night's drama. Maybe they could just sit at her café and swill coffee.

He changed into his favorite jeans, the ones that fit like a second skin and were worn soft as suede, along with a gray tee and a forest green chamois shirt. Enough to make it look as if he'd made an effort, but warm and comforting against his skin. *Like wearing a security blanket.* He gave a little snort.

He strolled to P-Town through a lull in the drizzle, taking his time about it. He liked the feel of the earth under his feet. He was still surprised sometimes to glance down and see how long his legs were, how well-built his body. Every so often he still felt like that runt of a kid who used to run home and cry over being bullied by Troy Baker and his mouth breather buddies.

Jesus. Troy Baker. Jeremy hadn't thought of him in years. When Jeremy escaped Bailey Springs for the softer air of Oregon, Troy was still there, changing oil and rebuilding engines. By then he'd knocked up some girl and hurried to marry her. Jeremy had no idea what had happened to Troy after that.

Ptolemy called a greeting as soon as Jeremy entered P-Town. "Hey, Chief!" Today he wore a sleeveless black denim shirt and skinny black jeans.

"That look's kind of subdued for you, isn't it?" Jeremy asked when he reached the counter.

"Yeah." Ptolemy sighed heavily. "My dissertation and I had a knock-down-drag-out this morning. I'm going monochrome in protest."

"Well, I hope you two kiss and make up really soon."

"Thanks, Chief." Ptolemy poured one of Jeremy's usual oversized mugs of coffee and slid it across the counter. "I hear you and Rhoda have plans tonight."

"Yeah. I was thinking of chickening out, though."

"Don't. A dose of Rhoda will do you good."

"Maybe." Jeremy gave Ptolemy a little wave before wandering across the shop and settling in his favorite seat near the window. He noticed right away that the guy in the leather jacket had returned, again bent over his table with his back to Jeremy. This time he huddled with a thick paperback, a large hardcover book, and a spiral-bound notebook. He was drumming his pen on the notebook, but Jeremy couldn't tell from this angle whether the guy was deep in thought or spacing out.

"Hey," Rhoda said, appearing in front of Jeremy and interrupting his thoughts. Her quilted dress was bright purple, as were her stockings, and she'd wrapped a lime green scarf around her neck. She plopped herself down, mostly blocking his view of the man with the books, and glared. "Seriously? You're considering backing out of Bosnian food? Burek, my friend. And that amazing bread."

Jeremy smiled at her. "Not to mention the wonderful company."

"So? Why not, then?"

"I just…." He ran fingers through his closely shorn hair, then pounded the heel of his hand against his forehead. "Do you know what I did last night?"

"Not a clue."

"I sewed thirty-five stitches into Donny's arm."

It was hard to surprise Rhoda, but that did the trick. "Donny the asshole ex?"

"The very same."

"Did you slice him up so he needed those stitches?"

Jeremy couldn't tell whether she was worried or hopeful that he might have been responsible for Donny's wounds. "Nah. Someone else did me the favor. I found him at my doorstep last night, beat all to hell."

"Who did it, then?"

"I dunno. I didn't even ask. I mean, knowing him, he probably had people lining up to smack him around."

"And he couldn't go to the hospital to get patched up?"

Jeremy shrugged helplessly.

"Oh, Jer." She shook her head mournfully. "Tell me you just stuck a needle in him and sent him on his way."

"Um… not exactly."

He ended up telling her the entire story, including the part where Donny showed up naked and drunk in his bed and Jeremy ended up sleeping on the couch. "My body's still kind of sore. I need a longer couch."

"You need to kick him back out of your life."

"I did. I mean, he was leaving anyway. He says he's heading to his sister's. I gave him some money and a jacket, and if I'm lucky, he'll stay put in California."

Rhoda was silent a moment, clearly deep in thought. Then she nodded decisively and stood, scraping her chair on the floor. "You're going out tonight, baby boy. But not for Bosnian. I have something else in mind. Let me go make a couple of phone calls."

"But I don't—"

"Pshh!" She held up her hand to silence him. "No arguing. I'll kidnap you if I have to, Jeremy Cox."

He fell back in his chair, groaning, although he was enormously grateful for a friend who fussed over him. "Fine."

She marched away like a general heading into battle. That was when he saw the man in the leather coat, twisted around in his seat, staring at him, mouth hanging open.

CHAPTER FOUR

IF QAY was going to be honest with himself—and he generally was—he was disappointed to arrive at P-Town and discover that Captain Caffeine wasn't there. But the man's absence was probably for the best, because Qay was supposed to be studying, not ogling. And with the help of a generous cup of coffee, he accomplished quite a lot. Knowledge was slowly seeping into his broken old brain, although fuck knew if he'd be able to pour it back onto the page come exam time.

When he heard the conversation taking place behind him, he lost all interest in Mill's thoughts about liberty. What caught his attention first was the man's voice. Pleasantly deep, it carried a hint of the twangy drawl Qay remembered from his childhood. Most of his youthful memories were painful, but sometimes he missed the accent—a unique mix of the Midwest and West with a dash of the South.

As he paid attention to the content of what the man was saying, Qay realized the guy was talking about a visit from his fucked-up ex. That was interesting for two reasons. The speaker was obviously gay, and he'd apparently done the ex a solid, even though—judging by Rhoda's interjections—the ex was a jerk. That made the man sitting behind Qay sound like a true white hat, and it was slightly gratifying to know that Qay wasn't the only person with a shitload of issues. At least nobody was trying to slice and dice him.

At this point in the conversation, Qay was pretty certain who was talking to Rhoda. Who else but Captain Caffeine, right? But Qay couldn't look around to confirm the identity without making his eavesdropping obvious. Then Rhoda called the man by name, and Qay's heart stuttered.

Jeremy Cox?

A detailed memory hit Qay: a kid a couple of years younger than him, tow-haired and slightly pudgy. Quiet. The kid kept his head down and his mouth shut, but every time a teacher called on him, his intelligence was clear—he was light-years smarter than Troy Baker and his gang of morons, who used to torment the boy for sport. That boy's name had been Jeremy Cox. He'd sat in the back row next to Qay, a little island of exiles among the other students, and he used to sneak shy glances. When Qay looked back at him, maybe spared him a rare smile, Jeremy would blush red as a fireplug.

Surely that runt of a boy from Kansas hadn't grown up to become Captain Caffeine, rescuer of past boyfriends and coffeehouse fixture in Portland, Oregon. Yet even back then, his face had the promise of real beauty, once he lost the baby fat and gained some experience. Qay especially remembered gray eyes, each pale iris encircled by a darker rim.

He couldn't help it—he turned around to look.

Just then, Rhoda walked away and left a clear line of sight between Qay and Captain Caf—Jeremy Cox, who stared at him with brows drawn together in a frown. Qay braced himself for an attack that didn't come.

"Do we know each other?" Cox asked. He tilted his head slightly. "Sorry, I kind of suck at names. But you look familiar."

Qay almost told him. But the person Cox thought he knew was long dead, drowned in the Smoky Hill River, and Qay had no intention of resurrecting him. Especially not for Jeremy Cox, who'd grown up into a strong, gorgeous man who worried about douche bag exes and probably spent his spare time rescuing cats and helping little old ladies cross the street.

"I don't think so," Qay lied.

"Are you sure? I work for the park department, if that helps. Name's Jeremy Cox."

Park department? Qay would have bet everything in his wallet he was a cop. "Doesn't ring a bell. I'm Qayin Hill." Then he remembered the way he'd just been staring at Cox. "I sort of overheard you talking about what happened last night."

"Are you twisted out of shape because I'm gay?" A slight threatening note had crept into Cox's voice.

Qay chuckled ruefully as he shook his head. His neck was getting sore from craning around. "Nope. Swing that way myself. I was just thinking that not many people would have put up with that guy like you did."

Cox gave him a long, scrutinizing look, making Qay squirm uncomfortably. Even if Cox didn't figure out who he once had been, he could certainly see who Qay was now: used and timeworn, poor, hunched over schoolbooks in a delusional fugue. And when Cox stood with his coffee cup in hand, Qay was sure he intended to turn away in disgust.

Instead, he walked around to the other side of Qay's table and gestured at the empty seat. "Can I?"

Fuck. Qay nodded dumbly, and Jeremy sat.

Close up, he was even more handsome. He wore his hair very short, but not because it was thinning, and it was only a few shades darker than the flax yellow he'd had as a kid. His face had weathered a bit with time and life, developed a few crags and lines, but he was one of those lucky bastards whom age flattered. He'd probably be handsome when he was ninety. The schoolboy shyness was long gone, of course. Now he stared at Qay with a frank confidence.

"Qayin?" he asked.

"With a Q. It's Cain in Hebrew. Most people call me Qay."

Jeremy smiled at him, wide and toothy. "I'm just boring old Jeremy with the potentially embarrassing last name."

Yeah, Qay remembered that from when they were kids. Another unfortunate boy in their math class was named Sonny Butt. His name came right before Jeremy's in roll call, which meant that by the time the poor teacher got to Brenda Cummings, most of the class would be hooting with laughter.

"You could always change it," Qay suggested.

"Nah. You know that Johnny Cash song 'A Boy Named Sue'? It's kind of like that. Made me tough. Besides, if the worst thing a person can say to me is that I have a funny last name, I think I'm doing pretty well." He snorted. "Anyway, I consider myself lucky. My parents almost named me Richard."

"What's wrong with that?"

"Dick Cox?"

Qay laughed so loudly he startled himself, and when Jeremy joined in, well, it felt too damn good. "It would make a pretty good porn star name," Qay pointed out.

"I'll keep that in mind if I decide on a career change." He cocked his head to get a better angle for reading the title of Qay's books. "Philosophy?"

"Yep. I'm the world's most geriatric student."

"Hey, that's cool! I thought about going to grad school a few years ago, but... I guess life got in the way."

Grad school. Fantastic. "This is just community college."

"It's still really cool. Are you majoring in philosophy?"

"Psychology," Qay mumbled.

"I liked my psych classes. I was a bio major."

"Guess that makes sense for a park department guy."

Jeremy shrugged. "I don't do as much bio as I'd like. The educators do most of the fauna and flora stuff. I'm, um, a ranger."

Ding-ding! So Qay's intuition hadn't been far off after all. "A cop."

Jeremy screwed up his face and looked oddly uncomfortable. "Nonsworn. I do a lot more than law enforcement. And even most of the cop stuff involves things like making sure people pick up after their dogs."

"Do you like your job?" Qay asked, genuinely curious.

A broad smile rewarded him. "I do. I guess there are more important things I could do with my life. Bigger things. But I like to think I make a small difference."

"Well, I'm sure you do better than me. I sweep up at a window factory."

"If you keep people from cutting themselves on glass shards, that's making a difference."

Qay had no idea how eyes the color of fog could be so warm. And seriously, was there any limit to Jeremy's perfection? Maybe he was secretly a serial killer. Or the kind of person who clipped his fingernails in public.

While Qay was considering Jeremy's potential hidden faults, Jeremy stared at him, his mouth scrunched up thoughtfully. "Have you had dinner?" he asked eventually.

"Um, no."

"Rhoda and I—she owns this place—she and I are going to eat. Will you join us?"

Completely taken aback, Qay was momentarily speechless. "Uh...." He swallowed. "I don't want to intrude."

"You're not. And if you don't come, Rhoda is going to try to fix my life. I don't think I'm strong enough for that tonight. I'd appreciate a human shield."

He was either sincere or a fabulous actor.

Qay glanced down at his faded long-sleeved shirt and frayed jeans. "I'm not really dressed for anything but fast food."

Jeremy held out his arms to indicate his own casual attire. "We'll find somewhere we meet the dress code. Please?"

"But... why? Why me?"

For a moment Jeremy said nothing. Then he shrugged. "Dunno. I swear I know you from somewhere. And I could use a distraction to get the Donny disaster out of my mind. You're interesting."

First off, this wasn't a date. And second, Qay was way too old and way too depleted to feel giddy about this. But he couldn't hide a small grin. "If you're sure—"

"Hundred percent positive," Jeremy said, the laugh lines at the corners of his eyes crinkling. "Just give me a few minutes, okay?" He took his coffee cup and walked away.

Qay expected Jeremy to keep on walking right out the door. Maybe the invitation was some kind of weird payback for the bullying he'd endured as a child. Keith had never tormented him—but then he'd never stepped in to back him up either. Jeremy didn't leave the café, however. He walked to the counter and entered into a conversation with Rhoda. It was a pretty lengthy chat, and although Qay couldn't tell what they were saying, they kept glancing his way. Jeremy looked happy, and Rhoda seemed intrigued.

When Jeremy strode back to Qay, his long legs covering ground quickly, he was smiling. "You ready?" he asked.

Qay willed himself to remain chill and took a deep breath. "Sure."

CHAPTER FIVE

HE KNEW Qay from somewhere—Jeremy was sure of it. Jesus, what if Jeremy had arrested him back when he worked with the bureau? That seemed unlikely, however, since Qay was being so friendly. It drove Jeremy a little crazy that he couldn't place him.

Rhoda was surprisingly agreeable to expanding the size of their dinner party, and she suggested a casual Mexican place on Hawthorne. Because the rain had stopped and the distance was only about a half mile, they decided to walk. As they did, Jeremy snuck glances at the man beside him. Qay was tall, almost as tall as him, and broad-shouldered but thin. His straight hair tended to hang in his face until he pushed it away in a habit so deeply ingrained that he probably never noticed it. He had dark hazel eyes, deeply shadowed, and a lush mouth in a slightly narrow face. He wasn't conventionally handsome, yet he had an odd sort of fragile beauty that was unusual in someone his age—which, Jeremy reckoned, was roughly the same as his.

Neither Qay nor Jeremy said much during their walk to the restaurant. Rhoda, though, had plenty to say, most of it concerning the dire parking situation in this part of town and the city's refusal to do anything about it.

"You know what the problem is? Portland lets money-hungry developers tear down houses and build condos in their place, and it doesn't make the builders provide any parking for the people who move in. So instead of one family with a garage, now you have four, maybe six families and nada. Nothing but street parking."

"I think they want people to bike or use buses," Jeremy said, more to keep her going than because he had any real feelings on the matter.

"Well, goody for them. Except the people who move into the condos are too snobby for buses and only bring out their bikes on weekends, when they can wear their cycling clothes that show off their asses. When they go to work or shopping, or when they're schlepping the kids to Cantonese lessons or raku class, these people drive. So they all have cars, and they park the cars on the streets so that customers or visitors have nowhere to go." She turned her head and pointed at Qay. "Where do *you* park?"

He looked embarrassed. "I don't have a car."

"Good. People like you should live in those condos."

"People like me can't afford them."

Rhoda laughed. "Hell, neither can I. I think they're all transplants from California anyway. They get Oregon plates as soon as they move here, but you can tell. Californians."

"I live in a condo and I'm not from California," Jeremy pointed out.

"Yes, but you bought when prices were reasonable and you have a parking garage. Besides, you're still a foreigner."

He knew she was teasing, so he stuck out his tongue. "I may have been born in Kansas, but I've lived here over half my life. I think I'm a naturalized citizen of Portland by now. Where are you from, Qay?"

Qay looked uncomfortable. "Nowhere in particular. I've moved around a lot."

Because Jeremy was looking at Qay, he tripped over an uneven spot in the sidewalk. "Damned tree roots," he muttered as Rhoda and Qay laughed.

Rhoda knew the owner of Diablo Verde, so even though it was Saturday night, they were seated at once. "Interesting," Qay said, craning his head to look around. The décor included local scenes and buildings done in the style of bright Mexican folk art: skeletons dancing on the lawn of the Pittock Mansion, smiling multicolored suns hanging over Mount Hood, giant lizards and winged hearts crossing the Fremont Bridge. It was hard not to be cheerful in this restaurant, especially with the wonderful smells wafting from the open kitchen.

Their waitress had purple hair and several facial piercings. "What can I get you to drink?" she asked.

Rhoda glanced around the table. "Pitcher of margaritas?"

Jeremy was going to agree, but Qay winced. "Um, just water for me, thanks," he said.

Without batting an eye, Rhoda nodded. "How about we compromise with agua fresca? Guava?"

"Sounds good," Qay said, looking relieved. He waited for the waitress to leave, then ducked his head. "I, uh, guess I should tell you, I can't drink. I got a black key tag a few years back."

Jeremy wasn't really surprised. Qay looked like he'd gone more than a few rounds with life and had sometimes barely made it back to his feet before the bell rang. He admired a person who kept on fighting, as Qay clearly had. "No problem," Jeremy said. "And good for you for sticking to it. Donny—that asshole I patched up last night—never could. Never really even tried."

Qay stared at him for a moment and then, having reached some kind of decision, nodded slightly and took off his leather jacket. He hung it on the back of his chair and seemed to relax a bit more, his shoulders loosening and his back growing straighter.

The three of them studied the menu until the waitress returned to give them drinks and take their orders. After that, the conversation had a surprisingly natural flow. Rhoda went on another small tirade, this time against something she saw on *Fox News* while sitting in a doctor's waiting room. Qay asked Jeremy about his job and appeared interested in the answers. But Qay generally sidestepped questions about his own history, so Jeremy stuck to safer subjects like school and food.

By the time Jeremy was halfway through his mole, he'd figured out that Qay was really smart in a self-effacing kind of way, and that he was at least three times more interesting than Jeremy had hoped. He was funny too, although sometimes he hunched his shoulders as if he hadn't intended to let certain words slip out.

And dammit, Jeremy *knew* him. Something about the fall of his black hair streaked with silver, or maybe the way the corner of Qay's mouth would lift in a lopsided grin.

Over a shared plate of mango sopapillas and a second pitcher of agua fresca, Qay sat back in his chair and gave Jeremy a long look. Then he turned to Rhoda. "How come you want to fix his life? Sounds to me like he's doing pretty well."

While Jeremy groaned theatrically, Rhoda grinned from ear to ear. "No, honey. I know he's flashy on the outside, but believe me. He's a fixer-upper."

"Because of, um, that guy?"

Rhoda opened her mouth to answer, but Jeremy beat her to it. "Donny. And I hadn't heard a peep from him in five years. Until last night." He said the last sentence with a heavy sigh.

"So he just shows up all beat to hell, trusting you to put him back together?"

"I'm guessing he had nowhere else to go. Look, here's the thing. Donny is a nice guy." Jeremy held a hand up to silence Rhoda's protest. "He *is*, at his core. He just…. He drinks. A lot. And he won't—or can't, I don't know—do anything about it." That had been the worst of it, really. If Donny had been a through-and-through asshole, Jeremy would have dumped him much sooner and never looked back. But it hurt to see such potential in a person traded away, drop by drop.

Qay nodded knowingly. "We're all nice guys when we're not using, man. But if it's been so long—and he obviously hasn't cleaned up his act—why did you help him out?"

"He didn't have anyone else," Jeremy replied, knowing it sounded lame. Qay probably thought he was a patsy who rolled over for any sad sack who knocked on his door. Jeremy wasn't like that. But Donny, well, he was different. Jeremy had been in love only twice. The first time was back in college, when they were both too young to settle down and had gone their separate ways after graduation. The second time was Donny.

"It's cool that he has you," Qay said after a brief pause. "Most addicts run through their friends pretty fast, and then there's nobody around when shit gets rough. Maybe he'll even dry out this time."

"Maybe. Did you run through your friends?" He knew it was too personal a question to ask someone he'd met only two hours before.

But Qay didn't even flinch. "Never really collected 'em to begin with." He kept his chin up while he said it and looked Jeremy right in the eyes. And dammit, Jeremy was *so* close to placing him.

Rhoda's voice was uncharacteristically soft. "So when shit gets rough for you?"

"I bootstrap it."

Jeremy wasn't close to his parents, but he'd never been completely, absolutely on his own. Mom and Dad did what they could, given their limited worldview. And he'd always had at least a couple of good friends he could rely on—good enough to help him move, listen to his troubles, give him a ride to the airport when he needed one. If he'd ever been desperate for a place to crash or a loan to tide him over until next payday, they'd have done it. He couldn't imagine being all by himself in the great big world.

"You're hella strong," Jeremy said.

To Jeremy's surprise, Qay laughed. "Hella? Really?"

"Two of his rangers are from California," Rhoda said. "They've taught him bad habits. That's what happens when you hang out with Californians."

They finished off the last of the sopapillas, and Jeremy snagged the bill, bringing protests from both of his companions. "Hey, this is my intervention. I ought to pay." And he could afford it. Rhoda could too, but he guessed it might be a stretch for Qay. Besides, Jeremy was the one who'd extended the invitation to begin with.

The waitress took Jeremy's credit card and hurried away, but Qay stared at Jeremy. "I still don't get why you need an intervention. Donny showed up, you gave him a hand, he left, end of story. Right?"

While Jeremy wished the waitress would return quickly so they could leave—and end this discussion—Rhoda leaned toward Qay. "I had tonight planned before the Donny thing. Donny was just the icing on the fucked-up cake."

"Mmm. Fucked-up cake. My favorite." Qay shot her a wink. "I've had more pieces of that than I can remember." And he rubbed his belly, which was almost too lean.

"Jeremy is deep in the abyss of ennui," Rhoda continued, as if Jeremy wasn't sitting right there.

Qay snorted. "Is that worse than the Cliffs of Insanity?"

"Much. Because Westley is not waiting at the top for our Jeremy. Instead, he—"

"Okay, enough with the *Princess Bride* metaphor," Jeremy interrupted. "I'm not Buttercup. And I'm not eating bad cake. I'm just... I don't know. Midlife crisis?"

Rhoda shook her head. "No, honey. That's when you buy a Corvette and date someone far too young for you. Your problem is that you're lonely and a little jaded. You see the same problems day after day at work, no matter how hard you try. And then you come home to an empty apartment. Maybe that would be fine for some people, Jer, but not you. You're the kind of man who needs... connections."

"I have friends," Jeremy said, although he knew that wasn't what she meant. She just raised her eyebrows at him, and he looked down at his napkin, which he'd been methodically tearing into strips. He set it on the table.

Qay had been listening and watching intently. "Do you have a solution for him?" he asked Rhoda. "'Cause that's kind of the point of an intervention."

"Ah. But the first step is admitting you have a problem, right? That's where we are tonight. Fess up, Jeremy."

Squirming under their combined scrutiny, Jeremy stared at a colorful cut-paper banner that hung near the ceiling. "It's not a problem. It's a situation. Nothing I can't handle."

Rhoda huffed at him, and Qay remained silent.

As they walked back toward P-Town, Rhoda changed the subject completely and kept up a running commentary on the condition of the front gardens they passed. She disapproved of anything too formal, and she was also antiweed. When Jeremy pointed out that some weeds were both botanically interesting and potentially useful for food or medicine, she reached up to pat his cheek. "Always rooting for the underdog."

The café was open late on Saturdays, and from the looks of things through the big front windows, it was a hot spot tonight. Ptolemy had help from two other baristas, but still Rhoda said, "I think I'll see if they could use a hand. Thanks for dinner, Jer. Think about what I said. And Qay, I'm really glad you went with us. I hope you come around often." She hugged Jeremy and patted Qay's shoulder before heading inside.

Qay and Jeremy remained outside, Qay gripping the strap of his backpack and shuffling a foot on the sidewalk. "Thanks for inviting me," he said quietly.

"I'm glad I did. But I'm sorry you got subjected to the Pathetic Jeremy Cox Show."

A smile curled the corner of Qay's mouth. "I'm just relieved to learn you're mortal."

Standing there, Jeremy felt not just mortal but big and dumb and clumsy. He scratched his head. "Um, do you think…. After what Rhoda said, you probably think I'm going to chain you up in my closet or something. I promise, I am not as needy as she made me sound. But I'd like to get to know you better. Another dinner, maybe? Without Rhoda and her attempts to fix my head."

Qay didn't immediately refuse or run screaming down the street. Instead, he looked conflicted. Then he squinted at Jeremy. "You want to go on a date with a junkie after what you went through with Donny?"

"I want to go on a date with *you*." It was an honest answer. If Qay was telling the truth, he hadn't used for years. In any case, there was clearly a lot more to him than a history of addiction. Something about the guy made Jeremy's heart beat a little faster, made him want to find a way to peel away the grief and wariness so evident on Qay's face and reveal the man inside.

"A date." Qay gave a small laugh. "I'm not sure I've ever been on one. I sort of skipped that developmental phase." He briefly chewed on a hangnail. "The thing is, I'm not just a junkie. I'm also an ex-con. Nothing earth-shattering. Just got caught holding a couple of times over the years. And that's not the worst of it. I'm crazy too. Spent time in more than one mental hospital. I'm just bad news, Jeremy Cox. You ought to walk away. Fast."

Taking a gamble, Jeremy instead took a step closer to Qay, then another. "Don't want to." He pushed the hair away from Qay's face, leaned in, and brushed their lips together. Not a passionate kiss by any means. It was more of a nibble, a little taste to see if they suited each other. Which maybe they did, because Qay rested a hand on Jeremy's shoulder and squeezed.

Then the kiss was over. Qay dropped his hand, Jeremy took a step back, and they looked at each other solemnly. "Fine," Qay said. "A date. But I pay, all right?"

"Deal," Jeremy said. He wanted to do a celebratory lap around the block but stood his ground. "When? I'm free every evening."

"Saturday. That'll give you a week to change your mind. We can meet here at seven, all right? And if you want to back out, that's cool. I'll understand."

"I won't want to."

Qay didn't look convinced, but he nodded slightly. "Saturday at seven, then."

"Good luck on the test."

That made Qay shoot him a quick, surprised grin. "Thanks, man. I'll need it." He tapped his head. "It's all up here, but getting it back out again onto paper, that's a struggle." He strolled away in the direction opposite Jeremy's loft, his lanky frame throwing shadows in the pools of light from lamps and shops.

Rhoda was watching from inside the café, a mug in one hand. She waved at Jeremy with the other, and he waved back. Thought about going inside but decided not to. A walk, he concluded. That was what he needed.

He'd strolled all the way to the curve near Mt. Tabor when his phone rang. He fished it from his pocket hesitantly, knowing late-night calls were never good news.

"Chief Cox?" said the gruff voice on the other end. "Captain Frankl here."

Jeremy knew Frankl from his time at the bureau, and they'd interacted numerous times since Jeremy joined the park department. They were hardly best buddies, but they got along. "What's up, Captain?"

"I need to see you. Got a body for you to ID."

CHAPTER SIX

IT WASN'T like in movies or TV shows, where some horrified spouse or parent gets dragged into a morgue and a stony-faced guy in scrubs peels back a sheet to reveal a corpse's face. Fact was, few bodies needed identifying to begin with, because even when people dropped dead by their lonesome, they usually had something on them to say who they were. Jeremy had been to the coroner's office a couple of times when he was still with the bureau, but it wasn't really set up for public viewings. He was relieved to be meeting Captain Frankl at a McDonald's this time.

Frankl got there first. That was also good, because if Jeremy had been forced to wait, squirming on the plastic seat and pretending to drink bad coffee, his stomach would have had time to twist into several extra knots. As it was, he already felt as if a Russian gymnastics team was practicing in his gut.

"Sorry to do this to you," Frankl said as soon as Jeremy sat opposite him. Frankl was thin-faced and a few years short of retiring. He had droopy eyes that always looked sad.

Jeremy nodded his gratitude for the sentiment. "I know it's not your favorite part of the job."

"Never gets any better." Frankl sighed noisily, slurped at whatever was in his paper cup, and pulled some photos from a jacket pocket. He set them facedown in front of Jeremy. "This is pretty much a formality anyway. We know who he is. But he didn't have any ID on him, and without any family members nearby...." He shrugged.

During the short drive over, Jeremy had tried to steel himself for this. His first thought when Frankl called had been of Toad, the kid he'd recently pulled off the street. Sure, Toad had seemed happy enough with the welcome he'd received at Patty's Place, but that didn't mean he hadn't rabbited a short time after. Didn't mean he hadn't OD'd or gotten jumped or pulled a psycho trick or just leaped in front of a bus.

But almost immediately—and with a good dose of relief—Jeremy had rejected that notion. Frankl wouldn't call him if Toad showed up dead. Hell, the bureau didn't even know Jeremy had ever met the kid, and the staff at Patty's Place would be a much more logical direction to turn for recognizing a teenaged corpse.

No, Jeremy knew perfectly well whose face he was going to see when he flipped over those photos.

"Where did you find him?" he asked quietly.

"River."

"Shit. How—"

"Take a look first, okay?" Frankl sounded exhausted, but his voice held compassion too.

Jeremy turned over the topmost photo.

Donny looked… bad. But he'd looked that way when he left Jeremy's house with his face swollen and bruised. He didn't look much worse in the picture, although his closed eyes were slightly sunken and the pale sheet under his head didn't do anything for his grayish complexion.

Jeremy stared for a moment or two, remembering when he'd run his fingers through that brown hair, when that mouth had been opened in laughter, when he'd watched those eyelashes flutter in ecstasy. Then Jeremy set the photo on top of the others and pushed them gently back to Frankl. "It's him." He was pleased his voice didn't waver.

Frankl sighed again. "Yeah. One of my guys thought he recognized him. And the jacket he was wearing, it had your name on the label."

Jeremy's favorite pullover looked like a lot of other gray hoodies, so in order to avoid mix-ups at the gym, he'd used a Sharpie to scrawl J. Cox on the inside.

"Were you two still together?" Frankl asked. "I thought I heard—"

"We weren't. We broke up five years ago. I hadn't even talked to him until last night."

Frankl's sad eyes sharpened. "You saw him recently?"

"He showed up at my place last night. He, uh, he was pretty banged up."

"The ME said those wounds were a day or two antemortem," said Frankl thoughtfully. "What happened to him?"

"He didn't tell me, and honestly, I didn't want to know. He was pretty desperate. Refused to go to a hospital. So I patched him up a little and let him crash at my place overnight. I gave him some money and clothes in the morning. He told me he was going to go stay with his sister in California." It was the last statement that made Jeremy's eyes sting and his throat feel thick. He'd never really expected Donny to head south and get his shit together, yet an optimistic corner of his heart *had* hoped exactly that—had wished for Donny to be clean and safe and happy. Now those wishes were dead.

Jeremy closed his eyes and bowed his head. "He was a good man. He fucked up so much, but deep inside...." He couldn't finish the sentence, but he was grateful for Frankl's nonjudgmental silence. No way did Jeremy want to lose his composure in front of a cop in the middle of a fast-food restaurant.

After taking a deep, shuddering breath, Jeremy looked at Frankl. "Willamette or Columbia?" he asked.

"Willamette. Boater found him this afternoon, caught up in some debris near the Fremont Bridge. But shit, Cox. I shouldn't be telling you this. You're the last guy we know of who saw him alive."

Jeremy wanted to weep from pure exhaustion. "Am I a suspect, Captain?"

After a long, steady look, Frankl shook his head. "No. I guess you could be, but.... Look. We all know Donny Matthews had been associating with some real scumbags. We busted Donny a couple of times, you know?"

Jeremy hadn't known that, but he wasn't surprised. "Did he do time?" he asked, worried because prison was not a good place for an ex-cop. Then Jeremy remembered that it didn't matter. Nothing mattered anymore, at least from Donny's point of view.

"Nah," Frankl said, shaking his head. He took another noisy pull of his soft drink. "It was minor shit and nothing stuck. But some of his buddies were into bigger stuff. Jesus. I've been on the job almost thirty years, and when I see what drugs do to people, I still want to weep."

"Yeah." Jeremy *had* wept over it in the privacy of his home. Not just over Donny throwing away their future and his own promise, but over the men and women whose lives lay in wreckage. And especially over the children—the kids like Toad who never had a chance.

But even as Jeremy's throat constricted again, he thought of Qay Hill. Drugs had damaged him too—Jeremy could see that in the tenseness of his shoulders and the lines on his face. But Qay had survived and, as far as Jeremy could tell, was waging a damned hard fight to get somewhere. It was good to remember that not everyone lost that war.

"How did he die?" Jeremy asked quietly.

"Gunshot. What kind of weapons do you own, Cox?"

"None." He wasn't a fan of firearms, and he'd turned in his sidearm when he resigned from the bureau. "Murder or suicide?"

"Unless he figured out how to shoot himself twice in the back and then dump himself in the river, I think murder's a pretty safe conclusion."

In the back. Had Donny been running from someone, or was he taken by surprise? Was he scared, those last minutes of his life, or did death claim him unexpectedly? Had he died quickly?

God, Donny. He'd shared Jeremy's bed for years. At one time Jeremy had known every inch of Donny's body, every sound he made. He'd known that Donny had a secret thing for Disney movies and could never pass a dog without stopping to pet it. He'd known that Donny's father was a macho, abusive asshole.

"Are you going to be okay, Cox?"

Until Frankl asked that question, Jeremy didn't realize he was rubbing his face. He let his hands drop to the tabletop. "Yes. Sorry."

"Don't apologize. You cared for the guy. It's nice that someone cares."

"Shit. His sister. Somebody needs to tell her."

"You?"

Jeremy shook his head. "She hates my guts. Better for it to come from you." He fought the urge to hide his face again. "I don't have contact info for her, but I can give you her name and town. You should be able to track her down easily."

"Okay. That'll work."

Another thought struck Jeremy. "I don't know.... Donny didn't always get along with her very well." And she could be a bitch, but he didn't say that. "If she refuses to make any, um, plans for... for the body...." His voice hitched, and he wished he had a soft drink to wet his throat.

"Burial plans?" Frankl asked.

"Yeah. If she won't make any, will you let me know? I'll take care of it." Because Donny didn't deserve to end up cremated and forgotten.

"Sure."

Wanting very badly to be in his own bed, buried in blankets, Jeremy sat up straight. "Do you need anything more from me, Captain?"

"Not tonight. We'll probably be asking you a lot more questions, especially about last night. But that can wait. Get some sleep, Cox."

"That's my plan."

The gymnastics in Jeremy's stomach had stopped, but a giant chunk of lead had replaced them. It took a huge effort to stand, to shake Frankl's hand, and to drag himself out of the restaurant and to his SUV.

When Jeremy got home, he didn't go straight to bed. He considered searching his cupboards for any alcohol Donny might have missed, but he rejected the idea. Then he thought about calling Rhoda, but the hour had grown late and he didn't want to wake her. He ended up curled on the couch, watching one of the DVDs Donny had abandoned when they broke up. This one was *The Incredibles*, which had always been one of Jeremy's favorites too. He might not have been married with kids, but he empathized with Bob Parr, the superhero dad.

The movie ended, the DVD menu screen hovered, and still Jeremy remained awake.

On Friday, Donny had been alive, had been on this very couch, and now he was dead.

Jeremy shouldn't have let him just walk out the door like that. Someone had beaten Donny, had slashed him with a knife. Jeremy should have taken him to a goddamn hospital. If he had, Donny might very well be in jail right now, but better there than in the county morgue.

Unwanted images of Donny kept flashing through Jeremy's mind. Not the living man, but the corpse. Cold and alone, stretched out on stainless steel in that chilled room in Clackamas, all the secrets of his body exposed to the medical examiner.

What if Jeremy had given in to Donny's drunken advances and fucked him? Would Donny be alive now? Or... shit. Jeremy could have thrown him into the SUV and driven him to California, bitchy sister notwithstanding.

There were a *lot* of things Jeremy could have done. Instead, he'd just stitched him up, given him cash and a jacket, and said good-bye.

Jeremy eventually fell asleep on the couch, the lights and the television still on.

CHAPTER SEVEN

QAY SPENT half of Sunday dithering over whether to study at P-Town. In the end he decided against it. Not because he wouldn't be welcome—he now accepted that Rhoda truly didn't mind if he parked himself in her coffeehouse all day. But if he *did* go there, Jeremy Cox might show up, and then Qay would never be able to concentrate on his books. Even if Jeremy didn't make an appearance, Qay would keep looking for him. So he stayed home, his thoughts often wandering to Jeremy.

It wasn't just that Jeremy was hot, although Jesus *Christ*, he really was. Big and built, with the kind of smile that sent a heart into palpitations, and an easy way of moving that showed he was both powerful and comfortable in his oversized body. But he wasn't a macho asshole. Instead he was unexpectedly sweet, funny, slightly self-effacing, and as willing to listen as he was to speak. When Qay had spit out a good part of the truth—a history of drugs, jail, and mental hospitals—Jeremy had barely blinked. He said he still wanted to go on a goddamn date with Qay, and fuck if he didn't seem sincere.

All in all, Jeremy presented the most appealing package Qay had ever encountered. But as he tried to concentrate on the tyranny of the majority, something else preoccupied him. What kept Qay's mind wandering were memories of Jeremy Cox as a kid.

He'd been short then and slightly pudgy. With the unerring instinct of predators, the school bullies had picked on Jeremy unmercifully. Maybe they'd sensed he was queer even before Jeremy recognized those feelings in himself, or maybe it was enough that he was quiet and smart and shy. In any case, Jeremy had weathered that misery with an attitude of mixed resignation and resolve, which Qay had admired from afar. Nobody bullied Qay, but if they had, Qay would have responded viciously.

The other thing that had struck him about young Jeremy was that he'd never been afraid of Qay—at least not the way the other kids were. When Jeremy looked at him, Qay had never felt like a freak. In fact, Jeremy's fleeting glances and adorable blushes had been Qay's first hint that someone might find him attractive. That realization had helped him through some very dark days.

Qay hadn't set foot in Kansas since his teens. And it had been years since he had thought about Jeremy. Mostly he avoided thinking about Bailey Springs at all.

Shit.

He slammed the textbook shut and stalked to the kitchenette. He wanted a beer, a shot, a pill… something. Instead he poured himself a glass of milk, grabbed a bag of chips, and stomped back to his slightly wobbly kitchen table. Right now Jeremy Cox didn't matter. Bailey Springs didn't matter. Qay's entire miserable, fucked-up history didn't matter. What was important was mainlining enough John Stuart Mill so that when Qay took the exam, he could vomit up enough knowledge to pass the class.

Yeah, because a C or higher in philosophy was going to make his life ever so much better.

HE DIDN'T sleep well Sunday night. For a long time he lay awake in the dark, imagining all the possible ways he might fuck up his life again—starting with failing his test so spectacularly that the community college would permanently ban him from campus. They'd hang signs in the hallways, a big red slash over his face.

Even when exhaustion overtook him, he had unsettling dreams. Nothing clear enough to remember, but he kept waking up sweat-soaked and breathing hard, the blankets twisted into a fabric prison around him.

He got out of bed earlier than usual and, after showering and dressing, gave his textbook a disgusted look and stomped outside into the drizzle. He'd never been a fan of exercise; drugs and poor eating had kept him skinny. Now that he was clean and his diet was better, he still remained lean. His parents had been slim, so maybe it was good genes. It was nice to know he might have inherited at least one good thing from them. He wasn't a gym bunny, but this morning he needed some exercise to clear his head.

He walked without a destination in mind, first down toward the river, then through the light industrial area north of the Ross Island Bridge. Aside from drivers, he didn't see many other people, which was fine with him. He eventually ended up very close to the Marquam

Bridge, where he stared out at the gray water of the Willamette, which looked nothing like the Smoky Hill River.

When he grew tired of the view and his clothes were wet enough to chill him, he trudged back toward home. He didn't stop at his apartment, though. Instead he continued up Belmont, where the cheery front windows of P-Town beckoned him inside. Jeremy wasn't there, and neither was Rhoda, but the smell of coffee was welcome. Qay ordered a large cup and splurged on one of the pastries arrayed attractively in the glass case. He took a seat near a corner, under a painting of a beautiful blond man swimming naked in a pond, and sipped meditatively. He couldn't have explained why, but he felt more at peace here in the coffeehouse than in his own apartment.

He was still lost in thought when Rhoda sat down across from him, startling him slightly. "You look a little damp," she said, cradling a mug of what smelled like herbal tea.

Qay looked down at the floor, where his dripping coat and soaked shoes had formed puddles. "Sorry. Didn't mean to make a mess."

"It's only water, honey. And it's one of the hazards of running a business in Portland, so don't worry about it. But do you want a towel? Can't have you catching pneumonia."

"I'm fine," he said, smiling shyly. He wasn't used to being fussed over; it was kind of nice.

Rhoda tsked disapprovingly and leaned forward. "Did you take your test yet?"

"No. Class is at four."

"Well, I'm sure you'll do fine."

"I'm glad one of us has confidence in me," he said with a small chuckle. And then, because he didn't really want to think about the exam anymore, he changed the subject. "You seem to be here all the time. Owning a coffeehouse must be exhausting."

To his surprise, she laughed. "Exhausting? Darling, I'm living my dream. Don't look at me like that. I'm serious." Still smiling, she flapped a hand at him.

"But...." He looked around. P-Town was a pleasant place to be sure, filled with the lovely smells of coffee and pastries and the friendly burbling of conversations. It was an attractive space too, with cheerily mismatched furniture, whimsical paintings, and warm lighting. But it was still just a café.

"Oh, I know," Rhoda said. "Most people dream of fancy mansions, exotic travel, worldwide fame. But not me. I'm a homebody who prefers eclectic and comfy to expensive, and I'm sure I'd get super bitchy if I had to deal with paparazzi. I work seven days a week in my obscure little corner of the world, and I couldn't be happier."

She looked happy, Qay thought. Even when she'd been railing about new construction and people's front garden choices, she'd clearly been enjoying herself. She wore contentment the way someone might wear a favorite sweater.

"How did this get to be your dream?" he asked.

It must have been the right question, because she beamed and patted his hand. "I used to work one of those soulless corporate jobs. I made decent money, but every moment in the office was miserable. I just counted the minutes until I could go home—and once I got home, I dreaded going back to work. I even hated the clothing I had to wear. Dull and colorless and uninspired." Today she had on a bright dress printed with an assortment of pies. Her hot-pink cardigan matched her stockings, and her gold shoes each sported a large metal strawberry.

"I like the clothes you wear now," Qay said sincerely. They were as bright and quirky as she was.

"Me too. While I toiled away in my dungeon, I fantasized about doing something else entirely. I wanted a business of my own so I could dress however I liked and decorate to my taste. I wanted a place where interesting people would come, stay awhile, and chat. I'm a busybody, Qay, and I adore hearing life stories. So when I came into a little money, I opened P-Town." She sighed, her smile slipping just a little. "The original plan was for my husband to run it with me, but he died less than two years after we opened."

"I'm sorry."

Rhoda shrugged. "Eh. Sometimes the fates fuck with us. But I showed 'em! 'Cause even without Tim, I went on. I get up every morning and I can't wait to get to work. If I walk out of here and get run over by a truck, well, at least I spent the last years of my life doing exactly what I wanted to."

After a moment of thought, Qay nodded. "I get it. Not all dreams have to be glamorous. And I'm glad for yours. I like this place. I feel welcome here."

"And you are, honey! Because that was a part of my vision too. Some of my regulars drive Mercedes, and some of them can barely scrape together enough change for a cup of coffee. You see those two gals over there?" She pointed at a pair of gray-haired ladies seated near the window. "They do cat rescue. They meet here every Monday to strategize where to park their newest bundles of fur. That man over there in the suit is a judge who drives across the river at least twice a week to have his sack lunch here. The blond guy reading the newspaper is a musician. He plays here twice a week. Some of my customers seem truly ordinary, and some, well, they're stranger than you could imagine. But every one of them is interesting, and they all feel at home here. I feel like I spend my days in a large and slightly profitable living room!"

Before he could answer, she stood and grabbed his cup. "Be right back."

He watched as she made her way across the floor, greeting nearly everyone she passed. She paused for a minute or so with the cat ladies, both of whom, Qay now saw, wore sweatshirts printed with pawprint motifs. When Rhoda finally returned, she carried not only his refilled mug, but also a pitcher of cream and a plate containing an oversized cookie. "Salted caramel and brown butter," she announced as she set everything on the table.

"But I—"

"I need your input. A new bakery dropped off a bunch of samples this morning. I can't carry everything, but I'm considering expanding my cookie offerings. They have some interesting flavors. With my waistline, I can't afford to try them all, and both of my on-duty baristas are vegans, so I'm temporarily deputizing you."

"Do I get a badge?" Qay asked.

"Next time." She pushed the plate a little closer to him. "So? Do your job, man!"

He dutifully took a bite and chewed. His eyes widened. He'd spent a good part of his life subsisting on generic brands, dollar-store finds, and stuff from the discount bin, so he was hardly qualified to judge gourmet goodies. But this was *good*. Even if his mother had been the type to bake—which she wasn't—she never would have come up with anything this tasty. He took a second bite. "Amazing," he said after he'd swallowed. "Sell these."

Rhoda nodded. "Good work, deputy." She sipped delicately at her tea.

Qay added cream and sugar to his cup and took a careful sip. He wasn't a connoisseur of coffee either, but hers was excellent. It wasn't even a distant relative of the swill he'd choked down in various institutions over the years.

"What's your dream?" she asked suddenly. He had the impression she'd been working up to that question for some time.

"Mine makes yours seem la-di-da. Stay sober. Stay in my own home. Stay employed."

"Is your class part of that dream?"

He winced and spent a moment pretending the cookie crumbs were fascinating. "The class is... a pipe dream. I mean, even if I pass it, and the next class, and the one after that, and even if I miraculously get an associate degree before I keel over from old age, it's not.... None of it's going to get me anywhere."

"Hmm," she said, pursing her lips. "Well, it'll get you better educated, and that's a good goal in itself."

"Great. So I can be a well-educated janitor."

"Nothing wrong with that, if you're content. But you know what? Sometimes dreams change. They evolve. Maybe yours will."

Qay doubted that. He'd never been a dreamer. It wasn't the sort of thing that was encouraged in the Moore household back in Bailey Springs—or in any of the places where he'd been locked up.

Rhoda tapped her short fingernails on the table. They were painted to match her cardigan and tights. "Nobody has to aim big," she said. "But I think you have to aim *somewhere*, or you end up lost. That's Jeremy's problem right now. He's chasing himself in circles because he doesn't know where else to go."

Since Qay didn't know Jeremy well enough to judge the truth of that, he simply shrugged. "He's smart. He'll find his way."

"I hope so." She gave him a sly grin. "I think he needs to share his ambition with someone else. Some journeys shouldn't be made solo."

Qay shook his head. "Some journeys shouldn't be made with ex-junkie losers."

"We all have our faults, honey." She broke off a piece of his cookie, popped it into her mouth, and after a moment, nodded. "You're right. This one's a winner. Now I have some bills to pay, which is *not* my favorite part of this dream. Good luck with the test." She sailed away with a smile.

His shoes were still slightly damp when he emerged from P-Town, but he was sugared up and well caffeinated, and the anxiety had receded to manageable levels. Apparently the butterflies in his stomach could be charmed with salted caramel. He returned to his apartment for his backpack, then trotted to catch the city bus to campus.

When he'd first visited the community college, he'd felt acutely self-conscious. School had always been a painful place for him even when he was a child, and now he was old enough to have a college-age kid. He'd very nearly run away before entering the registration office. But the staff there had been friendly and nonjudgmental, and his professor— an elderly hippie with a penchant for digressions about politics—was cool. The other students were fine too. None of them treated Qay like he was an outcast, and when the professor assigned group work, the other students listened to what Qay had to say.

If only he could pass today's goddamn test.

He sat in his usual seat near the middle of the room and took out paper and pencils. The professor was old-school, which meant laptops weren't allowed. Just as well for Qay, who hadn't yet saved up enough to buy one and was forced to borrow the school's computers when he had to write papers or use the Internet.

The seat to his left was vacant, but a pretty young woman sat on his right. She was painfully young—probably not yet out of her teens—and the first time she'd been in a group with Qay, she'd addressed him as *sir*. Luckily he'd managed to convince her to switch to a first-name basis, but she still tended to be deferential.

"I am so nervous!" she whispered in a thick Russian accent. "I do not think I understand anything."

"I'm nervous too."

"You! But you know everything."

He snorted. "Hardly."

"You do. When I ask you things, you explain them to me better than the book. Sometimes you explain them better than Professor Reynolds. Not so many big words."

He was going to tell her that knowing wasn't necessarily the problem with him; demonstrating that knowledge on paper was the issue. But the professor cleared his throat loudly and held up a stack of papers. "Are we ready, people? Do you have your thinking caps on? Make sure you answer the questions completely. Don't space out halfway through. And you can take off when you're finished, but keep the moaning and groaning to a minimum."

As Reynolds began to hand out the exams, Qay straightened his back and took several deep breaths. His grip on the pencil was so tight the wood threatened to crack. Reynolds gave him a friendly pat on the shoulder after handing Qay a test, and Qay tried to manage a smile in return. His mind wasn't blank—it was a whirling, dizzying mess, like a tornado spinning through a Walmart. For a terrifying moment, he couldn't even read the printed questions, and when he managed to decipher the first one, he couldn't find a single word with which to answer.

Describe Mill's thoughts on the tyranny of the majority. Give an example of this philosophy at work in modern America. Briefly discuss the potential pitfalls of attempts to contest the collective will.

Oh, who the fuck knew? Reynolds might as well have asked Qay to explain Einstein's theory of relativity in Sanskrit.

The thing was, Qay wasn't stupid. While he was locked up after the jump from the bridge, one of his shrinks had given him an IQ test and pronounced him in the gifted range. Qay's father hadn't believed the results. "If he's so damned brilliant, how come he kept flunking all his classes?"

The shrink had launched into a discussion about anxiety and depression, but Dr. Moore hadn't bought a word of it. "He does it on purpose," he'd insisted as Qay—then still Keith—sat sullenly beside him. "Just like the drugs and the sex and the suicide attempts. He does it to be defiant."

After giving Keith a quick sympathetic look, the psychiatrist had gamely attempted to convince Dr. Moore that Keith was not, in fact, just an insolent prick. It didn't do any good. A few days later, Keith's parents had dragged him to a different facility, this one with a razor-wire perimeter and a staff whose philosophy was in alignment with Dr. Moore's.

Those memories did nothing to settle Qay's mind. What the fuck had he been thinking when he registered for this class? He'd been delusional, that's what. He should check himself in to the nearest psych ward.

But then he recalled sitting in P-Town Café, Rhoda's good coffee close at hand, and Jeremy sitting nearby. If Qay concentrated, he could picture his textbook open on the table in front of him, Mill's muttonchopped, hollow-cheeked face staring up at him. *On Liberty. There is a limit to the legitimate interference of collective opinion with individual independence: and to find that limit, and maintain it against encroachment, is as indispensable to a good condition of human affairs, as protection against political despotism.*

Holy shit. Qay *knew* this. His pencil flew over the paper. He didn't need to rack his brains to come up with an example, because he immediately thought of the Supreme Court's overturning of the Defense of Marriage Act. Sure, maybe a majority of voters had thought that same-sex marriage should be banned, but a majority of the justices concluded that the ban unjustly interfered with people's liberty.

Once Qay passed the hurdle of that first answer, the others came easily. His only problem was writing fast enough to keep up with his racing mind and succinctly enough to have time to complete all the questions. He hoped Reynolds would be able to decipher his scrawl, but Qay had seen some of his classmates' handwriting, and he figured an experienced professor probably had magical powers to read scribbles.

When time was up and Qay handed in his exam, he experienced a surprisingly light heart. He smiled at Reynolds and wished him a good week. And then, still grinning, he hurried out into the rain to catch his bus home.

CHAPTER EIGHT

FOR A day or two after the exam, Qay wandered around feeling a little high, in a totally positive and nonaddict sort of way. He felt... good about himself. Confident. It was weird. He didn't even care when Stuart was his usual dickhead self at work. Qay just gave him an insincere smile and laughed when one of his coworkers mimed something obscene behind Stuart's back.

But Qay's good feeling began to fade as the week wore on and he didn't see Jeremy. Qay went to P-Town nearly every evening to study and unwind from the job, and although the atmosphere was great and Rhoda always chatted happily with him, Jeremy never showed. Qay skipped the coffeehouse on Wednesday because there was live music and crowds, neither of which were conducive to hitting the books. But he was back on Thursday and again on Friday—and Jeremy wasn't.

"You're scowling," Rhoda said, ignoring the Friday-night bustle and settling herself at Qay's table. She had a large brownie, which she broke in half before scooting the dish closer to him. "Here. Have some. The calories won't count for me if I eat off your plate."

"I wasn't aware that it worked that way."

"Oh, it totally does, honey. Just like calories don't count when you eat straight out of the fridge or while you're on vacation." She popped a bite of the treat into her mouth.

"Well, will they count for me since I'm eating off the plate you just gave me?"

"Yep. But that's okay because you could use a few extra pounds. It all evens out, you see. It's the calorie-equalization rule. Haven't you learned anything in college?"

She made him laugh despite his somber mood. "I guess I haven't gotten to that class yet."

At the next table, two men were making goo-goo eyes at each other over their books. One of them was brunet and wearing an eye patch, the other was a regular at P-Town, and the pair of them were disgustingly adorable.

"Scowling again," Rhoda pointed out.

"Sorry."

"You're not sweating another test already, are you?"

"No. I just…. Have you seen Jeremy?"

Now it was Rhoda's turn to frown. "I haven't. And he usually comes in at least a couple of times a week. I texted him Wednesday to ask if he wanted me to save him a seat for the music, but he said he was busy. He didn't say with what."

Qay chewed on his lip, decided the brownie would probably taste better than his own flesh, and took a large bite. "He's avoiding me," he said with his mouth full.

"Bullshit. I'm sure he—"

"Look. I don't have his number. Call him and tell him he's free to cancel for tomorrow, and I won't go psycho on him, and he can come back here and hang with you. You're *his* friend, after all."

Rhoda was good at rolling her eyes. She also did a *pfft* for good measure. "I'm your friend too, and he's not going to cancel. I swear, you are absolutely awash in misplaced pessimism."

"Not misplaced," he muttered.

"You do your homework, Qayin, and eat your brownie, and then go home and get a good night's sleep. I promise Jeremy will be waiting for you tomorrow. With bells on."

JEREMY WAS not wearing bells. He had on a nice pair of jeans that showed off his long, muscular legs, and a pale green sweater that brought out the gray of his eyes. And he was there, waiting at P-Town with a cup of coffee, when Qay walked in Saturday at three minutes to seven. Jeremy's expression was drawn and tired, and Qay was positive he planned to cancel—until Jeremy caught sight of him and his face brightened.

"You made it," Jeremy said, standing as Qay approached the table.

Oddly shy, Qay nodded. "Uh, yeah. You too."

They stood awkwardly. Qay's cheeks were warm, and he felt as if everyone in the café was staring at them. Finally Jeremy chuckled. "Let's see if we can handle this like grown-ups, okay? Because in about five more seconds, Rhoda's going to come over here and intervene."

Qay followed Jeremy's gaze across the room to where Rhoda stood glaring at them, arms akimbo. Her expression broke the tension slightly, and Qay laughed too. "I'd rather she not."

"Me too. So how about dinner? Are you hungry?"

Because Qay's stomach had spent the entire day tying itself in knots, he hadn't eaten a thing. He wasn't sure he'd be able to choke down anything now that the date had officially begun. But he was also fairly positive that an official first date generally involved a meal of some kind, so he smiled gamely. "Yeah. I'm paying, remember. But you choose the place. I, uh, don't really know local restaurants well." Or at all, in fact. His limited finances meant P-Town was the only place he ate besides home and work.

Jeremy rubbed his jaw thoughtfully. "Is there anything you definitely hate?"

"Nope. I'm not really dressed for fine dining, though." He'd worn his nicest clothes—his newest jeans and a white button-down.

"Neither am I. I'm not really a tie-and-suit-coat kind of guy."

Qay didn't own either of those things. He smiled. "So do you have a place in mind?"

"Yeah. We'll have to drive there, though. Is that okay?"

"You'll have to play chauffeur."

"Done."

After Jeremy shrugged into his jacket, they waved at Rhoda and left the café. The rain had stopped but the air was crisp, so they walked quickly. Jeremy's long legs covered a lot of ground. A few blocks from P-Town, Jeremy led them into an underground parking garage that was empty except for a big black SUV, the kind that looked like it belonged to the dictator of some Eastern European country. A sign painted on the wall indicated that the parking spot was reserved.

"Wow, your own private spot," Qay said.

The SUV's lights flashed as Jeremy unlocked it. "I live here. Top floor's mine."

Qay glanced up, as if he could magically see through several layers of building. He was willing to bet that Jeremy's apartment was in an entirely different league than his own musty basement. Hell, *Jeremy* was in an entirely different league. But when Jeremy grinned and held the passenger door open, Qay slipped inside.

The interior of the vehicle was showroom-spotless and smelled of leather and—just a bit—of aftershave. Qay could have sworn he'd lived in apartments with less space. When Jeremy turned the ignition, the radio began to play the Red Hot Chili Peppers, which made Qay smile. He wouldn't have pegged Jeremy as a fan.

Jeremy piloted them smoothly out of the garage and into traffic. It was distracting, being so close to his big body within the relatively intimate confines of a car.

"Have you really never been on a date before?" Jeremy asked, his voice a pleasant low rumble.

"Not exactly. I've had hookups." And not even any of those for years.

"I dated girls back in high school. Went to the prom and everything. A few guys after that. But it's been a while."

Qay wondered which girls he'd dated. By then, Qay himself had been long gone, nothing but old rumors remaining of him in Bailey Springs. "Anyone since what's-his-face? The guy you stitched up?"

They were stopped at a light. Jeremy turned to look at him, his face unexpectedly bleak. "Donny. And no."

For several minutes they remained silent. Eventually Jeremy took the Morrison Bridge on-ramp and passed over the river into downtown. The city lights looked festive, and although Qay knew that people like him—junkies, the homeless, the mentally ill—roamed the streets, he didn't see any. It was as if Jeremy's mere presence was enough to make everything better. Urban improvement personified.

Jeremy entered another parking garage, this one multistoried and absent a specially reserved spot. He had no problem finding a place to berth the SUV, though. Grinning, he grabbed Qay's hand while they strolled down the street. "You're not opposed to a mild PDA?" Jeremy asked.

It took Qay a moment to decipher the acronym. "Isn't that what first dates are for?"

A few blocks later, they cut through a little park. There, in the dark, were some of the people Qay had been expecting: several men and women with shopping carts, shapeless coats, and dogs. "Chief!" called a grizzled man sitting on a bench and smoking a cigarette.

Jeremy brought them to a halt. "Hey, Ramon. How are you feeling?"

"Pretty good, pretty good."

"But it's too cold for you to be outside. You're going to end up in the hospital again. What happened to that bed I found you?"

Ramon shook his head and patted the mutt curled up beside him. "They wouldn't let me keep Princesa, Chief. You know I ain't about to leave her behind."

"That's fine on a dry night, but it'll start raining again soon."

"I'm all good as long as Princesa's with me. I'm all good."

Jeremy huffed. "Let me see if I can find you a place that accepts dogs, okay? If I do, will you stay there?"

"Sure thing, Chief. But you ain't supposed to be working on a Saturday night."

"I'm not. I'm on a date." Jeremy lifted his hand, still clasped with Qay's. It was embarrassing, but Qay didn't let go.

Ramon gave Qay a narrow-eyed look. "You be good to him, you hear? He's good people."

"I will," Qay promised. He figured it was too dark for either man to see his blush.

After exchanging a few brief pleasantries with the other people, Jeremy continued towing Qay down the sidewalk. They emerged from the park and, a short distance later, entered a busy restaurant. Happy-looking people sat in orange vinyl booths, eating large mounds of food and talking loudly enough to maintain a dull roar.

Jeremy paused just inside the door. "It's not very romantic," he said uncertainly, as if the issue hadn't occurred to him before.

"I like it." It smelled good, and Qay preferred it to someplace with tablecloths and soft lighting, where he'd no doubt feel awkward and ignorant.

He was rewarded with Jeremy's blinding smile. "I'm glad. The food's great and the décor is unpretentious."

"You're still a Kansan at heart, aren't you?"

"Jeez. Maybe just a little. Although I'm not in Kansas anymore, Toto."

Once they were seated, they studied the menus. Qay realized that his stomach had settled and everything sounded appealing. He ended up ordering a shepherd's pie, while Jeremy asked for a mac and cheese dish that managed to contain three different kinds of pork products. On a whim, Qay told the waiter he'd like a chocolate milkshake. Jeremy said he wanted the same.

After the waiter left, Qay said, "I haven't had a decent milkshake in years."

"Oh, you'll be happy with this one. Maybe not quite as good as Mr. Hoffman's, but a close second."

Shit. Had Jeremy caught Qay's wince? Qay tried for a steady voice. "Mr. Hoffman?"

"He owned the pharmacy in my hick town. There was a soda fountain there, just like in *It's a Wonderful Life*, because that's the way we rolled in Bailey Springs. And Mr. Hoffman made truly awesome malts and shakes."

That was true. But Mr. Hoffman was also close buddies with Dr. Moore, way back when. He didn't mind filling the dizzying array and volume of prescriptions that the good doctor wrote for Mrs. Moore. Or hanging out with the doctor in the evening and downing a whole lot of booze. And if the doctor's only surviving son happened to make an appearance while Doc Moore was sloshed? Well, Mr. Hoffman didn't bat an eye over a solid backhand or a healthy kick in the ribs. Hell, Mr. Hoffman once helped Dr. Moore set the son's dislocated arm.

"Are you okay?" Jeremy asked, interrupting Qay's dysfunctional train of thought. Qay imagined that his thought trains resembled the one Casey Jones drove in the Grateful Dead song.

"Yeah. Sorry. Just hungry."

Jeremy nodded and leaned back in his seat. Their booth was a big one, but he dwarfed everything, as if he were a model made at a larger gauge than the rest of the world. "So you haven't been in Portland for long?"

"About six months."

"What brought you here?"

"Nothing specific. I'd passed through here a few times, and even though my head was pretty far up my ass back then, I liked the place. Now that I have my shit together—more or less—it seemed like as good a place as any to plant a few roots. How'd you get here?"

"College." The corners of Jeremy's lips lifted into a small smile. "I got a scholarship. And to be honest, it was as far as possible from home. Once I got here, I never left."

The waiter appeared with their drinks. The shakes were too thick to drink with a straw, so Qay dug in with a spoon. "Fuck. That *is* good."

Then, knowing he was treading dangerous ground, he asked, "You weren't happy in Kansas?"

Jeremy snorted loudly. "I was a short, fat nerd who got picked on a lot. And that was long before I was out. My parents.... They're not horrible people or anything. I just think they'd have been a lot happier if Dad hadn't knocked Mom up when they were in college. As for the town itself, it's boring. I think the lack of excitement is partly to blame for the popularity of rumormongering. They have no empathy for anyone who doesn't fit in."

Qay almost told the truth right then. He really did. But then Jeremy licked his spoon, and the sight of his tongue made Qay's belly clench and his mouth snap shut.

"So," Jeremy said brightly. "Let's repress the difficult childhood, shall we? It's time for first-date stuff. Um, what's your favorite movie?"

Repression it was. "*Shawshank Redemption*," Qay said. "*Fargo. Edward Scissorhands.*"

Jeremy licked his spoon thoughtfully. "Acceptable. I prefer *Raising Arizona* to *Fargo*, though."

Their food arrived shortly—it was delicious—and they talked easily about music and television shows and which movie stars they'd totally do, given the chance. Jeremy talked about some of his favorite outdoor spots and hesitantly suggested that maybe sometime they could go on a hike together. Quay tentatively agreed that it sounded like fun. Then he gave Jeremy a play-by-play of his philosophy exam, followed by a tirade against Stuart the asshole manager. Qay didn't know if these were the kinds of things people usually talked about on dates, but he was having fun. Jeremy was too, judging by his laughter. Some of the earlier shadows had left his face.

Considering the amount of food they put away—including pie for dessert—the bill was surprisingly reasonable. Qay felt absurdly proud to pay it. He'd never treated anyone to a good meal before.

They strolled back to the parking garage via a route that bypassed the park but took them past a brightly marqueed theater and an exceedingly raucous bar. Jeremy again held the passenger door for Qay, this time adding a deep bow. But when he climbed into the driver's seat, he didn't start the engine right away. He seemed to be considering something. Finally he turned to Qay, who could barely see him in the darkness of the garage.

"Are you up for a little drive?" Jeremy asked quietly.

"Sure."

Jeremy took them on a roundabout route out of downtown and up into the West Hills. They passed mansions that teetered on stilts, they drove through the expansive Washington Park, and they saw a lot of trees. Qay had never been in the hills before; he'd had no reason to, and transportation was slightly tricky. It was a pretty area. Sometimes the road had gorgeous views of the city lights below them.

He didn't know if Jeremy had a destination in mind or was driving aimlessly. Either was fine with him. But then Jeremy pulled the SUV to the side and cut the engine. "Park's closed to cars this time of night. I suppose I could pull rank and drive us in there anyway, but I don't mind walking."

"After all that food, walking's a good idea."

They sauntered hand in hand up the road until they reached the top of the hill. Most of the summit was covered in grass, although stands of trees ringed the area and a circular pavement with a low stone wall lay near the center. The place appeared to be deserted, maybe due to the chilly night. But as they stood within the stone wall, looking out at the city, Jeremy rested his arm across Qay's shoulder, and Qay didn't feel cold at all.

"Quite a view," Qay observed lamely.

"Nothing like in Kansas, I can tell you that."

Somewhat daringly, Qay leaned against him. Christ, Jeremy was so strong! Touching him, Qay found it easy to pretend that none of his troubles were important, that nothing was real except the very solid man at his side.

"This is nice," Jeremy said after a while. "I like that you're good at being quiet. Shit. That came out weird. What I mean is, you're fun to talk to. But you're the kind of guy who doesn't think every minute needs to be filled with conversation, and that's great."

Qay was unused to praise and had to chew on this for a few moments. "I guess you're easy to be quiet with." Jeremy had such a large presence that words weren't all that necessary.

"My exes didn't think so. Fuck. I probably shouldn't talk about exes on a first date, huh?"

"Go ahead," Qay said with a soft chuckle. "We're both too old to pretend we don't come with baggage. Hell, I have a whole cargo jet full, and mine is a lot uglier than Donny's."

Jeremy tensed against him before sighing heavily. "Donny's dead." He said it so quietly that Qay thought he'd misheard.

"What?" He turned to look at Jeremy, who gazed resolutely at the skyline.

"He's dead. Murdered. They found him floating in the Willamette last weekend."

A body floating in a river. Qay's dinner threatened to make a sudden reappearance. He swallowed hard. "Shit, Jeremy! And here I am, making you drag me all over the city on a date, and—"

Jeremy grabbed Qay's shoulders. "Don't. I *want* to be here with you. Looking forward to it was the only thing that got me through this craptastic week. Tonight's been.... We ate at a diner and took a little drive, and it's been *amazing*." And he bent in for a kiss.

Oh God. Jeremy tasted like chocolate and berries. His lips were soft, and firm hands cradled Qay's skull. He thrust his tongue into Qay's mouth, but he wasn't one of those assholes who needed to prove their manhood by drilling his tonsils. Jeremy had an agile and playful tongue, teasing Qay's tongue and nuzzling his teeth. Qay felt dizzy, as if he were balanced at the top of the world, so he wrapped his arms around Jeremy for balance. And Jeremy must have approved, because even though he didn't break the kiss, he managed a groan from deep in his chest.

Qay had no idea how long Jeremy's dry spell had been, but his own had lasted eons. A beautiful man—a *good* man—touching him, wanting him, was almost more than Qay could bear. He'd expected so little from life, had received so little, but how could he have thought he could survive without human contact? Jeremy's kiss sparked all the synapses that had once responded so eagerly to drugs. Qay's mind *sang*, and as his cock filled and he felt Jeremy's answering hardness pressed against him, Qay very nearly started ripping at their clothes.

But goddammit if the one little bit of his brain that was sane and responsible didn't choose that moment to speak up. *Don't fuck him over*, those bastard cells scolded. *Don't be Donny.*

With his biggest show of willpower since he'd kicked drugs, Qay pulled out of Jeremy's grip. The light was poor, so he squinted to get Jeremy into focus. He saw a muscular, handsome ex-cop with kiss-swollen lips—but he also saw the ghost of a shy little boy and the vulnerability of a man whose lovers had hurt him. And now one of those lovers was dead.

Qay had made a shitload of mistakes in his life. Lying to Jeremy Cox didn't have to be added to that list.

"I have to tell you something," he said.

He heard Jeremy's breath catch. "Nothing good has ever come after that statement," he said.

"I know." Jeremy was going to abandon him here at the top of the West Hills once the words were out. Qay would never be able to go to P-Town again, which meant he'd lose his favorite coffeehouse and Rhoda, who was becoming a friend. All Qay would have would be the memory of a nice dinner, a pretty drive, and one earthshaking kiss.

No, that wasn't true. He'd also have a little more self-respect because he'd know he'd done the right thing. Even if it hurt.

"Are you going to leave me hanging?" Jeremy asked. "Because I'm really a rip-off-the-Band-Aid kind of guy, and I'd rather be hit sooner than later."

Qay backed up a little and bumped into the wall. He wasn't trying to prolong Jeremy's agony. He just couldn't force his mouth to shape the right words.

"I've had Mr. Hoffman's milkshakes," he finally blurted.

Jeremy goggled at him, as well he might. It had possibly been the single most idiotic statement ever uttered by mankind. "What was that?" Jeremy asked slowly, as if he were speaking to a three-year-old who only understood Urdu.

"I'm…. Fuck. I'm from Bailey Falls too. I'm sure you don't remember me, but—"

"Keith Moore."

They stared at each other, equally dumbstruck.

Jeremy recovered first. "You are. You're Keith Moore."

"I was. Haven't been him for a long time."

Stepping back as if he'd seen a ghost—which, in a way, he had—Jeremy shook his head. "You…. The bridge. You died."

"Keith Moore died. Qayin Hill was born." And like all births, it had involved blood and pain.

When Jeremy's expression hardened, Qay's heart broke.

"You knew who I was before we met, and you never said a goddamn word. Was it fun playing me like that?"

"It's not like that," Qay said softly, unable to explain his cowardice or his efforts to deny the connection between the man he was now and the fucked-up kid he'd once been.

With a loud growl, Jeremy whirled around and stomped away. Qay waited for him to march back to the SUV and drive off. Their trip up to the hill had been circuitous, and Qay had no idea how to get home. It looked like he was facing a long walk.

But Jeremy stopped halfway across the paved circle. With his back still turned and his hands fisted at his sides, he called out, "Let's go."

A proud man would have refused. Would have disappeared into the darkness. But Qay had little pride, so he followed several paces behind Jeremy down the hill to the waiting vehicle. Jeremy did not hold the passenger door open for him, but at least he waited until Qay was belted into his seat before pulling away.

The drive back to downtown was a lot faster than the outbound journey. Not a word was exchanged until they were midway across the Morrison Bridge, and then Qay couldn't help himself. "I'm sorry."

Jeremy didn't even grunt in reply.

No parking spaces were free in front of P-Town, so Jeremy stopped about half a block past the café. He kept the engine running and stared resolutely ahead. Qay took off the seat belt, opened the door, and started to climb out. But he paused with one foot on the pavement. "You grew up well, Jeremy. You deserve better than the Donnys and Qays of the world." Then he slid out and shut the door. The SUV pulled away.

As Qay headed toward his apartment, he hoped he had the balls to make it the few blocks home without stopping for a drink.

CHAPTER NINE

JEREMY SPENT a good chunk of Monday in meetings with people from various city bureaus: Development Services, Planning and Sustainability, Risk Management, and of course Parks and Recreation. At issue was a developer that wanted to tear down a bunch of fairly decrepit old houses and defunct businesses in the North Macadam area to build high-density housing with extensive communal outdoor spaces. Almost everyone agreed that the project was a good idea in general, but contention existed over who should manage those open areas. Some of the parties thought the property should be held and controlled by the eventual homeowners' association, while others wanted at least some of the space to be deeded to the city for parkland. Jeremy had no opinion on the matter, but since he and his rangers were bound to get involved to some degree whatever the outcome, he got roped into the meetings.

He fucking hated meetings.

But even as lawyers and other people in suits droned on, as PowerPoints were shown, as sheaves of paper were exchanged, and as gallons of coffee were consumed, Jeremy reflected that this was one of the best days he'd had in over a week.

The days following Donny's murder had been nothing short of miserable. What felt like half the police bureau had wanted to question him—the same dull interrogation, over and over again. They'd gone through his apartment twice in search of evidence. Not because he was a suspect; Jeremy was certain nobody believed he had anything to do with Donny's death. But the detectives had a faint hope that Donny might have left something behind that would solve the case. As it turned out, all he'd left were empty booze bottles, ruined clothes, and used medical supplies.

Worse than the police business, though, were the arrangements for Donny's remains. His bitch of a sister refused to have anything to do with the planning, even though it was Frankl who spoke with her and not Jeremy. A gay ex-cop brother had been bad enough in her eyes, but a murdered gay ex-cop brother was just too much. That left Jeremy to decide what do with Donny's poor abused body—the same body he'd once held close, had once made love with. Jeremy had eventually settled on cremation and no service. It would have twisted his heart to be the only one attending Donny's funeral. He still hadn't decided what to do with the cremains, which meant an urn full of Donny now sat in his living room, haunting him.

All week as he'd weathered that crap and shown up for work, he'd looked forward to his date with Qay. The date had gone beautifully too. Qay was interesting. Funny in a dry sort of way. Smart. And he showed surprising depth of personality even in the short time they'd spent together.

And that kiss! It was bad form for the chief ranger to get naked in the middle of one of his parks, but Jeremy had been damned close to doing just that. It was as if touching lips with Qay closed some kind of circuit and activated every nerve in Jeremy's body. He'd never before gone so quickly from possibly interested to desperately needing.

Until Qay admitted that he'd been lying to Jeremy all along. That had sent Jeremy's hopes into a fatal tailspin.

On Sunday, Jeremy had exercised until he couldn't anymore. Then he'd sat in his big, comfortable living room, staring at Donny's urn, brooding over the wreckage of his personal life. He'd loved Donny but in the end had done nothing to save him from drugs and death. He'd seen promise in Qay, who'd turned out to be nothing but an illusion.

So by comparison, a day of meetings was a walk in the park. So to speak.

The final adjournment occurred just after five. "We're heading out for a few drinks," said one of the city attorneys, a tall woman with elaborately braided hair. "Join us?"

"Thanks, but I have stuff to take care of at home." A bald-faced lie, but more socially acceptable than admitting he wanted to go home and wallow.

"Next time." She threw him a wink. He didn't think she was flirting with him; in fact, he vaguely remembered that she had a wife. Maybe he just looked like someone who needed a bit more social interaction. Which he probably did, if he were in the mood.

Battling rush-hour traffic on the way home did nothing to improve his disposition. He intended to go to the gym, work his muscles until they screamed, go home to nuke something for dinner, and crash. If he was lucky, he'd exhaust himself enough to fall asleep immediately.

A few spa customers were still parked in his building's garage, but he didn't see anyone as he climbed the stairs to his apartment.

His front door was unlocked.

For a ridiculous, preternatural moment, he thought he might step inside to discover Donny alive and well, smiling winningly, ready to joke about how he'd fooled the entire police bureau. What Jeremy found instead was his home in shambles.

The furniture was slashed and overturned. The TV lay facedown on the floor, shattered glass scattered widely. His laptop was next to it in a twisted snarl, and the speakers were nothing but crushed-in hulks. In the kitchen he found every glass and dish broken, food containers opened and overturned, his Keurig reduced to meaningless bits of plastic and wire. All of his clothes were tossed from the closet and drawers. The toilet had been cracked and was leaking water onto the floor. And Donny.... Oh, fuck. The metal urn lay on its side, the ashes scattered everywhere.

Jeremy was trained to handle emergencies calmly. He took several deep breaths before pulling out his phone and dialing Frankl's number.

Frankl answered on the first ring. "What's up, Cox?"

"Someone broke into my apartment and tossed the place. I have a feeling this has something to do with Donny."

"Shit. You all right?"

"I wasn't home."

"Be right there."

Jeremy sat in the stairway and waited for the sirens.

SOMETIME AFTER the cops arrived, Jeremy called Rhoda. She showed up about fifteen minutes later, a giant coffee in one hand and a bag containing a SuperSteak burrito in the other. "Eat," she ordered, stopping his nervous pacing by shoving the bag against his chest.

"Not hungry."

"Bullshit."

She glared until he sat at the top of the stairway; then she set the coffee next to him and pulled the burrito from the bag. He had to admit the food smelled damn good.

Rhoda waited for him to eat several bites. "How long will they be in there?" She waved at the open doorway, through which they could see a nest of evidence techs, patrol officers, and detectives.

"A while."

"Will you be able to sleep there tonight?"

He shook his head. "Whole place is trashed. I'm going to have to…. Fuck. I'll have to hire a cleanup crew, a dumpster, contractors. I need to buy new everything." Thinking about it made his head ache. Not because of the expenses; he was insured. And not because of the damaged items, per se. With the exception of poor Donny's remains, nothing in the apartment held sentimental value. He could replace it all. But God, the hassles he was facing.

Rhoda sat beside him. "Stay with me, sweetheart."

"That's really nice of you to offer, but I'm going to get a hotel room."

"Why? I have a spare room. I promise I'll give you your space and not get all up in your business. Heck, I'm barely home anyway." She gently nudged his arm with her shoulder. "Or we can have pajama parties and paint our nails. Your call."

Despite his misery, he managed a small chuckle. He sobered immediately, though. "Somebody murdered my ex. And it's pretty likely that the same somebody ransacked my apartment in search of God knows what. What if that someone decides I'm carrying the God-knows-what and they come after me? I'm not bringing trouble into your home, Rhoda."

She frowned at him. "Are you in *danger*, Jeremy Cox?"

"I was a cop for over a decade. I can handle it."

"Donny was a cop for over a decade too."

Instead of answering, he took another bite of burrito. It was good. Rhoda waited patiently as he chewed and swallowed. Yet another uniformed cop came huffing and puffing up the stairs, his cell phone in one hand. He grunted a greeting, and Rhoda scooted closer to Jeremy so the guy could pass.

As soon as the cop entered the apartment, she nudged Jeremy. "He's cute. Does he lean your way?"

"Don't even."

"That's right. You have your heart set on Qay. I don't blame you. He's—"

"He's a fraud."

He might have said that louder than he intended. Rhoda blinked several times, then sighed heavily. "Oh, honey. I liked him. What happened?"

"Don't want to talk about it." He was aware he sounded like a surly teenager. But dammit, within the space of a week and a half, he'd had a gory surprise visit from his ex, that same ex had turned up as a floater, his apartment had been trashed, and his battered heart had suffered another bruising. He was entitled to surly.

"Fine. Keep it bottled up, big guy. But are you positive he's as bad as you're making him out to be? I have a good eye for fuckwads—it's my superpower—and he doesn't strike me as one at all."

Instead of answering, Jeremy finished the burrito. He wiped his greasy hands on a couple of paper napkins, shoved the napkins into the bag, and tossed the lot in the general direction of his door. What was a little more garbage added to the general devastation?

He stood, his coffee clutched in one hand. "I promise, I'll fill you in on every humiliating detail later. But right now I just can't wrangle enough brain cells. I'm going to see if the goons in there will let me grab a few things, and then I'm heading for a quiet, impersonal hotel."

"All right, tough guy." She stood and cuffed him lightly on the arm. "Get some sleep. And call me if you want to talk."

Thankful to the tips of his toes for a good friend like Rhoda, he bent to kiss the top of her head. "You're a saint."

"That's me. Our Lady of Perpetual Caffeine."

He lifted his coffee cup in salute.

Rhoda left, and another hour passed before he was allowed into his apartment. The place didn't look any better after being taken over by a herd of policemen who'd apparently dusted every square inch for fingerprints. At least someone had turned off the bathroom water so the toilet wouldn't flood the whole building.

Frankl sat on one of Jeremy's kitchen stools, looking as exhausted as Jeremy felt. "You don't really need me around, do you?" Jeremy asked.

"Nah. I have your statement. If I need anything else, I know how to get hold of you. You got someplace to go?"

"Marriott."

"Okay." He pointed at the open front door with its busted lock. "We're not going to be able to secure your apartment when we leave."

That made Jeremy laugh humorlessly. "'S okay. There's nothing left to steal and it's already trashed."

Frankl nodded unhappily, and Jeremy left to gather his clothing and whatever toiletries remained unscathed. His only suitcase had been destroyed, so he ended up shoving his things into a big plastic garbage bag. Classy.

"Good luck with it," he called to Frankl while crossing to the front door, the bag cradled in his arms.

"Yeah, thanks. Hey, Cox?"

"What?"

Frankl looked uncomfortable. "You were a good cop. You're a good man. I'm sorry this shit is happening to you."

"Thanks, Captain. Donny didn't deserve it either, you know?"

"Yeah."

Jeremy trudged out the door, hoping the hotel would provide a bit of rest.

DESPITE A comfortable mattress and enough pillows to bed down every park ranger in the city, Jeremy didn't sleep well. He spent a long time tossing and twisting on the mattress before standing at the window in his boxer shorts, staring blankly at the river. The same river, of course, where Donny's corpse had been discovered.

But then his thoughts turned to another river, half a continent away. Sometimes the Smoky Hill River ran low and sluggish. But after a summer storm, the water could be swift and muddy, hiding rocks, tree branches, and whatever debris was washing downstream. Kids went swimming in the river, but not when the water was high, and they sure as hell never jumped in from the Memorial Bridge. Not if they wanted to live, anyway.

God, what had led Keith Moore to leap into the river that summer day so long ago? And how the hell had the waters of time swept him back into Jeremy's life?

Jeremy thought about that lean, quiet boy in the back of the classroom. He'd seemed very tall back then, and he'd snarled at everyone... except Jeremy. Sometimes he even gave Jeremy the hint of a smile, as if they shared a secret. Which they apparently had, although Jeremy hadn't realized it at the time.

People called Keith a hoodlum—and worse. Some kids even claimed he was a Satan worshipper who stole neighborhood cats and sacrificed them to demons. Young as he was, Jeremy had known that was bullshit. Something in Keith's speckled eyes had echoed

Jeremy's own loneliness, and Jeremy had seen sadness and maybe a little fear, not wickedness.

Well, now he knew one thing for sure. Keith Moore—or rather, Qay Hill—was a goddamn liar.

After returning to bed, Jeremy had a few hours of fitful sleep, interrupted by unsettling dreams that slipped away every time he awoke. Falling. He kept dreaming about falling. When dawn broke, he seriously considered calling in sick to work. But then he realized he'd spend the entire day dealing with the break-in and stewing over the shitstorm his life had become. Better to keep occupied. He showered and dressed in one of his uniforms, then headed to the elevator in search of breakfast.

The workday ended up blessedly busy. He led a fall nature walk at Kelly Butte, where a revegetation project had just been completed. He told some squatters in Forest Park that they couldn't camp there, and he warned them that he'd issue them a park exclusion if he caught them again. He gave them a list of homeless shelters but doubted they'd use it. Then he headed to Patty's Place to talk to Evelyn, the director, about a summer work program they'd been planning. The idea was to give some of her kids jobs that would get them outdoors and, if everyone was lucky, teach them skills in communicating positively with the public.

"How's Toad?" he asked over his fourth coffee of the day. They were sitting in her bright, cramped office, where stacks of papers and pamphlets always teetered on the brink of avalanche.

She dimpled at him and bounced slightly in her chair. She was pushing sixty but had all the youthful energy of a twenty-year-old. "He's doing great! We've already got him attending school and showing up for counseling. He's pushed a few of the rules, but I figure a little pushing is a good sign. Means he's comfortable here. I'm gonna have to watch him 'cause he's crushing pretty hard on Juan, but I think this child's gonna be just fine."

One of the thousand points of tension in Jeremy's body loosened. "Juan. I'll be damned." Juan was an absurdly nerdy boy who'd magically maintained an air of innocence even after months on the streets. Nearly a year ago, Jeremy had discovered him sleeping in the little park near the central library. He'd taken Juan out for dinner, and during the entire meal, Juan had talked nonstop about *Minecraft* and *Doctor Who*. Although Jeremy was furious at parents who would reject a sweet kid like that, he had been gratified when Juan settled in immediately at Patty's Place.

Evelyn shook her head fondly. "I'm not sure Juan realizes how Toad feels about him. Juan probably just thinks Toad's extra enthusiastic about video games and sci-fi. They're real cute together, but Toad's fragile for now. He needs to get his head together before he goes looking for love."

Jeremy reflected that the same could be said for him. Except if he didn't have his head together now, with forty-four staring him right in the face, his prospects weren't good.

After leaving Patty's Place, Jeremy drove to Kenilworth Park to talk to a couple of his rangers about some stolen bicycles. His next stop was a community garden not far away. The plots were dormant for the winter, but he'd been meaning to take a quick look to make sure everything was in order and to eyeball a possible expansion for spring. Finally he stopped at an outdoor equipment store to finagle a donation of some hats, gloves, and sleeping bags. Once a month his agency took part in an event for the homeless under the Burnside Bridge. Over the course of the evening, participants received a hot meal, haircuts, and basic medical checks. Whenever possible, the rangers gave out clothing, blankets, and other supplies.

Off and on during the day, Jeremy made a series of phone calls to his insurance company and tracked down a cleaning service. He might need some major renovation work on his walls, floors, kitchen, and bathroom, but he wouldn't know for sure until the mess was cleared. He texted Rhoda several times just to let her know he was fully functioning.

When his workday came to an end, he met a locksmith at the apartment. The guy shook his head ruefully at the damage, and Jeremy tried not to look closely at what remained.

He planned to head back to the hotel and collapse, but he figured he owed Rhoda at least a quick hello first. She worried about him. He left his SUV in the garage and walked over to P-Town.

Rhoda spied him as soon as he walked in the door. "I love a man in uniform," she said, batting her eyelashes dramatically.

He looked down at himself. "What, this old thing?"

"What can I get you, honey? Big old joe?"

"Rhoda, I'm pretty sure the stuff flowing through my veins is at least eighty percent arabica at this point. I just wanted to let you know I got my lock replaced, the cleaning crew will be there in the morning, and I'm heading back to the Marriott."

"And I bet you haven't eaten anything all day," she said as her eyes narrowed dangerously.

"I did too!" He'd had a bagel-and-sausage thing for breakfast.

"Liar." She took his hand and tugged him to the nearest vacant table, then pushed at his chest until he sat. "Don't move." She disappeared into the back of the café.

Fuck. He didn't have the strength to fight her.

Rhoda returned ten minutes later and set a paper bag and a large plastic cup in front of him. He expected the bag to contain another burrito—SuperSteak was just down the street from P-Town—and was surprised to find a container of pad thai instead. She was perfectly aware that pad thai was one of his comfort foods; he'd eaten a metric ton of the stuff right after breaking up with Donny. "What's in the cup?" he asked suspiciously.

"Smoothie."

"What kind?" The liquid was green and opaque.

"Kale, spinach, banana, apricot, and berries."

He must have made a face, because she patted his shoulder. "Vitamins, iron, and potassium, Chief. You'll only feel worse if you don't eat well."

So he ate, and he obediently drank the smoothie, which tasted only half as awful as he'd expected. Meanwhile Rhoda circulated among the tables and helped Ptolemy behind the counter, but like a moth hovering around a porch lamp, she always returned to Jeremy's side. It was irritating but also kind of nice.

When he'd demolished the noodles and downed every green drop of his drink, Jeremy stood. "How much do I owe you? And for last night too."

"Don't be an ass, Jeremy. Go get some rest before you drop right here in the middle of my café and I have to hire a backhoe to get you out." She cocked her head. "Does your hotel have pay-per-view porn?"

He managed a small smile. "Why? Were you planning to come over?"

"If I'm going to watch pretty boys screwing each other, I'll do it at home on my high-def big-screen. Now go."

WHEN HE walked past the hotel registration desk, the night clerks did a double take at his uniform but greeted him cheerily, and he waved back. Then he was in his comfortable but soulless room with the river flowing beneath the window.

He would need to get moving early in the morning to meet the cleanup crew. Then he had a full day at work—more meetings and a training session for two new rangers—and probably more insurance crap to deal with. He needed to buy a new laptop, because checking e-mail on his phone was a pain in the ass due to the small print. He'd been in denial about reading glasses for some time.

As he stood at the window, a tidal wave of anger washed over him, red-tinged and bitter-tasting. He was angry at whoever had murdered Donny and destroyed his apartment. He was angry at Donny for getting himself killed, for repeatedly spurning Jeremy's offers of help, for breaking Jeremy's heart. He was angry at Laura for not caring enough about her brother to make fucking funeral arrangements. He was angry at the Portland Police Bureau for not identifying Donny's issues earlier and getting him treatment and counseling that might have saved his career. He was angry at Toad's parents and Juan's and his own—and every mother and father who didn't love their children enough. He was angry at Rhoda for fussing over him when he didn't deserve it. He was angry at himself for failing Donny and getting old and being weak and wallowing in his misery. And he was angry at Qay Hill for not being the man Jeremy thought he was.

With a roar, Jeremy pulled his arm back and rammed a fist into the wall beside the window. Something cracked loudly.

Oh, fuck. He didn't know at first whether the sound had come from the wall or his hand. Through a haze of pain, he peered at the wall. It was fine, and he was lucky—he wouldn't be paying damages to Marriott. Or maybe he wasn't so lucky, because his knuckles were bleeding and his hand felt as if he'd hit it with a sledgehammer.

He spent an eternity staring dumbly at his hand, watching the droplets of blood form and travel across his skin to fall onto the carpet. He would have to buy some stain remover the next day, or else he'd be paying damages after all. He hadn't thought to pack a first-aid kit in his garbage bag, but Donny had pretty much decimated his supplies anyway. Besides, doctoring his own right hand would be a bitch.

In the end, he roused himself enough to shamble to the bathroom. The water hurt like hell as he washed his hand. "Serves you right, moron," he muttered. Then he remembered he had a small emergency kit in the glove box of the SUV. The hotel garage felt as if it were a million miles away, and the walk back seemed even longer. But he spread some disinfectant over the wounds—more stinging—and awkwardly stuck a couple of large Band-Aids on the worst of it. By then his hand was swollen and throbbing. He took another journey out of his room, this time only to the ice dispenser down the hall, and finally sat in the room's comfy armchair with his hand in the ice bucket.

During the entire time he was doctoring himself, his mood continued to seethe. But the ice must have cooled his disposition as well as his hand, because as the pain began to numb, so did his temper.

His thoughts turned to Qay.

First he remembered the goddamn kiss, the kiss that had blown his mind. But that was only hormones and horniness and a dry spell long enough to kill a camel. They'd had a good conversation, though, where Qay's quiet sense of humor broke through unexpectedly, like the Portland sun on a December day. And Qay liked many of the same movies that Jeremy did and most of the same music, and he got it when Jeremy made slightly obscure jokes. There was the way Qay listened to Jeremy's tame work exploits as if they were exotic adventures, and the way Qay seemed to appreciate even the smallest gestures of respect. Jeremy remembered Qay's admission that he'd never really been on a date before. The shy pride Qay showed when he paid the bill at Perry's Good Eats. The comfortable manner in which Qay snuggled up against him while they looked at the view from Council Crest. Qay's self-deprecation and worry over his philosophy class, even though he was clearly a smart man.

And the subdued way Qay apologized to him while they were driving home. No excuses, no anger, no whining. Just… *I'm sorry.* And the resignation of a man who'd expected little and received even less.

What had Qay said before getting out of the car? *You grew up well, Jeremy. You deserve better than the Donnys and Qays of the world.*

For the first time, Jeremy thought about *why* Qay hadn't admitted his identity from the beginning. In the heat of his shock, Jeremy had accused Qay of playing him, but even then he'd known that wasn't true. Seriously, what kind of evil scheme involved engaging your victim in fun conversations, buying him dinner, and kissing him senseless? Qay hadn't asked Jeremy for one damn thing.

Maybe… maybe Qay was ashamed of his youth. More ashamed than he was of his addictions and criminal record and poverty, which he'd offered up to Jeremy almost as soon as they met. Maybe his time in Bailey Springs was too painful to think about. Maybe it was just as he'd said—Keith Moore died in the Smoky Hill River. Maybe Qay's reticence had nothing to do with that idiot Jeremy Cox and a lot more to do with whatever baggage Qay had been dragging around for almost thirty years.

And Jeremy had to admit that Qay had come clean eventually. Without any pressure from him, and before they'd even finished their first date.

Fuck.

Jeremy's hand had stopped hurting, but now his chest ached like a son of a bitch.

CHAPTER TEN

SATURDAY NIGHT after his first and only date, Qay went home, climbed into bed, and fell into a coma. The lack of consciousness was a relief. But now Sunday gaped before him, and that fucking day had teeth. It had been years since he was so tempted to get high. Only two things stopped him. One was the conviction that if he used again now, he wouldn't stop until he was dead. The other was morbid curiosity: he wanted to know how he'd done on the damn philosophy exam.

So instead of finding something to drink, pop, smoke, or shoot up, Qay spent Sunday huddled in his basement, watching crap on TV. Television was a safe enough drug. By the end of the day, he had no idea what he'd watched, but he'd survived another sixteen hours, which was something. He ate macaroni and cheese that tasted like the box it came in.

Monday was slightly better because he had a sense of purpose. He had no test that week but he studied anyway, reading the textbook twice so the words might sink in. William James, John Rawls, and Bertrand Russell. Booyah.

He missed P-Town and Rhoda, and he missed Jeremy with an intensity completely out of proportion to the extent of their now-defunct relationship. One date night, incomplete, did not make for True Love. They hadn't even become real friends yet, for Christ's sake.

On Monday afternoon Qay took a bus to school. He got to class early and sat in his usual seat, body clenched with anxiety. He kept his head bowed to avoid eye contact with the Russian girl, Professor Reynolds, or anyone else. As a result, he startled slightly when Reynolds set a sheaf of papers on Qay's desk.

"I'd like to speak to you after class, Qay."

Fuck. His grade must be so miserably low that he wouldn't pass the course. That was what Reynolds was going to tell him, along with the news that the college had banned him from registering for anything else in the future, seeing as Qay had the intelligence of a ground squirrel.

Reynolds was already well into his lecture before Qay dared to look at the front of his test.

Outstanding work.

Qay spent a good five minutes puzzling over the possible meanings of the word *outstanding*. He suspected there must be a definition he wasn't familiar with. Perhaps it was a word like *sanction* or *cleave*, which could mean one thing and also its exact opposite. Maybe it was a synonym for *horrible* or *appalling*.

But when he finally paged through the exam, he saw the red-inked scrawl at the bottom of the last page: *100%*.

Holy shit.

Qay couldn't breathe. He literally couldn't breathe. He was going to fucking die right there in the middle of philosophy class, and the coroner would write "unexpected success" as the cause of death. When he finally pulled oxygen into his lungs, the sound was loud enough for the Russian girl to give him a concerned look.

Professor Reynolds had made other comments on the paper, some of them quite extensive, but Qay couldn't process them now. His head was spinning.

Whatever happened in class that day was lost on him. He felt more buzzed than he ever had on drugs. All he could do was hold his exam and think about those shocking bits of red. Outstanding. One hundred percent.

He waited in his chair as class ended, tucked into himself, still half expecting Professor Reynolds to tell him the grade was a mistake. The other students made a lot of noise as they packed up their gear and shuffled out of the room. Several muttered unhappily about their grades. When the room fell silent, Qay looked up and saw Reynolds waiting patiently for him at the front. He wore a Janis Joplin T-shirt under a sport jacket that had seen better days, and his gray ponytail had come slightly loose.

"Hey, Qay."

Qay managed a weak smile. "Hi."

"C'mon up."

"Okay." Clutching his exam, Qay made his way to the front. If his life had a soundtrack, heavy piano chords would have been playing right then. *Dum-dum-dum-dummmm.*

Reynolds shoved a manila envelope into his backpack, which looked ancient, and grinned. "That's quite an accomplishment," he said, waving a hand toward the papers Qay held.

"It is?"

"I've been teaching this class for almost twenty years. In that time, I've awarded exactly five perfect scores. Yours is the sixth."

"I…. It is?" Way to sound intelligent.

"Qay, I'm going to make a wild guess here. Life's kicked you around some, right?"

"A little bit."

"Yeah. But you pulled your ass out of the fire and now you're reaching for more."

Well, that was a succinct summary of the last few years. Qay nodded.

"I'm impressed, man. Doing that takes balls of steel, and I know it's hard as hell. Do you have long-term plans?"

With a degree of sadness, Qay remembered the conversation he'd had with Rhoda about dreams. "I don't know. Sobriety, stability, solvency."

Reynolds laughed loudly. "Not a bad start, man. Not bad at all. But I think you need to aim higher. What're you majoring in?"

"Psych."

"Okay, that'll work. And how close are you to finishing your associate degree?"

Qay shrugged. Three hundred years was an exaggeration, he supposed. "Not very."

"What if I could talk to a friend at Portland State and get you in there? And get you out of some of the rinky-dink intro classes you don't really need?"

"I…." Qay realized he was gaping and attempted to look less like an idiot. "That's nice of you. But I can't afford—"

"I bet we can get you a scholarship. Qay, what you need to do is get a bachelor's degree and then get yourself into grad school. If you can pull off an exam like this in my class, I'd love to see what you can do when you're really engaged."

"But you don't understand. This test was a fluke. I never—"

"Nobody writes like this as a fluke. You had shit standing in your way before, but the day you took my exam, you got past that shit. The real you came out to play, man. And the real you has a hell of a brain. You just need to find a way to coax him out more often."

Unable to form a response, Qay simply blinked, which made Reynolds chuckle. "Yeah, this'll take you a while to process. That's cool. Come see me when you're ready, and I'll pull some strings. You know, if a guy wants to kick back and live a low-key life, no problem. My son fixes cars during the week and plays in a band on weekends. Lives in a trailer on some acreage in Boring, and he's happy as a dog with two tails. So, good for him. But if a guy wants more, and if he's capable of it, then it's a pity and a waste if he doesn't give himself the chance to get it."

"Thank you," Qay said at last. "It means a lot to me that you're saying this."

Reynolds nodded. "Somebody gave me a similar speech, back in the days when I was smoking too much weed and thinking I could change the world just sitting around and bullshitting with my stoned buddies. I'm glad I listened to her."

Qay rode home on a regular old TriMet bus, but it felt as if he were floating. He replayed Reynolds's words in his head. Scholarship? Fucking graduate school? A hell of a brain? Jesus.

The only thing dampening Qay's mood was knowing he had nobody to share his good news with. He ached to tell someone: one of only six perfect scores in twenty years. A glimpse of a future he'd never imagined for himself. But he couldn't face Rhoda again, and he sure as hell couldn't face Jeremy, so that left... who? Stuart, his asshat supervisor? Yeah, Stuart would give a flying fuck.

Okay, then. Qay would just have to bask in the warmth of his own accomplishments. He'd give himself a high-five. In fact, he'd celebrate that night with a decent dinner.

So that was what he did, stuffing himself with pasta at an Italian place a few blocks from home and following up with gelato. No espresso, though. He had to be up early in the morning for work.

Qay didn't often bemoan his lack of electronic gadgets, but when he got home that evening, he truly wished he owned a computer. Or a smartphone. Or a DVD player. Or anything that would have allowed him to plug into some porn. Yes, he had some stroke mags stashed away in his apartment, and even a few books with some pretty hot erotica. But tonight he wanted real bodies, and if he couldn't touch them, it would be nice to at least watch them move, listen to the sounds the men made. Pretend for a short while that he wasn't alone.

He ended up naked in bed without any props and with nothing to keep him going but his hands. He used his hands well, though. And if he thought about Jeremy and that electric kiss while he got himself off? Well, nobody could blame him, and he was due a little self-indulgence.

"HILL, GET over here." Stuart's voice rang out across the shop floor, strident even over the sound of machinery. Qay sighed, let go of the trash bin he'd been wheeling, and walked over. A few of the other employees shot him sympathetic glances. They thought Stuart was a shithead too, but there wasn't much they could do about it.

Stuart pointed to a stack of boxes. "These labels are supposed to go over there." Now he pointed to the far end of the room.

"You told me to put them here."

"No, I didn't. Pay some fucking attention for once, Hill." Stuart flounced away like a pissed off prima ballerina.

Sighing again, Qay found a nearby handcart, piled the boxes of labels onto it, and took everything to the spot Stuart had indicated. He headed back to his abandoned trash bin, but before he'd rolled it more than five feet, Stuart planted himself in the way.

"I put the labels where you told me," Qay said mildly.

"Well, good for you, Einstein. But you didn't clean up the lunchroom."

Technically, cleaning the lunchroom wasn't one of Qay's duties; it was Barry's. But Barry had called in sick that day, which meant the task should have fallen to Stuart. Apparently Stuart had decided to delegate.

"Fine," Qay said. "Just let me get rid of this trash, and—"

"Now, Hill. Shoulda been done an hour ago."

Qay spent quite a while taking care of people's discarded bags and cups and napkins, wiping down the tables and chairs, and mopping the floor. He even cleaned out the coffeepot and the microwave, neither of which Barry appeared to have tackled in some time and both of which looked on the verge of birthing new life forms.

He glanced at the clock when he returned from dragging the trash bin outside. Only ten minutes to go. Thank God.

But Stuart was waiting to ambush him. "Bathrooms next, Hill."

Also not Qay's responsibility. "It's almost time to clock out."

"I don't give a shit. You shoulda thought of that earlier."

Qay wanted to kick Stuart's ass up to his shoulder blades. But one thing he'd learned long ago was that officious pricks were everywhere, and if you let them get under your skin, you'd only hurt yourself. Besides, it was Friday night, he had no plans, and he wasn't in a hurry to get anywhere. If he stayed late, he'd get a little overtime, and that would be nice. He'd love to be able to save up some money for a cheap laptop.

"I'll get right on it," Qay said.

The women's restroom took very little time to clean. Few women worked at the window factory, and the ones who did were evidently quite tidy. The men's room was another story, though. A gross story. One of the other employees came in to use the facilities while Qay worked, and Qay watched him miss the trash bin entirely as he tossed his paper towel. "Men are pigs," Qay muttered, picking the trash off the floor.

He didn't finish the bathrooms until nearly six. By then the machinery had been shut down and everyone was gone except the security guards and Gaylene from accounting, who preferred to arrive late and leave late whenever she could. Qay clocked out, donned his coat, and waved good-bye to the guards.

Night had fallen some time ago, and the black sky spit cold, stinging raindrops, making Qay shiver as he descended from the loading bay onto the street. He had to walk a couple of blocks to his first bus; he'd be soaked and miserable by then. Wouldn't it be nice if someday he could afford a car? Although he'd always lusted after muscle cars, he'd be happy with even the most basic little econobox as long as it ran and kept him dry. He certainly didn't need anything as burly as the dark SUV parked a few yards away.

Just as he realized that he recognized the SUV, the driver's door opened and a big man in a green uniform slid out. Qay froze in place. The man walked over until he was just out of arm's reach, and then he stopped.

"You worked late," Jeremy said.

"What… what are you doing here?"

"Waiting for you."

"But…. Why…. How did you…?" As usual, Qay was eloquent when flustered.

Jeremy's grin was small and tight, but it was there. "We're getting soaked. Can we have this conversation in my car? I'll crank the heat."

Not trusting himself with words, Qay simply nodded. When Jeremy held the passenger door open, something lively fluttered in Qay's chest.

They sat silently in the SUV for a long time, fogging the inside of the windshield. The radio was off, but the fan blew full blast. Qay watched rain droplets fall from his hair onto his lap. They left little circles of darker blue on the denim.

"Stuart is an asshole," Qay finally said.

"Your supervisor?"

"Yeah. That's why I worked late." He snuck a peek at Jeremy from the corner of his eye. "Have you been here since five?"

"Four thirty, actually. And I've had to pee for at least half an hour."

"I could probably talk the security guard into letting you into the factory. The bathroom's pristine. I just cleaned it."

"I guess I can hold it a little longer."

Qay nodded. He glanced at Jeremy's right hand, which lay on the console between them, and saw that the knuckles were scabbed and slightly swollen. "What happened?" Qay asked.

"Stupidity."

They were quiet again, the pause dragging on long past awkward. Then Jeremy cleared his throat. "How did the exam go?"

Qay couldn't stop a wide smile. "I aced it. The prof even kept me after class to tell me I'm brilliant."

Jeremy looked as happy about this news as Qay felt. "Hell yeah, you're sharp as broken glass."

"Appropriate comparison."

"I tried."

A little of the tension between them eased. Qay picked at a thread on his slightly frayed jeans, then stopped himself and drummed on the armrest instead. "Why are you here?" he asked, looking through his window into blankness. "And how?"

"I used to be a cop, remember? You told me you work at a window factory in Northwest, which narrowed it down. I made some phone calls." He snorted a laugh. "Didn't want to get you in trouble or let you know what I was up to, but I remembered Stuart's name and asked for him. I found him yesterday. Pretended I was a bill collector when he came to the phone. He was just about in tears—kept insisting he'd paid what was due on his credit card."

The thought of Stuart nearly crying over an imaginary unpaid debt cheered Qay more than it should have. "So that's the how. What's the why?"

"I have… questions. And an apology, if I can man up enough to spit it out."

"Apology? For what?"

Jeremy gave him a long look. "Let's go somewhere, okay? I can piss and we can eat and… and we can talk."

Maybe he was courting disaster, but Qay nodded. "All right."

He thought Jeremy might take them to the restaurant where their disastrous date had begun, or maybe to P-Town. Instead, Jeremy drove deeper into Northwest Portland before parking under some enormous trees on Quimby. He led Qay to a diner that was even less upscale than Perry's, but it was crowded, which was a good sign. Besides, nobody gave Qay's work clothes a second glance. The host clearly recognized Jeremy. "Chief! Good to see you! It's been a while."

"Too long. Can you find a quiet table for my friend here? I need to see a man about a horse."

The host—a pudgy young guy with cute dimples—giggled. "Sure thing." He grabbed a couple of laminated menus and, still smiling, took Qay to a corner booth. "Something to drink?" he asked when Qay was seated.

A little chill remained in Qay's bones, so he ordered a coffee. Then he pretended to study the menu and tried not to worry that Jeremy had changed his mind and ditched him. He was relieved when, a few minutes later, Jeremy slid into the opposite seat.

"I'm in the mood for breakfast for dinner. You mind?" Jeremy asked.

"No, it's fine."

"Good. Although to be honest, right now I'd give a kidney for a genuine home-cooked meal. I've been eating at restaurants all week."

"Your personal chef is on strike?"

Jeremy scrunched up his face. "Been staying at a hotel downtown. Long story, and not why we're here."

Qay would have liked to hear that story, especially if it delayed a rehash of the unpleasant scene at Council Crest. But the host came by to fill their mugs with coffee and take their dinner orders. Qay asked for a bacon and cheddar scramble, while Jeremy opted for pancakes and sausage. "Which I'll probably regret tomorrow," Jeremy sighed.

"Why?"

"Because the fitness center at the hotel isn't nearly as good as my gym, and exercising there sucks. Dragging myself across the river to my usual gym also sucks."

"Why are you at a hotel?" Maybe Qay could still steer the conversation into less turbulent waters.

Pretending that the salt shaker was fascinating, Jeremy avoided Qay's gaze. His mouth was compressed into a tight line and shadows lurked in his pale eyes. "Somebody broke into my place and trashed everything. Took a couple days just to get it cleaned up, and now I have a bunch of repairs to do. And shopping for new… everything."

Fuck. "Are you okay?"

Jeremy gave him a quick glance. "I wasn't home at the time."

"And if you were, you'd have kicked their asses, I bet. That's not what I meant. I mean…." Qay squirmed uncomfortably in the vinyl booth. "Emotionally. You've had a hell of a week. Me and Donny and then this."

"This *is* Donny. The fuckers who broke in were probably the same ones who killed him. They didn't steal anything—they were looking for something."

"What?"

Jeremy shrugged. "Drugs? Money? The Holy Grail?"

"That's—"

"Why'd you jump?"

Qay was startled enough to jerk back. And then it was his turn to be enthralled by condiments, only he fixated on the little bottle of chili sauce instead of the salt. "Because I wanted to die," he finally murmured.

Which wasn't the complete truth. His shrinks had pressed the matter: why walk nearly two miles to the Memorial Bridge when his household contained enough pills to kill himself many times over, when the kitchen was full of sharp objects, when his father's hunting rifles were conveniently within reach? Back then, Qay had struggled to find the words to explain. If the fall from the bridge had been fatal, the Smoky Hill River would have washed his body far away, so Bailey Springs couldn't imprison him even in death. The shrinks accepted that explanation, and it had been a true one. Years later, though, Qay realized he'd had another motive as well. That bridge was high. Before he died, he'd wanted to fly. Briefly, sure, but he had that fierce moment of exultation and freedom.

"That town could be hell," Jeremy said, his voice pitched low. "I remember. But you were almost eighteen. What was so bad you couldn't wait it out a little longer?"

"Like you did?" Qay said, sounding bitter in his own ears.

"I guess."

"You had scholarships waiting for you. You had this damp little city ready to call you its own. I had nothing." He'd been a loser who couldn't pass tenth grade math, a delinquent, a nutcase who stole his mother's pills and his father's booze.

Jeremy reached over and settled his huge, warm hand atop Qay's. "What was so bad?" But he knew already, or at least suspected. Qay could tell by his intense stare.

"Why do you even care?" Although Qay made his voice sound hostile, he couldn't bring himself to pull his hand back. "I lied to you, remember? Played you."

"You weren't honest with me, and I was pissed about it. But then I got my head straight enough to realize that the universe doesn't revolve around me. You don't want anything to do with Keith Moore, so you pretended he never existed. You were protecting yourself, not trying to hurt me. So this is where that apology comes in. I'm sorry I had a tantrum. I reacted badly, and you didn't deserve it."

Qay could count on one hand the apologies he'd received in his life, so perhaps he could be forgiven for how he responded to this one. "What if the lie *was* because of you?"

Jeremy blinked and opened his mouth, but before he could say anything, the waiter appeared with their dinners. He didn't bat an eye at the big man in the ranger uniform touching the hand of the scroungy-looking guy across the table. Qay could have fed a small army with the food on his plate, which smelled delicious. But he didn't dig in, and neither did Jeremy, who'd been given pancakes proportionate to his size.

"Because of me how?"

After gently dislodging his hand, Qay shrugged. "You're Captain Caffeine."

"Captain Caffeine?" Jeremy said, bemused.

"You're handsome and ripped. You have a cool job with a sexy uniform, and everyone knows you and calls you Chief. You drive a dictator car. You have great friends like Rhoda. You're practically perfect in every way. I know I'm not much, but I am something, and I fought really fucking hard to get this far. I wanted you to see what I've made myself into. Not that piece of shit I was in Kansas."

For a long moment, Jeremy simply gaped. Then he gave his head a slow shake. "There is so much wrong with that little speech you just gave, I don't even know where to begin." He closed his eyes, then opened them again as he puffed out a lungful of air. "Eat while I think about how to deal with that."

Until he started digging into his food, Qay didn't realize how hungry he was. Turned out he was ravenous, and the scramble was delicious. He shoveled forkfuls into his mouth while Jeremy did much the same. Jeremy could put away a lot of pancakes really fast. "Point one," Jeremy said after swallowing a bite of sausage. "I'm so far from perfect it's not even funny. Dead ex, remember? Burglarized apartment. Not to mention I'm forty-three—which is seventy-five in gay years—and single, and if you want to know what my love life has been like, well, I refer you back to the dead ex."

"But I—"

"Point two! You *are* something. I saw that from the first. I can tell that you're strong and you have a lot of pride, and fuck, I always knew you were smart. Even when you were flunking biology. I know a few things about addiction and mental illness, thanks to the job and poor Donny, so I have a crystal clear idea how hard you've worked to get where you are. I couldn't do it, Qay. I'd just fall apart."

He took a breath, shoved in more sausage, and talked with his mouth full. "Point three. You were never a piece of shit. Ever. Do you remember what I was like? I practically had *punching bag* tattooed on my forehead. You were one of the few people in that place who didn't treat me like crap. I, uh…." His speech stuttered to a halt and the fair skin of his face reddened. "This is embarrassing. You were my first crush."

Qay couldn't stop a smile. "I know. I knew back then."

"You…. Really? *I* didn't even realize what was going on yet."

It had been sweet, one of the few solid anchors in Keith's life. Jeremy was almost a foot shorter than Keith was back then, with corn-silk hair that hung in his eyes when it got too long, and an adorable smattering of freckles across his face. He'd sneak looks at Keith and his cheeks would color—just like they were now—and he'd fight to hide a goofy grin.

"I could tell. Didn't feel that way about you 'cause you were *young*. But I liked you. Used to wonder how you'd turn out if you survived high school."

"You hardly even spoke to me." Jeremy sounded accusing, maybe even slightly hurt.

"Kept my distance. They treated you badly enough already. The last thing you needed was to be associated with me. I guess I could have had your back some of the time, but not always. Troy Baker and his gang of idiots, they'd have found you anyway and punished you twice as hard for being my friend."

Standing back from Jeremy had been difficult. He could have used someone bigger and tougher in his corner, and Christ knew Keith was dying for one good friend. Maybe if he'd had that, he wouldn't have jumped off the bridge. Or maybe he'd have dragged young Jeremy Cox down with him.

The waiter appeared with more coffee. "Can I get you anything else?" He cleared their plates, magically emptied. Qay had no idea how he'd consumed so much in one sitting.

Qay was going to say no, but Jeremy grinned. "We'll split a cinnamon roll."

"You've got to be kidding," Qay said after their waiter had gone.

"They're good. Besides, the way we're tearing our chests open here, I think we deserve some empty calories."

"That sounds like an argument Rhoda would make."

Jeremy smiled. "I think I stole it from her."

They sipped their coffee. Taking a rest, like coming up for a few lungfuls of air before submerging below the waves again. But then Jeremy nearly left Qay gasping with six quiet words: "I missed you after you jumped."

"You shouldn't—"

"Everyone gossiped, but nobody seemed to know the truth. I didn't even know if you were still alive. I guess… I guess I kind of hoped that eventually I'd hear good news about you. I didn't expect to run into you in P-Town, though." He picked up the salt shaker and peered at it like a jeweler inspecting a diamond. Qay loved watching his hands—they were big and wide, with long, blunt-tipped fingers and those small scabs on his right knuckles. His fingernails were slightly ragged. Definitely not a manicure guy.

He set down the salt and licked his lips. "What did happen? After the bridge? Besides Keith becoming Qay, I mean."

"That… took a while. I hurt myself pretty badly. Internal injuries, broken bones. Once I was stable, my father shipped me to a hospital in Iowa, probably because nobody knew us there. After that, I spent a good long time in mental hospitals." He laughed humorlessly. "I had issues when I went in there, but I was really nuts by the time I got out."

"How did you get out?"

Qay gave him an evil grin. "I ran away. Yes, I am a genuine escapee from a loony bin. They caught me a few months later—I was living on the streets and easy to catch. But I was well over eighteen by then, and I fought commitment. My father tried to get me locked up again. For once luck was on my side. Judge let me go. I went far away and never looked back."

That had been the last time he saw his father, who'd been red-faced with fury, his lips drawn back in the grimace that had terrified Keith as a child. But Dr. Moore couldn't touch him that day in the courtroom, not with the judge and bailiff watching. It had been Keith's only triumph over the bastard. He'd renamed himself that same afternoon.

"What happened with your parents after that?" Jeremy asked, as if he'd read Qay's thoughts.

"No idea. That was our last contact."

"Are they still alive?"

Qay lifted one shoulder. "Don't know and don't care. I told you. Their son died in the Smoky Hill River." Well, their younger son had. Their older one died years before that, and in a considerably more corporeal way.

The cinnamon roll arrived—enormous, of course—and Jeremy paused with his fork hovering over the mountain of sugar. "Do you think we've unearthed enough of our skeletons this evening?"

"God, yes."

"Then I propose we leave the rest of the bodies buried for now. We can always dig 'em up as we get to know each other better. Um, assuming you'll forgive me for being an asshole and will want to know me better."

Qay wanted that like his lungs wanted oxygen. He smiled and dove his fork under Jeremy's to spear a chunk of sweet roll. "There's nothing to forgive you for," he said between chews. Because if Jeremy could talk with his mouth full, Qay had no intention of being Miss Manners.

They finished eating at last but lingered over coffee for a long time. Jeremy paid. "I'm driving you home," he announced when they were back out in the stinging rain.

"You'll have to cross over to the east side and come back again."

"Big deal." Jeremy opened the passenger door and gestured grandly.

As they crossed the Burnside Bridge, Jeremy settled a warm hand on Qay's leg. "Don't suppose you want to come shopping tomorrow? Furniture mostly, and a laptop. I'll wait until I'm ready to move back in to get everything else."

"I have to work," Qay said with real regret. He'd never been furniture shopping—certainly not with an amazing man.

"That sucks. Then... the forecast says Sunday will be dry. Come hiking with me."

"Hiking?"

Jeremy nodded enthusiastically. "Yeah. We'll do a nice easy one. Please? I really need to get out of town for a few hours, and I'd rather do it with you."

Qay could hardly refuse that, especially when his belly was full and round and Jeremy's hand was so comfortably heavy on his thigh. "Okay. Hiking."

Jeremy's smile made the promise worthwhile.

Qay directed him to his house, and Jeremy coasted to a stop in front of the driveway. "Nice place."

"I have the basement. Not so nice."

"Well, at least it's livable." Jeremy's mouth quirked. "If you want a little more luxury for a few days, you can always come stay with me at the Marriott."

Oh, shit. Qay had a sudden clear image of Jeremy—uniform off, body sprawled invitingly across a big hotel bed. *Bad idea*, he reminded himself. *You'll fuck things up.* And because his desire not to screw up whatever time he might have with Jeremy outweighed his desire to just screw Jeremy, Qay shook his head ruefully. "I have to be at work at eight tomorrow."

"I guess you better get your beauty rest, then. But I'll pick you up at eight on Sunday, all right? Dress warmly."

"Sounds good." Qay dismounted from the SUV but paused before closing the door. He looked back at Jeremy, so big and competent behind the wheel of his oversized vehicle. "I really am sorry about the mess with Donny. And I don't care how much shit has fallen on you lately. You're still Captain Caffeine." He slammed the door, waved to Jeremy, and headed to the basement.

Chapter Eleven

JEREMY WOKE up very early Saturday—alone in the big hotel bed. He felt refreshed after sleeping well for the first time in over a week. When he pulled back the curtains to look outside, he discovered a steady rain, the kind that formed shoe-soaking puddles and ran beneath jacket collars. He thought about Qay having to take two buses to work, only to be bullied by Stuart. And Jeremy had an idea.

He showered and dressed quickly, jogged down the hallway, bounced on his feet in the elevator, and hurried to the parking garage. Saturday morning traffic was light, so it took very little time to drive to P-Town, which opened early. Rhoda wasn't there, but Ptolemy was, resplendent in a hand-knit sweater and peasant skirt, a floral barrette in her hair.

"Your dissertation must be treating you nicely," Jeremy said. "You look great."

Ptolemy rolled her eyes. "It's not. I'm trying to seduce it into cooperating."

"Sounds like a good plan." He held out the big thermos he kept in his SUV for when he spent a long day outdoors. "Would you fill this, please? And I'll take a couple of those chocolate-looking things on the top row. To go."

After filling the thermos, Ptolemy wrapped the pastries and slid them into a paper bag. She added napkins, packets of sugar, creamer cups, and wooden stirrers. Upon Jeremy's request, she also tucked in two paper cups with sleeves and lids. "Saturday morning adventure?" she asked as she rang up his order.

"Surprise breakfast for a friend."

"That cute dark-haired guy?"

"That's him."

She nodded. "I approve. He has big textbooks."

Qay's house was a short drive away. By then it was a little past seven, and Jeremy didn't know when Qay left for work. He hoped he hadn't missed him. There were no parking spots available, but nobody was driving on the street this early, so Jeremy idled directly opposite Qay's door.

Qay had his head down when he emerged and didn't see Jeremy right away. When he did catch sight of the SUV, his eyes widened. As he hurried through the downpour, Jeremy leaned over and pushed the passenger door open.

"What are you doing here?" Qay asked.

"Saving you from the discomfort of public transportation, just for this morning."

The sky might have been dark, but Qay's smile was brighter than August sunshine. "You didn't have to get up so early on your day off."

"Didn't have to, but I did. C'mon. You can eat on the way."

With a bemused grin playing around his lips, Qay fastened his seat belt. He seemed delighted with the pastry and even more so when Jeremy instructed him to fill a paper cup from the thermos. "I've never had a chauffeur before," Qay said as he ate. "It's nice."

"Just don't expect me to wear a suit and black cap. I hate suits."

"I'd rather see you in your ranger uniform. It's sexy."

"So you've said." Jeremy knew he sounded a trifle smug, but it was nice to be admired. And the uniform did look good on him.

They chatted lightly as they crossed town, and they got to the window factory early enough to spend some time just sitting, drinking coffee and watching the rain sheet down the windshield. Qay seemed reluctant to leave when it was time to go. "Thanks for this. It was nice." And then he surprised Jeremy by leaning over and briefly pressing his sweet-tasting lips to Jeremy's. "Really nice." Then he was darting through the rain, leaving Jeremy grinning like an idiot.

JEREMY DID not enjoy furniture shopping. He had specific tastes and didn't like it when salespeople tried to talk him into crap he didn't want. He didn't like fussy or ornate, but he wasn't a huge fan of modern either. He wanted good quality, and he wanted the furniture to be comfortable, because he actually intended to use it, goddammit. When he was a kid, the living room contained a couch patterned in gold, cream, and brown, with cushions that would never lie straight. He was strictly forbidden from bringing food anywhere near it. It gave him immense satisfaction as an adult to eat on his couch—and do several other activities that would have given his mother a stroke.

He finally found a sectional in pale gray. It had clean lines and, the saleswoman assured him, stain-resistant fabric. It was large enough for even a man his size to stretch out. He picked up some other pieces as well: an armchair, a coffee table, a dining table with chairs, a side table that could double as a desk. None of the headboards satisfied him, so he ordered a simple frame to go with the new box spring and mattress. It would tide him over until he found a headboard he liked. The store promised to deliver everything to his apartment in two weeks. By then he hoped the damage would be repaired.

The furniture hunting took a good chunk of the day. Normally Jeremy would have been grouchy about it, but he kept remembering the look on Qay's face that morning and the cotton-candy touch of Qay's lips against his. It hadn't been an incendiary kiss like their first one, but it had been sweet and ripe with promise.

Over an afternoon coffee at P-Town, Jeremy replayed that morning kiss in his head, not caring if Rhoda spied his dopey smile. Once he regained a little energy, he intended to look for a new laptop, a task he anticipated with even less enthusiasm than finding a new couch. In the meantime, he sipped his coffee and grinned idiotically and allowed his gaze to float around the room.

Two tables over sat a young family, a father and mother with a baby and a little girl about kindergarten age. The youngster pouted theatrically over something—she was good at it—and her parents patiently tried to cajole her back into good humor. When the father pulled a ridiculously silly face and settled a paper napkin on his head, the girl couldn't hold out any longer. She erupted into noisy giggles.

It was a cute scene. But as Jeremy watched, his smile faded. To the best of his recollection, his own parents had never joked around with him. They had never been cruel, but even when he was young they treated him seriously, as if he were another adult, albeit a small one. Being trapped into marriage by an unwanted pregnancy had apparently killed all their frivolity and joy.

That was bad. But even worse was Qay. Keith, really. He hadn't specified why he'd felt imprisoned and hopeless in Bailey Springs—so hopeless that he believed death was his only escape. But Jeremy had a good inkling. The expression on Qay's face when he talked about his father was one Jeremy had seen before. Many of the homeless kids he encountered at work bore that same expression. Jeremy had no idea of the type or extent of abuse Keith had suffered at his father's hands, but the wounds were still deep and open thirty years later.

Dammit, Jeremy should have suspected something back in high school. No kid was as troubled as Keith Moore unless something serious was going on. Jeremy was smart—he should have figured that out. And Keith would have had nowhere to go for help. The Moores were pillars of the community. Mrs. Moore was involved with most of the local civic and charitable organizations, and half the town's residents relied on Dr. Moore for medical care. It was unlikely that Jeremy could have magically convinced the authorities to do something to protect Keith, but he could have at least been a friend. Fuck. A pair of sympathetic ears might have been enough to save Keith from decades of pain, but Jeremy had let his shyness get in the way of reaching out.

"You look like you're ready to kill someone," Rhoda said. He'd been so busy with his thoughts that he hadn't noticed her approach.

"Not quite. But I'd love to go back in time and shake some sense into my younger self."

She laughed. "You and pretty much everyone else on the planet, honey. Hell, I had a nightmare once that I'd received Divine Judgment, and my punishment was to endlessly relive every dumb thing I did when I was a kid. It was awful."

"This dumb thing affected someone else's life."

"Yeah, those are the worst ones. It's bad enough I did things to screw myself up, but I hate thinking about the ways I messed up other people." She patted his shoulder. "We're human, baby. Comes with the package."

She was right, but he didn't feel any better about it. "I bought furniture," he said, knowing it was a non sequitur. "And I'm about to go computer shopping."

"Sounds like a productive weekend."

"I guess. I'm going hiking tomorrow."

"Solo?" she asked, tilting her head slightly.

"With Qay."

That made her eyebrows rise. "He's not a fuckwad?"

"He's not. Your superpowers didn't fail you. I was the one at fault. But I apologized and he's forgiven me."

"Oh, I'm glad. And I'm also glad he and I can be friends again. Tell him to come back."

A bit of Jeremy's former good mood returned. Qay deserved a friend like Rhoda on his side. "I will. He'll be happy about it."

Laptop shopping turned out to be relatively painless. In fact, the new one was a lot nicer than his old one, with a faster processor, more memory, and better screen resolution. He got a pretty good deal on it too. He took his new purchase back to the hotel and sat with it for a while, trying to decide whether to pick Qay up after work. Dinner together would be nice, and while the rain had stopped, Jeremy's SUV beat TriMet any day.

In the end, though, he decided it would be too stalkery if he showed up tonight. He didn't want to overwhelm Qay. They had all of Sunday to be together. So he worked out at the fitness center, ordered from room service, and spent the rest of the evening playing with his new computer.

ON SUNDAY morning Jeremy nearly bounced out of bed. Even though he was about to spend the day outdoors, most likely getting sweaty and muddy, he showered. Then he put on his hiking gear, which he'd fortunately salvaged from the devastation in his apartment. He jogged to his SUV.

P-Town opened late on Sundays, which was too bad. He figured he and Qay could stop for a quick breakfast somewhere else on the way out of town. When he pulled up to Qay's house—nearly ten minutes early—Qay already stood at the curb, grinning. He held a large paper bag in one hand.

"Morning," Qay said when he climbed into the car. "Um, am I dressed okay? I don't exactly have REI in my closet."

Jeremy inspected him. Scuffed work boots, jeans, a gray sweatshirt, and the leather jacket. Not the best, but they were only doing a light hike today. "You're fine," Jeremy said with a reassuring smile. "We're walking about five miles. There's some elevation gain, but nothing crazy. Will your feet be comfortable in those boots?"

"I wear them all day at work, so I guess so."

"At least you'll be safe if there's glass on the trail."

Qay snorted. "True." Then he rustled in the bag. "It's not P-Town, but last night after work, I picked up a couple of things at the store. Um, muffins, sandwiches, granola bars.... I wasn't sure what you'd want."

That was about the sweetest thing anyone had done for Jeremy in a long time. The silly grin reappeared. "Actually, a sandwich would be great. How about if I hit drive-through for coffee?"

"Captain Caffeine strikes again." Qay's smile was audible in his words.

Fed and energized, they headed northeast. Qay didn't ask where they were going, and Jeremy wasn't sure whether that was a good thing or bad. Maybe it meant Qay trusted him, or maybe it meant Qay was passively resigned to taking whatever came to him. In either case, he seemed content to gaze out the windows as they zoomed along the freeway in the light Sunday-morning traffic. This wasn't the most scenic part of town, but he likely didn't come this way often.

Just after they reached Troutdale, Qay twisted in his seat to face Jeremy. "If you don't let me change the radio station, I'm going to lose my mind."

Jeremy hadn't really paid any attention to the music. "What's wrong with it?"

"I'm not a thirteen-year-old girl."

"You don't have to be to like this song." Jeremy was arguing for the sake of form. He didn't know who the singer was, and the song itself was innocuous and forgettable. It was just background noise. But he enjoyed Qay's impatient huff.

"No, probably some twelve-year-olds listen to it too. For fuck's sake, Jeremy. I don't have much sanity as it is."

Jeremy passed an eighteen-wheeler with a giant photo of french fries on the side, then an old van hand-painted with bright swirls and squiggles. "You could sync my phone with the stereo. I think I have Justin Bieber and One Direction on my playlist." A bald-faced lie that, as he'd hoped, made Qay groan loudly.

"I didn't realize you're a sadist," Qay said.

"Only on weekends. It's a hobby."

Another snort, and then Qay reached over and began to fiddle with the radio controls. "There must be something decent," he muttered as he scanned through the wavelengths. He seemed about to settle on Led Zeppelin, which would have been perfectly fine with Jeremy, but then Jeremy's phone rang. It was a generic ringtone, not the ones he'd assigned to Rhoda, his work contacts, or Nevin Ng, whom he occasionally joined at the gym or to watch basketball games. He ignored it, leaving the phone untouched on the console next to him.

"Phone's ringing," Qay said mildly.

"Uh-huh."

Qay tapped the armrest. "Not going to answer it?"

"Not unless it's you. I'm spending today with you."

"I don't own a cell phone, so I know it's not me."

Jeremy briefly glanced away from the road toward Qay. "Really?"

"Don't need one. Who'd call me? My apartment has a landline."

"I'd call you."

Qay laughed softly. "I believe you. And I could call you when I needed my next chauffeur service."

I'd service you anytime. Jeremy had just enough sense not to say that out loud. By then the ringing had stopped and Robert Plant was bellowing out "The Lemon Song." Jeremy barely managed not to sing along with the innuendos.

"How do you—" Qay began. He stopped when the phone rang again.

"What does the screen say?" Jeremy asked him.

Qay picked up the phone and peered at it. "Frankl."

Jeremy's buoyant mood crashed and his stomach tightened. "Fuck! Could you do me a favor and put it on speaker?"

After a moment of fumbling, Qay did, and then he turned down the radio. "What's up, Captain?" Jeremy asked loudly.

"We got a good lead."

"Don't tell me you found prints in my apartment."

"No. Patrol got called on a criminal mistreatment charge. Guy turned out to have an entire pharmacy in his bedroom, along with a few other items he wasn't supposed to have. And his girlfriend's kid might not survive, so this guy's facing a long haul as a guest of the state. He's in the mood to talk."

"Shit," Jeremy said. He'd heard stories like this plenty of times—seen them himself when he worked for the bureau—but they still made him ill.

Frankl sounded equally disgusted. "Pretty much. Look, I need to talk to you. There's stuff you need to know. I can meet you at Mickey D's again."

"Can we do it tomorrow? I'm… tied up today."

"Yeah, okay." Frankl clearly wasn't pleased with the delay. "Meet me there at nine. And be careful, Cox. Keep an eye out."

Shit, *shit*. "I will. Thanks, Captain."

For a minute or two after disconnecting the call, Qay was silent. Then he cleared his throat. "Criminal mistreatment? What's that?"

"Child abuse. The fucker they arrested beat the shit out of his girlfriend's child." The words tasted bitter.

Qay made a noise deep in his throat and turned away. Jeremy imagined he wasn't finding the greenery beside the road all that interesting. The better view was out Jeremy's window, where the Columbia River rolled on like liquid steel. Jeremy lifted his coffee cup and swallowed the cooling dregs, and he wished he knew what to say that would make things better.

"My father...," Qay began, but he didn't finish the sentence. It hung heavily between them.

Jeremy set down the cup and reached for Qay's leg. "I know."

"Yours?"

"My parents never laid a finger on me. They punished me by sending me to my room without anything to read."

Jeremy couldn't decipher the meaning of Qay's answering sigh. "I thought about killing him," Qay said. "I even planned different ways. I could slip something into his bourbon, maybe greet him at the door one afternoon with his hunting rifle in my hand. I was going to kill her too. She didn't hurt me, but she knew what he did, and she... she just turned away. Popped a few of her pills and pretended everything was hunky-dory." He was still talking to the window, but he pressed his thigh slightly into Jeremy's touch. The denim of his jeans was worn soft as suede.

"Why didn't you?"

"I was chicken. I knew if I did it, I'd spend the rest of my life in a cage, and I couldn't face that. I preferred to die. Of course, I ended up in a cage anyway. But I finally got out." He turned to look at Jeremy. "You're a cop. You still want to hang out with me after I told you this?"

"I'm a park ranger, not a cop. And yeah, I really do."

Qay turned up the radio and leaned back in his seat. Jeremy couldn't see, but he thought Qay might be smiling. But then something must have occurred to Qay, because he switched the radio off completely. "What that guy said.... Are you in danger?"

"I know as much about it as you do."

"Then shouldn't you meet with that Frankl guy?"

"Tomorrow. I'm sure I'm safe out here, and today is officially our second date. I want it to end better than the first one."

"The first one was good until the last part," Qay said quietly.

"It was."

A short time later, Jeremy pulled into a parking lot. It wasn't crowded on this cold morning, so he had a good choice of spots. "Multnomah Falls?" Qay asked. "I've seen photos but never been."

"It's a nice little hike. Do you want anything to eat or drink before we go? There's a visitors' center." He pointed at the large stone building. "They have espresso."

"Nope. I'm good."

Jeremy had brought some bottled water in a daypack. He stuffed his first-aid kit in there too—because you just never knew—plus a well-worn trail map and the leftover food from Qay's stash. Then he adjusted his coat and hoisted the pack onto his back. "Let's go," he said after locking the SUV.

They set out at a leisurely pace. They weren't in a hurry, and if Jeremy had gone at full speed, he wasn't sure Qay could keep up. Not only did Qay undoubtedly have much less experience hiking than he did, but his work boots were no match for Jeremy's expensive day hikers. Anyway, it was nice to poke along, greeting a few other walkers and looking closely at everything they passed. Some of the views were breathtaking, and Jeremy and Qay paused to admire them, but Qay seemed just as interested in smaller things like rocks and trees.

"Weird," Qay said, not quite touching a tree branch where tiny tufts of bright green stuck out among small gray lobes.

Jeremy moved in for a closer look. "The green parts are moss. The gray is felt lichen. *Peltigera collina*."

Qay's eyebrows rose. "What's the tree?"

"Oh, that's easy. *Pseudotsuga menziesii*. Douglas fir. They're not true firs, though, despite the common name. The genus is *Pseudotsuga* instead of *Abies*. They're sort of in a category of their own."

"Do you know *all* this stuff?" Qay waved his hands widely, indicating everything, apparently.

"Not all of it. I'm better with biology than geology, for one thing, and if it's something obscure, I may be stumped. Douglas firs aren't obscure."

"Jesus."

Jeremy wasn't sure whether Qay was impressed or overwhelmed. "Have I nerded you out?"

Qay responded with a wide, easy grin. "I find nerds kinda hot even when they don't look like Marvel heroes. I just don't know how you can know so much."

"I was a bio major. Plus it's my job, sort of." Jeremy closed the space between them and bent a little to whisper in Qay's ear. "Hot, huh?"

"Uh-huh."

"Hmm. *Dysphania pumilio. Ailanthus altissima. Ambystoma gracile.*"

"Is that Latin dirty talk?" Qay asked with a low chuckle.

"Nope. An herb, a tree, and a salamander."

The chuckle turned into a laugh. "I have no idea how to counter that."

"You could whisper sweet philosophy nothings in my ear. Or… hell. Just stand there and smile like that. That's good enough for me."

"That's ridiculous," Qay said, ducking his head.

"Is not. Jesus, you used to give me just a crooked little lift of your lips and make my heart go pitty-pat long before I had a clue what that meant. Yours is the gold standard by which I've been measuring smiles for thirty years."

Qay snorted and pushed lightly at Jeremy's chest. "You have more sap than all these Douglas firs put together. C'mon." He moved ahead on the trail.

As they walked farther, they encountered fewer people. A lot of folks just tromped around near Multnomah Falls, skipping the many smaller falls in the area. That was just fine with Jeremy, who enjoyed having the trail—and Qay—to himself. Sometimes he and Qay purposely bumped into each other, sometimes one of them tapped the other's arm to point something out, and in a flat section where the trail widened, they walked hand in hand. They didn't say much, and when they did speak, their voices were hushed, as if they were in church. Jeremy preferred to listen to the natural sounds around them—the drip of water, the rustle of leaves, the twitters and rasps of birds—and Qay either shared that preference or was willing to humor him.

They stopped at a trail junction and sat on big rocks to eat some of Qay's food. It wasn't fancy, but everything tasted better outdoors, especially after some decent exercise. And with good company.

"Feet holding up?" Jeremy asked.

"Not too bad. These boots are damned heavy, though." He jerked his chin in the direction of Jeremy's feet. "Yours look pretty snazzy."

"There are some things I refuse to skimp on. Footwear is one of them."

"And vehicles?" Qay asked, mouth quirked.

Jeremy's cheeks heated. "It is, uh, kind of over-the-top. But I really do need four-wheel drive for the job, and the city got me a deal on it."

"It's comfortable. And big. Overcompensating?"

Jeremy threw a wrapper at him.

Qay ducked, laughed, and scooped the wrapper up. "No littering, Chief. You'll make Smokey the Bear mad." He threw the wrapper back, and Jeremy caught it.

"It's Smokey Bear, no *the*, and he doesn't give a shit about littering. He hates fire. It's the stereotypical Indian who doesn't like litter, and he doesn't get angry. He just cries very majestically."

With an incredulous expression, Qay muttered, "Nerdgasm." But then he stood up and ran his palm across Jeremy's short hair. Just a quick touch, but electrifying nonetheless.

They passed many waterfalls. Thanks to the recent rains, the falls rushed at full flow, spraying Qay and Jeremy with their mist and forming little rainbows in the cold winter sun. At one point, Qay stood with his toes at the edge of a drop-off, his face angled up to the falling water. Jeremy remained watching him from several yards back. He wondered at how beautiful Qay looked, and yet how vulnerable.

Near the end of their hike, they came to the big stone bridge that was so beloved of photographers and tourists. Qay leaned over the railing and gazed down at the pool between the upper and lower cascades of Multnomah Falls, and Jeremy pressed close to him.

"Don't sweat it," Qay said. "I'm not considering jumping."

"Do you ever?"

At first Jeremy didn't think Qay would answer. It had been an intrusive question, probably far too much for a second date, even though they'd already shared confidences. And maybe Qay wouldn't want to reveal a weakness in himself. But then Qay shook his head. "Not anymore. I did for a long time after I left Bailey Falls. Tried a couple times when

I was locked up in the booby hatch, and even after I got free…. Shit. I used heavily for years. That was hardly more than a really slow suicide."

To reward Qay for his honesty, Jeremy leaned more heavily against him and dropped a kiss on the side of his head. Qay's hair was damp, the gray strands shining like threads of silver, and he smelled deliciously of forest and coffee and herbal shampoo. Jeremy moved back slightly. "How did you stop?"

Qay tucked his hair behind his ears and rubbed his hands together as if he were cold. "I'm not sure. I didn't have a grand epiphany. I just… I think I just got tired. It's this fucking nasty circle, you know? I started using to dull the pain, but the drugs only caused *more* pain—and quitting was even worse. There's only two ways out of that trap, and one of them is in a coffin. I didn't have any big plans for myself or anything. Didn't want to change the world. Still don't, which you can pretty much tell. I guess I just decided staying alive for one more day was plan enough."

Jeremy had to chew on that. He understood what Qay was saying. Hell, other people had told him similar stories. No big hallelujah moment—just a quiet determination to get dressed and get through the next twenty-four hours. And then the next. What Jeremy didn't see, though, was how Qay had managed to come so far on his own. As far as Jeremy could tell, nobody had championed Qay's cause or steadied him when he stumbled.

"I have a plan," Jeremy said after a long silence.

"Oh?"

"Dinner somewhere nice. And according to my plan, first we stop at your place so you can clean up, then we go to the hotel for my turn to scrape off the dirt, then we eat." It made sense because the restaurant he was thinking of was downtown, so they'd pass by Qay's apartment first. And Qay didn't work on Mondays, so they wouldn't have to call it an early night. Jeremy was willing to lose out on some sleep.

Qay looked doubtful. "My place is a dump."

"And mine is literally in shambles."

"It's my turn to pay for dinner."

"Done," Jeremy said, feeling victorious.

IT WAS pretty clear Qay would have left Jeremy outside his apartment if he could have. But Jeremy kept close on his heels as they went up the sidewalk, and when Qay unlocked the door and turned to look at him, Jeremy flashed his very best puppy-dog eyes. Qay rolled *his* eyes and gestured him inside. "I warned you."

The door opened to a tiny landing with a worn vinyl floor and scuffed yellowish walls. Directly ahead lay another closed door, and a flight of stairs descended to the right. The stairs creaked as Jeremy and Qay walked down. Qay unlocked the door at the bottom.

The basement was dark and slightly musty, with mismatched thrift-store furniture and paneled walls. But what really struck Jeremy was the amount of stuff: little knickknacks of every description and hanging magazine pictures of landscapes and cats and underwear models. And books. Books everywhere, piled crookedly and splayed pages-down atop furniture.

"Told you," Qay muttered, his cheeks red.

"Have you read all of these?"

"No. I… I find them. Sometimes they're a dime each at the Salvation Army, or maybe a quarter at someone's yard sale. Or in a giveaway box in front of a used-book store. I have a hard time just leaving them there." He sighed. "And once I get them home, I can't let them go. And— What?"

It was, perhaps, the most charming thing Jeremy had ever heard, and he couldn't help his big, dopey smile. "That's sweet."

"It's slightly pathological. I have a tendency toward anxiety disorders. I don't want to end up one of those people who gets buried alive by his piles of old junk mail."

"I'd dig you out."

Qay gave him an inscrutable look. "I'm, uh, going to shower. Make yourself at home." He waved vaguely before heading into what must have been his bedroom. A moment later he emerged with a stack of clothing in his arms, only to disappear again into his orange-tinted bathroom. He shut the door with a hollow click.

Jeremy ambled through the living room, picking things up, examining them, and putting them down. He couldn't discern a theme to the things Qay had collected: figurines of animals, people, supernatural creatures, and vehicles; ashtrays, tiny ceramic cups, and wooden mushrooms. The books were mostly—but not all—fiction. The genres included westerns, spy thrillers, mysteries, chick lit, fantasy, sci-fi, historical, romance, and literature. Qay even had cookbooks, although anything much more complicated than a grilled cheese sandwich would clearly overtax the tiny kitchenette.

Just as Jeremy began to leaf through what appeared to be a young adult novel about a circus performer, he heard water running in the bathroom, and he froze. Qay was *right there*, on the other side of that flimsy door. Jeremy could reach that door in just a few strides, could yank it open—he hadn't heard a lock engage—and then he would see Qay naked, his lean body shrouded slightly in shower steam, his long black hair slicked back from his face. And then Jeremy could—

No.

Jesus God, that scenario appealed to him. He was pretty sure Qay would go along with it too. After all, Qay had spent the day flirting as openly as Jeremy had. He'd called Jeremy sexy and hot, and when they walked on the wider parts of the trail, Qay reached for Jeremy's hand as often as Jeremy reached for his.

Jeremy could slip into the bathroom, strip off his clothes, and clasp Qay's wet body to himself. They could fuck—Qay bent over the edge of the sink, maybe, or leaning up against the slick shower wall—and it would likely be spectacular. After all, Jeremy had practically come in his pants the first time they goddamn kissed.

But then where would that lead them? They were only partway through their second date, with a few little not-dates besides, but Jeremy possessed a firm conviction that they could have more. If he could only be a little patient, if the rest of his life would stop imploding, if Qay didn't spook and run, the two of them could *be* something. Something a lot more important than a fast bathroom fuck.

He would wait.

CHAPTER TWELVE

WHEN QAY got out of the bathroom, his hair still damp against his neck, Jeremy sat on the couch with a book in his hands. "Trapeze artist," Jeremy said, holding the book up.

"Uh-huh," said Qay, who didn't know what the hell Jeremy was talking about. "Look, if you want to borrow it, go ahead. I have plenty of others to keep me busy."

"I don't read much," Jeremy answered, looking abashed.

"You used to." Back in high school, Jeremy would finish the work before anyone else, then pull out a paperback. Other kids gave him shit about it, but Keith had thought the books an improvement over his own classroom activities, which mostly consisted of doodling, fidgeting, and scowling into space. He hadn't picked up the reading habit himself until the tedium of institutionalization forced it.

"Yeah. I just… I left that Jeremy behind, I guess. I didn't kill off the little loser. Just, you know, locked him up in a trunk somewhere."

"That's too bad. I liked him."

Jeremy looked thoughtful for a moment, then smiled slightly, stood, and tucked the book into his coat pocket. "Ready?"

"I guess. This is as dressy as I get." He wore the same white button-down and new jeans from their first date, which was possibly a major relationship faux pas. But he didn't have alternatives, and anyway Jeremy didn't seem to mind.

"I've already shared my thoughts on formalwear. C'mon."

As soon as Qay realized which hotel was Jeremy's, he felt intimidated. Not that he expected Jeremy to stay in the kind of dump Qay had often called home, but the Marriott was big and shiny, with an aura of expense accounts and platinum credit cards. The concierge greeted Jeremy with "Evening, Chief!" as they passed.

Jeremy's room daunted Qay as well. It wasn't huge, but it wasn't tiny like some of the cracker boxes where Qay had once lived. The bed was made up neatly with a crisp white duvet and piled with enough pillows for half the city. Stylish abstract art hung on the walls, the TV was a huge flat screen, and the window commanded a lovely view of the river. Jeremy had left little clutter lying around, and if he'd been messy, the maid had dutifully tidied everything up. But as Qay looked uneasily around, he realized that the room was missing any personal touches. Sure, it was only a temporary place for Jeremy to sleep, but even at his most nomadic, Qay had always had books and a few odds and ends scattered around. An interesting-looking rock, perhaps, or an advertisement he'd found appealing. Maybe just a few fast-food wrappers folded into shapes. Anything at all to mark the space as his and announce to the world that he existed.

"I'm gonna hop into the shower," Jeremy said. "Need anything?"

"No. I think I'll just enjoy the luxury for a few minutes."

"It's a nice bed. Feel free to bounce on it." Jeremy winked at him before disappearing into the bathroom.

Qay didn't bounce. He walked to the window and stared out, pretending he wasn't imagining Jeremy stretched out on that big mattress, his long limbs just barely fitting. And God, what about Jeremy naked in the shower, all those bulky muscles in view, his pale skin dripping. He didn't seem the type to wax, but his body hair would be pale. His nipples were probably pink, and his cock—

This was not a productive train of thought. The good thing about middle age was that he didn't have to let his dick make so many decisions for him. He could wait.

When Jeremy emerged from the bathroom with a towel wrapped precariously around his hips, Qay very nearly abandoned that resolution. Jesus, he was every bit as gorgeous as Qay had imagined, with bulging pecs, a washboard stomach, and just the hint of a blond treasure trail disappearing beneath the white terry cloth. Most men in their twenties would have envied his physique; for a man reaching his midforties, he was nothing short of magnificent.

"Forgot my clothes," Jeremy said.

"Holy crap."

Jeremy blinked, then allowed a slow smile to spread over his face. "Yeah?"

"You were this tubby little kid."

"I had a hell of a growth spurt. And I spend a lot of time in the gym."

"And you have personal access to the Fountain of Youth."

Jeremy shook his head. "I feel every damn year of my age."

Qay decided that Jeremy was the human equivalent of his SUV: big and powerful, flashy, yet with substance behind the bling. On the other hand, Qay resembled a used car. Not the real clunkers that would die on you after a few hundred miles, but he'd been used, and used hard. He'd accumulated scratches and dents, his upholstery was a little stained, and his paint job had lost some shine. He was still reliable—still kept motoring away—but he was the kind of car you'd want to trade in as soon as you could afford something better.

"We could postpone dinner," Jeremy said quietly. He prowled a few steps closer, so that Qay smelled the almond and citrus scents of his soap and shampoo.

Qay wanted to tear away the towel and press himself against all that bare skin. He wanted to feel Jeremy's big hands on his shoulders, his back, his ass. God, it had been so long, and he ached to drown himself in human contact—nearly as much as he sometimes ached for a needle or a pill.

"What do you want from me?" he asked, his voice cool and even.

Jeremy didn't hesitate. "Everything."

Qay's knees went weak, and he sat heavily on the bed. In a tiny voice, he said, "I'm not pretty. I have scars."

"You're…. I can't take my eyes off you. Not since I first caught sight of you. But I don't care what you look like." He bit his lip. "I can't tell you what it is about you. I mean, it's not like I can break you into your components and say, '*This* is what gets me going. This piece right here.' But you really do, Qay."

Overwhelmed, Qay couldn't respond at first. Then he pulled himself together. "You really want…. Look. If you're trying to get into my pants, it's not that big a challenge. I'll unzip and bend over right now, and then we can go our separate ways. But don't take me for a ride, okay?" He had no pride; he wasn't above pleading.

Something seemed to set in Jeremy's storm-cloud eyes. He'd made a decision. "The only place we'll ride tonight is to dinner. I want…. Jesus. My life's like a tornado lately and I'm discussing deep thoughts wearing nothing but a towel. Let's give us some time. We're worth it."

Qay answered him with a smile.

THEY ATE at the kind of place Qay never would have chosen on his own: white tablecloths, man-bunned waiters, a menu full of phrases like "locally sourced" and "sustainable." But the prices were surprisingly affordable and the food damned good.

"Do you know every restaurant in town?" Qay asked, spearing more coconut lime snapper with his fork.

"Nope." Jeremy was midway through an elk burger, which Qay found absurd. Elk? "But I eat out a lot."

"I guess you have to, living in a hotel."

"Even before that. I can cook, but it hardly seems worth it when it's just me." Then he froze with his burger poised halfway to his mouth. "Thanksgiving."

"What?"

"It's next week. I'd forgotten."

Qay shrugged. He paid little attention to holidays.

But Jeremy nodded resolutely. "You're joining us."

"Us?"

"Rhoda does a thing. Her son drives down from Seattle—with a date, if he's seeing someone. And because it's Rhoda, there's always an interesting collection of other people. International students, newcomers to town, singles… whatever. I don't know where she finds them all. We have a ton of food. And this time, *I* get to bring a date." He beamed.

Qay had eaten institutional Thanksgivings—dry turkey and mashed potatoes from a box—and the ones served by shelters and soup kitchens. But the last time he'd had a home-cooked holiday meal had been in Bailey Springs, with the bird roasted perfectly and served on a garnished platter. And with his father sloshed before the second helping and his mother medicated nearly comatose.

"Rhoda won't mind?"

"Mind? She'd probably drag you there herself. I'm sure she'd have asked you already if she'd seen you this week. She told me she was glad you didn't kick me to the curb."

Qay smiled. He'd missed her. "Should I bring something?"

"Dunno. We can ask her later."

That settled, they finished their dinner.

Jeremy didn't drive them back to the hotel after their meal. Instead, he took them straight to Qay's place. They remained in the dark of the SUV, quiet and peaceful. Until Qay ruined it. "You're meeting that cop tomorrow."

"I guess so."

"I'm going with."

Jeremy had been facing forward, staring at the windshield, but now he turned to face Qay. "What? No! You don't need to get all wrapped up in my shit."

"I've shown you the skeletons in my closet." Not all of them, perhaps, but enough. "Something's going on with you, and I want to hear about it. Unless you don't want that cop to know about me."

Jeremy made a rude sound with his lips. "I was out long before I left the bureau, and who I'm dating is none of Frankl's business anyway. Besides, I want people to know about you. You can be my trophy boyfriend."

A herd of tiny elephants galloped across Qay's chest. "Boyfriend?" He'd never been that before. Not really.

"Yeah, I know it sounds kind of lame at our age. But *lover*? That's too… salacious. And we haven't done more than kiss. *Partner* sounds like we're in business or walking a beat together, *significant other* is awkward and long, *sweetheart* is something your granny calls you on Valentine's Day, *bae* is out of the question, *companion* is your dog, *beloved* is from a Harlequin romance, *paramour* is—"

"You've thought about this a lot," Qay said, laughing.

"It's a serious question."

It was. "I can live with *boyfriend*, I guess."

"I can too."

"And your boyfriend is going with you when you talk to that cop."

Jeremy sighed loudly. "Fine. I'll pick you up at eight forty-five. It doesn't count as a date, though."

"Fair enough."

They were silent again. Qay didn't want to get out of the car and return to his lonely, cat-piss-scented basement. But if he didn't get his ass in gear, his resolve would erode and he'd end up rutting in the SUV like a teenager. "Our second date went well, I think."

"Me too."

"Pretty scenery. Partial nudity, but PG rated. A good meal."

"And no tantrums," Jeremy added. Then he leaned over the console into Qay's space.

And Christ, Qay could only resist so far. He used both hands to pull Jeremy's head closer so they could kiss. Maybe Jeremy tasted a little of elk—Qay didn't know—but mostly his lips were sweet from the crème brûlée they'd shared, and his mouth was hot as a furnace, consuming until nothing remained of Qay but burning embers. Jeremy's hands were hot too, even through Qay's jacket and shirt, and his face was just a bit rough with late-night whiskers.

Jeremy moved one huge palm from Qay's back to his crotch. Qay would have been embarrassed by how quickly he'd grown hard, but then Jeremy *whimpered*—a needy little sound that made Qay shudder like he had the DTs. Jeremy broke the kiss and leaned his forehead against Qay's. They were both panting.

"I think we've earned an R rating," Jeremy said hoarsely.

"I'm... I'm going to go before we get to X."

Qay could feel Jeremy's nod. "But I'm hoping we'll get there soon anyway, when we both know we mean it. And I think it'll be so, so worth it."

Qay thought so too.

CHAPTER THIRTEEN

QAY'S HEART lifted as soon as the familiar black SUV appeared on his street. He hadn't expected Jeremy to bail on him—Captain Caffeine wouldn't do something like that—but maybe he hadn't believed in Jeremy 100 percent. But here it was, 8:50 on a Monday morning, and Jeremy had arrived. So had the rain, an impatient little patter that dripped from rooftops and danced up and down the sidewalk. Qay hurried over to Jeremy's car.

"Did you have sweet dreams?" Jeremy asked as Qay buckled up.

"Want to know the truth? I jacked off like a fifteen-year-old."

Jeremy laughed so hard he nearly had to pull over. "Me too," he said in between guffaws. "God, we're quite a pair, aren't we?"

They were a pair. Huh.

"Do you have to work today?" Qay asked.

"Yeah. But I can be late. It's a perk of being chief. You have another exam?"

"Not until after Thanksgiving. I'm supposed to be working on a term paper right now, so I'll need to get to school early."

"How come?"

"No laptop."

"Ah." They were at a red light, so Jeremy looked at him. "Must be hard to be a student without one."

"Eventually I'll have to figure out how to swing one. If I don't flunk out."

Jeremy blew a raspberry. "Right. Aren't you the guy with the perfect test? You won't flunk out."

Qay wanted to tell him that one good score did not a brilliant academic career make. Qay still had ample opportunity to choke. But he decided he'd only sound as if he were fishing for compliments or desperate for reassurance. Anyway, the computer issue was a serious one. His pay was enough to afford his apartment, bus fare, and the necessities of life, with, lately, an occasional restaurant dinner. A laptop was out of the question.

The McDonald's parking lot was almost empty. Jeremy pulled into a spot between a Prius and a primer gray muscle car and cut the engine. "Are you sure you want to subject yourself to this?"

"Positive."

Over the years, Qay had spent a fair amount of time in fast-food restaurants. If you were quiet and relatively clean, usually no one cared if you sat there for a long time, nursing bitter coffee or a cup of Coke. The bathrooms were generally clean. And all fast-food joints had the same grease-and-sugar smell, the same plastic tables and chairs, the same noisy youngsters squealing over cheap toys.

This particular McDonald's was quiet. The kids working there looked bored, one of them wiping mindlessly at the stainless-steel counter while another refilled the straw dispensers. Three old men sat together near a window, arguing amicably in a foreign language, and a young guy with a lumberjack beard sat near them. He was reading a newspaper. An older woman shared a booth with a younger one who must have been her daughter, both of them looking tired and blank. Long night at work, maybe, or a long drive. Maybe a disaster in their lives. And at a table far from everyone else, a man in a sport coat watched Jeremy and Qay closely. Qay would have ID'd him as a cop from a mile away.

Jeremy led Qay to the cop, who looked surprised. "Captain, this is Qay Hill. My boyfriend. Qay, Captain Frankl."

Frankl shook Qay's hand and they exchanged some terse pleasantries. Qay would have been put off by the man's close scrutiny— it felt as if he were psychically tapping into Qay's entire rap sheet—but his head was still spinning from the use of the word *boyfriend*. Yes, he and Jeremy had discussed that magic word the night before, but it was one thing to joke about it in the privacy of the SUV and another to use it in public.

He sat down as Jeremy took the chair next to him.

"Are you sure—" Frankl began.

But Jeremy interrupted. "He argued that if something's up with me, he has the right to know. I think he's right."

Although Frankl's expression clearly showed his skepticism with this conclusion, he gave a weary shrug. "Suit yourself."

"How's the kid?" Qay asked abruptly. They both stared at him. "The one who got beaten?"

Frankl's gaze shifted slightly, as if his opinion of Qay had just gone up two notches. "Not good. She's just a baby. Docs say if she survives, she'll have permanent brain damage."

Jeremy's jaw was gritted so tightly, Qay could almost hear it creaking. Qay's own fists clenched in his lap.

"Is the DA going to nail the fucker?" Jeremy growled.

"Probably. DA agreed to drop the drug charges so the perp would talk, but child endangerment is going to stick. The scumbag will plead it out, but he's still facing hard time."

"Good."

Frankl nodded his agreement. "But in this case the scumbag's been a stroke of good luck for us. Turns out he's buddies with the man Donny crossed. Good enough buddies to know what the man's been up to."

Jeremy relaxed and leaned back in his chair, as if discussing this part was more comfortable for him. "Who is he?"

"Guy named Ryan Davis. He's not very bright, but his family has some money. He's pretty high up in the food chain, but he dabbles—drugs, whores, gambling, ID theft. Wherever he can make a buck. Our perp doesn't know exactly what Donny had going with Davis, but it wasn't anything good."

"Figured that much." Jeremy leaned forward, his eyes sharp and intent. He'd probably been a good policeman. Compassionate and not too quick to judge, yet also smart and focused. Qay had encountered a few officers like that during his drug years—cops who saw the human beings beneath the track marks.

Frankl, on the other hand, looked as though he'd rather be doing something else. Golfing, maybe, or drinking beer and watching a game on TV. "What we do know," he continued, "is that Donny stole something from Davis. Some kinda computer files that Davis doesn't want anyone to see. Donny had 'em on a thumb drive, supposedly, and after he and Davis had a falling-out, Donny was trying to blackmail him."

"Shit," Jeremy groaned, looking pained. He rubbed his forehead. "What a stupidass thing to do, Donny. God. So Davis was looking for this thumb drive at my place."

"Yeah. And our source says he didn't find it. So you—"

"Wait. If he wanted the thumb drive back, it seems like killing Donny's not going to help matters. Not if Donny's the only one who knew where it was."

"I told you he's not exactly a rocket scientist," Frankl said. He sipped his coffee and made a face. Qay considered buying coffees for Jeremy and himself, but he didn't want to miss the conversation. Maybe when they were done at McDonald's, he'd go to P-Town. He was looking forward to a reunion with Rhoda.

"Our rat doesn't know exactly what happened with Donny that night. He thinks Davis was supposed to meet him and give him some money, but Davis sent a couple of goons instead. Once they got there, maybe something spooked 'em. Maybe Donny had second thoughts and turned around to leave. Maybe the goons were just too damned stupid to follow instructions. In any case, they shot him. When they searched the body, they didn't find the drive. From what we hear, Davis was not happy." Frankl gave a death's-head grin. "And I guess Davis figured out that Donny had paid you a visit and hoped maybe Donny left the thing with you."

Jeremy sighed and shook his head. "If he did, I don't know anything about it."

"If he did, he hid it damned well, because Davis's guys didn't find it."

None of this was fair, Qay thought. Jeremy hadn't done anything but be a stand-up guy, going way above and beyond for his fucked-up ex. He shouldn't have gotten pulled into this mess. Jeremy deserved rainbows and unicorns and fireworks, not drug dealers and murders and burglary.

"If you know so much, why isn't Davis in jail?" Qay asked. He sounded hostile but couldn't help it.

"Because an informant's tip isn't enough," Frankl answered, clearly irritated. "If we're going to make a murder charge stick, we need more. And I'm confident we'll get it. But while we're working on it, we have to be careful not to tip Davis off. He already knows we have his pal in custody, and that'll be making him jumpy."

That made some sense, but it sure as hell didn't make Qay happy. He scowled at the guy with the lumberjack beard. He hoped one day beard styles would come back to haunt hipsters the way that mullets haunted some men Qay's age.

"So Davis is after me now?" Jeremy's voice was calm, matter-of-fact.

"We think so. You're his best bet on finding that thumb drive."

Jeremy nodded and stroked his square chin. "I guess I am."

Qay's head hurt, and he wanted to have a tantrum—to stand up and scream and kick things. He wanted to smash the stupid plastic chairs onto the tile floor, and he would have if he were younger and still using. After that, of course, Jeremy wouldn't want him. But dammit, Qay was slowly cluing in that Jeremy *might* want him, which was a certifiable miracle. And now this bullshit with Davis was getting in the way.

"I'll meet you outside," Qay said tightly. Without waiting for an answer, he fled the restaurant. Head bowed against the rain, he leaned on the SUV and tried to calm down. It wasn't easy. His heart raced, his lungs felt too tight, and despite the cold air, he was sweating. It took all his self-control not to sprint out of the parking lot and up the street, running until he collapsed.

"How can I help?" Jeremy's voice was warm, and his hand was nicely heavy on Qay's shoulder.

Qay liked the question. Not *What's wrong?* or *Are you okay?* but an offer of assistance.

"Sorry," Qay mumbled, not meeting Jeremy's eyes.

"Don't be." He clapped Qay's shoulder. "Let's get the hell out of here."

"Did Frankl—"

"He told me everything I need to know. C'mon."

Qay felt like an idiot. He was the one who'd insisted on tagging along, and yet he ended up hyperventilating in the parking lot like a drama queen. Fortunately Jeremy's presence had a calming influence, as if the gravitational pull of that big body was enough to counter Qay's emotional tidal waves. And when they sat together inside the SUV for several minutes with the radio soft in the background, that was nice too.

"Breakfast?" Jeremy eventually asked.

"Don't you have to work?"

"It can wait. It's too wet for any park-related emergencies this morning."

They quickly agreed on P-Town. Qay sat back in the comfortable leather seat with his eyes closed and felt his frantic heart slow to a reasonable speed. The swish of the windshield wipers helped—back and forth, steady and even.

When they got to Belmont Street, Jeremy found a spot close to the café. He didn't get out of the SUV right away. "You good with being in public? If not, I can get us stuff to go and—"

"I'm fine." A firming of resolve. "I want to see Rhoda."

Rhoda greeted them both with a wide smile and added an enthusiastic hug for Qay. She smelled wonderful. Qay wondered why nobody sold eau de coffeehouse as a perfume. "I'm glad to see you boys worked things out," she said. "Our Jeremy is pigheaded, but he's not stupid."

Jeremy protested weakly while the three of them walked to the counter. Qay was a little disappointed that Ptolemy wasn't working. Ptolemy was his favorite barista—interesting, funny, and whip smart. But the two kids on duty this morning were cute too. The boy had dimples, and the girl's green hair was in pigtails. She poured coffee for Jeremy and Qay while her coworker heated some eggy things that Rhoda insisted weren't quiches but sure looked like them to Qay.

Rhoda joined them at a table. She tried to ask some serious questions about the Donny thing, but Jeremy derailed her, maybe for Qay's benefit. "Have you decided what Qay should bring next week?" Jeremy asked her.

It took a moment for Qay to understand what Jeremy was talking about, and then he was a little shocked—pleasantly so—that Jeremy had already discussed Thanksgiving with Rhoda.

For her part, Rhoda looked pleased. "I've been thinking about that. What are you good at, Qay?"

"You mean… cooking?"

"Uh-huh."

"Ramen. Which is about the most I can handle in my kitchenette anyway. But I can buy something to bring. I'd like to."

She looked thoughtful. Today she wore something vaguely steampunk in style, with watch-gear earrings and a magnifying-glass necklace. "How about if I put you in charge of entertainment?" she finally asked.

"Um… what does that mean?" Because if he had to sing or put on some kind of show, they were all sunk.

"Well, we don't do movies because nobody can ever agree on what to watch, and the karaoke attempt of ought-nine was an unmitigated disaster. Generally we end up with some kind of game, although sometimes we do a craft project."

Jeremy nodded sagely. "Last year we etched designs on wineglasses. Mostly obscene designs. Mine got ruined in the break-in."

Rhoda leaned over to pat his arm. "If you really want to, we can make more penises this year."

"That's okay. I think Qay should be creative and come up with something new."

Qay shook his head. "I'm not sure I can outdo genital-themed stemware."

"I have faith in you, honey," said Rhoda with a grin.

After breakfast—the not-quiches were very good—Jeremy drove Qay home. Once again they paused in the idling SUV. Then Jeremy made a funny, hoarse sound. "How many dates do you think it takes before we can have sex? Not that this was a date. But I'm not up to saving myself for marriage."

"Little late for that, isn't it?"

"Well, I'm not eligible for a purity ring. But when you sleep with someone you care about for the first time, that's almost like losing your virginity, don't you think?"

"Who *did* you lose it with?"

Jeremy chuckled throatily. "Gary Baker."

Qay goggled. "Troy Baker's little brother? But Troy Baker—"

"Was a shithead. I know. He made my life miserable. But Gary was kind of sweet, actually. We were on the football team and—"

"You played football?" It was a morning for surprises, apparently.

"Qay, look at me. I grew eight inches during sophomore year and kept on growing after that. My parents just about went crazy trying to feed and clothe me. And since I somehow grew mass as well as height, Coach Williams decided he needed me for football instead of basketball. I wasn't that great, but I was big."

Qay imagined Jeremy in a letterman jacket. Or better, in tight pants. "So Gary…?"

"Was a year younger than me. And like I said, he was sweet. I was already fairly sure girls weren't going to do it for me, so when Gary offered to go down on me in the locker room one day, I didn't say no."

Locker room. Shit.

"How about you?" Jeremy asked.

And Qay had to answer because he'd raised the damn subject to begin with. "I was thirteen."

Jeremy hissed. "That's young."

"I know. And the guy…. Sometimes I hung out at that café alongside the highway. Remember the place?" The Burger Hut. A very *greasy* greasy spoon. "I'd bum cigarettes off people or, if they looked likely, see if they had any weed to sell me. One day this guy showed me some pills and some bud, said I could have them if I bent over for him. I figured it was worth it."

There. Now that was out in the open. Qay hesitated to even look at Jeremy, but when he finally dared, he saw compassion and sadness, not disgust. "Four dates," Jeremy announced. "And it will be like a first time for us both, okay?"

Qay managed a weak laugh. "Okay. It's already been a long time for me." As in nearly seven years. Jesus, seven years with no human contact, not even the fast, impersonal kind.

"Good. So we'll do something Saturday after you get off work, and then Sunday makes our fourth. And you don't have to get up early on Mondays."

"You do."

Jeremy winked. "I'll take a vacation day."

Four dates. Qay could do that.

CHAPTER FOURTEEN

A WISE man would have spent the next several days worrying about Ryan Davis and his possibly evil plans, but Jeremy wasn't especially wise. He thought instead about Qay. Oh, he did other things too. He park-rangered as diligently as ever. He ran before work and exercised in the hotel fitness center. He paid a quick visit to Patty's Place—technically to discuss the summer work program, but covertly to check on Toad, who was doing well. Twice Jeremy thought he saw a gray Toyota tailing him—once when he was running and once while he drove. He caught the plate number the second time and called it in to Frankl. He stopped by his loft frequently to make sure repairs were on track. He was getting tired of hotel living.

But mostly he thought about Qay.

Sometimes those thoughts were dirty. He imagined Qay naked, fantasized about what they might do together after their fourth date, and wondered what kinds of noises Qay might make during lovemaking. God, it had been so long since Jeremy had enjoyed more than a casual hookup. He wanted to bed down with someone he cared about and luxuriate in the touch of skin. He longed for more than the usual push and pull. He needed tenderness, affection, familiarity. When Jeremy had these kinds of thoughts, he masturbated. He hadn't yanked his crank so much since he was a teen.

Sex wasn't the only thing on his mind. As he worked out in the fitness room and went about his workday routine, he considered Qay's reaction during the meeting with Frankl. One minute Qay had seemed calm, if unhappy, and the next he was rushing for the door. By the time Jeremy caught up to him, Qay was paper-pale and looked as though he was going to vomit. Jeremy hadn't known what to do for him, and Jeremy had felt so terrible he nearly panicked as well. In the end, though, his presence alone seemed to help settle Qay. A relief for Jeremy, but also sobering. How much could he really do to help Qay, especially with his own life in shambles?

The third matter haunting his thoughts was an amalgam of the other two. He lusted after Qay—that was reasonable enough—but he'd lusted after plenty of men before. This was different. He hadn't fallen in love often, but when he did, he fell fast and hard. And now, at the very least, his feet were teetering on the brink. Absurd, considering he and Qay hardly knew each other, but since when did love make sense? Jeremy had taken anatomy classes in college. He'd seen the inner workings of a human heart, yet he still didn't understand how the heart really worked. At least when it came to love.

On Thursday afternoon the week before Thanksgiving, he patrolled some of the parks downtown. In his experience, life became more difficult for many people as the holidays loomed. Homeless people suffered with worsening weather, the mentally ill struggled with additional stress, kids and parents resurrected old arguments or found new ones. Part of Jeremy's job was to help stem the bits of these crises that spilled into the city's public spaces. And he endeavored to do so despite his distraction. His mind kept wandering to Qay, wondering whether they could truly have a future together.

He saw a young man hunched on a park bench, his knit cap pulled low. Maybe just a college student, or maybe not. Jeremy started toward him but stopped as his phone rang. He glanced at the display and sighed slightly with relief.

"Nevin! How're you doing?"

"I'm doing fine, unlike you, asshole. I just heard about the shit you've been wading through. Why didn't you tell me?"

"Because it's not your jurisdiction." Jeremy and Nevin had worked the same precinct when they were patrol officers. Nowadays Nevin was with the Family Services Division, mostly investigating cases involving abuse of elders and other vulnerable adults.

"But I'm still your friend, dickwad. That makes it my jurisdiction. And fuck, man, I'm really sorry to hear about Donny. He was a bastard, but he didn't deserve to end up dead. You sure as hell didn't deserve to end up shouldering his crap."

Jeremy smiled. Nevin Ng was renowned in the bureau for his spectacularly foul language. "Thanks," Jeremy said simply.

"Did you run yet today?"

"No. Did some weights."

"Pussy. Okay, you're going to meet me at six and I'm going to run your ass off."

"But—"

"Six. Where're you staying?"

Jeremy sighed as he gave in to the inevitable. "You're the detective. Shouldn't you be able to figure that out yourself?"

"Well, I could track you down now and beat it out of you, but then you'd be too fucked up to run. Where, Germy?" Nevin was the only person on the planet who could get away with that hated old nickname, and that was only because the alternatives were worse.

"Marriott by the river."

"Well, la-di-dah and fuck me sideways. See you there at six." Nevin disconnected the call.

Shaking his head fondly, Jeremy continued walking toward the kid.

THERE WASN'T much point in showering before a run, so after dropping off the park kid in Beaverton—one of the kid's friends had offered him a warm place to crash—Jeremy hurried back to the hotel and changed into sweats. No point eating now either; he'd catch something later. A few minutes after six, he was standing outside the lobby and bouncing on his toes when Nevin appeared.

Ten years younger than Jeremy, Nevin was a small man, his compact body coiled like a tightly wound spring. He'd grown up in some kind of hellish environment he refused to talk about, he could outfight much larger men, and he latched on to cases as doggedly as a pit bull. He had a famously active libido and would screw any man or woman who was willing and able. He was also unfailingly gentle and caring to people who needed it the most, especially the elderly and other vulnerable victims of crime. He and Jeremy got together every few weeks, sometimes with other guys for beers and a basketball game, sometimes just the two of them at the gym or out for a run.

Nevin jogged up to Jeremy and slugged him in the bicep. "C'mon, princess. I've already got a half mile on you." Without waiting for a reply, he took off.

Even though Jeremy was nearly a foot taller and much heavier, they made surprisingly good running partners. Jeremy's strides were longer, but Nevin had more zoom. They jogged side by side on the darkened sidewalks, sometimes separating to avoid pedestrians. They ran up Waterfront Park and past Union Station, then through the worn streets in the industrial zone near Qay's window factory. Jeremy was dripping sweat and breathing hard as they raced through Northwest Portland to the edge of the West Hills, but they stayed in the flat area and came back through downtown, ending on the sidewalk outside the hotel.

"Wuss," Nevin said as Jeremy bent, clutching his knees and gasping. "That wasn't even five miles."

"You're out of breath too," Jeremy wheezed.

"Bullshit. I'm just pretending so you don't feel bad, old man." Nevin grinned and leaned against the wall of the hotel.

"You're such a giver."

"Damned right."

After a few minutes, Jeremy was able to stand upright again. He grinned crookedly at Nevin. "You always bring a ray of sunshine into my dreary day."

Nevin could be adorable when he tried, like right now. "You are all lucky the gods saw fit to grace you with my presence." He bowed slightly. But then his gaze caught something toward the street and the smile slipped from his face. "Did you notice—"

"That gray Toyota? Yep. I was a cop too, you know."

"He's been following us since—"

"Since we began. I know. I saw him the other day too. He's not especially sneaky."

Nevin took a few angry steps toward the street, then spun and marched back. "Well? What are you going to do about it?"

"What can I do? He's not breaking any laws."

"You stupid shit! He's probably—"

"He probably has something to do with the Donny mess. I know." Jeremy let out a long breath. "But what good is it going to do anyone if I confront him or call Frankl? I know he's there, and I'm being careful. They're not going to mow me down in the street with a machine gun or anything. They want information, not another corpse."

Nevin narrowed his eyes and kicked the wall. "Douche bags. I could go get my piece and—"

"And that would solve everything, Nev."

Another kick to the wall, this one hard enough to make Jeremy wince. "Goddamn motherfucking cocksucking sons of whores."

To be honest, Jeremy had been slightly concerned about the car tailing him. But he wasn't truly alarmed, and Nevin's worry on his behalf was sweet, if expletive-filled.

Jeremy walked over and settled his hand on Nevin's bony shoulder. "Thanks for the run. Join me at Rhoda's next week?" If Nevin had any family, he never mentioned them. He'd joined Jeremy at Thanksgiving celebrations before, although not every year.

"Nah. I, uh, got plans."

"Don't tell me you have to work. Avoiding crappy shifts is supposed to be one of the benefits of moving off patrol."

Nevin surprised the hell out of him by looking embarrassed. "I'm going somewhere."

"Somewhere?"

"Dinner." When Jeremy just waited, eyebrows raised, Nevin snarled. "Nosy fucker, aren't you? I'm invited to dinner at a fancyass house in the hills. I have to wear a fucking suit. And then I have to pretend like I'm goddamn civilized because I'm meeting the parents. All right? Satisfied now, asshole?"

Delighted, Jeremy grinned. "Whose parents?"

"This… this guy. Colin. He's fruity as a nutcake and he prances around with his twatty graduate degree and his fancy-schmancy everything, and the only reason I can stand to be near him is he's got a spectacular ass and he's hung like goddamn Pegasus." He glanced up at Jeremy, scowled, and looked away. "And he's also a pretty good guy," he muttered.

To the best of Jeremy's knowledge, Nevin had never reached the parent-meeting stage with anyone. "Way to go, Nev. Mazel tov."

"Bitch." Then a wicked grin appeared on Nevin's face. "But what's this I heard about you and some dude?"

Police officers gossiped worse than teenage girls, so Jeremy wasn't surprised rumors about Qay had reached Nevin. "Some dude," he affirmed. "It's speculative at this point, but with a real likelihood of a positive outcome."

Nevin punched him in the chest, almost hard enough to make Jeremy *oof*. "Glad you're getting some, Sasquatch. You've been needing to get laid for a good long time."

Jeremy opted not to tell him about the four-date rule.

Although Jeremy invited him for dinner that night, Nevin declined. Well, he actually said, "Nope. Sorry, farmboy. Colin's got plans and he'll bust my balls if I'm late."

"I wouldn't want your balls busted."

And then, for just a brief moment, Nevin let his inner self peek through, the kind man who made sure old ladies were safe and who would sit for hours playing Go Fish with learning-disabled young people. "You be careful, Germy Cox. Watch out for the bad guys. You deserve that positive outcome, you know?"

Knowing it was best not to draw the thing out, Jeremy nodded. "Good luck with Colin's 'rents. Knock 'em dead." He bopped Nevin's bicep—but lightly—and turned toward the hotel entrance, already looking forward to a hot shower and room service.

CHAPTER FIFTEEN

SATURDAY'S DATE was relaxed and easy. Jeremy parked the dictatormobile in front of Qay's house—having miraculously found a parking spot there—and they walked over to P-Town for a quick hello to Rhoda. They continued strolling up to Hawthorne, then paused in front of the Bagdad Theater. "Will this be okay for you?" Jeremy asked, looking worried. The Bagdad showed movies and served food, but it was also a pub.

"I can go into places that serve alcohol," Qay said patiently. "We've been in some already, remember?"

"Yeah, of course. But none of them were quite so aggressively boozy."

"Thanks for the concern, but I'm good. I'm not craving." Which was true, to a point. Right now in Jeremy's presence, Qay had no desire to use. But all week he'd been itchy and restless, jonesing worse than he had in years. He'd even gone to a Narcotics Anonymous meeting after work on Friday, something he hadn't felt the need to do in a long while. Not for the first time, he regretted that his history of addiction precluded Xanax or other antianxiety meds. But it would do no good to pick up a new habit.

Looking uncertain, Jeremy squinted. "I don't want to tease you. Tempt you. Except with me, that is." He tried an eyebrow waggle.

But Qay was slightly pissed off. "I won't dive headfirst into the stout, I promise you. Besides, I'm responsible for whatever choices I make—not you."

"Okay. You're right."

Once they got inside, Qay honestly had no interest in drinking. Drugs had always been his worst weakness, not alcohol. *Thanks, Mom.* He was content to follow Jeremy through the ornately themed lobby to the snack counter, where they bought pizza, popcorn, and soft drinks. Then they continued into the theater itself. Comfy chairs, Qay was pleased to note. The movie started almost immediately.

The film was a spy thing. Fun, but not great. The lead actor was handsome. The best part, though, was holding hands with Jeremy in the dark, passing the popcorn back and forth, sometimes making out a little during the slow parts. It was as if they were high school kids again, although two boys would never have gone out so openly in Bailey Springs in the 1980s. Snuggling against Jeremy, Qay felt young for the first time in… possibly ever.

Even as the movie rolled, Jeremy ran popcorny fingers through Qay's hair and hummed inaudibly to himself—Qay could feel his chest rumbling.

Afterward they strolled down Hawthorne, chatting contentedly about nothing in particular. Sometimes they paused to peer into shop windows, and sometimes they read restaurant menus and planned future outings. The weirdest part was that Qay felt a part of something. Part of a pair, part of a community. That was new.

"Four dates, huh?" Jeremy said when they'd returned to Qay's house. They were leaning against Jeremy's SUV, neither of them eager to part.

"That's less than twenty-four hours away."

"I might be able to last that long. Especially if we start the date a little earlier. You up for another hike? This one closer to home."

Qay had never been a nature lover, but he'd really enjoyed their visit to the falls. Of course the main attraction had been Jeremy, so animated as he pointed out mushrooms and ferns and slugs. "I'd like that," Qay said. "And then can we go on a quest?"

"That sounds like an adventure. What are we questing for?"

"My contribution to Thanksgiving."

"Ah. I think we can manage that." Then Jeremy ducked his head shyly, which was an interesting look on such a big, confident man. "Hey, Qay?"

"Yeah?"

"Since we're waiting for the fourth date and all, I want tomorrow to be worth the wait. Not a… quick thing, you know?"

Qay laughed uncomfortably. "I've been flying solo for a long, long time. I don't think I'm going to be able to avoid quick."

"That'll be two of us. But there's nothing stopping us from a second act. I want all night. A sleepover."

With a shiver not attributable to the night chill, Qay nodded.

Obviously pleased, Jeremy crossed his arms and bumped his shoulder against Qay's. "I'd like to spend tomorrow night at your place. Please."

"But you have that fancy hotel room, and my apartment's—"

"Screw the hotel room. It's sterile. Your place may not be the Ritz, but it's a home. That's what I want for our first time."

He looked so damned earnest that Qay shivered again, then leaned against him for warmth. "My place it is."

They finished the evening with a scorching kiss that wasn't quite sex but sure as hell came close. Qay walked to his door with his jeans uncomfortably tight, swollen lips tingling, and Jeremy's hungry gaze nearly devouring him.

He needed a cold shower.

QAY SPENT most of Sunday morning cleaning his apartment. It was cluttered but not truly dirty, and he wasn't worried that Jeremy would call things off over a few dust bunnies. But he was jittery, and scrubbing the place down kept his twitchy muscles occupied. Three separate times he had to collapse onto the couch, drop his head to his knees, and practice the deep breathing exercises his last shrink had taught him.

A shrink. Fuck. He hadn't seen one in a while. He was fairly sure that the insurance policy from his employer would pay for one, but even if the copay didn't break him, Qay would have to find a good therapist. He'd also have to find time to get there, which was a challenge without a car and with work and school. And he wasn't confident that going through all those hassles would help him. He'd seen plenty of counselors and psychologists and psychiatrists. He'd memorized their schtick long ago, so he could do the exercises and recite his mantras on his own. Hadn't he gotten this far by himself? He didn't need some dude with a string of letters after his name telling him what to do.

While Qay dusted his apartment, he seriously considered getting rid of some of the little objects lying around—chucking them into the closet or maybe the trash bin outside. He picked up the nearest item, a rectangular tin box imprinted with the Union Jack. Judging by the interior smell, it had once held tea, but it had been empty when Qay found it on the sidewalk near his apartment shortly after moving to Portland. He liked the box. He'd never been to the UK and never would, but the box was a kitschy little reminder that an entire big world existed out there, somewhere. He set the box down.

Next to it lay a piece of driftwood the length of his hand. It fit smoothly in his palm, a bit like a magic wand. He'd picked the wood up a few years ago on a windswept beach. It still smelled slightly of salt. He put that down too.

He lifted a plastic toy—the genie from Disney's *Aladdin*. The small figurine had likely once been a fast-food kid's meal prize, and it was a little dingy. It had been on the floor of a hole-in-the-wall taco shop near LA. He found it exactly one month after he went clean. No, he couldn't throw that away either.

In the end, he cleaned under and around all his stuff but then set every piece back in place. He straightened the wobblier book piles, though, and threw away a couple of magazine pages that had faded during their stay on his walls. He replaced them with new ones: David Beckham in his white underwear, a Stetsoned cowboy selling overpriced jeans, a lush landscape of a waterfall cascading into a pool. The last one made him smile.

Jeremy arrived shortly after one, his short blond hair glistening with water droplets. "It's damp. Still up for a walk?"

"I won't melt." Qay already had his boots on, so all he had to do was slip into his jacket. "Do I need anything else?"

"Nope. This will be an urban hike."

And it was. In fact, the trail Jeremy chose in Forest Park was paved, which was probably best considering the weather. Even still, it was soon easy to forget they were within the boundaries of a large city. Mist hovered among the trees that surrounded them, and Qay felt as if they were trekking through a Tolkien novel. He was almost ready to believe that they would encounter an elf or a hobbit around the next bend. They didn't, although they met a lean older guy with a gray beard and fancy waterproof gear.

"Chief!" the man called when they neared one another. Jesus, did everyone in town know Jeremy?

Jeremy smiled and gave the guy one of those one-armed hugs. "It's great to see you, Len. It's been a while. This is Qay." He turned slightly.

"Qay Hill, meet Len Coleman. He used to be a supervisor for the parks department."

Coleman gave Qay a friendly handshake. "Retired a couple years back, but as you can see, I never really left the parks."

"I can see why," Qay said. "It's a beautiful place."

"Is the Chief here trying to recruit you too?"

Jeremy cut in. "Nope. Just showing my boyfriend around because he's sort of new to town."

There was that word again, and Coleman's grin didn't fade. "The great outdoors is a good way to a man's heart. Works up an appetite." He winked.

Jeremy blushed slightly, which was adorable. After a few minutes of chitchat, Coleman wished them well and set off in the direction from which they'd come. Qay and Jeremy walked in silence for a minute or two.

"You really don't give a crap who knows about me, do you?" Qay finally asked.

"Why would I?"

"I'm not the best catch."

Jeremy stopped suddenly and grabbed Qay's shoulders. "For crap's sake. Stop with the self-deprecation. You're awesome. I thought you were hot shit back in high school, and now that you've grown into yourself? You're smart and interesting and sexy as fuck."

"I come with baggage."

"Who doesn't? Especially at our age. Anyone who hits his forties with nothing in his past to regret has done a piss-poor job of living. I mean, look at me! My recent regret showed up dead and is responsible for siccing a bad guy on my tail."

That didn't make Qay feel much better, but he didn't say so. Instead, he set his jaw. "Fine. No more criticizing myself."

"Good," said Jeremy, who still held his shoulders. "Because I think we ought to be concentrating on a happy ending to our date." He leaned in to kiss Qay—a lingering caress of lips upon lips.

Qay was slightly breathless when they separated. "I warned you. If we 'concentrate' like that, the happy end's going to come way too soon."

"There are no medals for sex endurance, Qay."

They held hands as they resumed the walk, their skin slightly clammy due to the moisture in the air. Jeremy occasionally paused to point out something interesting or to slap a name on flora or fauna, but mostly they enjoyed the sounds of the wintering forest.

Both of them were chilled by the time they returned to the SUV. Jeremy cranked the heat, and as they waited for the windows to defog, he rested his hand on Qay's thigh. That contact did more to warm Qay than the fan did.

"Thanks for the walk, Jeremy. I liked it."

"There are over eighty miles of trail in Forest Park. When the weather improves, we can see them all. I'll show you a few of my favorite spots."

When the weather improves. That was months away. Qay had had lovers before—men who spent a few nights or even a few weeks with him. But he was an addict and so were they, and the only future they'd thought about was their next fix. Most of them hadn't been bad people. But Qay had been killing himself slowly, and so were they, and they all knew there would never be a spring together. And here was Jeremy, blithely assuming more and later and better. It was terrifying.

"Qay?" Jeremy's voice roused Qay from his brief reverie. "Why that name?"

"Qayin is the Hebrew version of Cain."

"Yeah, you told me that. Why that name and not George or Tristan or Marcel?"

Qay turned his head to look at him. "Marcel?"

"Sure, why not? Or if you were going for Old Testament names, there's always Jedidiah or Shem or Boaz."

"Seriously?"

"My parents were big on Sunday School. I guess some of it stuck. You?"

Qay shook his head. "They made me go for a while, but I never paid attention. I only remember the highlights. Apples, floods, Sodom and Gomorrah, stuff like that."

"Then why choose a biblical name, and a Hebrew one at that?"

It was too hot in the SUV. When Qay reached over to turn down the fan, his hand shook. "I don't want to talk about it. Can we go shopping now?"

Surely Jeremy noticed that Qay's voice was sharp and tight, the vowels clipped. But Jeremy didn't comment on it. "Of course. I know just the place." To Qay's relief, he started the engine and turned up the radio, Aerosmith blaring as they pulled away.

They ended up back on the east side in a cavernous store with a bare-beamed ceiling and huge murals on the walls. A big part of the space was occupied by goods for sale. Shelves, counters, and display cabinets contained every game imaginable, and many Qay hadn't imagined at all. Board games, yes, but also video games, puzzles, cards, and complex systems of miniatures. The store also contained many tables, quite a few of them occupied by people gaming. There was even a food area with snacks and drinks.

"My inner nerd loves this place," Jeremy explained.

"I didn't know you had an inner nerd."

"Are you kidding? You knew me when I was fourteen. That little geek is still buried inside this bigger package." He ran a hand down his impressive chest.

"Oh, I knew that. I just figured your nerd was pretty much outer. Guys who spout Latin on a date? Nerds." Qay grinned lasciviously. "Nerds are hot."

Jeremy waggled his eyebrows in return, then made a gesture that encompassed the whole store. "What do you think you want to bring?"

Qay had played games in various institutions when he was younger. Endless droning games of checkers and chess, Monopoly, Parcheesi, and Yahtzee. Better than twitching away in the corner or sinking into a drugged haze, but not by much. He'd played cards too; everything from Go Fish and War, to poker, blackjack, bridge, and hearts. And lots and lots of solitaire. "Cards?" he said hesitantly. Not that solitaire made a great holiday group activity.

But Jeremy brightened. He led the way across the store to a stacked display of oblong boxes. "This," he said decisively.

Qay read the box. "Cards Against Humanity?"

"Yep." Then Jeremy briefly described how to play.

It sounded fun, so Qay grabbed a box. "Sold. Let's go."

Jeremy grinned brightly. "You seem eager, Qayin Hill."

Eager, petrified. Sometimes it was hard to tell the difference. "I think we've successfully completed phase two of date four. Now we just need dinner, and—"

"Takeout. There's great Thai just a few blocks from your place."

"Thai to go."

THE THAI place was just a block away from P-Town, and Jeremy couldn't find a place to park.

"We could just go to my place and walk," Qay offered.

"Nope. Got a better plan." Jeremy pulled into the parking garage beneath the building where he lived. After turning off the engine, he looked at Qay. "I know you're kind of in a hurry. Me too. But are you up for a brief detour? I can show you my loft-in-progress."

Oh. Qay wished very much that he could have seen the place before it was trashed, because then he would have gained a little more insight into Jeremy. A person's living space said a lot about him. Like Qay's basement, which was old and cheap and full of useless crap.

"I'd love a preview," he said.

Jeremy took his hand to lead him up the three flights of stairs. There was nothing special about the stairwell, just concrete steps, bare white walls, and an unmarked door on each floor. When they reached the top floor, Jeremy hesitated a moment before undoing the lock.

"Everything okay?" Qay asked.

"Yeah. I had a couple of unpleasant surprises here lately. I guess the associations are bad. But then you know all about that, Mr. Psych Major." He gave Qay a half grin before using his key.

The first thing Qay noticed was the size of the apartment, easily three times the square footage of his basement place. He was willing to bet that during the day, the high ceilings and big windows kept it bright and airy. There were no furnishings yet, and the kitchen was still in shambles, but the white walls smelled of fresh paint, and the concrete floor was stained an attractive mottled brown.

"Wow," Qay said. "It looks high-end."

Jeremy shrugged. "I got a good deal when I bought it, and I had great insurance coverage. C'mon. I'll show you the rest."

The bathroom was big enough to host a Roman orgy, with an oversized tub and a huge shower enclosure. The tile work wasn't complete and the toilet was missing.

"I miss my bathroom," Jeremy said wistfully.

The bedroom was large, but not as supersized as the bathroom. Right now it was nothing but bare floor and pristine walls. Jeremy stood in the middle, looking around carefully. "I bought a mattress set but not a headboard. And since I want the dresser to match, I don't have that yet either. I guess I'd better make a decision soon. God, I hate shopping."

"What kind of gay man are you?"

Jeremy walked up to him, grabbed his hand, and yanked him close. "A very butch one," he rumbled.

Qay stole the kiss before Jeremy could offer it, but Jeremy didn't seem to mind. In fact, he pulled Qay impossibly closer and settled his hands over Qay's ass. It was too bad that several layers of fabric—jacket, shirt, jeans, boxers—prohibited skin-on-skin contact, but those big palms felt good anyway. Qay worked his hands under the hem of Jeremy's coat and gave his ass a squeeze. Fuck. Talk about buns of steel. If they were this glorious covered by denim, what would they be like bare?

Qay had always enjoyed kissing. Oral fixation, maybe. But kisses didn't usually make his entire body hot and tight, didn't make all the anxieties and miseries and unmeetable needs temporarily recede, didn't make him want to give in and give himself over. Until now.

They broke apart, panting, lips tingling. "We better go. The floor would not be comfortable," Jeremy said.

Although he was nearly past caring about discomfort, Qay nodded. "Thai food. Thanks for the tour."

"Maybe when it's ready and all the shit I ordered gets delivered, you can help me set things up."

"Do I look like the interior decorator kind of queer?"

Jeremy laughed. "Man, we're really letting our team down with our inadequate homosexuality."

"Let's get naked in my bed and prove we can still be gay."

They took the steps at a run.

THEY CARRIED their plastic bags—smelling of chilies and peanut sauce and cilantro—through the drizzle to Qay's apartment, laughing like teenagers who'd just TP'd someone's house. Qay's hand shook with cold and excitement, making it difficult to turn the lock. Jeremy's hot breath on his nape didn't help matters.

Once they were finally inside, Qay grabbed plates and cutlery while Jeremy arranged foam boxes on the table. Giddy with hormones, they had gone a little overboard ordering, and Qay would be eating leftovers until Thanksgiving. They heaped their plates with noodles and curry and rice, then sat on the couch to eat.

"I don't know if having a huge meal before sex is such a great idea," Qay said doubtfully, although he didn't stop shoveling food into his mouth.

Jeremy pointed a fork at him. "We need it. Stamina."

Qay had eaten better since meeting Jeremy than he had in a long time. Maybe he should start worrying about getting more exercise. He walked a lot at work, and jittering burned a lot of calories, but he didn't run or hang out at the gym like Jeremy did.

For a few more minutes, Qay turned his attention to his pad gra prow. When he glanced up again, Jeremy was gazing at him with a bare hunger that had nothing to do with Thai food. "I like watching you eat," Jeremy said, a slight hoarseness to his voice.

"Why?"

"Imagining other things you might do with that mouth. Wondering what you taste like."

Qay set his plate down. "I think we should clean up." He hadn't spied any roaches in this apartment, but he better not tempt fate by leaving food out. Besides, if he didn't cool down a little, one touch of Jeremy's hand would be enough to burn him to ashes.

Jeremy helped him stick the leftovers into the fridge and rinse the dishes, then used his big body to trap Qay against the kitchen counter. "Appetizer," he said before leaning down to drag his tongue slowly across Qay's neck. If Qay hadn't been pinned in place, his knees might have given out. "Shit," he groaned.

"Yeah." Jeremy's pupils had taken over most of the iris, and his gaze burned with an intensity rarely seen in the sober. A slight flush colored his cheeks.

But then he moved back a step—almost a stagger—and ran fingers through his shorn hair. "Is it usually like this for you?"

Qay shook his head. "Never."

"We… we ought to understand this, you and I. I know about hormones and neurotransmitters and what makes a body work. And your professors, they've taught you about the philosophy of what draws people together, right? And the psychology of attraction? So what's this thing we have?"

"I don't know. Don't have a name for it." Oh yes he did, but believing that name would be stupid beyond all comprehension.

"We hardly even knew each other back then, and Jesus—we're not in Kansas anymore. Neither of us is the same person we were then."

Qay thought for a moment. "Maybe we are. Just a little, I mean. You have the bullied, nerdy kid still inside you, and I'm the sullen misfit." His laugh jangled. "Maybe more than a little bit, in my case. And yeah, I'm more than Keith was. Less than him too. But he's still here." He'd never admitted that to himself, let alone said it out loud. The idea should have terrified him, but instead it was a relief. Like maybe he'd been regretting killing Keith off.

"Maybe we don't need to understand it," Jeremy said after a pause. "'Cause it's real, isn't it?"

"Unless I'm delusional again."

Jeremy started forward, but Qay stopped him with an outstretched arm, palm to Jeremy's chest. "I've told you this, but you need to see it." He began to unbutton his shirt. His hands shook so badly that the task was difficult, but when Jeremy reached forward to help, Qay batted his hand away.

One advantage of living in Portland was that you could wear long sleeves year-round and rarely would the weather be hot enough for anyone to question it. Qay's skin was a secret he kept to himself. He didn't much like looking at it either.

He finally got the shirt unfastened and let it drop to the floor. He pulled off his plain white T-shirt, then stood with arms spread, displaying himself. He knew what Jeremy must see: scrawny torso, pasty skin, a dusting of dark hair going gray. A few scars, most of them souvenirs of his landing in the Smoky Hill River. Badly drawn tattoos, each symbolizing something he'd thought was important while he was high or drunk or frenzied but none of them meaning anything to his sober, sane self. Small craters and puckered lines on the insides of his elbows and forearms.

Jeremy didn't wince or draw back, which was a small surprise. He worked his gaze slowly over the details of Qay's bare upper body as if it were a crime scene he must analyze.

"I've seen junkies before," Jeremy said softly. "Interacted with lots of them when I was a cop, and I still do now that I'm a ranger. I know what track marks and prison tats look like, and I—"

"So no need to look at me." Qay crossed his arms on his chest and drew in his shoulders.

"If you'd let me finish," Jeremy said, stepping nearer. He gently grasped Qay's upper arms with his big, hot hands. "I don't see a junkie when I look at you. I see *you*—Qayin Hill—a fascinating man who's gotten under my skin faster than I would have thought possible."

Some of the thrumming fear within Qay quieted, mostly because he read nothing but sincerity on Jeremy's face. Well, sincerity and the embers of lust. But Qay couldn't just let it lie, couldn't get the rest of the way naked and have fulfilling, amazing sex with this perfect man.

"You haven't asked about my HIV status," Qay said.

Once again, Jeremy didn't flinch. "You haven't asked about mine."

"You're Captain Caffeine. Lethal viruses wouldn't dare come near you. But I did every fucking thing you're not supposed to do. Unsafe sex. Dirty needles. For years, Jeremy." He laughed bitterly. "Did you know that the CDC lists vulnerable populations for exposure to HIV, and I belong in nearly every damned one of them?"

"Are you healthy, Qay? Are you getting the right treatment?"

Fuck. If anything, Jeremy moved a little closer as he spoke. He shifted his hands to Qay's cheeks and stared intently into his eyes.

"I'm negative," said Qay, feeling foolish. "I don't know how the hell that happened, but I am. It's like God figured out I was trying to kill myself again, and he purposely fucked me over by making me live."

Jeremy's next exhalation was shaky. "So you're not—"

"No. I was negative the last few times I got tested, and I haven't slept with anyone since then. But if I was positive—"

"I'd be sad. And scared for you. But I'd still do this." He leaned forward for a long, intimate kiss. "And I'd still beg you to come to bed with me. Now. Please?"

Qay shivered as Jeremy's warm hand closed over his. Then he looked him straight in the eye and nodded his assent.

CHAPTER SIXTEEN

ALMOST SINCE they'd met, Jeremy had considered the possibility—no, the *probability*—that Qay was HIV-positive, and the idea had scared the crap out of him. Qay didn't always take the best care of himself, and Jeremy didn't know what kind of health care he had access to. Qay's diet was iffy, he tromped around in the rain, and between work and school, he was often stressed and exhausted.

So when Jeremy learned Qay was negative, he could have sobbed with relief. But crying like a baby was a good way to ruin what was left of the mood, and Jeremy refused to do that. Instead he let Qay, bare-chested, lead the way to the bedroom. He'd made up the bed very precisely, which caused the corners of Jeremy's mouth to rise. "That looks inviting," he said.

Qay blushed. "Hospital corners. One thing you learn when you spend time locked up."

Jeremy was about to answer, but then he remembered something. "Don't move." He ran into the other room, where his coat hung over the back of the couch, and pulled a small paper bag from the inside pocket. After returning to the bedroom, he dumped the bag onto the bed. A dozen assorted condoms fell out, as did a fairly large bottle of lube.

Qay stared at the colorful pile, wide-eyed.

"I don't think I'm Captain Caffeine, but I'm definitely Mr. Safety," Jeremy said. And that was true. Even in his two committed relationships, he'd insisted on safer sex. Which turned out to be a wise decision in Donny's case, at least, considering that he was sleeping around.

Qay began to laugh, and suddenly he looked years younger. He dug into one of the two mismatched nightstands and came out with a double handful of wrapped rubbers. And he did Jeremy one better—Qay had *two* bottles of lube. "I went shopping the other day."

"Looks like we were both optimistic," Jeremy said through his own laughter. It felt good to be lighthearted.

And that was when Qay again surprised him with a kiss, this one ravenous. They didn't just tangle tongues; Qay also nibbled sharply on

Jeremy's lower lip and dragged his tongue across the late-evening rasp of whiskers. "It's been a really, really long time," Qay said shakily, leaning his body against Jeremy's.

How long was long? Jeremy didn't want to know. He decided that tonight he'd make Qay forget—even if temporarily—every unfair thing life had dealt him.

Jeremy slowly stroked Qay's back, feeling the chilled skin warm under his touch. Qay warmed too, pressing against Jeremy more firmly and wrapping his arms tightly around his torso. They still wore jeans, but Jeremy felt Qay's cock hard against his own. When Qay snuffled at the junction of Jeremy's neck and shoulder, Jeremy suddenly remembered they'd been walking through Forest Park that day. "Do you want me to shower?" he asked.

"God no! You smell amazing. Like... pine trees and rain and lime juice." As if to emphasize his point, Qay licked Jeremy's neck slowly, lingering over the pulse point.

Fuck. Jeremy wanted more of that, which meant he needed more bare skin. He tried to take off his sweater without losing contact with Qay, but that didn't work well. They ended up tangled in each other's arms until Qay chuckled, pulled the sweater over Jeremy's head, and tossed it aside. Next he tackled the button-down Jeremy wore underneath, but when he saw an undershirt beneath that, Qay clicked his tongue. "How many damn layers do you have? Am I just going to keep undressing you until there's nothing left? Are you actually teeny-tiny in there, like a matryoshka doll?"

"Nope. That's it. On top, anyway."

When they were chest to chest, Qay started licking again—neck, collarbone, shoulder. But when he got to a nipple, Jeremy groaned. "I'm... I'm hella sensitive there."

Qay looked up at him with delight. "Really? How sensitive?" He punctuated the question with a tender nibble that made Jeremy's knees wobble.

Gently, Jeremy pushed Qay's head away. "Sensitive enough that if you keep it up, this show's gonna be over quicker than either of us want."

"You can come just from this?" Qay gave both nipples a gentle pinch, then cackled gleefully when Jeremy moaned and threw his head backward. "Jesus, you *can*!"

Jeremy would have begged at that point, but he wasn't sure for what. Stop? More? He grunted instead, then quickly popped his fly and pushed his jeans and underwear down to his thighs. He was rewarded when his cockhead bumped against Qay's flat belly and Qay hissed.

"Fair enough," Qay said. He stepped back and stripped off his remaining clothing as Jeremy did the same, and then they simply stared at each other. It was weird. Jeremy knew that good genes and the gym had made him attractive. He'd been called sexy many times and was used to the heated need on a lover's face. Yet he still felt slightly surprised to be wanted, just as he was sometimes surprised to glance in the mirror and not see a chubby, geeky little boy.

As a teen, Keith Moore had been rangy—all long limbs and wide shoulders, a boy still waiting to fill out. But although Qay's shoulders were still broad, he had never really filled out. His body was wiry, with tight muscles and firm pale skin. Even his cock was taut as it jutted from the dark curls at his groin. Despite the badly done tats, the track marks, and his other scars, he was beautiful, making Jeremy's heart speed and his nerves thrum.

Talking stopped, at least in any coherent form. They still made plenty of noises, some of which were words—*yes*, *please*, *God*, *more*, *fuck*. Most of the condoms and all three bottles of lube ended up on the floor, the neatly arranged bedding quickly became a tangled mess, and their bodies grew heated in the chilly room.

Qay's ass felt almost unbearably tight, even after Jeremy took great care to prep him, and his long neck looked so vulnerable as he bent his head back on the pillow and gasped. He dug his heels into Jeremy's ass, urging him to go deeper and faster. And although the sensation of his cock being welcomed and surrounded was fantastic, other heady sensations bombarded Jeremy. The sight of Qay's straight dark hair fanned out on the pillow, his hazel eyes focused so intensely on Jeremy's. Qay's gasps and moans and whimpers, the slap of skin against skin. The odors of sweat, precome, and forest. Jeremy felt his climax build. Qay had been stroking himself in rhythm with Jeremy's thrusts, and now Jeremy wrapped one of his hands around Qay's so they grasped Qay's cock together. The skin of Qay's belly was smooth and tender—and that bit of softness against his knuckles finally carried Jeremy, shouting, over the edge.

Qay came just a moment later, growling breathlessly while his hot spend spurted between them.

Jeremy was reluctant to pull out of Qay's body, but when he did, he couldn't do much more than roll onto his back and wheeze. Qay took charge of the cleanup, bringing a plastic wastebasket for the used rubber and then a couple of damp washcloths. He seemed jittery and intent on more chores, so Jeremy caught his hand. "Will you come to bed? I forgot to warn you. I'm a cuddler."

"Of course you are," Qay said with a smile. He turned off the light and would have made it to the bed uneventfully if he hadn't stepped on the slippery pile of wrapped condoms. Instead, he stumbled, swore, and collapsed onto Jeremy with a thump.

Jeremy grabbed him tightly, and they laughed as they attempted to arrange the blankets and each other. At last Jeremy had Qay exactly where he wanted him: spooned back against Jeremy and wrapped in Jeremy's arms.

"You smell good too," Jeremy said after burying his nose in Qay's hair.

"One thing I like about the window factory is that it's not stinky. I worked at a poultry processor for a while. God, it took months to get the reek off me. The only thing worse than that was my stint at a recycling plant."

"Well, now you smell like sex. And Thai food. Which make an oddly appealing combination."

Qay chuckled and adjusted his body slightly, resting more firmly against the warmth behind him. Jeremy wasn't a kid with a superhero refractory time, but Qay's firm round ass against his cock was nearly enough to get Jeremy going again. Maybe later. After a nap. He yawned loudly.

Qay yawned as well; then he laughed. "We're very exciting."

"Don't want exciting," Jeremy murmured into Qay's tender nape. "I want this." Because the sex had been wonderful, but holding Qay close was even better.

Qay made a throaty noise that might have been either agreement or skepticism.

Despite being warm and postorgasmic, Qay was still tense, his muscles coiled as if he might spring from bed any second. Yet he also leaned back into Jeremy's embrace as if he would never leave.

And that was how it must always be for Qay, Jeremy realized with a start: eager for stability, comfort, and affection, yet worried that none of those things were real or lasting. Well, Jeremy would just have to do his best to encourage the positive emotions and chase away the fears.

"I'm glad we waited," Qay said sleepily. "Was worth it."

"Amen."

Jeremy slowly rubbed his hand along Qay's arm and lean flank, across his chest, over his thin, soft belly. Qay melted a bit more, his breathing evening out. Jeremy thought he'd fallen asleep, but then Qay spoke. "Did you know about the Diegleman place?"

The question was such a non sequitur that at first it made no sense, but then the name resurrected an ancient memory. "In Bailey Springs, you mean?"

Jeremy felt Qay's nod.

"It was supposed to be haunted," Jeremy said.

"It wasn't. It was just a run-down farmhouse. Abandoned years before we were born, I think."

Jeremy frowned as he tried to remember details. "I just remember a field."

"Yeah, they tore the house down after...." Qay swallowed loudly. "Teenagers used to go there to get high or to fuck, but that was when we were little. When I was eight, nine years old, I spent a lot of time there, just sort of poking around. I think that farm dated back to homestead days. I'd find all kinds of interesting shit there—old tins and bottles and stuff. Once I found a bunch of coins that had been buried in a coffee can."

Qay fell silent, which gave Jeremy the opportunity to imagine a very young Keith Moore, skinny and dark-haired, poking around the dirt and weeds in search of treasure. The image made him smile, yet it also thickened his throat, because at eight or nine, shouldn't Keith have been running around with other kids?

"A lot of the time, I'd just bring a book to the Diegleman place and read, or sometimes I'd draw in a sketchpad. The older kids didn't come until night, so I had it to myself during the day. It was... peaceful. Did you have a spot like that?"

"My room. On weekends and vacations, I'd spend all day in there. Just come out for meals." His mother never minded; in fact, she'd always seemed relieved that Jeremy entertained himself so easily. When his father got home from work, he'd sometimes yell at Jeremy to get his lazy butt outside for a change. But neither of his parents ever raised a hand to him. He didn't have to go somewhere else just to feel safe.

Qay nodded again and shivered. Jeremy sensed the cold wasn't to blame, and he held him tighter. "I wasn't supposed to go there," Qay said. "It was less than a mile from home if you walked along the railroad tracks, but my parents put it off-limits. Dangerous, they said. I don't know why—they weren't big on explaining reasons behind the rules. I ignored them. I went all the time. I used to dream that when I grew up, I'd buy the Diegleman place, fix up the house, and live there. I even imagined what colors I'd paint the walls, how many dogs I'd have and what breeds... all that crap."

He sounded so young and wistful. All Jeremy could do was hold him.

Then Qay shook again—a shudder instead of a shiver. "It was August and I was twelve. It was a miserably hot day. Remember the kind? The air so thick and heavy it weighs you down. If I was a smart kid, I'd have stayed in my house with the air-conditioning. But it was Saturday and my father.... That kind of weather always put him in a bad mood. Fuck, *everything* put him in a bad mood. So I went to Diegleman's and sweated while I read. By late afternoon I saw thunderclouds piling up to the west, but I didn't worry about them. I guess I figured I'd be fine in that old house. If worse came to worst, there was a storm cellar, but it was so full of spiders I don't know if I'd ever have braved it."

Jeremy remembered watching those Kansas storms roll in. The sky to the west would get darker and darker with angry purple clouds, but he'd still be safe in the sunshine for a while. Then the temperature would drop and everything would go eerily silent as the sky took on a green tinge. When the clouds finally reached him, blotting out the light, he'd be thankful for a strong roof over his head. Although those storms could be scary, they were also exhilarating—lightning bursting overhead like fireworks and thunder shaking the marrow of his bones.

Jesus. Even in the darkness of a Portland basement apartment, he could see storm clouds rushing in. Still, he prompted Qay with a question. "So you stayed at the farm that day?"

"Yeah." The answer came out as a sigh. "I did. My parents heard the weather forecast and sent my brother to fetch me. He never went to Diegleman's because it was against the rules. Kevin obeyed all the rules."

His brother. Oh, shit. Another dusty memory reared its head and glared at Jeremy. There had been *two* Moore boys, hadn't there? And a family tragedy.

"Kevin's fourteenth birthday had been just a few weeks earlier. Our parents got him a Walkman. Remember those things? Nobody else in Bailey Springs had one yet—hell, Kev might've had one of the first ones in Kansas. He thought he was such hot shit. He wore it all the fucking time."

Another pause, another shudder that devolved into muscle twitches, which Jeremy tried to smooth away. But just when he thought Qay would never finish the story, Qay took a deep breath. "There were two ways to get to Diegleman's from our house. If you stuck to streets and roads, it was longer than if you walked the tracks. And Kev was in a hurry to get me because those clouds were coming in fast. He could've walked alongside the tracks, but in August the weeds were tall. It was easier to walk the rails. So that's what Kev did."

Oh. Oh *fuck*.

"Qay—"

"He never even heard the train. Didn't feel it coming either. The engineer said Kev never so much as turned to look behind him. I guess he was too into his music."

Jeremy knew Bailey Springs, so the image was clear in his head: a teenager trotting along the railroad ties, bopping his head to Bruce Springsteen or Bob Seger. Behind him, the yellow locomotive just finishing the curve and the engineer blowing the horn in vain.

Just as Jeremy was pushing that vision away, a realization struck him. "Qayin. Cain. Shit, Qay. You didn't kill your brother." He was surprised by the shakiness in his own voice.

"That's what the shrinks told me too. But Kevin died because of me. I know it. My parents sure as hell knew it."

"Your parents—"

"Before Kev died, Dad had a hair-trigger temper, especially when he drank. But he only drank on weekends. And the worst he'd do was backhand me. Mom was usually there for me when he lost it, though. She didn't try to stop him from hitting me, but afterward she'd give me an ice pack, maybe get me a bowl of ice cream. After Kev died, though.... After he died, Dad drank every night. He hit harder too." Qay barked a humorless laugh. "Good thing he was a doctor, because he could patch me up if it was worse than bruises."

Jeremy couldn't remember if he'd known Keith then, but he'd seen Dr. Moore around town. His grandmother was one of Dr. Moore's patients.

One time, Jeremy accompanied her to an appointment, and when Dr. Moore spied Jeremy in the waiting room, he'd given him a lollipop. Jesus, why hadn't Jeremy realized what a twisted fuck the man was? Qay had nobody to tell about the abuse, but Jeremy could have—

"Mom changed too," Qay said, interrupting Jeremy's thoughts. "Kev's death broke her. She still kept up with all her clubs and things, but only because Dad kept her drugged to the gills. At home when she saw me, she'd just turn away."

Because he needed to, Jeremy repeated what he'd said before. "You didn't kill your brother."

Qay ignored him. "I understand addiction and mental illness. Christ, I understand them inside and out. But they were no excuse for my parents to…. At least my problems never fucked up anyone's life but my own."

Oh. Another reason why Qay was so skittish. If he let someone in close, he risked hurting them. Even Jeremy could figure that one out.

"You're not them," Jeremy said. "Just because you have issues doesn't mean—"

"Like Donny? Look what his issues did to you."

It was Jeremy's turn to sigh. "You're not Donny either. Anyway, I can take some hurting. I'm a big boy."

"You're not as powerful as you think, Captain Caffeine. Every superhero has his kryptonite."

It wasn't the time to argue, so Jeremy remained silent. But dammit, he *was* strong. He'd worked fucking hard to make himself that way. He squeezed Qay a little tighter, just to remind him.

"I don't remember the funeral," Qay said. "Not the church part anyway. It's a blur. But I do remember standing at the gravesite. My tie was so tight—strangling me like a python—and I had to wear a suit, so I was melting in the heat. I wanted to melt. Just… become a puddle and sink into the grass. But Mom stood there like the goddamn ice queen, and Dad might as well have been made of granite. They didn't look at me. They were burying the wrong son."

"Jesus, Qay—"

"They told me so, later. Each of them. *It should have been you.* And nobody… nobody comforted me. My big brother was dead and nobody even…." The sound that followed was more like a groan than a sob, and it broke Jeremy's heart.

Jeremy gently urged Qay to roll over. Qay buried his face in Jeremy's shoulder, and Jeremy cradled him in a firm embrace. Qay's body quivered, but he didn't cry. And he didn't release Jeremy.

Inside every man was the boy he used to be. No matter how much bigger he'd grown or how many miles he'd traveled. No matter how high the bridge from which he'd leaped.

After a time, the nature of their mutual embrace changed. Jeremy had been circling his hands soothingly over Qay's back, but when Qay shifted his head and began to suck and lick Jeremy's skin, Jeremy moved his palms gradually downward. Seemingly pleased by that, Qay undulated against him and then focused his attention on Jeremy's nipples. Maybe those sensitive little nubs of flesh were Jeremy's kryptonite, because his mood abruptly shifted from comforting to voracious.

This time, they didn't even make it to the condoms, which was okay because they didn't need penetration. Qay worked Jeremy's nipples with lips, tongue, and teeth, and their slick cocks rubbed and jostled as Qay and Jeremy rutted against each other. Considering how little time had passed since their first round, they reached their peaks surprisingly quickly. Qay came first, but that didn't stop him from continuing his devotion to Jeremy's chest while firmly stroking Jeremy's dick, and soon afterward Jeremy cried out his own climax.

Stuck together with drying come and tangled limbs, they slipped effortlessly into sleep.

Chapter Seventeen

JEREMY AWOKE, slightly disoriented, to the smell of coffee. Qay stood beside the mattress with a steaming mug in his hand. His flannel pants hung low on his hips, and his plain white tee was tight across his chest. "Rise and shine, sleeping beauty."

"Morning?" Jeremy asked, because it was hard to tell.

"Yeah. Don't you need to go to work?"

Work. Shit. It was Monday, wasn't it? He hadn't set the alarm on his phone the night before. He wasn't even sure where the phone was. He'd shed it along with his clothes. And although he'd intended to take a vacation day, he'd decided against it—with the holiday coming, he had a lot to do. Feeling groggy, he struggled to sit up. First he took the coffee with a grateful smile, and then he saw the red LED numbers on Qay's ancient clock radio. "Shit. It's almost eight."

"I thought about waking you earlier, but you're cute when you're asleep. And I like having you in my bed."

That made Jeremy grin. "I like being here. And if I don't shift my ass, I'm never going to leave."

Qay leered. "If you *do* shift your ass, I won't let you leave."

"Twice in one night wasn't enough to tide you over?"

"I have a long, long dry spell to make up for."

Jeremy swallowed some milky-sweet coffee and winced—it was hot and definitely not up to Rhoda's standards.

"How long?" Not a comfortable subject, perhaps, but better than reviving Qay's childhood memories.

Qay sucked on his teeth and looked away. "Almost seven years."

"Seven years? Seven *years*? Holy fuck!"

"Wrong expletive," Qay said with a snort.

"But how did you—"

"I know how to masturbate, Jeremy. I'm sort of an expert on it, in fact."

Jeremy shook his head. "Not the same. You haven't even had a quickie? A hookup?"

"I haven't so much as kissed another person since I got sober, and that was seven years ago." Qay looked amused by Jeremy's astonishment. "And it didn't kill me. I mean, I wasn't exactly a monk. I looked at porn. Um, sort of a lot sometimes."

"I realize abstinence isn't fatal. But *why*? Jesus, Qay. You're really good-looking. It wouldn't be hard for you to find someone who's willing."

"It's not, but that's not the point. I had plenty of sex when I was younger. Some of it I was even sane and sober enough to remember afterward. It felt good at the time—scratching an itch. But the same could be said for heroin and oxy and the other shit I used. And none of that was good for me." He shrugged. "It was killing me."

Jeremy downed the rest of the coffee in one scalding chug, then stood. He was still naked, with his and Qay's dried come flaking off his skin. But Qay didn't protest when Jeremy pulled him into a hug. "I'm not heroin," Jeremy murmured into Qay's ear.

Qay chuckled and squeezed Jeremy's ass. "No, but you *are* tempting me."

Jeremy eventually showered and left for work, but not before a long, nerve-tingling kiss. He swore he could taste Qay all morning.

TUESDAY WAS dry but cloudy and nut-freezingly cold. It was one of the rare times Jeremy disliked having an outdoorsy job. True, it was nothing like the below-zero temps he'd endured in Kansas, but he'd lived in Portland for a long time and had acclimated to the more moderate climate.

He tromped through the South Park Blocks with his breath pluming and his gloved hands stuffed in his parka pockets. He was tempted to head straight for the nearest coffee place and barricade himself inside, but he had work to do, especially since he'd lost an hour lazing in Qay's bed on Monday and a four-day weekend was coming up.

In weather like this, the only people dallying in parks either lacked the mental capacity to get in out of the cold or had nowhere else to go. That meant Jeremy and his rangers were busy making sure everyone was safe. When possible, they shepherded people back home. When there was no home, they tried to help find shelter.

Jeremy spotted a figure slowly wobbling through the park and sighed. He had the feeling this one was going to involve more than a phone call to a relative or caregiver. From the back, he couldn't tell the person's gender, but he or she was underdressed, wearing decaying slippers, ragged jeans, and a lumpy oversized sweater. The person's medium brown hair looked hopelessly snarled. Jeremy hurried to catch up.

A bronze Teddy Roosevelt watched from his horse as Jeremy drew abreast of the person. "Hey," Jeremy said mildly. He knew his size and uniform could intimidate, so he worked hard to be nonthreatening.

The person—a man, Jeremy could see now—stopped, peered up at Jeremy, and swayed on his feet. Sores dotted his hollow-cheeked face, and when he opened his mouth, he showed badly rotted teeth. But he probably wasn't past his thirties, Jeremy guessed. Likely a good ten years younger than Qay.

"It's awfully cold today. Do you have somewhere you can go to warm up?"

The man made an unintelligible grunt.

Jeremy spoke slowly and soothingly. "I'm not a cop. I can't arrest you. I'm just worried about you." Although he knew of a few available shelter beds, no shelter would take in anyone this obviously zonked. That left him few options. "I can take you to Good Sam. They'll make sure you stay warm." The hospital wouldn't be thrilled to have this guy turn up, but they'd make sure he didn't OD or die of hypothermia, at least for a few hours.

"No," the man said and began to walk away.

Jeremy reached for his arm, at which point the guy swung at him. It was a clumsy attempt, off-balance and badly aimed, so it was easy for Jeremy to duck out of the way. That pissed his assailant off, though, and he flailed at Jeremy wildly, spitting and growling like a rabid monkey.

It was difficult to subdue him without harm. Jeremy ended up with scratches on his face and a couple of fresh bruises. But eventually he was able to capture the man's wrists in a set of flex cuffs. He was required to carry the restraints but rarely had to use them. Holding the guy's arm to keep him from bolting, Jeremy managed to dig out his phone and call the boys in blue.

The pair of patrol officers who showed up a few minutes later were absurdly young. But Jeremy knew them fairly well, and they were decent sorts. He happily handed over his prisoner. "He's not really dangerous," Jeremy said. "Just tweaking and scared. Maybe you can just let him warm up a little and chill out?"

The cops exchanged a quick look, then both nodded. It was the square-bodied blonde woman who spoke. "If you're sure, Chief. But if we take photos of your face and get a statement from you, I'm sure the DA could get an assault charge to stick."

"What good would that do anyone? Don't bother."

The cops nodded again, probably relieved to avoid paperwork and looking forward to hanging out for a while inside the nearby warm jail. "Do you want a medical check?" the woman asked.

Jeremy patted his glove against his stinging cheek. "Nah. I can clean this up myself."

"Sure thing. Happy Thanksgiving, Chief."

"You too. Stay warm." He even managed a smile for the prisoner, now slumped in defeat.

He walked the several blocks to his SUV, started the engine, cranked the heater, and rooted in the glove box for his small first-aid kit. He used the mirror to cleanse the wounds and apply antiseptic, then scowled at the results. Okay, so maybe he was slightly vain.

He sat there for a time, thinking about the guy who'd just been hauled off to jail. Poor bastard. Maybe someday he'd seek help getting clean, but not today, and his outlook wasn't good. Fuck. Jeremy dry-rubbed the uninjured parts of his face. As miserable as work might be on a day like this, at least he had a home to go to. Well, a nice hotel room anyway. And he had people who cared about him.

At that point his thoughts naturally turned to Qay. How many times had he been left out in the cold, literally or figuratively? By Jeremy's count, Qay must have spent two decades masking his fears and sorrows with drugs, bouncing between institutions. What if Jeremy had encountered him in a park during those years? Would events have transpired as they had today? Jesus, even imagining that made Jeremy's stomach clench.

He heaved a long sigh and checked the time. Almost two hours until Qay got off work. At least he could keep him warm tonight.

QAY LOOKED neither surprised nor especially thrilled to discover Jeremy waiting outside the window factory. He wandered over and opened the SUV's passenger door but didn't get inside. "I can get home by myself. Been doing it a long time."

Jeremy frowned. Qay's jacket was too light for these temperatures. "You *can* get home by yourself, but you don't have to. C'mon."

For a moment he thought Qay was going to refuse, and Jeremy wasn't sure what he'd do then. Instead Qay squinted at him. "What the hell happened to your face?"

"Get in and I'll tell you over dinner."

Somewhat reluctantly, Qay complied. Jeremy tried not to look smug when Qay leaned forward to place his palms close to the heater vents. "I'm paying," Qay said a little sullenly.

"But you paid when—"

"*I'm paying.*"

"Fine."

They ended up at Burgerville, where they each ordered a big burger and shared onion rings and sweet-potato fries. Despite the cold, Qay ordered a pumpkin milkshake. "So," he said after a noisy slurp. "Face?"

"Nothing big. Just an unhappy member of the public."

Qay had been slumping, but now he sat up straight. "Some fucker did that to you? Who the hell attacks a park ranger?"

Very quietly, Jeremy said, "An addict who doesn't want help."

"Oh," said Qay, melting back and ducking his head.

Jeremy grabbed the milkshake cup, stole a sip, and gave it back. "Change of subject. How was class last night?"

Qay perked up. "Professor Reynolds talked to his friends at Portland State. They might be able to get me in for spring semester—with a scholarship."

"That's fantastic! How many classes would you take?"

"I don't know. Depends on whether I have a laptop by then. If I do, I can take one course on campus and one online, I think. I should be able to manage that."

Jeremy mentally calculated the chances that Qay would have a conniption if Jeremy bought him a laptop for Christmas. High. But a few weeks remained—maybe Jeremy could think of a way to finesse it. "That's really exciting, Qay."

"And completely terrifying." He pushed his hair back from his face. "Reynolds said I can maybe take some tests, and if I score high enough, they'll waive some of the general education classes. But shit, that means I have to do well on the tests. Fat chance."

"You got a perfect score on your last exam," Jeremy reminded him.

"That was an outlier. A rare phenomenon, like Halley's Comet or St. Elmo's fire."

"Dude. In two sentences you just used a five-dollar word and referenced statistics, astronomy, and meteorology. Or possibly a Brat Pack movie. Either way, very impressive. Only a smart guy would be able to do that."

Qay grinned slightly but then shook his head. "I know I'm not stupid. I just can't get shit from here"—he thumped his head—"to paper. It gets all twisted up along the way, or else I panic and just go blank."

A few of the fries remained. Jeremy snagged them and popped them into his mouth. "That's good, because stupidity is permanent. Test anxiety we can work with."

"We?"

"We can do some relaxation techniques. Together. I bet you could find me very, very relaxing." He waggled his eyebrows for emphasis.

Qay's answering smile was wide and lecherous. "Maybe we should practice that tonight."

And they did.

AS TEMPTED as he was by Qay's warm, pliant body stretched out under the blanket, nude and slightly sweaty, Jeremy got dressed. Tomorrow was going to be a long day, and he needed some rest. Besides, he didn't have a change of clothes with him or any other sleepover supplies.

"I'll pick you up Thursday at one," he said. "Don't forget the Cards Against Humanity."

"At one. Um, I've been meaning to ask. Is there a dress code?" Qay worried his lip.

"Well, you know Rhoda. She's apt to wear just about anything. Two years ago she wore an orange-and-brown dress with a turkey appliqué on the chest. That's going to be hard for her to top. I'll be in jeans and a sweater."

"Okay. Thanks."

Jeremy dropped to his knees so he could land a kiss on Qay's forehead. "You'll be fine whatever you wear. And you'll have a good time. Rhoda adores you, and wait until you meet her son, Parker. He's the most adorable little twink you've ever seen. He's like a sparkly unicorn.

I don't know who else is coming this year, but I promise you'll impress them with your good looks and wit."

"I'll impress them with something," Qay muttered.

Another kiss, this time to the tip of Qay's nose. "One o'clock." Jeremy groaned slightly as he rose to his feet. He was not getting any younger.

Qay waved lazily at him. "I'm too comfortable to see you out. Sorry. The upstairs door will lock on its own."

"You have Friday off?"

Qay blinked at him. "Yeah. And Saturday."

"Perfect. After dinner at Rhoda's, we'll head to the Marriott, climb into bed, and not get out until Sunday night at the earliest. We'll order room service when we grow faint."

God, he'd give everything he owned just to keep that smile on Qay's face.

WEDNESDAY BROUGHT more rain and slightly warmer temperatures. That was a relief, because Jeremy wasn't in the mood to deal with snow. It was rare in Portland, but when it fell, it was always a nightmare. Between the hills, the scarcity of snow removal equipment, and the local drivers' inexperience, massive traffic jams and multicar pileups were just about guaranteed.

In skin-numbing drizzle, Jeremy spent the morning checking in with his rangers, making sure everything would stay as quiet as possible over the holiday. After a quick lunch, he drove to a grocery store in Northeast, where he picked up donated feast supplies. With his SUV full of bags and boxes, he drove to Patty's Place, where Evelyn greeted him with a hug. "We can always count on you to come through for us, Chief."

"I've seen how much food your kids can go through in one sitting. You need all the help you can get."

A few of the kids trotted out to help carry everything in. Jeremy grinned broadly when he recognized one of them. "How's it going, Toad?"

Toad wore a bright sweater that reflected his cheerful mood. "Really great, Chief. You were right about this place. They get me here."

"I'm glad. I've heard good things about you from Evelyn. You're going to be someone."

Toad beamed. "Me and this guy, Juan, we're making a video game where you get to travel to another planet and kill off these, like, alien zombie bad guys, and if you win that planet, you go to another. It's sick. We're gonna be millionaires."

Comparing this enthusiastic, colorful boy to the subdued one he'd recently had lunch with, Jeremy felt warmed through. "Will I get a copy when it's finished?"

"Sure. We'll even give you a discount!" Toad laughed, hefted a couple of bags of potatoes, and hurried into the house.

Later that afternoon, as Jeremy drove across town, he contemplated lost souls. There were so many of them in the world. So many just in this one city! And all he could do was offer meager help to one at a time, like using tweezers to relocate a sand dune. Even the ones Jeremy could assist might have already suffered for years. Toad was a lucky case. Jeremy had spotted him right away, hopefully before rejection and the streets could do irreparable damage. But then there was Qay. Such a remarkable man, yet so long adrift that even if offered safe harbor, he might never recognize his own worth and allow himself to anchor comfortably.

Jeremy badly wanted to call Qay—or at least text him—simply to remind him that Jeremy cared. But Qay's only phone was his apartment landline. Shit. Could Jeremy get away with buying him a cell phone for Christmas too?

Once his regular work duties were completed, Jeremy returned to the hotel to shower, shave, and change into a clean uniform. Then he trudged back to the parking garage, lost in thought. He would have walked, but the weather was nasty and he couldn't quite shake a gloomy, uneasy feeling. It was as if one of the city's pewter-colored clouds had slipped in through his ears and parked over his brain. Normally he looked forward to his pre-Thanksgiving tradition with Malcolm, but tonight he wished he could get together with Qay instead. Not for sex—although sex would be good too—but for the company and conversation. And for the opportunity to spend a few more hours building the rudimentary structure they'd begun.

Jeremy had met Malcolm, his first love, during their sophomore year in college when they were paired up as chemistry lab partners. Mal was a small, intense young man with enough energy to rival a nuclear power plant. He had been involved in every activist group on campus and was also a perfectionist who slaved over every assignment, dissatisfied by anything less than stellar grades. He slept only a few hours each night. He later admitted that when they first met, he'd assumed Jeremy was a dumb jock. But Jeremy proved otherwise, and he and Mal were soon head over heels. They got an apartment together their junior year. Jeremy assumed they were heading toward permanence, but then he started at the police academy and Mal joined the Peace Corps—and that was Jeremy's first broken heart. Well, second if you counted Keith Moore.

After bouncing around for years, Mal had ended up back in Portland, where he'd settled down to open a vegan restaurant, the Green Elf. Jeremy ran into him not long afterward—he was still with the bureau and Donny back then—and although the passion of youth was gone, they remained on friendly terms. Jeremy was too carnivorous to eat often at the Elf. But every year on the night before Thanksgiving, he joined a group of "celebrity waiters"—the mayor, the chief of police, various local media people—who served a meat-free and cost-free feast to the elderly, the poor, and the lonely. It was fun. Usually.

Jeremy found a parking spot in Old Town close to the Elf. The restaurant was crowded already, even though the meal hadn't yet begun, so he hurried to the kitchen to check in. Mal dashed about in the midst of chaos, directing employees and volunteers with all the confidence and authority of a seasoned general. He spied Jeremy immediately and called him over. "Jacket off and apron on, big guy. The hordes need feeding."

After executing a salute, Jeremy hurried to obey.

Although free meals weren't hard to come by at this time of year, the Elf's was a favorite. At first Jeremy had been surprised to see street people get so excited over quinoa and chickpeas, but an old lady wearing a half-dozen ancient shirts and cardigans had set him straight. "I get tired of the same ol' food, jus' like rich people do. It's nice to eat somethin' new." And Mal always presented an interesting menu, including items like mushroom pot stickers, millet-and-kale-stuffed pumpkin, eggplant tacos, and persimmon salad.

By the time the guests had finished their chocolate avocado truffles, hemp ice cream, and almond-butter cups, Jeremy was exhausted, but he still had to help with cleanup. Scrubbing dishes shoulder to shoulder with a very well-known drag queen was enjoyable, and the bites of food he'd managed to grab had been tasty. But he really wanted to head back to the Marriott, order a pizza (extra cheese and extra meat), and crash.

No. What he really wanted was to collapse onto Qay's mattress in his dank, cat-piss-scented apartment and hold him close. Dammit.

JEREMY WOKE up early on Thanksgiving morning feeling restless and worried, although he didn't know why. Maybe Qay's anxiety was contagious. When a long session in the fitness center left him sweaty and sore but no more settled, he stood indecisively in the middle of his hotel room. He wanted to go see Qay, but it was well before their appointed meeting time. Jeremy was afraid that if he hovered, he'd end up chasing Qay away. A blanket up to your chin was cozy; a blanket over your face could smother you.

Maybe he needed a run. Not a long one, since he'd already worked out, but enough to loosen the kinks in his emotional state. But as he was reaching for his sweats, his phone rang. Frankl. Shit.

"Happy Thanksgiving," Jeremy said when he picked up the call.

Frankl made a grumbling noise.

Jeremy tried to keep the tone light. "I take it you didn't call to wish me a good holiday?"

"Happy fucking Thanksgiving, Chief. I got bad news for you."

For a brief but soul-searing moment, Jeremy was positive Frankl was going to tell him something awful about Qay. His heart pounded and his throat felt tight as he pictured Qay leaping off the Fremont Bridge and being found floating facedown somewhere on the way to the Columbia River. "What is it?" he managed to choke out.

"Laura Gifford's been murdered."

The relief at not hearing Qay's name was so complete that at first Jeremy didn't process the rest. And then it took him a couple of beats to remember who Laura Gifford was. "Donny's sister?"

"Yeah. We've been in touch with the PD down there while we've been investigating the case. They called to say Mrs. Gifford was found dead in her home last night."

"Fuck." Jeremy sat down hard on the bed. He'd never cared for the woman, and he'd lost any remaining respect when she refused to make arrangements for Donny's remains. But she didn't deserve to die. "Are you fairly certain this is related to Donny?"

"Can't ever be a hundred percent, but yeah. Her place was ransacked just like yours, but it didn't look like a burglary. And look, I talked to her after we found Donny, and she sounded like a bitch. But I don't think she was bad enough for anyone to want to murder her. And, uh, she'd been roughed up before she died. Heart attack, their ME says."

"Roughed up?"

Frankl sighed. "Yeah. She was pretty banged up."

Jeremy propped his forehead on his free hand. "Holy fuck."

"We've been keeping an eye on Davis, and it wasn't him. She died a couple days ago, but that scumsucker hasn't left town in weeks. Means he's got goons willing to travel to do his dirty work. Also means he's still looking for that thumb drive and is willing to be real nasty to get it."

"You can't bring Davis in?"

"Not yet. Don't have enough to tie him to this mess. If we can nab whoever's responsible for Mrs. Gifford, that would help a lot."

"How can I help?" Jeremy asked.

"Just watch your back. That's why I called."

After mutual promises to fill each other in on further developments, Jeremy ended the call and lay flat on the mattress. Watch his back. How completely fucking useless. He wanted to be *doing* something, dammit.

He *could* be doing something, he realized. He could go to his loft and see if, as the contractors had promised, it looked like it would be ready for habitation by the middle of next week. He could make a list of what he'd need to buy besides furniture. Kitchen supplies, mostly, but he'd been thinking of a couple of area rugs as well. He could measure for them. True, visiting his place wouldn't do anything to help solve Donny's and Laura's murders, but it would keep Jeremy occupied for a while instead of stewing uselessly. And when he was done, he could stop by Qay's place early—could honestly say he'd been in the neighborhood—without being too much of a stalker.

Reenergized, he hopped to his feet.

In the shower, he remembered his plans for the long weekend with Qay, which involved making the most of his large, comfy hotel bed. Even thinking about it made him hard, and he ended up jerking off under the Marriott's endless supply of hot water. Good to take the edge off, he decided as he shaved and dressed. Proximity to Qay made him feel like a horny teenager, and it would be nice to think about something besides sex while they were at Rhoda's.

Rhoda's. Hmm. He'd skipped breakfast and was getting hungry. He'd jammed a few things into the minifridge in his room, but none of them appealed at the moment. He'd just endure an empty stomach until dinner, then make up for it with triple servings of everything.

Jeremy's contribution to the feast was nonalcoholic drinks. He'd been shopping a few days earlier and now had a box filled with sparkling cider, juices, and soft drinks. He hefted the box and headed to his SUV. The hotel garage was especially busy with drivers arriving and leaving, probably due to the holiday. Traffic across town was heavy too. He was glad he wouldn't have to drive far to get to Rhoda's house; she lived just a couple of miles from P-Town.

At least he had the garage under his apartment to himself. He trotted up the flights of stairs and had a quick look around. The bedroom and living room were finished, as was the bathroom. He trailed a loving hand over the edge of his bathtub—big enough even for him—and eyed the shower speculatively. Yes, he and Qay could easily fit in there together. His hot water wasn't as limitless as the Marriott's, however. Maybe they could share the tub instead.

Unlike the rest of the apartment, the kitchen wasn't quite complete. The contractors hadn't yet installed the sink fixtures, lighting, or appliances. None of those things should take long, though, so the place actually might be ready by Wednesday.

Jeremy pulled out a pad of paper and a measuring tape. He noted the dimensions of the rugs he'd need, then made an exhaustive list for the kitchen. Very few of his things had escaped destruction, so instead of weeding out the good from the ruined, he'd asked the cleanup crew to dump it all. As a result, he needed everything: dishes, glassware, cutlery, cookware, and gadgets. He wasn't actually much of a cook—it didn't seem worth the effort when it was just him—but he liked all those obscure little items they sold in kitchen shops.

His stomach grumbled, causing him to glance at his watch and smile. It was just after noon. Surely that wasn't too early to barge in on Qay. He was so distracted with those thoughts that he forgot his tape measure and list until he was halfway to the garage, and he had to bound back up the stairs to retrieve them. But the dark cloud seemed to have evaporated, and his mood had lifted considerably from earlier that morning. Soon he'd be spending a long weekend with his boyfriend.

Whistling happily, he descended to the garage, thinking about the soft skin on Qay's belly even though the rest of him seemed so tough. Jeremy pulled the key fob from his pocket and was about to press the

Unlock button when he heard something rushing at him from behind a wide support pillar. He spun around, but before he could get a good sense of what was happening, a loud pop and buzz echoed through the space, and something struck his leg.

He bellowed and fell as his entire body clenched in an agonizing muscle spasm. When he gained partial control, he was hit again, this time in the chest. A large man dropped onto Jeremy's rigid body, pinning him in place, and as Jeremy feebly tried to scream for help, the man slapped a thick cloth over the lower half of Jeremy's face.

A heavy smell assaulted him, burning the sensitive tissues of his nose and throat. Even as he tried to struggle free, the Taser hit him a third time—in the leg again. This time he could only groan as the blackness swallowed him.

CHAPTER EIGHTEEN

STUART WAS a colossal ass. Qay had known this for some time, of course, but the days before Thanksgiving cemented it. Because the factory would be closed Thursday through Monday—paid holidays, hooray!—Stuart apparently decided Qay should do a week's worth of work in two days. Not *Stuart*, of course. He mostly marched around and shouted orders like a little dictator.

And then on Tuesday, the son of a bitch saw Qay getting into Jeremy's SUV after work. First thing Wednesday morning, before Qay had even finished slipping on his work gloves, Stuart planted himself in his way. "Who was that in the flashy SUV, huh? Your boyfriend?"

Qay looked him straight in the eyes. "Actually, yes."

That must have caught the fucker by surprise, because his jaw dropped and he blinked a few times. "You're a faggot?"

"Jesus, Stuart. Hasn't anyone told you it's 2015? Let's pretend we're not still living in caves, shall we?"

Stuart sneered, but seemingly unable to fashion a response, he spun and marched away.

That wasn't the end of it, though. He spent the better part of the day smirking at Qay and asking him things like "Which of you is the woman?" and "Do you put on a cute pink dress after work?" Qay did his best to ignore the little prick, because as far as he was concerned, this brand of homophobia was all about Stuart's insecurities regarding his own masculinity and sexuality.

Qay had never come out to his coworkers, not because he was embarrassed or afraid but because the subject had never come up. He wasn't close enough with any of them to discuss personal matters. But aside from Stuart, nobody seemed to care about his revelation. In fact, the other guys appeared more annoyed with Stuart's antics than Qay was. When Stuart minced in front of Qay and asked him loudly if he was a size queen, Barry said, "With all the questions, I'm beginning to think you want to sleep with him, Stuart." Everyone laughed—everyone but Stuart—and that was the end of the harassment, at least that day.

One of the reasons Qay remained calm despite his tyrant supervisor was that he felt unusually mellow after Tuesday night. Okay, lots of good sex after a seven-year drought helped too, but just the memory of Jeremy's calm, even presence was enough to soothe Qay's tangled nerves.

By late Wednesday, Qay was more than eager for a dose of that palliative. He was even a little disappointed when he clocked out and didn't find a black SUV waiting for him near the loading dock. Then he remembered that Jeremy had an event that evening. Still, the Marriott wasn't that far from the window factory; Qay could walk it easily. And he could wait in the lobby until Jeremy returned, and then—

No. The poor guy would be tired. And after all those long years of waiting, Qay could damned well wait one more night.

He took the buses home.

QAY WOKE up much earlier than necessary on Thursday. He was never good at sleeping in, at least not when his body was free of pharmaceuticals. Too... buzzy with energy, with nerves. And this morning was especially bad because he had dinner to worry about.

Rhoda was wonderful, and he trusted her not to invite any assholes. Still, a houseful of strangers was intimidating. What would he talk about? They might all have fascinating careers, while he swept up glass in a window factory. Maybe they'd all traveled to interesting places, whereas he'd wandered here and there and hardly remembered most of those times—and even if he did, he wouldn't want to talk about them.

Shit. Maybe he'd just hide behind Jeremy and hope nobody noticed him.

He was also concerned about the availability of alcohol. He could only resist temptation so much, especially when his nerves rattled like an old jalopy. Rhoda had actually offered to declare the day booze-free, which was awfully nice of her, but Qay had declined. People liked some wine with their festive meal, and Qay didn't want to be the dickhead responsible for depriving them.

He could play sick, right? Pretend he had a terrible cold. Only then Captain Caffeine would undoubtedly—and heroically—insist on skipping dinner to nurse Qay through his illness, and Qay would feel like a bag of shit.

When fretting threatened to escalate into an anxiety attack, Qay cleaned his apartment. Dusting was a good way to burn a little energy and keep his twitchy muscles occupied. But soon his dungeon was as spotless as it was ever going to get, and he was still trying not to hyperventilate. A walk, he decided. A brisk one.

After leaving the house, he headed down toward the river—almost as if he were being drawn in Jeremy's direction. Which he knew was a stupid idea. But he felt a pull, and even when he reached the river and stared across—he couldn't see the Marriott from this angle—he yearned to keep on going. To choose a bridge and cross it, not in order to plunge into the frigid water below but to keep on going until he landed in Jeremy's arms.

"Fucking idiot!" he said out loud and then was glad nobody was near enough to hear him. He didn't need a trip to a padded room. Psychosis had never been his gig anyway. Although now here he was, shivering on the bank of the Willamette, thinking that he was falling in love with Jeremy Cox. And if that wasn't crazy, nothing was.

The last fall he'd taken was off the Memorial Bridge—he'd never fallen in love. He wasn't the type. Love meant opening yourself to someone else, and Qay was wound up so tightly he couldn't even open himself to himself. He'd had temporary partnerships over the years, arrangements that lasted as long as they were mutually beneficial and then ended when someone went to jail or rehab or the psych ward, or ran out of drugs or money or patience. He certainly hadn't loved any of those men. Hell, he barely remembered most of them, and they'd surely forgotten him.

Even if Qay *did* do love, it was absurd to believe such a thing was possible with a man he barely knew. Except… he did know Jeremy, didn't he? Not just because of the past couple of weeks, and not because they'd shared some classes during a previous life.

Qay closed his eyes and listened to traffic humming on the elevated freeway. Everyone in a hurry to go home for Thanksgiving.

Home.

And that was it, wasn't it? For almost thirty years, Qay had not set foot in Kansas. But then he found Jeremy, who was one of his few youthful memories not tinged with pain. Jeremy was home, but with all the bitterness and sorrow winnowed away. That was why Qay knew him so well. *That* was why Qay loved him.

Qay wandered for a long time, choosing streets randomly. In a modest residential neighborhood south of Powell, he admired the front gardens that were now mostly dormant and the decorative fish-scale shingles on some of the houses. He walked through a good-sized park with sports fields and a playground, and he wondered what things Jeremy would point out to him if he were there. That thought made him smile. Then he headed north and wandered through Ladd's Addition with its confusingly laid-out streets, expensive bungalows, and tall leafless trees. He wondered what it would be like to live in a fancy house like these and not dread going home, to feel welcomed and warm and safe.

Fucking idiot. This time he kept the words to himself.

It was nearly noon when he returned to his basement. He made himself a can of tomato soup, more for warmth than nourishment, and sipped it from a mug while pacing his small living room. His stroll had kept him slightly preoccupied for a time, but now his anxiety returned full force, chewing at his innards like some prehistoric beast. Sweat droplets began to form at his hairline as his heart beat a frantic salsa rhythm and his chest grew almost too heavy to move. He was dizzy, shaky on his pins, and although he was terrified, he also felt as if he were floating up near the popcorn ceiling, watching himself fall to pieces.

He set the mug on the kitchen counter and dashed to the toilet, where he proceeded to puke his guts out. Long after everything he'd recently consumed was flushed down the plumbing, he still dry heaved. When that had run its course, he leaned nervelessly against the cold porcelain and yearned to be somebody—anybody—else.

Like an old man, he pulled himself to his feet. He rinsed his mouth at the sink, brushed his teeth, and rinsed again, all the while carefully avoiding his reflection. He knew he'd be pale and hollow-eyed like a zombie extra in a bad horror flick. It was almost one o'clock. He needed to change.

Dithering over clothing options was stupid, especially for a guy like him. It wasn't as if he owned that much, and he sure as hell wasn't a fashionisto. He dithered anyway. Eventually he settled on his nice jeans and a red sweater he'd found the week before at a thrift shop. It was soft and comfortable and looked brand-new. When he'd worn it on Saturday, Jeremy said it nicely set off his complexion and the color of his hair. And yes, apparently Qay had a bit of vanity in him after all, because the compliments had made him blush and smile.

He was a fucking idiot: sappy thoughts of Jeremy, and Qay calmed the fuck down. Not all the way, but the pterodactyls in his stomach morphed to butterflies, and his heart decided it could stay in his chest after all.

Qay detoured to the bathroom to attack his hair. Every time he looked at it, he saw more silver strands, but at least it wasn't receding. He'd always wondered a bit about his hair. His mother's was mousy brown and, when she had gone a little long between hairdresser appointments, prone to curls. His father's, which had thinned by the time Qay hit his teens, was also brown, but with a slightly reddish tinge. Kevin's too. But Qay's was straight-on black. When he was little, he imagined he was a changeling abandoned among the Moores, and he'd used his hair as evidence. But when he mentioned it to his brother, Kevin rolled his eyes. "We have Indian blood in us, dummy. That's where your stupid hair comes from."

Fuck. He usually couldn't even think about Kevin without wanting to barf. Either his stomach was done with that for the day, or his pillow talk with Jeremy had been slightly cathartic.

And speaking of Jeremy, where was he? Qay glanced at his watch. It was just a few minutes past one, but Jeremy had always been punctual. Superheroes didn't stoop to tardiness. Thinking that maybe the SUV was waiting for him in the street because there was no place to park, Qay threw on his shoes and leather coat, hurried up the stairs, and opened the door to look outside. No black SUV. No Jeremy.

Qay went back into the basement to wait.

By 1:20, Jeremy still wasn't there, and Qay was starting to lose it again. He'd paced back and forth, he'd packed and repacked Cards Against Humanity in its plastic bag, and he'd run up and down the stairs six times.

At one thirty, Qay called him. The phone rang for a bit before going to voice mail. Qay left a lame message. "Uh, hi, Jeremy. I thought you said one. Could you call me with an ETA?"

Maybe there had been some kind of park-related disaster, he told himself. He turned on the TV and flipped through the channels, but if anything terrible was happening in the Portland park system, there was no coverage. He clicked off the TV and tossed the remote onto the couch.

He would have sold his soul for a pill, a hit, a shot... anything to insulate him just a little from the claws tearing at him from the inside.

When two o'clock came and went, Qay decided that Jeremy had obviously had enough of Qay's bullshit and wanted nothing more to do with him. Jeremy was probably over at Rhoda's right now, scarfing turkey and stuffing and telling Rhoda that Qay was too high maintenance and not worth the bother.

That thought sent Qay running to the bathroom again, only this time his stomach had nothing to eject.

He eventually steadied himself against the nausea and dizziness, and perhaps his brain decided it was time to wake up, because he realized there was no way Captain Caffeine would treat him like that. Jeremy might get sick of him, but he'd be a gentleman about it. He'd take Qay to dinner somewhere, give him an it's-not-you-it's-me speech, and probably even drive him home afterward. He wouldn't ditch Qay on Thanksgiving without saying a word.

So where the fuck was he?

None of the possibilities flashing before his mind were good ones. Traffic accidents. Freak medical conditions. The Marriott collapsing into a giant sinkhole. Or….

Fuck.

Goddamn whatshisface, the guy who killed Donny. Ryan Davis.

Qay tried Jeremy's phone four more times in rapid succession but got nothing but voice mail. He sat on a kitchen chair, his head bent down to his knees, and tried to breathe. "A panic attack's not going to help Jeremy, nimrod," he told himself between panting gasps. "Man the fuck up."

Tackle it like a school assignment, like a calculation handed to him in statistics or an essay assignment in philosophy. Analyze the problem and logically find solutions. Dissociate his brain from the out-of-control emotions and think clearly.

The first useful idea that came to him was Rhoda, but he quickly dismissed it. He didn't have her phone number, he had no idea where she lived, and P-Town was closed. There was no way for him to get hold of her.

Okay then, what about the Marriott? Qay owned an old-fashioned paper phone book, the kind that was dumped on the front sidewalk once a year. He might have been the last person in North America to use one, but he had no smartphone or Internet at home. Besides, he'd have hated to throw it away, full as it was with names and places. Now, he used it to look up the hotel.

The perky woman he eventually spoke with told him she couldn't tell Qay whether Mr. Cox was in his room.

"Please. It's an emergency," he begged, knowing he sounded melodramatic.

"I can try calling his room, sir."

"Okay. Thank you."

A few moments later, she was back on the line. "He's not answering, sir."

Fuck. Not that Qay had expected Jeremy to pick up, but there had been a faint hope he'd simply taken a nap and not yet awakened. "Can you.... If you see him, can you give him a message? Ask him to call me. It's urgent."

She agreed, and Qay left his number before hanging up.

He knew the room number, so he could head downtown and knock on Jeremy's door himself. But that would take time, and he had the feeling it wouldn't get him anywhere. After a few more moments of agonizing consideration, he thought of Jeremy's loft. Maybe that was where he was. And since Davis had already wrecked the place, he certainly knew its location.

Feeling relieved to be doing *something*, Qay raced out of his apartment and toward Jeremy's. He covered the distance in record-setting time. All the businesses he passed were closed, giving the area a slightly forlorn appearance. No lights shone through the windows at the top of Jeremy's building either, but Qay entered by way of the parking garage, planning to take the stairwell to the apartment.

He stopped in his tracks when he saw the SUV.

For a few seconds, relief flooded him. Jeremy *was* here! But that emotion was short-lived, because as Qay drew closer to the vehicle, he spied two things on the concrete beside it: a key fob and a cell phone. The phone was crushed.

LATER—MUCH LATER—WHAT astonished Qay most was what he did after finding Jeremy's keys and ruined phone. Or rather, what he *didn't* do. He didn't vomit up the nothing in his stomach or collapse in a quivering heap on the cold concrete floor. He also didn't go running out to find the one bar open on Thanksgiving or the one dealer who hadn't taken the holiday off. Those were all fucking miracles.

What he did do was stand for what felt like hours but was probably less than a minute, assessing his options. He needed to call the cops. And not some beat cop who knew nothing about Jeremy and Ryan Davis, who was pissed off about working this afternoon, and who would either dismiss Qay's concerns or just drag things out until it was... fuck, until it was too late. Qay needed to talk to Captain Frankl. And that required a phone.

Just about any other day of the year, he could have run to a nearby business for help, but of course that wouldn't work now. He could run home and use his landline, but that would take too long. Seconds counted. He could—

His attention was caught by the door to the stairwell. Those stairs led not just to Jeremy's loft but to the offices below it. They'd have a phone.

Qay sprinted up the stairs. He tried the door to the spa and found it securely locked. One floor up, the door to the office suite was also locked, but it was a cruddy hollow-core model. Thankful for heavy boots with thick soles, Qay drew back his leg and kicked as hard as he could. The door cracked satisfyingly but didn't give. Two more solid blows and then, ignoring the shards and splinters, he rushed inside. Finding a phone was easy.

The 911 operator was skeptical, and Qay had to fight hard to maintain his cool, but he explained as calmly as possible. He didn't mention the breaking and entering; he could deal with that later. Finally the dispatcher said she'd have Frankl call him back. Qay gave her the number printed on the phone.

Waiting for that call proved the longest minutes of his life. He almost sank to his knees in gratitude when the phone rang.

"Frankl. Who's this?"

Qay's answer tumbled out in a rush. "Qay Hill we met at McDonald's that fucker's kidnapped him!"

"Say that again. Slower."

Better to get to the point. "Jeremy's gone. Kidnapped." *Please, please kidnapped and not simply dead.*

Frankl swore loudly and colorfully. "You're his boyfriend?"

"Yeah."

"Hang on."

Qay bounced from foot to foot as he waited another eternity. He'd never in his life prayed, not even when he was little and his parents dragged him to church. Now he wished he knew how. All he could manage was a simple mental plea: *Please, God. Please, God. Please, God.* Over and over until Frankl picked up again.

"We're on it," Frankl said, sounding breathless. "Where are you? I'm gonna have some of the guys come meet you."

"Jeremy's building. It's at—"

"I know where it's at. Sit tight." Frankl disconnected the call.

Qay hung up too. And *then* he threw up.

CHAPTER NINETEEN

JEREMY WOKE up groggy and freezing, every muscle in his body aching and the mother of all headaches pounding through his skull. His mouth tasted burnt and bitter, and—

Fuck!

He was standing, but ropes held him securely against something hard and heavy. Blinking to clear his vision, he struggled to get loose. He was rewarded with a blow to the head that almost threw him back into unconsciousness, but he fought desperately to remain aware.

"Fuck!" he bellowed.

"Shut up or I'll hit you again."

It took a few more minutes before he was calm enough and alert enough to more fully assess his situation. He was inside a cavernous space that contained machinery, tall shelving, and long worktables. The huge room seemed to contain only four other people, all of them men. One wore a security guard uniform, but judging by the deferential way he positioned himself, he wasn't in charge.

"*You're* Ryan Davis?" Jeremy asked, thick-tongued. The boss of this little crew was young—definitely not past thirty—with a full beard and a goddamn waxed mustache. He was considerably shorter than Jeremy's six-four, had a slightly stocky build, and was stylishly clothed. His skin looked sallow in the overhead fluorescent lights. He held a handgun pointed casually at the floor.

As Davis smirked, Jeremy quickly took in additional details. At least one of the goons was armed, and while Davis appeared calm, his men were twitchy. Jeremy had been stripped to nothing but socks and boxers, which accounted for his shivering. He couldn't tell for sure, but he was fairly certain he was tied to one of the round concrete pillars that supported the ceiling.

Time. He needed to buy time. "How'd you get a big guy like me tied up like this?" he asked as calmly as possible. "Must've taken all four of you."

Ryan frowned. "Shut up! I'm asking the questions, not you."

Jeremy tried another solid tug on the ropes. Nothing. God, his head hurt. "We can be civilized human beings about this, you know."

"Fuck you. You know what I want, asshole. Where is it?"

"I don't know what you want because you haven't told me."

"But you know who I am," Davis spat.

"You're a motherfucker who's going to rot in prison." It wasn't the wisest thing to say to someone with a gun, but Jeremy was cold and sore and scared, and he held a deep conviction that he wouldn't make it through the day alive. So he wasn't surprised when Davis whacked the side of his head with the gun barrel.

Jeremy grunted and blinked away the black swirls in his vision.

"Where the fuck is it?" Davis yelled, sending flecks of spittle into Jeremy's face.

Time for a new tactic. "If I had it, don't you think I'd have turned it in to the cops long ago?"

Judging by his expression, that thought had never occurred to Davis. Fantastic. In addition to being morally bankrupt, the guy was a moron. In Jeremy's experience, stupid criminals were the most dangerous.

Taking advantage of the momentary confusion, Jeremy tried to distract Davis further. "You know, whatever's on that drive might have sent you to prison for a while, but now with a murder rap, you're looking at life instead."

"I didn't kill that faggot!"

"You didn't have to," Jeremy said, ignoring the slur. "It's called felony murder. If somebody gets killed in furtherance of a felony you're participating in, you're just as liable as the guy who pulled the trigger."

Davis took a moment to chew on that—possibly decoding all the big words—then turned to his buddy in the security uniform. "That true?" he demanded.

The guard shrugged. "I don't know, man. All I got is a GED."

"Dumbfuck." Davis returned his attention to Jeremy. Then he raised his chin a bit. "So if I'm up for that anyway, I might as well off you. They can only sentence me to life once. It's like buy one, get one free."

"Buy one get two, you mean. Remember Donny's sister?"

"Never met the bitch."

Jeremy sighed. "Look. I'm a park ranger—that's law enforcement. You kill me and you get the death penalty." That was a lie. A park ranger didn't count as law enforcement because he wasn't a sworn officer, and in any case, Oregon hadn't executed anyone for nearly twenty years. But Jeremy figured Davis wouldn't know that.

When Davis hesitated, Jeremy decided to push his luck and expand the lie into full-fledged fantasy. "You know how they execute people here? Electric chair. I used to be a cop, and once I got to go down to Salem and watch them fry someone. *Zhzhzh*. You know those bug zappers people put on their porches? It was like that, only a man takes a lot longer to kill than a mosquito."

Davis's men shifted uneasily, exchanging glances with one another. But Davis only sniffed. "There's worse things than death anyway. We got this place to ourselves all weekend. I'll just torture it out of you."

That wasn't much of an improvement over getting shot. Jeremy tried his best to think of any way to talk himself out of this mess, but he was so fucking *cold* and his brains felt as if they'd been scrambled by a rototiller. "I don't know where the goddamn drive is," he said tiredly. "Donny never mentioned it. I never saw it. I had no idea it existed until after you wrecked my place."

Thud! Davis hit him with the pistol again. And this time Jeremy blacked out.

HE CAME to consciousness gasping and spitting out water. Frigid liquid dripped down his chest, chilling him all the way to the bone. He was so cold he could barely work his jaw.

Davis stood in front of him with a plastic bucket, looking smug. "It's not bedtime yet. We still have some talking to do." Slowly, he set the bucket down. Then he pulled a pack of cigarettes from his jacket and a lighter from his expensive pants. He shook out a cigarette, lit it, and tucked the other items away. "We can do this the easy way, or we can do it the hard way," he said.

Shit, a moron *and* apparently a fan of bad gangster movies. "Don't want to do it at all," Jeremy said through chattering teeth.

"We'll start simple." Davis closed the distance between them and pressed the burning end of his cigarette into the center of Jeremy's chest.

Jeremy bellowed. He wasn't sure which was worse, the searing pain or the stench of his own scorched flesh. He didn't really have time to think about it, because Davis pushed the cigarette against him again and again, and when that one burned out, he lit another. After a while, the small wounds coalesced into one excruciating agony that grew with every heartbeat.

How could he be burning and freezing at the same time?

When Davis ran out of cigarettes, he stood behind Jeremy and broke his fingers. One by one, starting with the pinky on Jeremy's left hand. He stopped before he got to the thumb, and he walked around to face Jeremy, who slumped in his bonds. Davis roughly lifted Jeremy's chin. "I want a drink. Give you time to think about the upside of talking. Otherwise, when I come back, we'll try something new. Maybe… see how hard I can squeeze your balls before they burst." He gave a small, evil smile before kneeing Jeremy in the crotch.

This time, Jeremy grayed out. He was vaguely aware of Davis walking away and the sound of conversation, but his mind couldn't track it. Didn't matter anyway. Nothing mattered except the cold and the pain and…. Oh God. Qay.

What if this sick fucker knew about Qay and decided that was where the thumb drive was?

Moaning deep in his throat, Jeremy pulled at the ropes. He'd been scared since he woke up in this place, but the realization that Qay might be in danger was enough to ramp him up to full-blown terror. Despite the pain, exhaustion, and cold, adrenaline surged through him. He was *strong*, dammit! He wasn't that fat little loser who got bullied in school, whose parents didn't find him worth their attention, who never reached out in friendship to the handsome, lonely boy who shared the back row of his classrooms.

He wrenched his body with all his might, but the ropes held.

And then he did the only thing that remained to him—he opened his mouth and screamed his frustration and anger and fear. And his despair over having failed Qay.

His cry sounded ragged and hoarse even as it echoed around the vast room.

Davis walked slowly toward him with a beer in his hand and a snarl of a smile. "Had a good think, fag? Decided whether you want to end your life as a eunuch?"

"Fuck you," Jeremy rasped through a sandpaper throat.

Although Davis opened his mouth, his no doubt witty reply was lost to eternity when two doors crashed open with resounding bangs.

Davis dropped the bottle and whirled around. His thugs took off running in separate directions. Commanding shouts rang out. Jeremy yelled, "They have guns!"

And as if to prove his point, that fucker Davis pulled out his gun and shot him.

Jeremy didn't even scream when the bullet tore through the front of his left shoulder. He already hurt so much that he merely grunted and gritted his teeth, then endured the heated drip of his blood as it flowed down his chest.

The rest came to him in flashes. More gunshots. Lots of yelling. Someone standing in front of him, saying something Jeremy couldn't begin to process. And then he was falling—

No. Several arms caught him, laid him on a stretcher, covered him with a thermal blanket.

"Qay?" he whispered. But if anyone answered, he was too far gone to tell.

CHAPTER TWENTY

JEREMY'S BUILDING swarmed with patrol officers, every damned one of whom had a million questions for Qay. He didn't want to answer any of them—he just wanted to know what the hell was going on with Jeremy. But if these cops knew, they wouldn't tell him. They just kept badgering him until he sank down onto the cold floor of the parking garage and fought to breathe.

"Mother Mary's tits, you flaming pricks! This guy didn't hurt anyone. Give him a moment of fucking peace!" Qay glanced up. The yelling came from a small, handsome man in a natty suit. A detective, Qay supposed vaguely.

"He broke into the offices," said one of the uniforms, pointing up at the ceiling.

"So he could call 911, fuckwad. Go. Do your job. Write up an assload of useless reports." The detective made a shooing motion before turning to Qay and crouching on his haunches. "Your name's Qay Hill?" he asked in a considerably softer tone.

Qay nodded mutely.

"I'm Nevin Ng, and I'm Jeremy's friend." He stood and held out a hand. "Let's blow this shithole, okay? Where's your car?"

"No car. I walked."

"Then I'll give you a ride home. C'mon."

After a moment's hesitation, Qay took the offered hand and used it to haul himself up. Ng was strong and took Qay's weight easily. Then Ng glared and swore at a few of his colleagues, who parted like the Red Sea and cleared a path to the garage exit.

Under different circumstances, Qay would have laughed when he saw Ng's car: a classic GTO in a purple so dark it was almost black. Ng unlocked it and waved him to the passenger side. The upholstery was black and absolutely pristine, and the car smelled a little like Old Spice.

Ng reached to turn the ignition, but Qay stopped him with a hand on his arm. "Have they found him?"

"Don't know yet. But I got friends who promised me an update as soon as they know anything."

Qay's sigh was more like a groan as he fell back against the plush seat.

"Are you his speculatively positive outcome?" Ng asked.

"Wh-what?"

"Are you and Germy Cox doing the nasty?"

"Don't call him that!"

Ng grinned slightly. "You are. And you give a damn about the big dolt." His smile faded and he shook his head. "I told that asshole to be careful. Thinks he's a goddamn superhero."

"Captain Caffeine," Qay agreed, slumping forward with exhaustion. He'd burned all the energy from his body.

"Ha! Captain Caffeine! I like it. Where to, princess?"

Ng didn't comment on Qay's shitty apartment. Instead, he settled Qay on the couch and made them both some tea. Which was a hell of an achievement, because Qay could have sworn he didn't have any tea. But Ng handed him a steaming mug and sat next to him with a sigh. "Hell of a fucking mess," Ng muttered.

Qay nodded numbly. His hands were the only parts of his body he felt connected to as they gathered heat from the cup. The rest of him floated weightlessly in a deep black hole.

Ng must have felt obligated to fill the silence. "This isn't even my beat, you know? I catch the whoresons who beat up grannies or rape people they think can't tell on 'em. Kidnapping, murder, drugs... those are for the fuckheads in vice and homicide. And if they'd done their jobs, we wouldn't be here right now." He barked a laugh. "I guess I should be thankful. This shit saved me from the most painful Thanksgiving ever."

Thanksgiving. Even the thought of food turned Qay's stomach. He had forgotten all about their plans. "Rhoda," he said, his voice flat despite his concern. "She was expecting us. I don't have her number."

"God *damn* it," Ng swore, but not at Qay. "Drink your tea, man. I'll be right back." He took his tea into the kitchenette and talked quietly into his phone for a while. Qay didn't bother trying to listen.

Ng returned and plopped down beside him. "I talked to Rhoda. She wants to know if you're holding it together."

Qay gave him a bleak look, and Ng shook his head. "You got some booze around here? Couple shots might chill you a little."

"I'm an addict. Clean seven years, but…."

Instead of looking disgusted, Ng clicked his tongue. "That sucks balls. Good for you, though. Seven years is like moving a fucking mountain with a teaspoon."

There was no way to respond to that except with a nod.

A thought formed in Qay's sluggish brain. "If they're so eager to find that thumb drive, how come they didn't touch Jeremy's SUV? It was right there in the garage, and Donny could have stashed it there."

"Dunno, man. Douchecanoes like Davis don't think logically."

Qay nodded slightly. He used to know douche canoes like that.

They sipped their tea.

When Ng's phone rang, Qay startled so badly he sloshed the contents of his mug. He chewed his lip bloody as he watched Ng talk, but the detective's grave face gave nothing away. Then Ng ended the call, tucked his phone away, and gave Qay a long look. "He's alive," he finally said.

Qay moaned.

"He's alive but he's in shitty shape, and they've got him in the ER right now."

Qay jumped to his feet, ignoring the remains of his tea. "Where?"

"I can take you, man, but—"

"Please!" If Ng refused, Qay would find out which hospital and get there himself, holiday bus schedule or not. He'd run if he had to.

"Yeah. Yeah, okay, dammit. Let's go."

If Ng spoke during the drive, Qay didn't register it. He had no idea what neighborhoods they passed through or which direction they were headed. He simply sat in the purple GTO and wondered if someone could die from a daylong anxiety attack.

He seemed to lose Ng shortly after their arrival at the hospital, but Rhoda was there, and she swooped in to give Qay an unexpected and robust hug. "Sweetheart!" she said. "You look like death. Have you eaten anything today?"

He stared vacantly at her. "Jeremy?"

"In surgery. Serious but stable. He'll pull through, honey."

Qay drew in a shuddering breath, then another, and then he couldn't stop shaking. Rhoda sat him down on a plastic chair and waved away a nurse who assumed Qay was a patient. "I'm sorry," he said miserably when he could speak again.

"Don't give me that. It's been a terrible day and you deserve to fall apart. But Jeremy's going to be all right, and so will you."

He hung his head miserably.

Rhoda bustled away, and when she returned a few minutes later, she thrust a packaged muffin at him. "It'll taste like crap, but you need to eat."

Because he didn't have the energy to argue, he opened the plastic, broke off a piece of pastry, and stuck it in his mouth. He didn't taste it at all. "You're missing your dinner," he said.

"I had one serving, which was plenty. I like the leftovers better anyway. Parker's holding down the fort at home, and that's good for him. He just broke up with his latest boyfriend, so he's feeling a little lost."

Qay wished he'd had the chance to meet Rhoda's son. Jeremy had good things to say about him.

The muffin disappeared magically into Qay's stomach, and Rhoda brought him a Coke to wash it down. "No coffee?" he asked.

"I'm willing to commit certain atrocities, but serving vending machine coffee isn't one of them." She smiled faintly. Today she wore a long-sleeved dress with a peacock-feather print and matching earrings. She'd arranged her hair in a complicated style.

"You look really nice today, Rhoda. Um, not that you don't usually look nice, but today you're extra nice and those colors are great on you." Oh good. He'd lost control of his tongue and was babbling inanely.

But she beamed and patted his arm. "You're a good one for sure, Qay."

He was still considering how to respond when Ng reappeared with Frankl at his side. Ng was tight-faced and angry, but Frankl just looked exhausted. "Are you Rhoda Levin?" Frankl asked.

She stood and nodded. "Yes."

"I'm Captain Frankl from the police bureau. Let's go somewhere quieter."

Qay remained seated as Frankl began to walk away, but Rhoda gestured impatiently. "Come on, Qay. You too."

"He's not listed as an emergency contact," Frankl said.

"Only because Jeremy hadn't gotten around to it. These two care about each other. Qay needs to be there."

Maybe Frankl would have argued, but Ng huffed. "Don't be a prick, Frankl. Jeremy told me himself he's got a serious thing for this dude. Qay gets to go."

When Frankl shrugged wearily and stalked away, Qay allowed Rhoda to tug him upright. As they walked through the hospital, Qay was stunned by what had just happened. Jeremy had said something to Ng about him—said it was serious. And both Rhoda and Ng had stood up for him. Nobody did that.

Two floors up and several corridors away, they ended up in another waiting room. This one was smaller, with a more hushed atmosphere. The furniture was upholstered instead of plastic, carpet lined the floor, and peaceful landscapes hung on the walls. A small group of people huddled in one corner, while an older man dozed by himself near a wall. Frankl led them to a circular cluster of chairs and motioned Rhoda to sit.

Qay sat too, but only for a few seconds. His nerves were crawling under his skin, so while the policemen spoke quietly with Rhoda, Qay paced the room, his shoulders hunched under his leather jacket. He heard bits and pieces of the conversation: burns, gunshot, broken fingers, hypothermia. He learned that Davis and one of his minions were dead, another was in surgery, and a fourth man was jailed. Frankl's men were busily searching the factory where they'd found Jeremy as well as Davis's house and just about every other place where the guy had stepped foot lately. At some point Qay would probably be relieved to know Davis was no longer a threat, but right now he simply paced. The silent family in the corner watched.

He was on his thousandth circuit of the room when Rhoda waved at him. "Why are you limping?"

Surprised, he stopped and looked down at his right foot. It hurt. He hadn't noticed.

"He kicked a fucking door in," Ng said.

"A door? Why?"

"To get to a phone and call for help. He's the one who figured out Jeremy'd been snatched."

"Honey!" She rushed over to drag him to a chair. Then she ran off, returning shortly with a doctor who insisted on examining Qay's foot. Bruised and mildly strained, the doctor said. He gave Qay an ice pack and told him to rest for a few days and keep the foot elevated. When the doctor seemed about to ask for paperwork and insurance information, Ng had a few quiet words with him. The doctor nodded and went away.

Now Qay couldn't pace anymore, and he couldn't get his boot onto the swollen foot. He leaned back in his chair, covered his eyes with an arm, and concentrated on not going insane.

"Here you go, hon." The soft words and a gentle tap on his shoulder brought him back to awareness. Frankl was gone, but Ng sat across from him, balancing a paper plate heaped full of food. Rhoda held a foil-covered plate out to Qay. "This is better than a machine muffin," she said.

He took the plate, removed the foil, and inhaled. Turkey with all the trimmings, still fragrant and warm. "How?" he asked.

"I had Parker come by with it. He brought you one of his slippers too. I bet you can get it on your bum foot." She pointed at the slipper in question, which sat on the chair next to him. The slipper was furry with a monster face appliquéd on it. Qay must have looked skeptical, because Rhoda laughed. "Your dignity will survive, baby."

"I don't have any dignity." And to prove it, he eased on the foolish slipper and dug into the food with the plastic cutlery Rhoda gave him. Everything was delicious. She'd even managed to conjure a hot spiced cider—nonalcoholic—which he hadn't tasted in years.

Shortly after Qay and Nevin finished eating, a doctor entered the room and headed their way. She was tall and thin, her black hair pulled back in a ponytail, and although she looked tired, a small smile played on her lips. "You are Mr. Cox's friends?" she asked. She had a slight accent, musical and pleasant.

They all nodded, and Qay remained seated as Nevin and Rhoda stood.

"I am Dr. Jalali, the surgeon. I am happy to tell you that Mr. Cox is doing quite well. He is in recovery now and should be able to receive visitors soon. Does he have someone to help care for him at home?"

"Yes," all three of them said in unison.

"Very good. Then he should be able to go home by Saturday. Perhaps even late tomorrow."

An enormous weight lifted from Qay's chest, making him feel buoyant. "He'll be okay?"

"Yes. His fingers will remain splinted, and he may require physical therapy for his shoulder when the wound has healed. The burns will scar. But he will recover fully."

Maybe his pitiful prayer had been answered. Qay wasn't even sure he believed in God, but he figured it didn't hurt to be grateful. *Thank you, God*, he thought. *Thank you so much. I owe you one.*

AFTER MAKING Rhoda promise to call if anything changed, Nevin went home—but not before he shook Qay's hand. "You're still fucking holding it together, man. Looks like for once, Germy chose wisely in love."

Qay and Rhoda sat and waited. She'd found a couple of paperbacks somewhere—maybe Parker had brought them—and she handed one to Qay. It was one of those fantasy novels with a complicated plot and impossible names. He was unable to keep track of any of it in his current state, but it was still nice to run his gaze over the sentences, even if they didn't make much sense.

A doctor spoke with the group of people in the corner. They looked relieved. But the outcome apparently wasn't as good for the older man, who was led weeping into a private room. Qay's heart ached for the guy, and he hoped that at least the man and whomever he was mourning had enjoyed a long time together.

Rhoda brought Qay another Coke. When he hobbled to the bathroom, an exhausted-looking nurse smiled at the ridiculous monster face on the slipper, and Qay felt a little better about his footwear.

He returned and collapsed into his chair with a sigh.

"Will you be all right, sweetie?" asked Rhoda, indicating his foot.

"Yeah. I don't have to work until Tuesday." Thanks to the ice, the ache had already diminished slightly.

"Good. Let's talk about what we're going to do with Jeremy. I have a plan, if you're up for it." She gave him an assessing look. "And I think you are."

"Jesus, Rhoda. Look at me. I'm a goddamn mess."

"You saved Jeremy's life today, Qay."

He breathed in so sharply it hurt. "I—"

"He was a big idiot who ignored everyone's warnings to be more careful, but you called in the cavalry. That qualifies you to take care of the fool."

"If I'd gone for help earlier, he might not have been hurt."

"So now you're supposed to be psychic? C'mon, Qay. I didn't do anything at all. When the two of you didn't show, I tried to call and got his voice mail. I figured either you'd had another fight, in which case he'd want to pout alone, or you were too busy in bed together to notice the time."

Qay felt his cheeks heat.

Rhoda chuckled and patted his shoulder. "It's okay. I'm a big girl. But do you want to hear my plan?"

"Sure."

"As soon as they spring him from this place, I'll give him a ride to the Marriott. You stay with him until you have to go to work."

"But I—"

"He's going to need help bathing, dressing. I'm absolutely positive he'd rather you do that than me."

Qay considered this. "Yeah, you're right." The question was whether Qay could keep his shit together enough to help.

"I'm always right, darling. Okay, then. We'll see what kind of shape he's in Monday night and go from there. He can stay in my extra bedroom if he wants to."

That decided, they waited until a nurse came for them. "He's awake. You can come see him, but just for a few minutes. He needs to rest."

Qay bounced out of his chair, then had to swallow an expletive when he landed on his sore foot. Rhoda just sighed and rolled her eyes.

JEREMY LOOKED awful—and yet beautiful, because he was alive, and because when he saw Rhoda and Qay, he gave them a woozy smile. His face was swollen, bandages swathed a good part of his head and body, and tubes trailed from his arm.

"When you're healed, I'm going to kick your ass," Rhoda said. "Idiot." Then she bent over and kissed him gently on the less puffy cheek. A plastic cup with a straw sat on the little bedside table. She picked it up and stuck it near his face. "Drink."

He took an obedient sip. "Thanks." His voice sounded as if it had been dragged through a gravel pit. "Is everyone all right?"

"Everyone but you. And the bad guys. Davis is dead."

Jeremy nodded slightly, winced, and sighed. "Such a waste." Then he turned his attention to Qay, who'd been hovering uncomfortably near the door. "You missed Thanksgiving."

Qay hobbled closer, shaking his head. "Not with Rhoda around. She made Parker bring plates of food."

"Why are you walking like that?"

Jesus Christ. The guy got kidnapped, tortured, operated on, and was probably doped to the gills, yet he still noticed Qay's limp. "I hurt my foot."

Jeremy tried to sit up, but Qay held him down. "Did Davis—" Jeremy began, and Qay realized Jeremy had feared for Qay's safety.

"Davis was never anywhere near me," Qay said soothingly.

"He hurt himself rescuing your reckless ass," Rhoda said. "He kicked down a door to get to a phone."

Jeremy frowned. "Was gonna buy him a phone. And a laptop. Have to be sneaky to make him accept them."

While Rhoda blinked, Qay just shook his head. "I think they've got you on the really good stuff, Jeremy." He was envious.

"You're good stuff. We weren't going to get out of bed all weekend." Jeremy looked mournfully at his splinted fingers.

Rhoda's cough sounded suspiciously like a laugh, so Qay ignored her. He took Jeremy's good hand and, remembering all the comfort he'd dreamed of when he was hospitalized, gave a warm smile. "We'll have time for that. We'll just reschedule. Did you know I get a week off at Christmas?"

"You for Christmas. Better than a laptop."

Jeremy's eyes dropped closed, and although he opened them a moment later, it was clear he was fighting sleep. Qay leaned forward and placed a careful kiss on his badly chapped lips. "Enjoy that stuff they have pumping through your veins. I'll see you in the morning."

"I'll tell you I love you in the morning," said Jeremy before his lids shut again. This time they stayed that way.

QAY LOATHED hospitals. He'd forgotten that on Thursday because he was too busy freaking out over Jeremy. But he emphatically remembered on Friday, when he spent the better part of the day at Jeremy's bedside. Qay tried to concentrate instead on Jeremy, and that worked fine when Jeremy was awake and needed entertaining or assistance. But when he frequently napped, still groggy from the pain meds, Qay had nothing to do but fret. He'd brought his schoolwork but didn't manage to get much done.

A doctor arrived late in the afternoon and spent a long time poking and prodding. Qay winced to see Jeremy's wounds but stayed close by as the doctor explained home care for the days after Jeremy's release.

"I can take care of myself," Jeremy grumbled.

The doctor—an older man with the bristliest eyebrows Qay had ever seen—shook his head. "No, Jeremy, you can't. And Qay has my permission to haul you back here if you don't follow my orders."

Jeremy raised an eyebrow, as if doubting that Qay could haul his bulky body anywhere, but Qay scowled. "I'll do it, even if I have to get Rhoda and Nevin to help." That threat must have been sufficient, because Jeremy sighed and nodded at the doctor.

"If you promise to be a good boy, I'll sign you out," the doctor said.

"Fine. I promise."

Rhoda drove them to the Marriott in Jeremy's SUV, which she'd retrieved from the parking garage. She handed Qay a duffel bag containing the spare clothes and toiletries he'd packed that morning before she took him to the hospital. When they got to Jeremy's room, she set down a big paper sack full of food. "It's mainly fruits and juices," she explained. "And some pastries from the shop."

"We can order room service," Jeremy protested from the bed. The short walk had exhausted him, and his face was drawn with pain.

"Of course you can. But I feel better if I leave you boys with provisions. Jer, do you have shoes you can get on one-handed? If not, I can—"

"Loafers. Ugly things, but I own them."

"You'll be back in your manly boots soon enough." She kissed Jeremy quickly on the cheek and then, to Qay's considerable surprise, tugged him down for a kiss as well. "Ring if you need anything. Even if I can't do it, Parker's here for the weekend and willing to be at your beck and call."

After she left, Qay helped Jeremy change out of the sweatpants and T-shirt Rhoda had brought to the hospital. He checked Jeremy's bandages, which looked fine, and settled him into bed. Jeremy blinked up at him. "Will you join me?"

"You're not in any shape for sex."

"I know. But we can cuddle, right?"

Even that was difficult due to Jeremy's injuries, but they eventually found a comfortable position with Jeremy lying flat and Qay draped over his good side, carefully avoiding the burns.

"I'm sorry," Jeremy said after a while. "I was stupid, and you could have been killed."

"Me? I was safe at home."

"They would have come after you next. Hell, if Davis wasn't such a pea-brain, they'd have taken us both. Then hurt you to get me to talk."

Qay sighed. "They hurt *you*."

"That's not the point. I'll be okay. But they would have gone after you next, and I couldn't do anything about it." His voice was strained, and Qay could feel the tension in his body.

"They didn't, and I'm fine."

They were both quiet for a long time. Then Jeremy sighed. "God, I feel zonked."

"Pain pills will do that to you."

"I hate not… not feeling in control."

Qay couldn't quite suppress a snort. "No big surprise there."

"But how could you—" Jeremy stopped very suddenly.

"How could I let myself get addicted to shit like that? Bad genes and bad decisions."

"No, I understand addiction. It's biology. What I don't get is how you could stand to have your head messed up like this. Just trying to think, it's like… like walking through thick mud."

"I don't know." That wasn't true. Qay had weathered his muddled head when he was high because cotton wool in his skull was better than the razor wire of his goddamn anxiety. He doubted Jeremy would understand that, though. He'd been tortured, for Christ's sake, and came out of it kicking himself for not being a better superhero.

Probably without even realizing, Jeremy stroked Qay's back. "Qay? If I tell you something, will you believe it's true and not just the drugs?"

"Yeah." Dope didn't stop you from seeing some things with clarity.

"Good. It's something I realized while I was in the factory. Guess it took some knocks to my head to get me to realize the obvious." Jeremy took a deep breath and let it out. "I love you."

Qay froze. He thought Jeremy had forgotten his promise from the night before. "You can't—"

"I *love* you. I know it's only been a couple of weeks, but that doesn't matter. I think the longer I know you, the stronger I'll feel about you. I'll fall a little more for you every damn day. But I'm already there, and you need to know that."

"I've never been in love with anyone," Qay said carefully.

"And I don't expect you to be where I'm at yet. You have more sense than I do. And more insulation around your heart."

Qay had no sense at all, and his heart was stripped bare. "I'm with you," he said quietly. "Right where you are."

"You feel the same way?"

"Yes. And it fucking terrifies me." There. He'd just handed his raw, vulnerable heart right over.

Jeremy pulled him tighter. "Love doesn't have to be scary, Qay. We're in it together, right?"

Because Jeremy made it sound as if they were facing a firing squad instead of a relationship, Qay laughed despite the knots in his stomach. Jeremy chuckled too, then groaned when the movement jostled his wounds.

Qay glanced at the bedside clock and sat up. "You're due for another dose." He stood and headed for the desk, where Jeremy had left the little paper bag containing his meds.

Jeremy struggled to sit up, and this time Qay was too far away to stop him. "Don't, Qay. I can skip it. No big deal."

Ignoring him, Qay filled a drinking glass from the bathroom sink and grabbed the bag as he crossed to the bed. He wordlessly set the glass on the nightstand, pulled out a pill bottle, opened the cap, and removed a pill. He held it out to Jeremy. "Take it."

"Qay—"

"Yeah, I want to fix right now. But you need this and you can't open the fucking bottle one-handed. Take it."

After a pause, Jeremy obeyed. When the pill was no longer in his hand, Qay felt a small rush of relief mingled with disappointment, but he watched Jeremy place the tiny thing on his tongue and wash it down with the water Qay handed him. Jeremy fell back on his pillows as if he'd just finished a strenuous task. "Thank you."

"You have to understand this about me, Jeremy. I'm *always* going to want to fix. And every time I see a pill bottle or a glass of booze, or every time the demons start trying to claw their way out of my skull, I'm going to want it even more."

Jeremy tightened his jaw. "I can do without the damn pills. I won't drink. And *I'll* be here when the demons are after you."

Qay shook his head and ignored the stomach roil, knowing Jeremy didn't get it. But now wasn't the time to argue, not while Jeremy was hurting and tired and partway out of it. They'd have plenty of time to travel this uneven ground later.

The meds made Jeremy sleepy. Qay helped him eat a little—part of a fancy sandwich Rhoda had packed, as well as some beef noodle soup from room service—then watched as Jeremy fell asleep. Even with the bandages and bruising and passage of three decades, Qay could see the boy he used to be. Same fair skin and pale hair, same wide mouth. And the poor sap was in love with damaged misfit Qay.

CHAPTER TWENTY-ONE

IT WAS a little like a honeymoon, only with subdued sex due to Jeremy's injuries. Even quiet sex was good, though. On Saturday morning, neither of them complained when Qay started out by rubbing ointment into the circular burns on Jeremy's chest and ended up licking his way down those taut abs to Jeremy's cock. And when Qay climbed into bed that night, both of them naked, Jeremy used his good hand to stroke Qay to a climax that had Qay gasping against Jeremy's neck.

Both men were restless by Sunday, so Qay helped Jeremy dress and arranged his arm in a sling, and they went for a slow walk around downtown. They strolled through a couple of Jeremy's parks, where he pointed out some of the features as proudly as if he'd put them there, and they had lunch at a quiet Lebanese place. After that, Jeremy grinned and insisted they visit Powell's bookstore, where Qay went into such sensory overload that they had to sit in the café and drink hot chocolate until he calmed. He ended up with three books, even though he didn't really need them and could barely afford them. He refused to let Jeremy pay and, in fact, insisted on paying for Jeremy's thick volume on plant evolution, thankfully at a used-book price.

As they were slowly walking back, a patrol car passed them. The officer inside waved at Jeremy, who waved back. The sight of the black-and-white started a chain of thoughts in Qay's head, and at the end of it, he asked, "Where do you think that thumb drive is?"

Jeremy gave him a sidelong glance. "Does it matter?"

"Might help the case against those fuckers. But mostly I'm just curious."

"I'm not sure the damned thing even exists. Planning ahead on something like that was never Donny's style. I bet he got desperate for cash and cooked up the whole blackmail scheme out of nothing. He was reckless enough to do something like that, and Davis was dumb enough to fall for it."

Qay shook his head, dumbfounded at the damage compulsion and lies could cause.

When they got back to the hotel, Jeremy needed a nap. Qay sat at the desk to do his homework, pretending the pain pills weren't just a few strides away.

Late that evening, Jeremy looked up from his book, which he'd been reading in the chair by the window. A wicked smile curled the corners of his mouth. "Will you help me shower?"

Qay would. He'd never showered with anyone before, and the hotel tub was crowded with the two of them, but who cared when all that warm, wet skin was right *there*. They had to be careful of the gunshot wound, which was fairly easy, but avoiding the burns was harder because they both yearned for attention to Jeremy's big, round nipples—Jeremy because they were one of his favorite erogenous zones, Qay because he loved how Jeremy moaned and clutched Qay's hair when Qay played with them. But Jeremy had plenty of other parts to play with, and they intrigued Qay too. When Jeremy leaned forward against the tile and canted his ass backward and Qay slowly lathered soap over those big, strong muscles, they both groaned with pleasure.

"God," Jeremy said when Qay slipped his fingers into the tight cleft. Jeremy looked over his shoulder at Qay. "Did you know sex releases natural endorphins? So if you fuck me right now, you'll be helping me heal."

Qay moved forward slightly to grasp Jeremy's hips and rub his own erection against that enticing flesh. He licked the knobs of Jeremy's spine and the point of his right shoulder blade. Slightly soapy; tasted good. "You want me to play doctor?" he asked hoarsely.

"Please?" Jeremy arched his back a bit, pressing his ass more firmly against Qay.

"Bed." Qay's foot and ankle were still a little sore, and the last thing either of them needed was to collapse in a twisted heap inside the slippery tub.

But when they neared the bed—Jeremy groping him one-handed the entire way—they realized their condom stash was at Qay's apartment. "I'll go find a drugstore," Qay said, but Jeremy caught him before he could move away.

"We'll be fine without. It's been almost eight months since I had sex with anyone else, and I tested clean just last week."

Qay raised his eyebrows. "You just got tested?"

"Yeah."

"Why?"

Jeremy pulled him flush against his body and nuzzled his neck, making Qay shiver. "I was hoping we'd be... I don't know. Exclusive. Real. Permanent. Can we be those things?"

Christ. Qay wanted that desperately, with a craving deeper than any he'd felt for drugs or alcohol. But a man as broken as he was couldn't make those kind of promises. Instead of answering, he kissed Jeremy, and if Jeremy took that as a yes, well, Qay could add that lie to the others on his conscience.

Standing naked beside the bed, they made out until Qay's foot throbbed and Jeremy growled with disgust over clutching Qay's ass with only one hand. They fell onto the bed harder than was advisable. Jeremy *oofed* but kept Qay pressed against him. "I do have lube. It's in the drawer, next to the Bible."

Qay opened the drawer and retrieved the little bottle. "I hadn't realized the Gideons had become so useful."

"They haven't. I bought it to fly solo when I was being too big of a dumbshit to talk to you."

"I think we can find a better use for it," Qay said, smiling.

"Much, much better."

With a slight grunt, Jeremy worked his way out from underneath Qay and turned onto his belly. He spread his legs invitingly and turned his head to look at Qay. "I'm waiting."

"That's not hurting your burns?"

"Who the fuck cares! Come on, Qay!"

Laughing, Qay scooted beside him and massaged those glorious glutes. "Figures you'd be a bossy bottom, Chief." Jeremy shot him an indignant look, and Qay retaliated with a light swat to one buttcheek. That made Jeremy wriggle demandingly.

After that, Qay ignored Jeremy's complaints and took his goddamn time slicking Jeremy up, easing tight muscles until they were more than ready to accept him. Jeremy was reduced to a string of mumbled pleas and attempts to fuck himself more thoroughly on Qay's fingers. Qay could possibly make him come like that: his fingers moving in and out of that tight heat, Jeremy squirming and humping against the mattress, emitting a chorus of expletives and moans. That would be fun. But Qay's dick really wanted to join the party, and Qay didn't think Jeremy had the stamina yet for a second round. So he withdrew his fingers, patted Jeremy's ass again, and smoothed the small of his back.

"Roll over, Jer."

He did so with surprising speed for a man who'd been shot three days earlier. He bent his knees, planted his soles on the mattress, and smiled widely. "You're so beautiful," he said.

Qay felt himself blush, which was absurd. "Is that those endorphins speaking?"

"Nope. Just calling it like I see it. And remember, I'm a trained observer."

With just a little difficulty, Qay managed to get a pillow under Jeremy's ass. Then he took a moment to admire what Jeremy was offering him. It might have been past Thanksgiving, but he was feeling supremely grateful.

He positioned himself between Jeremy's legs but didn't penetrate him yet. Instead, Qay rutted gently against Jeremy's body and captured his lips in a kiss. God, Jeremy always tasted so good! But as the movement of his hips sped a bit, Qay realized the pressure of his torso on Jeremy's burns wasn't a good idea—not that Jeremy seemed to be noticing any pain. He was rubbing Qay's ass and trying to raise his hips a little more.

"Are you ready for me?" Qay asked.

"I think I've been ready for you for years."

Qay drew back a bit, lined himself up, and slowly sank inside.

Holy Christ, so tight, so good. The look on Jeremy's face alone was almost enough to make Qay come. Gray eyes heavy-lidded, beautiful mouth parted, a delicate flush tingeing those broad, lightly stubbled cheeks. Qay wasn't fucking Captain Caffeine; he was making love with Jeremy Cox, a stunning man with a fine mind and a heart as big as the Great Plains.

When Qay was fully seated, every inch of him encased in Jeremy's welcoming body, they froze and their gazes locked. And for that one blessed moment, every one of Qay's nerves untangled, the demons disappeared, and the weight lifted from his chest.

"I love you," Jeremy whispered.

"I love you," Qay echoed. The first time he had ever uttered those three words.

They had to move eventually, and what followed was sublime, a dream clearer and more joyful than any drugs could give, a precious bit of perfection in an imperfect world.

They didn't clean up afterward. Qay wanted to wear Jeremy's spend on his belly and chest, even though he knew it would flake and itch. And although he must have been sticky and somewhat uncomfortable, Jeremy seemed content as well. He tugged Qay close, pulled up the covers, and breathed warmly against Qay's nape. "The universe can be so weird, darlin'."

Qay heard Kansas in the way Jeremy said that last word.

THEY SHOWERED together again Monday morning. Qay hadn't planned to have sex right then, but he couldn't resist Jeremy naked in front of him, so he dropped to his knees and blew him. Jeremy came and collapsed into Qay's arms, the water sluicing over them both. A few minutes later, Jeremy returned the favor, but he sat on the bed and leaned against the headboard while Qay crouched above him and thrust into his mouth.

It was a good way to begin the day.

But eventually they had to talk business. "Are you going to be all right on your own?" Qay asked. Jeremy was taking the whole week off to recuperate, but Qay had class that night and work in the morning.

"I'm fine. I'm getting really good at doing things one-handed. Thank God that asshole didn't go after my right hand. Rhoda can be here in twenty minutes if I get stuck."

"I could take a couple of days off." He couldn't afford it, but he was worried about Jeremy.

"Don't. Really, I'm doing great. Have you noticed? I stopped taking the meds Saturday night."

Of course Qay had noticed, because Jeremy hadn't asked him to open the pill bottle, which had mysteriously disappeared. "You got *shot*, Jeremy."

"It's nothing but a flesh wound." Jeremy winked. "And the day after tomorrow, I get to move back into my place. I'm really tired of hotels. Will you go shopping with me this weekend for kitchen stuff and…. Shit!"

"What's the matter?"

"I made a list of everything I needed. It was in my pocket when they snatched me." He sighed. "Guess I need to make a new one."

The guy got tortured, shot, and almost killed, but his biggest complaint was a lost shopping list. Qay shook his head in bewilderment. "Yeah, we can shop." Wasn't that what gay couples did?

But now Jeremy looked like he wanted to say something more and couldn't spit it out. He gnawed his lower lip and angled his vision toward the ceiling. "Um, Qay? I want you to think about something without freaking out."

Great. Qay immediately began to breathe fast. "Wh-what?"

"It's not a scary thing. Just something to contemplate. But…." He swallowed loudly. "You could move in with me."

Qay gaped.

Jeremy continued gamely. "You've seen the place—it's plenty big enough for two people to spread out. And you can pay rent or help with the utilities, or whatever. I don't care. I'd just really like to come home to you."

Qay's heart sped and his head swam, but he managed to not collapse. "I don't—"

"I know. It's sudden. You don't have to decide now. I mean, you've probably already paid rent for December, right?"

A slight nod.

"Right," Jeremy said. "So no use hurrying things. But you can help me pick out rugs and dishes and… stuff. Things you like. That way, if you do move in, it'll really feel like your place too."

Apparently only slightly daunted by the silence that followed, Jeremy shrugged, then winced. "I'm hella tired of the damn shoulder. Want to go for a walk?"

SHORTLY AFTER lunch they shared a passionate kiss. Jeremy was a talented kisser, although his broken fingers seemed to frustrate him. Then Qay gathered up all his clothing, schoolwork, and the various other belongings he'd scattered around Jeremy's hotel room and stuffed everything into his duffel and backpack.

Jeremy stopped him at the door. "Will you come by my place after work Wednesday?"

At least he'd said *my* instead of *our*. "Sure. Maybe you can come back to my apartment for dinner. I can do amazing things with ramen."

"I believe that. And look. I'm going cell phone shopping this afternoon, since mine's toast. Sometimes they have a good deal if you buy two. Will you throw a fit if I get you one?"

Qay thought about how much faster he could have called for help on Thursday if he'd owned a cell phone. And if he'd had Rhoda's number, he could have called her soon after Jeremy failed to show up. It would have saved Jeremy some pain. "I won't throw a fit. But I'm paying for mine."

"Done," Jeremy said with a grin.

One more kiss, and Qay left.

He stopped first at his apartment, which seemed especially dank and dreary after a long weekend at the Marriott. He dropped off his duffel, threw out some expired milk, and set out again, this time to school.

It should have been an interesting class. The subject this week was Nietzsche and Foucault on ethics and morality, and Qay had found the readings engaging. But several minutes into the discussion, someone brought up the subject of responsibility and self-blame, and Qay began to think about Kevin walking down the railroad tracks to retrieve his errant younger brother. Over the years he'd become better at pushing those thoughts away. But the past several days had been emotionally tumultuous, weakening his defenses, and now his thoughts spiraled from Kevin to his parents to addiction to crime to his job. The disaster tornado touched down next on Jeremy and stayed there, kicking up fears of all the ways Qay could fail him and all the things that could go wrong.

When Professor Reynolds announced a fifteen-minute break halfway through class, Qay gathered up his things and fled.

He got off the bus several stops early, partly because he couldn't sit still any longer, partly because he felt like he might puke. His hands shook and his legs were unsteady as he made his way down the sidewalk, and now the disaster tornado was joined by a berating chorus. *Fucking idiot couldn't even make it through class today. What's Reynolds going to think? What happened to your university plans? Weakling! Fuckup!*

Which was why, when he came to a tavern with neon beer signs in the window, Qay turned and went inside.

CHAPTER TWENTY-TWO

JEREMY WASN'T used to so much sitting around. It made him jumpy. He couldn't even play on his laptop easily without the use of his left hand. After Qay left on Monday, Jeremy tried reading, but he couldn't get into it. Finally he put on his shoes and spent a good fifteen minutes trying to tie the laces. He hoped the weather wasn't too cold, since he had to give up entirely on zipping his coat.

"How are you doing today, Chief?" asked the young woman at the reception desk.

"Pretty good, thanks."

"There was another article in the paper this morning. One of the suspects is being arraigned today."

Jeremy made a face. His kidnapping and the subsequent shoot-out had received a lot of media attention, especially after some enterprising reporter connected that mess to Donny's death. Rhoda and Nevin had both called the hotel room to warn Jeremy about what was going on in the press, and Jeremy had happily avoided turning on the TV or reading the paper over the weekend. Better for him that way, and *much* better for Qay, who'd had enough stress already. And since Jeremy's temporary living quarters remained known to only a select few, no news crews had camped out at the Marriott. Thank God.

"I'm going for a walk," Jeremy told the receptionist. "If my friends come looking for me, please tell them I'm not dead."

"You're not dead. Got it."

He ventured outside, head bowed slightly, and headed for Waterfront Park.

Fuck, he'd been such an idiot to ignore Frankl's warnings. He'd been so caught up with the giddiness of getting to know Qay, coupled with the devastation of Donny's death, that everything else had seemed unimportant. So he'd continued along with his head in the sand, and just as he'd sent Donny into the hands of a murderer, he'd gravely endangered Qay as well.

He'd learned his lesson. Davis was dead, and Jeremy would always remember now to put Qay's welfare first. Qay fucking deserved it, didn't he?

The gray water of the Willamette churned by, and Jeremy's thoughts were no more placid.

After a time he turned and headed west, away from the river. He bargained hard in the phone store, deciding he wasn't above a little flirting with the salesman if it meant Qay would get a good deal. The kid was half his age and kind of a ditz, but Jeremy left with two fancy new phones and a plan he hoped wasn't out of Qay's price range. The account was in Jeremy's name, but he figured if Qay insisted on paying—which he would—he could just write Jeremy a check every month. If all went well, Qay could just add it to the rent.

Fuck, the rent. Jeremy ambled toward the North Park Blocks and hoped he hadn't spooked Qay by inviting him to move in. It was sudden. But Jeremy had just come within inches of being killed, and maybe that had reminded him of the fragility of life. He took care of himself—he might have another fifty years in him. Or he could step off the curb and get hit by a bus. However much time remained to him, he didn't want to waste it dicking around. He wanted to spend it with Qay.

He waited for the light to change so he could cross Burnside. Three people huddled under an awning on the other side, passing a cigarette back and forth. He recognized the two men, but the young woman was new, and for a moment his heart sank. Sometimes it seemed that for every kid like Toad he pulled off the streets, two new hopeless people came to take his place.

When Jeremy came abreast of them, the men waved. "Chief!" the skinny one called. Randall—that was his name. "What the fuck happened to you?" Apparently these people weren't up on the latest news.

Jeremy waved his left hand slightly. "Bad decisions. Busted fingers."

"Naw, man, you gotta be careful! It's a tough ol' world."

"Don't I know it. Are you doing okay, Randall? You guys have a place to stay?"

"Yeah. Me an' Curtis been sleepin' at the men's shelter. But Lina here, she's new. She don't got nowhere."

Jeremy gave Lina a closer look. She was pale, with a fading bruise around one eye and a slightly swollen lip. He gave her what he hoped was an encouraging smile. "Hey, Lina. I'm off duty and out of uniform today, but I'm a park ranger. My name's Jeremy Cox."

"Park ranger?" she said in the same tone as if he'd announced he was a visitor from outer space. "This ain't a park."

He got this a lot. "Not here, no. But there are lots of parks all over the city, and that's my territory."

She still looked highly skeptical, but then the other man—Curtis—nudged her slightly. "It's true. He's a good guy, Li. Makes sure everyone's all right. He helped get my friend AJ into a program. Now AJ's got a job and everything. He volunteers at the shelter sometimes."

Jeremy remembered AJ but hadn't seen him in a couple of years. He grinned widely to learn that AJ was doing well. He'd been a heavy drinker with a truly sweet heart. "When you see AJ again, tell him hello for me."

Curtis nodded, and Lina thawed a tiny bit. She was really young, and although it was hard to tell with her bulky clothing, Jeremy suspected she was pregnant. "Do you have a place to stay, Lina?"

She looked down at her feet. "I was stayin' with a friend," she murmured. "That didn't work out."

"Yeah, that happens. Look, I know this place. Harbor House. It really is a house, one of those big Victorian things. It's only for women and children. I can call and see if they have a room free."

She narrowed her eyes. "What do I gotta do?"

"Follow the rules. They're pretty reasonable—no drugs, no fighting, no men in the house. Stuff like that. They can give you food and a safe place to sleep. Counseling if you want it. Medical care."

"I wanna keep my baby," she said firmly.

"They can help with that too."

He could see her wavering. Normally he'd have offered to give her a ride over there right now, before she could set her mind against it, but the doctor said he wasn't supposed to drive for two more days. At least the cute dimwit at the phone store had managed to transfer Jeremy's contacts to his new phone. "Hang on," he said. He stepped a few yards away, fished out the phone, and called the director of Harbor House. It was an awkward procedure one-handed, but the director answered and said yes, they had a free bed.

Smiling, Jeremy walked back to the little group. "They're holding a room for you, Lina. I'm going to write down the address for you. They're in Northeast but real easy to get to. The number twelve bus will get you less than two blocks away."

Lina wasn't exactly wildly enthusiastic, but she didn't say no. And when Jeremy found a piece of paper and pen in his pocket and scrawled the address, she took it from him, glanced at it, and tucked it away. It was the best he could do for her. Well, almost. "Do you need bus fare?" he asked her. She nodded slightly, so he pulled out his wallet and gave her a ten. Curtis and Randall watched carefully, so Jeremy handed Randall a twenty. "You guys'll have to split this. Promise me you'll spend it on food and not booze."

"We can get ourselves a couple good meals out of this," Randall said happily. Jeremy hoped that was what they'd actually do.

He wished them all luck, especially Lina. "You take care of yourself, Chief," Randall said. "Don't go breaking no more bones."

"I'll do my best to avoid it."

Jeremy continued his walk but couldn't help glancing back. The three of them still stood there, conversing closely. He wished he could just shove Lina into his SUV and take her to Harbor House. And drag Curtis and Randall somewhere they could dry out, making sure they stayed there until their alcoholism was under control, and then help them find decent jobs and stable homes and a life that wouldn't kill them young. He wished he could take Qay home and—

Shit. Qay. He was the most extraordinary person Jeremy had ever met, brilliant and complex. And sometimes when they were just sitting together—across the table over a meal, next to each other on the bed with books in hand—Qay would stop jittering. His muscles would loosen, an easy smile would play across his face, and he'd look happy and relaxed. It never lasted long, but those moments were beautiful. Qay would look at Jeremy as if he'd been given an unexpected and wonderful gift. Jeremy wanted those times to come more often and stay longer. He wanted Qay to find his much-deserved place in the world.

TUESDAY WAS endless. Jeremy walked several times. He had lunch at Perry's with two of his rangers, both of whom were a little starstruck due to Jeremy's newfound, albeit unwelcome, notoriety. He met Frankl for coffee after that. Frankl apologized for not moving in on Davis faster, but Jeremy understood. They couldn't pounce on the guy every time he left his house, and since his family owned the factory where they'd taken Jeremy, Davis's presence there wasn't particularly suspicious. "I'll need a formal statement from you," Frankl said as he played with the handle of his mug. "But it can wait a couple of days. Those scumbags aren't going anywhere."

"No problem. I have the week off. I'll be busy tomorrow, though. Moving back into my loft."

"Thursday's fine. You know, that guy… your boyfriend?"

"Qay?"

"Him. He saved your life."

Jeremy nodded. "I know." He'd tried to thank Qay for it, but Qay refused to discuss it. Even raising the topic of that afternoon was enough to send Qay heading for a panic attack, so Jeremy had let it drop.

"I had some reservations about him when you brought him to McDonald's. He looks… a little rough, you know? But damn, he came through for you."

"He did."

Later Rhoda met him for dinner, with Parker since he was still visiting, and the three of them had a nice meal. But Jeremy was distracted, thinking of Qay taking the bus home from work in the drizzle and eating alone in his basement. *Don't hover*, he lectured himself. *Give him some space to think.* Maybe by tomorrow Qay would decide that moving in was a good idea. If nothing else, Jeremy could give him the cell and that way they could stay in touch more easily. A text message now and then went a long way.

After Rhoda dropped him off at the Marriott, Jeremy began to pack up his belongings. He hadn't salvaged much stuff from his trashed apartment, but in the interim, his possessions seemed to have multiplied exponentially. He was going to have to put a lot of them into plastic shopping bags, which wasn't ideal. It didn't help that he had only one hand.

When he moved an untidy pile of T-shirts and uncovered a small object, he smiled and picked it up. It was a very ordinary seed cone, the three-pronged bracts sticking out past the scales. Qay had picked it up during one of their walks and smilingly asked what tree it came from. Jeremy told him it was from a Douglas fir, and Qay had tucked the cone into his pocket. Jeremy had no idea how the thing ended up in his hotel room.

He was still examining the cone when his phone rang. He glanced hopefully at the screen, but instead of Qay's number, he saw a 620 area code. "Mom?" he asked when he answered.

Her response was equally uncertain, her voice raspy from a lifetime of smoking. "Jeremy?"

Jeremy wasn't exactly estranged from his parents. He called them on Mother's Day and Christmas, they called him on his birthday. They didn't really have much to talk about. He wasn't interested in the latest gossip from Bailey Springs; they sure as hell didn't want to hear about the men he dated. He'd last seen them over ten years earlier at his grandmother's funeral.

"What's up, Mom?"

"I ran into Betty Ostermeyer at the market today, and she said her son saw you on the Internet. Did you get *shot*?"

Oh, holy Christ. "Yeah, Mom. But I'm—"

"I thought you said you're not a policeman anymore."

His parents had never approved of that career choice. They said it was a waste of his college degree and that he ought to be working in a lab somewhere or maybe teaching. "At least you could do those forensics things, like on *CSI*," his mother had said. He'd tried to explain that he wanted to help people who needed it the most, but neither of them had been convinced.

Now, he sighed. "I'm not. I'm the chief park ranger. This had nothing to do with my job."

"Betty Ostermeyer said you were taken hostage by a drug lord!"

"That's not quite true. And the gunshot wasn't life-threatening. I'm fine."

She was silent for a moment, then sniffed. "Crime is very bad in those big cities." For her, *big city* meant anyplace with more than two stoplights. Dodge City was a teeming metropolis.

"Portland is safe. This was a fluke, and it won't happen again."

"Well… I hope you're being careful."

"I am."

Another silence, this time longer. He could picture her sitting at the kitchen table, a cigarette and ashtray in front of her. Had they ever replaced that ancient corded phone that hung on the kitchen wall? Its cord was permanently tangled, but his mother used to straighten the kinks while she talked.

"Jeremy? Do you think you might come visit sometime? It's been so long. I'm sure you're busy, but your father's been sick, and…."

Jeremy cleared his throat and wished he had a hand free to rub his temple. “I’m sorry to hear about Dad, but I don’t know when I can get away. I have this week off because of the injury. I’m going to have a lot of work to catch up on.”

Jeremy cleared his throat and wished he had a hand free to rub his temple. “I’m sorry to hear about Dad, but I don’t know when I can get away. I have this week off because of the injury. I’m going to have a lot of work to catch up on.”

“But you’re really okay? You’re healthy? You don’t have that… that disease?”

For fuck’s sake. She wasn’t stupid—she knew the name perfectly well. “I’m HIV-negative. Other than some bumps and scrapes from last week’s adventure, I’m the picture of good health.” He wanted to tell her about Qay—that he’d found someone to love, someone who loved him. That things were still uncertain between them, but Jeremy was hoping for a happy ending. That their entire community had misjudged Keith Moore, had failed him. That Keith had struggled through hell to transform into the man Jeremy now loved.

But she would neither understand nor accept any of that, so he didn’t bother.

He sighed again. “How about you, Mom? How’s it going?”

“I keep busy. I can’t garden this time of year, of course, but I have my shows. Oh! Do you remember Mildred Walker? Your grandmother played cards with her.”

“Um… I guess.”

“Well, she died not too long ago. But before she did, her son Stephen retired early and came back from Kansas City to take care of her. Stephen’s a good ten years older than you. I don’t think you know him.”

“I don’t think so,” Jeremy replied as patiently as possible. He didn’t care about Stephen Walker or anyone else in Bailey Springs.

“Well anyway, she died but he stayed. And do you know what he did? He took up with a mechanic from Laupner! Moved in with him and everything. That man in Laupner was divorced twice and has grown sons and all. Tsk. I guess you can never tell.”

So the point of this story was that his hometown had spawned another practicing homosexual—as had, apparently, the neighboring town. “Did the world end? Has Bailey Springs and/or Laupner been inundated with hellfire and brimstone?”

She clucked her tongue again. “I saw Stephen Walker the other day. Fay’s Boutique was having a fancy do for the holidays. Cookies, mulled cider. It was very nice. And he was there to talk about some of his paintings—he’s an artist, you know—and I suppose to sell them.

His… well, that mechanic was there too. All dressed up. They looked really happy."

This time Jeremy paused before responding. "That's nice, Mom," he finally said.

"It is. Well, I'll let you go. Take care of yourself, Jeremy."

"You too."

For a long time after the call ended, Jeremy just stood there, holding the phone.

RHODA ARRIVED early Wednesday morning, towing Parker and Ptolemy in her wake. The first thing she did when Jeremy opened the door was hand him a large cup of P-Town coffee. "I can't carry things if my hand is full," he grumbled. And then he showed his true feelings by sniffing the aroma deeply. It smelled great.

"That's why I brought help. Ptolemy's on the clock, but Parker's slave labor."

"And I get an excuse to wear my butchest outfit," said Ptolemy, who sported combat boots, baggy jeans, a sweatshirt, a plaid hunting jacket, and a gray bandana tied across his forehead.

"I appreciate it, guys." Coffee in hand, Jeremy watched as everyone else hefted his stuff and carried it away. He did a final check to make sure he hadn't forgotten anything, left a hefty tip for the pleasant housekeeping staff, and closed the door firmly behind him.

"Checking out, Chief?" asked the young man at the desk.

"Yeah, you're finally getting rid of me."

"I hope you've enjoyed your stay."

Jeremy grinned. "If my home is ever trashed again by drug dealers who subsequently kidnap and shoot me, I won't think of staying anywhere but here." When he got a chance, he'd probably write to the corporation and commend the staff, who'd treated him well.

Rhoda and her crew piled all of Jeremy's crap into the back of the SUV. Then Rhoda and Parker climbed into her Mini. "Do you want me to drive?" Ptolemy asked, eyeing Jeremy's splinted fingers.

"I've gotta get back in the saddle eventually. May as well be today. The doc said it's okay."

In truth, driving was a bit of a challenge, and his shoulder ached a little when he moved the wheel. It was a short trip, though. He didn't even shudder when he reached the parking garage.

"I would have been so terrified," Ptolemy said, looking around the space.

"It happened too fast. I was plenty scared when I woke up tied to that post, though."

"But now you're cucumber cool."

He shrugged, which caused a subtle wince. "It's over with. He's dead, I'm not. I'm moving on."

Ptolemy shook his head. "Most folks can't move on so quickly from something that bad. It makes an impression, you know? Like a footprint in wet cement."

"I have friends who care about me. That makes a difference."

"Yeah, I suppose it does. Still, you have to find peace for yourself."

Jeremy was going to ask what that meant, but just then Rhoda walked into the garage with Parker. She'd left her car at P-Town and they'd walked over, bringing a box of pastries this time. Everyone but Jeremy grabbed armfuls of stuff. He led the parade up the stairs with his coffee in hand and put it down to unlock the door.

Everyone oohed and aahed over the revamped kitchen, which really looked great. They approved of the new fixtures and tile in the bathroom too. Their only complaint involved the walls, which were stark and white. Jeremy thought about the magazine pictures Qay had taped up in his apartment and smiled. "I'll decorate eventually," he said.

Then the furniture began to arrive. Jeremy's friends tried to be sneaky about admiring the burly guys who dragged everything up the stairs, but the delivery guys definitely noticed. There was excessive bicep flexing. Somehow Parker took charge of furniture placement, which was fine with Jeremy. He didn't care how stuff was arranged, since after he and Qay picked out some rugs, the contents of the living room would be moved around anyway.

Eventually everything was in place, the preening deliverymen were gone, and Rhoda and her crew had to leave. "Thanks for everything, guys," Jeremy said.

Rhoda patted his arm. "You owe us a big dinner when your fancy-schmancy kitchen's ready to go and your hand is back in service."

"Done." He walked them out and waved as they descended the steps. Then he closed the door and looked around.

He was home. It was damn good to be out of the hotel and back in his own space. But right now, that space felt empty—and not because of the bare walls and rugless floors.

He put away his clothing, then made a long list—again—of everything he needed to buy. Some of those things could wait, like a new TV and speaker system, while others were more urgent. His cupboards were literally bare. And he needed a few things just to get through the day: bedding, towels, toilet paper, a few pantry basics.

A shop not far away on Hawthorne sold high-end linens, and at first he considered going there. But parking would be a bitch, and if he walked, he'd have a hard time dragging his purchases home one-handed. So he trotted down to his SUV and drove to the mall, where he was able to buy some of the needed items. He stopped for groceries on the way back. It took several trips up and down the stairs to unload everything, but at least he was getting some exercise.

Jeremy put away the groceries and threw his newly purchased sheets into the new washing machine. By then he was ravenous. All he'd eaten that day was a P-Town croissant and, at the mall, a hot dog on a stick. But his shoulder throbbed and his head felt heavy, so he decided to lie down on the bare mattress for a short nap.

It was well past three when he woke up, the low sun casting long shadows through his uncurtained windows. At least it wasn't raining. His shoulder was a bit better and his head clear, but his stomach had decided it was never going to be fed and had turned itself inside-out in protest. He chugged some milk from the carton—hey, no glasses!—but that didn't help much.

Then an idea struck him.

He threw the sheets in the dryer, awkwardly put on his stupid loafers, and slipped into his jacket. Then he ran down the stairs, grinning the whole way.

HE LIKED to watch the traffic move around the streets near Qay's workplace. Lots of trucks rumbled by, and sometimes a train rattled past on the nearby tracks. That reminded him of Qay's brother, Kevin, and he wondered whether Qay could see or hear trains without anxiety overcoming him.

A steady stream of people was emerging from the local businesses by the time Jeremy arrived, but he knew Qay didn't get off until five, so he waited. But darkness fell, the stream reduced to a slow trickle, and still no sign of Qay. Jeremy checked his phone. Five fifteen.

Heavy dread settled in his chest, although he couldn't say why. Maybe because the place where he'd been tortured was only a few blocks away. He jiggled his legs as restlessly as Qay and waited.

At a little past five thirty, Jeremy got out of the SUV and trudged to the factory entrance. The door was unlocked, but when he stepped inside, the place was quiet, with only a few workers still there. "Can I help you, sir?" The uniformed security guard looked nothing like the one who'd been with Davis, but still Jeremy shivered slightly.

"I'm looking for Qay Hill," Jeremy said.

The guard frowned slightly. "Hang on." Then he turned and bellowed, "Hey, Stuart! Come here!"

A scrawny man appeared from around the corner. He couldn't have been past his twenties yet, but his greasy hair was already receding. He had a pointy chin and a red, pointy nose. "Whatta ya want?" he demanded, narrowing his eyes at Jeremy.

This must be Stuart. Jeremy wanted to kick his skinny ass for the way he treated Qay, but managed to sound civil. "I'm looking for Qay."

Stuart's eyes widened for a second; then his lips curled into a smirk. "You're the boyfriend." He said it in the singsongy voice of a schoolyard bully.

"Yes, Stuart, I am. Which of us are you jealous of?" Jeremy smiled sweetly.

It was fun to watch Stuart's face turn red and his smirk morph into a snarl. He started to say something beginning with *f*—either *fuck* or *faggot*, Jeremy guessed—but then apparently thought better of it. "I don't know where your *boyfriend* is, but when you see him, you can tell him his ass is fired. If he's too stupid to figure that out for himself."

Jeremy's blood ran cold. "Why is he fired?"

"Because the asshole hasn't shown his face since before Thanksgiving, that's why." An evil glee lit Stuart's features. "And you didn't know! I'll bet he's—"

Whatever else Stuart had to say, Jeremy didn't hear it through the rushing in his ears. He turned on his heel and dashed out the door, down the steps, and to his SUV. He dialed Qay's landline and let the phone ring a dozen times before he gave up.

He tried to drive carefully and within some semblance of the speed limit but didn't succeed. He crossed over the river in record time. Predictably, he couldn't find a parking spot near Qay's house. He circled the area several times, getting increasingly agitated, until he finally found a place two blocks away. As soon as the engine was off, he leaped from the vehicle and ran down the sidewalk.

Although he rang Qay's doorbell several times, nobody answered. So Jeremy trotted up the front stairs and rang the bell belonging to the first-floor tenant. A lady in her early thirties answered; a little kid peeked out from behind her legs.

Jeremy tried not to look like a serial killer. "Hi. I'm a friend of Qay's. Um, he's your downstairs neighbor. I haven't heard from him in a couple days and I'm a little"—*a lot*—"worried. Have you seen him?"

"Yesterday. He, uh, looked—" She stopped and glanced down at the child. "You stay the night with him sometimes, don't you?"

"Sometimes."

She nodded slightly. "How about if I just let you in?"

A small bit of relief shot through him. "I'd really appreciate it."

"Meet me by the door."

So he trotted back to the basement door, and shortly after he got there, she had it open and stood there without the kid.

"Thank you so much," Jeremy said.

"Sure. Just make sure you shut it when you go. I hope he's okay." She cast a worried look down the stairs before heading back to her own apartment.

When Jeremy reached the bottom of the stairs, he knocked. It was a cop knock, loud and imperious, but nobody answered. After hesitating for a moment, he tried the knob, which turned easily.

The apartment reeked of alcohol and vomit.

Qay slumped on the couch, unmoving, and for a heart-stopping moment, Jeremy thought he was dead. But then Qay slowly lifted his head, brushed his greasy hair from his face, and looked at Jeremy. Even from across the room, Jeremy could tell his eyes were red and shadowed, a stark contrast to his too-pale skin. "Go away," Qay said quietly.

Jeremy didn't go away, although he remained rooted in place for several moments. Finally he moved closer. "What the fuck, Qay?"

"Go away."

Jeremy looked around. The books and knickknacks were in disarray, and empty bottles littered the floor and the kitchenette countertop. He walked a few steps to pick up the nearest one and examine the label. "Great taste in wine, babe."

In a monotone, Qay said, "What's the word? Thunderbird."

"How drunk are you right now?"

"Not very. Ran out hours ago." Qay lifted his chin. "Wanna be a pal and get me some more?"

"Jesus Christ." Jeremy tossed the bottle onto the armchair and stepped nearer to Qay. He crouched to bring himself to Qay's level. "What the hell happened?"

"Nothing happened. I figured one drink, what could it hurt? It's just booze, not smack. Just one fucking drink. Is that so much to ask from life?" His voice started out bitter but ended up raw and wretched.

Fuck. Fuck, fuck. "You can't have one drink, Qay."

"Don't you think I fucking know that? Every goddamn day it claws at me, and I can't—I can't—" He growled and threw his head back against the cushion.

Jeremy tried to calm himself with a few deep breaths, ignoring the room's foul smell. "This is my fault. I'm sorry. I shouldn't have pressured you—"

Qay leaped to his feet, startling Jeremy so badly he nearly toppled onto his ass. "It's not your fault! It's not all about you, Captain Caffeine. This is *my* addiction. Mine." Qay hit himself hard in the chest. "*My* fucked-up head. Other people, when a fantastic man wants to build a relationship, when a good education gets handed to them on a platter, they can handle it. They're fucking thrilled. Not me. Never me." He made an inarticulate noise and began to pace the small apartment.

Deciding that chasing Qay would only spook him, Jeremy stood his ground. "It's not fair, but it's also not your fault. Life dealt you a shitty hand. But you're…. Look. Relapses happen. It's not the end of the world. I'll drive you to a meeting, okay? And we'll find you a counselor. I know some really good ones. You're not alone anymore. You have me."

Qay spun around and marched right into Jeremy's space. "Is that what I am? Another of your charity projects? Captain Caffeine saves the fucking world."

"Stop calling me that!" Jeremy's one good hand bunched into a fist—which promptly loosened when he saw the despair in Qay's eyes. "You're not a project, Qay. You never were. I love you."

"Did you love Donny?" The question came out as a hoarse whisper.

"Yeah, I did. But that was a long time ago. He's gone now and—"

"And that's my point. Love isn't enough, Jeremy. You should have learned that already. You can love someone with every ounce of your fucking enormous heart, but it's not enough. It won't cure what's in here." He knocked his own forehead with his fist. "Love doesn't save anyone. A man has to save himself, and I don't have it in me. I just fucking don't."

"You do!"

"Keith Moore never died. He's—*I'm* still here, more fucked-up than ever. Still falling off that goddamn bridge."

Jeremy felt as if he'd been flayed. Qay hadn't set a finger on him, yet this hurt worse than anything Davis had done to him. "Qay," he began.

"No. Go find someone who deserves you. Someone who's whole."

"I don't want someone else. I want you. You're—"

"You'll get over it." Qay tried to harden his expression to match his cold voice, but he couldn't hide the sorrow and desperation in his eyes. "You need to go now."

"Let me stay. I won't try to… to *do* anything. I won't say a goddamn word if that's what you want. I can just sit here with you."

Qay shook his head. "Go."

A toxic stew of emotions churned in Jeremy's gut, making him want to puke. Anger, fear, sadness, frustration, distress, worry, panic. He wanted to crush Qay in a tight embrace until Qay saw reason. But Jeremy didn't even have two good arms.

"I think… I think we both need to calm down," Jeremy said. *And sober up.* "Get our minds clear. Things will look better tomorrow."

"My mind is never going to be clear, and things will never be better."

"Qay—"

"Just *go*." Qay pushed Jeremy's chest with both hands. Not hard, but it hurt a little due to the healing burns, and Jeremy winced. Qay winced too, but his jaw was set.

Jeremy backed away. He stopped when he got to the door, but by then Qay had turned to stare at a wall, his back to Jeremy.

"I love you," Jeremy said.

Qay didn't answer.

JEREMY COULDN'T put the new sheets onto the mattress properly due to his broken fingers, a fact that didn't matter anyway because he couldn't sleep. He spent most of the night pacing his brand-new, empty apartment, cursing Qay, himself, the Moore family, and God. If it hadn't been so late, he might have called Rhoda to talk things out. But she'd done enough for him already, and he didn't want to disturb her sleep.

Sometime in the middle of the night, he remembered he was hungry. He hadn't bought anything substantial during his grocery trip, so he shivered in his boxer shorts in front of the open fridge, trying to find something edible. He ended up with bread and butter. Charming.

He kept asking himself what he could have done to avoid this mess, but no clear answer presented itself. Yes, he could have sprung the whole moving-in-together idea more gently, or he could have waited awhile, but he had the feeling Qay would have freaked out no matter what. And Jeremy couldn't blame him. Someone didn't spend four decades alone with his demons and then just launch into a sudden—and fierce—relationship. As far as Jeremy could tell, Qay had never been able to trust anyone, and he couldn't just set that instinct aside.

But as dawn crept tentatively through the windows, Jeremy seriously thought about what Qay had said. Had Jeremy placed too much faith in himself? Did he take on too much responsibility for the welfare of others? He wasn't a superhero, and he couldn't cure the world no matter how hard he tried. Couldn't even cure the people who were closest to him, like Donny.

But fuck, couldn't he *help*? Maybe a man had to cure himself—and honestly, Donny had never really tried—but he didn't have to do it by himself. A medal-winning marathon runner had to run every step of that race by himself. But he had a coach to help him prepare, to remind him to keep hydrated, and dammit, to cheer him on even when he stumbled. Qay had been running so long by himself; if only he'd let Jeremy support him.

Jeremy showered even though he'd forgotten to buy soap. At least he had shampoo. He shaved and dressed and had milk and plain bread for breakfast, just to silence the grumbling in his stomach. Maybe he'd head to P-Town later. But not now.

Ignoring the light rain, he walked to Qay's house. His shoulder ached from the cold and the restless night. His fingers were cold too, but there was no way to get a glove over the splints, and his bulky, immobile hand wouldn't fit in his pocket. Little droplets sprayed upward with every step, wetting the cuffs of his jeans. He was aware that a Portland winter was infinitely milder than the ones he'd endured as a boy, but still he was beginning to long for spring. Longer days. Warmth. New growth.

He turned onto Qay's street. Plenty of parking at this time of day, when most people had gone to work but the nearby shops hadn't yet opened. Had Qay ever owned a car? *That* was a useless question.

Jeremy drew abreast of Qay's house, took one look at the basement door standing slightly ajar, and knew the truth.

But he had to make sure. His cop's brain—no more banished from his psyche than the bullied little boy—demanded a thorough investigation.

Jeremy walked slowly down the basement stairs. The doorknob to Qay's apartment turned as easily as it had the night before.

The reek of cheap wine hung heavily in the room. Qay had gathered all the empty bottles into one corner and smashed them nearly to dust. The piles of books lay toppled, the magazine pictures were scattered over the floor in shreds, and every one of Qay's carefully collected trinkets had been swept off the tables and shelves. Many of them were broken.

Qay's backpack gaped on the couch, his schoolbooks and notes still inside.

Jeremy entered the bedroom where they'd first had sex, first slept together. Empty drawers gaped in the ugly dresser. The closet door stood open. A few clothes remained strewn on the floor and bed, but they were mostly Qay's work clothes. His favorite jeans were gone, as were his white button-down, his red sweater, and his ancient leather jacket. His duffel bag was missing too.

Qay was gone.

Chapter Twenty-Three

JEREMY KNEW the places in Portland where men gathered to drink cheap booze. He checked them all and described Qay to everyone he saw, but he found no sign of him. He tried the neighborhoods with the drug dealers too. Nothing. The entire time, he kept picturing Qay falling from a bridge—why were there so many goddamn bridges in Portland?—kept imagining him floating facedown in the Willamette. Jeremy reminded himself that if Qay intended suicide, he probably wouldn't have bothered to pack his duffel and take it with him. But that logic brought little solace.

Over the next couple of days, Jeremy stopped by Qay's apartment several times. Just in case. The upstairs neighbor barely knew Qay but was sympathetic, and she gave Jeremy a spare key so he could get in. While he was there, he cleaned out the refrigerator and carefully cleaned up the broken glass, even though his bad hand made the task difficult. He straightened the piles of books and placed the knickknacks back on the tables and shelves. Even the broken ones, because Qay never seemed to mind a few dents and scratches. Jeremy couldn't do much about the shredded magazine pages except throw them away. So he begged a couple of magazines from Rhoda, who always had a stack at P-Town, and carefully selected some new photos he thought Qay might like: scenic views, animals, and hot men. And then Jeremy hung them on Qay's walls.

He grew increasingly frantic as the days passed with no sign of Qay. On Sunday he gave in to desperation and called Nevin.

"'S up, Germy?"

"I lost him," Jeremy said plaintively.

"You lost— What the fuck, man?"

Jeremy tried to pull himself together. He was sitting in his SUV just off Burnside, hoping he could avoid a complete hysterical breakdown. "Qay. I lost Qay."

After a brief pause, Nevin sounded all business. "Chill out right *now*. Breathe. And tell me what the ever-loving fuck is going on."

It helped to be given orders, because Jeremy was suddenly tired of being in charge. As succinctly as possible, he told Nevin what had happened.

Nevin didn't interrupt; he waited to respond until Jeremy had spilled every searing detail. "Okay. Your boy freaked and then he split. You know we can't do a missing persons report, right?"

Jeremy did know. Unless foul play was suspected or the person was incompetent or a danger to himself or others, an adult had the right to pick up and disappear. "Can't you at least—"

"He have any friends or family around here?"

"He has nobody."

"Fuck. Well, I can ask around. You got a photo?"

Jeremy squeezed his eyes shut. "No." He hadn't taken a single picture of Qay. Other than that seed cone and the book, he had nothing tangible from their time together.

"Dial it down, Germy. You sound like you're about to fucking lose it. I'm on this, okay? If he's anywhere in the Portland metro area, I'm gonna find him and bring him back to you with a big pink bow on his pretty ass."

"Thanks, Nev."

"Yeah, yeah. Between this and your Thanksgiving fucktasm, you owe me so goddamn big, cowboy. You're gonna need to build a statue in my honor when this is all done, and stick it right in the middle of one of your damn parks."

Despite everything, Jeremy chuckled slightly. "So the pigeons can crap on you? No problem." And then, very belatedly, he remembered Nevin's Thanksgiving plans. "How's it going with that guy?"

"Colin? He's an overprivileged fairy who doesn't have a fucking clue what real life is like." Nevin sighed noisily. "And I can't get enough of him."

Jeremy hoped he'd someday meet the man who had apparently captured Nevin's feral heart. But right now, Qay was his priority. "Nev? Qay might be…. He's been clean for seven years, but he was a user. And he was drinking last week."

"Got it."

One of the things Jeremy liked about Nevin was that he didn't judge junkies and drunks. Although Nevin fiercely hated anyone who hurt other people—especially if the victims were children or otherwise vulnerable—he was pragmatic about addicts. "Just people on the wrong fucking side of biology, man."

By the time they ended the call, Jeremy was calm enough to trust himself in traffic again. But he was still scared to death.

JEREMY RETURNED to work Monday, which was a good thing. His regular duties distracted him just enough to keep him sane. And while he was out in the parks, he could keep an eye out for Qay and ask all the down-and-outers whether they'd seen him. None had. Everyone seemed to know about Jeremy's unpleasant adventure, though. Surviving torture and landing back on his feet even earned him a little cred with some of the tougher cases who previously hadn't wanted anything to do with him.

On Friday afternoon he went to Patty's Place with a load of donated clothing. Toad and some of the other kids made a huge fuss over him, examining his splinted fingers closely and begging for details about the kidnapping. He was reluctant to say much.

"Did the cops come in blazing away?" asked a girl with candy-cotton-pink hair and a sparkly nose ring. "Like, with Uzis or something?"

"I don't think the Portland Police Bureau uses Uzis."

"Well, was it the SWAT team? With the—"

"I'd just been pistol-whipped and kneed in the balls. For all I knew, I got rescued by clowns on a Rose Festival float."

The kids were still laughing as he made his escape to the office, where Evelyn waited. "Thanks for bringing those clothes, Chief. We need 'em."

"How are you guys fixed for Christmas presents?" These kids had dealt with enough shit already; they should at least get something to unwrap and call their own.

"Pretty good. I got one of the department stores to pony up, so each of these kids is gonna get a backpack with underwear, soap, pajamas… stuff like that. They'll get new shoes too."

He nodded. Some of them had come to Patty's with literally nothing but the clothes on their backs. But then he thought about Qay's collection of… stuff: little figurines, tiny mementos, things that had no purpose except to sparkle or shine or look cute. Reminders that even though life could really suck, it could also be frivolous. Proof to Qay that even when the world turned its collective back to him, he was there and he was real.

"Hey, Evelyn? I think these kids need toys too."

Her eyebrows rose. "You mean video games? We can't afford that."

"No, I mean... stuffed animals. Silly little things. I know they're teenagers, but... I don't know. Maybe they still have some little kid left in them." Because despite being in his forties, only recently had he realized that he'd never quite outgrown the child inside him.

Evelyn gave him a sweet, slow smile. "That's a real nice idea, Chief."

He headed to Target and filled his cart with trinkets—plush puppies, superhero action figures, shiny costume jewelry. Nothing expensive. But maybe enough to make some young people a little happier. He dropped the bags off with Evelyn, telling her to distribute as she saw fit.

"Our hero," she said as she walked him to his SUV.

He smiled at her, but his broken heart knew the truth. He wasn't a hero at all.

ON SATURDAY afternoon Nevin joined Jeremy for coffee at P-Town. Rhoda, wearing the most hideous Hanukkah sweater ever made, sat with them. Jeremy frowned at the dancing dreidels. "I thought they only did ugly Christmas sweaters."

"Are you kidding?" Rhoda scoffed. "The Chosen People don't get left out of that tradition. I own eight different ones."

The café bustled with shoppers needing a caffeinated pick-me-up and students cramming for finals. Rhoda refused point-blank to play holiday music, so Johnny Cash rumbled over the sound system instead. The air smelled of rain and coffee and cinnamon, and the taste of sugar lingered on Jeremy's tongue, reminding him of Qay's kisses.

Nevin had already given a progress report on the search for Qay. Not that there was any progress to report. Qay had disappeared without a trace.

"He must have left town," Jeremy said, tracing his finger through a few droplets of spilled coffee.

Rhoda patted his arm. "Maybe he just needed some space, honey. Maybe he'll be back."

Jeremy shook his head. Qay had abandoned his job, his schoolwork, and nearly everything he owned. He wasn't coming back.

Jeremy had been imagining him dead through suicide, accident, overdose, or violence. Those images were wrenching. But it was almost as bad to think of him huddled somewhere in his too-thin leather jacket, shivering and hungry and with nowhere to turn. God knew Jeremy didn't have to try hard to conjure those mental pictures; he'd seen the real version far too many times.

Nevin always ordered the darkest roast available and chugged it hot and black. Either his tongue was impervious to burning or he'd already permanently scorched it with his litany of expletives. Now he took his cup to Ptolemy for a refill and swigged while retaking his seat. "Let's consider your problem logically, man. If Qay's not here, he's gotta be somewhere else."

"Yeah, and that narrows it down to… the entire continental US, I guess. I doubt he has a passport."

"I don't believe people travel at random. Something pulls us toward a place, or some kind of shit pushes us away. What are his pushes and pulls?"

Running his fingers through hair that desperately needed cutting, Jeremy considered Nevin's words. They made sense. After all, Jeremy himself had been pushed out of Bailey Springs by a whole lot of cold shoulders and contempt, and he'd been pulled to Oregon by a scholarship and the chance to feel strong in his own skin. But how would this help find Qay? Jeremy was well aware of what had pushed him from Kansas— and now, what had pushed him from Portland—but the pulls? He didn't know Qay well enough for that. "I don't know if he has any pulls," he finally said.

Nevin rolled his eyes. "We all do, Germy. Even if sometimes we don't like 'em and don't wanna admit it. A week and a half from now? I'm going to a Christmas gala at Colin's parents' house. Me at a motherfucking gala! I'd rather eat raw banana slugs. But Colin says I owe it to him on account of missing Thanksgiving, and he's been making puppy-dog eyes at me, so I'm going. See? Pulled. And I bet you can guess what part of me he's yanking." He made an unnecessary gesture toward his crotch.

Rhoda cackled so loudly the people at the next table turned to stare. Then she sobered and looked contrite. "Sorry, honey," she said to Jeremy. "I know this is serious."

He waved away her apology. "Nevin's dick makes everybody laugh."

That made Nevin narrow his eyes and flip him off, and Rhoda laughed again. Nevin could shoot someone the bird with great panache. Jeremy felt a little better, just being around friends.

And then for no good reason at all he remembered the recent phone call from his mother and the way she'd rambled on about the guy with the mechanic lover—as if the story were important for some reason. What if a push could also be a pull? It was all he had to go on.

He looked up at Rhoda and Nevin. "I'm heading to Kansas."

APPARENTLY THE airlines were convinced that nobody in their right mind would want to travel from Portland, Oregon, to Bailey Springs, Kansas. Maybe they were right; Jeremy certainly wasn't in his right mind. But he needed to get there anyway. He ended up booking an early Monday flight to Wichita with a layover in Dallas. He hoped for decent weather since he'd have a long drive ahead of him after landing.

Arranging for time off from work was relatively simple; he had a lot of vacation time saved up. And other than that, leaving town on short notice was distressingly easy. He didn't even have a goldfish or potted plant to worry about while he was gone.

He'd intended to take a taxi, but Rhoda showed up at his apartment well before dawn—coffee in hand—and gave him a ride to the airport. "You travel light," she said as they zoomed down the Banfield. There was almost no traffic this early in the morning.

"I'm going to have to pick up a few things when I get there. I don't own winter-in-Kansas clothing."

"Are you staying with your parents?"

He shuddered. "No. I booked a motel. But I'll visit them. I mean, I guess I can't really fly all the way there and not see them." He was dreading it the way he'd dread a root canal without anesthesia, but he was a big boy.

Rhoda couldn't look at him because she was driving, but she reached over to pat his leg. Not that she had to reach far. Jeremy didn't fit very well in her tiny car. "I think that's a good thing, sweetie. I think if you didn't see them at least once more, well, someday you'll regret it."

He wasn't so sure about that. "They're strangers. I barely knew them even when I lived with them, and that was a long time ago."

"Mmm," she grunted, clearly not convinced.

When she reached the departures area, she leaned over to kiss his cheek. "Travel safely."

"Thanks, Rhoda. You're the best."

He retrieved his small bag from the back of the car and waved at her as she pulled away.

Jeremy flew very rarely, and as soon as he boarded the plane, he remembered why. Airplane seats were built for anorexic pixies, not guys who stood six-four and liked to lift weights. Because of his late booking, he ended up with a middle seat, which meant the people on either side glared at him for daring to be big. The flight attendant served breakfast—which Jeremy had to pay for—and then he spent most of the rest of the flight with the tray table digging into him and the remains of his plastic food slowly congealing. Compared to an airline, Davis had been an amateur at torture.

His flight to Wichita was delayed by a couple of hours due to bad weather somewhere. Jeremy stalked the airport corridor, ignoring the stares at his mangled hand and imposing size.

By the time he made it to Wichita and got a rental car, Jeremy was sore and exhausted. He was also nearly vibrating with nerves, having spent the day fretting over Qay. And *fuck*, but he'd forgotten what cold was. His recent stint with hypothermia should have been a reminder, but wet and mostly nude in the factory was like a trip to the Bahamas compared to December in Kansas. This was the kind of cold that froze your nose hairs, that made your one working hand stiff and unmanageable, that blew in through your clothing and flayed you to the bone.

Before he left Wichita, he found a Dillard's and bought a parka, a knitted hat and scarf, and heavy gloves, all discounted in preholiday sales. He'd only be able to use one glove, so in a fit of genius, he also purchased a pair of thick, stretchy socks. The saleswoman looked at him funny when he painstakingly pulled one of the socks over his left hand, but hey, it worked.

As he drove west in the last bit of light, Jeremy marveled at how monochrome Kansas was in winter. That was another thing he'd forgotten. Even though winter brought lead gray skies to Portland, many of the trees remained green and only some of the landscaping plants died back. And there were always ferns and moss and other small growing things. Here, though, the landscape consisted of brown grass and gray weeds sticking up through a light dusting of snow. Even the sky was pale blue until it darkened into night.

It didn't feel like home.

He arrived in Bailey Springs hungry and worn out. He decided to wait until morning to call his parents and search for Qay. Instead, he drove to the tired little motel near the highway. It wasn't the Marriott, but it was the only game in town, and at this point he'd love anything with heat and a bed.

The man behind the counter had been watching TV, but he slid off his stool as Jeremy approached. "Evening," the man said.

"Hi. I have a reservation. Jeremy Cox."

The clerk's eyes widened and his jaw dropped. "Jeremy *Cox*?"

Jeremy sighed. "Yeah. I called Saturday." The motel's website looked as if it had been last updated in 1995, so he'd decided reserving by phone was safer.

"Holy crap. We went to high school together, remember?"

Jeremy examined him. He was middle-aged and a good hundred pounds overweight, and the last few hairs on his scalp looked ready to jump ship any moment. His nose and cheeks were red with broken capillaries, and the rest of his face was pallid. "Sorry," Jeremy said, shaking his head. "It was a long time ago."

"It sure enough was. Man, I miss those days." The clerk stuck out his hand. "Troy Baker."

Now it was Jeremy's turn to gape. Troy Baker had led the little gang that made Jeremy's adolescence hell. "You used to call me Pansyass Germy Cox."

Troy managed to look both frightened and embarrassed. He moved his outstretched hand to the back of his neck and rubbed. "Yeah. That was just…. Kids are like that. My boys had a mouth on them too until the Army straightened them out."

Jeremy wanted to tell him how much those words had hurt, how miserable he'd been. But what was the point? Thirty years gone. And it looked as if fate had exacted its own revenge on Troy. Still, Jeremy couldn't quite let it be. "You called me faggot. And you were right—I'm queer as a three-dollar bill. Do you want to call me that now?"

After a few more moments of gawping and mumbling, Troy shook his head. "My little brother, Gary? He's one too. And he's... he's all right, you know?"

Jeremy could have informed him that he was perfectly aware of Gary Baker's sexual orientation, seeing as how Gary used to blow him regularly during their senior year—and twice, when they'd had the locker room to themselves, Jeremy had fucked him until their mingled cries echoed among the lockers. But instead he simply asked, "Can I have my room key, please?"

Fumbling a little, Troy got him checked in and handed him the key—the metal kind, hanging from a yellow plastic fob. Troy even managed a wan smile.

"Where can I get something to eat?" Jeremy asked.

"This late? You'd have to drive to Laupner. They have a Subway that's probably still open. We got a vending machine right near your room, though."

Fantastic.

Jeremy started to walk away but then stopped and turned back to Troy. "Do you have someone named Qay Hill staying here? That's Qay with a Q."

Blinking, Troy shook his head. "I ain't supposed to...."

Jeremy pressed up against the counter and loomed. In his best cop voice, he said, "I really need this information now."

"Yeah, uh, okay. I guess so. Since I know you." Troy poked two-fingered at his computer keyboard. "Nope. Not here."

Shit. "How about Keith Moore?"

This time Troy scrunched up his broad face in thought. "Keith Moore? Isn't he the guy who killed himself?"

In a manner of speaking. "Just check, please."

More pecking, then a slow shake. "No. Nobody with that name."

Although Jeremy hadn't expected it to be that easy, he was still disappointed. He gave Troy a small smile, hefted his bag, and headed for his room.

His dinner that night consisted of Cheetos, Teddy Grahams, those neon orange crackers with peanut butter between them, and a Three Musketeers, all washed down with Gatorade. In other words, not even the hint of a real food group, but he figured he consumed enough chemicals to embalm him alive. He showered with a fitful trickle of water and a sliver of soap, and dried himself with an undersized towel the consistency of cardboard. Then he lay down on the scratchy sheets in the overheated yet drafty room and almost immediately fell asleep.

DOWNTOWN BAILEY Springs hadn't been much when he was a kid, and it had dried up even more in the intervening years. At least Walmart hadn't yet arrived to eradicate the remaining businesses. Hoffman's Pharmacy was still there, as was Arnold Brothers' Hardware. Fay's Boutique had a festive holiday display in the front windows, and Jeremy wondered if the paintings were done by the guy his mother had told him about. To Jeremy's considerable relief, Louella's Café still graced Main Street, and while the pancakes, sausage, and hash browns were forgettable, the apple pie was still blue-ribbon quality. But the coffee sucked.

Although a few people stared curiously as he ate breakfast, nobody seemed to recognize him. All the faces looked vaguely familiar, but he couldn't come up with any names. He paid cash for his meal, bundled up, and braved the cold.

The Moore house was about a quarter mile from downtown in what passed for Bailey Springs's high-rent neighborhood. Big Victorians loomed over snow-dusted lawns. Christmas lights hung from most of the eaves, although they weren't lit at this time of day, and the sidewalks were neatly shoveled and carefully sanded. A nice little neighborhood. He could probably buy most of a block for what his Portland condo was worth.

He'd never been inside the Moore house, although he'd once followed Keith home—skulking a block behind him and feeling like a CIA operative—so Jeremy knew which house it was. A white-painted two story with fancy scrollwork and a wraparound porch, it had looked opulent and welcoming to Jeremy's young eyes. He used to wonder what the interior was like and which room was Keith's.

Now he turned the corner and spied the Moore house, and he immediately recognized that it was abandoned. The damage became more obvious as he drew closer. Most of the paint had peeled and the rest had grayed. Plywood covered the windows. The rooflines sagged, two pillars were broken, and the front stairs had collapsed completely. Nobody had lived there for a very long time.

He thought about the things that had been inflicted on Keith within those walls and he wanted to cry.

JEREMY'S PARENTS lived a couple of miles away in the "new" section of town. The modest houses had been built in the early 1950s for postwar couples who were starting their families. Originally, many of the residents worked in a candy factory nearby, but the factory had shut down around the time Jeremy was born. It burned to the ground when he was in grade school; he remembered watching the black smoke climb into the sky.

Now, he fetched his rental car from its spot near the diner and drove to his parents' house. It was smaller than he remembered, a brick three bedroom with a basement his father always planned to finish but never did. An old Ford Escort—still covered by the recent snowfall—took up the narrow driveway.

Jeremy took a deep breath, got out of the rental car, and marched up the stairs. He pressed the dimly lit doorbell. It was strange to ring the bell when he'd spent eighteen years passing in and out of that door, but he couldn't very well barge in unannounced.

An old lady in a green sweat suit answered the door, her sweatshirt decorated with sequined reindeer and snowflakes. With her curly gray hair, she looked remarkably like his grandmother, if only his grandmother hadn't died a decade earlier. This must be his mother.

"J-Jeremy!" She held a hand against her chest.

"I'm sorry I didn't call first, Mom." He did feel bad about it, but he'd been too worked up over Qay to deal with his parents.

"My... my goodness!" She shook her head as if to clear it and stepped aside. "Come in, come in!"

The front door opened directly into the cramped living room, which hadn't been redecorated since he was in high school. Everything still reeked of old cigarette smoke. The television was new, though, and his father sat in his old armchair facing the screen. He looked as if he'd been dozing, but there was an open book on his lap. His glasses sat on the little table beside him, along with a glass of water and a box of tissues.

While Jeremy's mother looked old, his father was ancient. He'd been a tall man—just an inch or so short of Jeremy's final towering height—and brawny, although his bulk had been going to fat by the time Jeremy graduated high school. But now he was gaunt and gray, with age spots dotting his high brow. He fumbled for his glasses and put them on. "Is that Jeremy?" His voice had thinned too.

"Hi, Dad."

The next part was awkward. Nobody exchanged hugs, but Shirley Cox took Jeremy's outerwear, sat him on the couch, and brought him a cup of instant coffee and a little plate of store-bought cookies. Frank Cox asked him how he'd gotten to Bailey Springs: which airport he'd traveled through, what kind of car he'd rented, and which route he drove.

His mother sat in her usual armchair, next to Frank but with the little table between them. When Jeremy was a kid, she always kept an ashtray there. It was gone now, so maybe she'd finally quit. "Do you want me to make up the spare room for you, Jeremy?"

"No, thanks. I'm staying at the motel. I didn't want to put you guys out." Not the entire truth, but polite.

"Well, it's not that much of a bother," Shirley said. But she didn't push the subject. For the first time, she seemed to notice the state of Jeremy's left hand. "Is that where you were shot?" she asked, looking slightly alarmed.

"No. They shot my shoulder. My fingers are broken."

So then he had to tell the story, although he gave them an abridged and expurgated version. They didn't need to hear the details of what Davis had done to him, and they didn't need to know about Donny, other than that he was an old friend. Even still, Shirley gasped a lot and Frank scowled.

"You seem to be doing very well after such an ordeal," Shirley finally said.

Jeremy almost laughed. He was not doing well at all, but Davis wasn't to blame for that. "It wasn't as bad as it sounds, Mom."

She brought him more awful coffee and more cookies—they were the Danish butter kind that came in a tin. A holiday gift from someone, he guessed. She also brought Frank a fresh glass of water and some pills, which he swallowed without explanation, then coughed.

"Will you be looking up some old friends while you're in town?" she asked when she returned to her chair.

Jeremy almost choked. "Mom, I—"

"Remember Lisa Wade? Of course she's Lisa Lamb now. She married and moved away years ago. Omaha, I think. Is that right, Frank?"

Frank grunted.

Shirley continued her story. "She visits her family, though. Maybe she'll be back in town for the holidays and you can meet up with her."

"I didn't come here to see Lisa," Jeremy said.

This time, Frank's grunt was louder. "I bet you didn't come here to see us either."

The wary politeness drained from Jeremy as suddenly as if someone had pulled a plug. He didn't care that the old man was sick. He didn't care that these people were his parents. He was raw and troubled and so goddamn *done*. "Maybe I'd want to visit if you acted like you love me."

Frank's scowl deepened and Shirley put her hand to her throat. "We do love you," she said.

"Throwing a few empty words at me isn't enough. You don't love who I am, the real me, and you never did." His eyes prickled, but he kept his voice steady.

Shirley made a choked little sound, and Frank pointed angrily at Jeremy. "You're upsetting your mother!"

"I'm upsetting— Do you know what it was like for me to grow up here? I got picked on every day of my life, and that was pure misery. But the worst part was when I came home crying—bruised sometimes, do you remember that?—and all you did was tell me to toughen up and learn to fight back."

"All this bullying crap they're going on about nowadays," Frank growled. "Like boys are delicate little flowers who wilt if someone calls them a name. You toughen up and take it like a man!"

"I wasn't a man, Dad; I was a little kid. And words do hurt. Sometimes worse than bullets." He set the coffee cup on the table in front of him. "I know I could have had it worse. You never beat me. But dammit! Complete strangers accept me for who I am and respect me for what I do, but you can't manage even that much."

Frank looked as if he wanted to get up from his chair, but he stayed seated. He leaned forward, however. "We taught you to fight your own battles."

Jeremy laughed bitterly. "That's great, Dad. Did it ever occur to you that I could have used somebody on my side? Not a... a superhero to save me. Just an ally. That's all I needed." Shit. He needed to get out of here and find Qay.

He stood and marched to the kitchen, where Shirley had hung his coat, hat, and scarf on a hook near the back door. After slipping into his parka, he scooped up the rest of his gear and walked back into the living room. These old people were strangers to him. Faintly familiar, like the rest of Bailey Springs, but that was all. They looked over at him—Frank furious, Shirley slightly teary-eyed—but neither moved to stop him. He was a stranger to them too.

But he had to tell them something more. "Do you want to know why I flew out here? Because I'm looking for Keith Moore."

Frank looked puzzled. "Isn't he the one who jumped—"

"Frank!" Shirley interrupted.

"Mom. I'm forty-three years old. You can talk about it in front of me. Yes, he's the one who jumped off the Memorial Bridge. Everyone said so much awful shit about him. You too; I overheard it. Did any of you ever ask yourself why a kid would do that? How much he had to be suffering if he felt like that was his best option?" His voice cracked on the final word.

"What does that hoodlum have to do with you?" Frank demanded.

"He wasn't a hoodlum. He was a boy, just like me. He was abused, Dad. And he was scared and sad and lonely." He still was. "He didn't have any allies either, and he wasn't about to get a scholarship offer from the West Coast, so he tried to find a different way to escape."

Shirley shook her head. "You're not making any sense. The Moores are all dead. The older boy with the train—such a shame!—and the younger with the bridge. Dr. Moore passed away several years ago. Not too long after that, Mrs. Moore…." She hesitated, then seemed to make up her mind. "Mrs. Moore committed suicide."

Well, shit. Not surprising that they were both gone, considering the condition of their house. Jeremy wondered if they'd had any regrets before they died. Did they mourn their lost son as much as their deceased one? And Qay—would learning of their deaths help set him free or frustrate him because they never saw the brilliant, beautiful man he became despite them?

Although Jeremy was still angry at his own parents, the urgency of his rage went away. They'd never truly see the man he became either. Their loss.

"Keith Moore didn't die," Jeremy said. "But he did escape. We ran into each other in Portland. And I love him. Not who I want him to be or who I imagine he could be. I love *him*. And I have to go find him now."

He fumbled the doorknob open—awkward, with his scarf and hat in hand—as his parents sat and watched. But before he walked outside, his mother called his name. "Jeremy! Don't you walk out on us! We're your family!"

Jeremy paused with his back to them. "Not really. But I wish you well. Have a merry Christmas, okay?" And he walked out into the cold.

He didn't consciously decide where to drive; the car seemed to pilot itself down his parents' street and out of their neighborhood. But then the road curved, and he wasn't surprised to see the Memorial Bridge in front of him. He parked on the shoulder, adjusted his coat and scarf, and got out of the car.

The wind that swept down from the Rockies and over the plains cut through even his new parka and thick hat. He covered everything but his eyes with the scarf, and yet he was still bitterly cold as he crossed to the middle of the bridge. It wasn't a fancy structure, just a utilitarian thing of steel and concrete, strung between opposing sandstone bluffs. Beneath him, ice rimmed the edges of the Smoky Hill River, but the water in the center ran free, gray as his own eyes.

He leaned on the concrete railing and looked down. The river was so very far away. It was easy to imagine a lanky, long-legged boy scaling the low barrier, balancing for a moment on the thin ledge, and then letting go. Falling, falling.

Jeremy buried his face in his arms and began to sob.

CHAPTER TWENTY-FOUR

QAY WAS nearly sober when he trashed his apartment. It wasn't alcohol that led him to break glass and tear pictures from the walls—it was anger. Anger at his parents, who'd broken him; at the world that had roughed up his shattered pieces; at Jeremy for almost getting killed, for being so goddamn heroic, for seeing Qay at his worst. But Qay's greatest rage was directed at himself, because he was weak and stupid and so incredibly fucked-up.

After he'd destroyed everything, when it all lay in shambles, Qay knew what he had to do. Run. Because he loved Jeremy—which was more than he'd ever hoped for. And because if he stuck around, he was going to drag Jeremy down. Just like Donny almost had.

He wasn't jittery at all as he collected a few items of clothing and toiletries and threw them in his duffel bag. He zipped up his jacket and ascended the stairs, his mind as calm and clear as a mountain lake. He wasn't even slightly anxious, because what did he have to worry about now? Everything was already gone.

He'd left his keys on the kitchen counter, knowing he wouldn't return. But he kept the door at the top of the stairs slightly ajar because he knew Jeremy *would* return. Qay had no way to cushion Jeremy's grief when he found him gone, but at least he could save Jeremy the hassle of borrowing the neighbor's key.

The night was cold, but Qay warmed up a good bit as he walked to the river, crossed, and trekked to the Greyhound station. He bought a ticket for the next bus, and an hour later he was on his way to Pendleton.

He had a little money saved up. Not much. Not enough to afford a motel. So he spent the next days sleeping on buses and in stations, cleaning up as best he could in public restrooms. It had been a while since he'd survived like that, but he remembered how. He didn't have a destination or plan in mind, and his only regret was that he hadn't thought to bring any books.

Well, not his *only* regret. Because with every single heartbeat, he missed Jeremy more.

If only he hadn't gone into that tavern—

No. He was bumping through the night on a bus and couldn't even remember where he was going, and he couldn't blame the tavern. Couldn't blame the whiskey he'd drunk when he was in there or the fortified wine he'd bought after. Couldn't blame his parents or bad genes or the fucked-up mess in his head. *He* had made the decision to drink that night. He had ruined everything he had worked so hard for. He had pushed Jeremy away and rabbited. The fault was all his own.

At a bus station somewhere east of Salt Lake City, Qay sat on a bench and had such a horrible shaking fit that a young guy in an Army uniform put away his phone and walked over. "You okay, man? Need me to call 911?"

Qay shook his head miserably and tried to talk through chattering teeth. "P-panic attack," he gasped. "I'm f-f-fine."

"You don't *look* fine." After hesitating a moment, the soldier sat next to him on the bench. He didn't say anything and didn't make contact, but he glared at anyone who stared too hard, and his silent presence gradually soothed Qay's nerves.

"Thanks," Qay finally murmured, shaken and pale but with his heart rate and breathing at normal levels. He no longer felt as if he were about to be engulfed by a tsunami.

"No problem. My mama gets those. She takes something for it. One of those pills with all the *z*'s and *x*'s? Says it helps her a lot."

Qay nodded slightly. "I can't take any of them."

"That sucks."

The soldier was twenty-two, maybe twenty-three, with dark brown skin and the kind of lips that looked as if they would lift into a smile any moment. His voice was surprisingly deep, considering his small stature.

"Are you going home for Christmas?" Qay asked.

Yep, there was that grin. "Yessir! My mama's gonna cook all my favorite dishes, and my girlfriend, well, she's waiting for me too." He winked. "You heading off to family too?"

"No. I'm running away."

The soldier looked at him carefully before reaching a decision. "I've got three hours 'til my bus leaves, and I'm hungry. Join me for dinner?"

Qay was hungry too. He was pretty sure he hadn't eaten since the previous day. And he hadn't yet bought his next bus ticket. "Sure."

They introduced themselves as they walked to a nearby greasy spoon. PFC Elijah Wilson was stationed at Fort Bliss and on his way to Sacramento. He'd done a tour in Afghanistan—which he said he'd rather not talk about—but he now worked with a supply unit, which he liked much better. "A lot closer to home," he said as he slid into a booth.

Elijah ordered a burger, and Qay asked for grilled ham and cheese with soup on the side. Then they regarded each other over the slightly sticky table. "Wanna talk about what you're running from?" Elijah asked.

"You don't want to hear my sob story."

"Sure I do. I got time to kill, and I'm tired of playing Temple Run. And man, I haven't talked to a civilian in months who wasn't also a relative. So hit me."

It was weird. Qay wasn't usually eager to spill his guts, but suddenly he needed to unload on someone, even some kid he didn't know and would never see again. Maybe especially that kid. So Qay told him everything, starting from the moment his brother got hit by a train and ending with the day he told Jeremy to go away. Elijah didn't flinch over anything—not attempted suicide and stints in mental hospitals, not shooting up smack, not falling for a man instead of a woman. He just listened, nodding as he chewed, until their plates were empty and Qay had no more words.

Then they ordered pie and coffee.

"Why don't you call him?" Elijah asked. "See if you can make things right? You can use my phone."

"I don't know his number." Qay was well aware it was a lame answer, and when Elijah lifted his eyebrows skeptically, Qay sighed. "I don't think I can make it right."

"You think he won't take you back?"

"Oh, I'm pretty sure he would. He'd want to save me. But… I don't think I can be saved."

"Because you relapsed?"

The waitress came by to refill their cups. She looked tired, but she smiled at them anyway before hurrying away.

"I guess one relapse in seven years isn't the end of the world," Qay admitted. After all, he'd stayed sober in the days since. "But I might have more, and I'm always going to be kind of crazy. Jeremy shouldn't have to spend his life trying to rescue me."

Elijah took a bite of his pecan pie and looked thoughtful as he chewed. "Maybe rescuing you is what he wants to spend his life doing. And you're not exactly a damsel in distress." He grinned. "I don't see you in a pink dress and tiara. You're mostly rescuing yourself. He's just there to give you help when you need it. One thing I learned in Afghanistan: there's nothing shameful in asking for support when you need it. It can save your life. And some guys? Easing other folks' burdens is what makes them feel strong."

Qay burned his tongue on the coffee. "You're awfully wise for someone half my age," he finally said.

"I grew up a lot in the Army. Had a lot of time to think. And you know what? Getting shot at kinda puts things in perspective."

"I bet it does," said Qay, thinking of Jeremy in the factory.

"Besides, like I told you, my mama's a little bit crazy too. She's had some real bad times. But my dad's been there, helping her get through those times, and she's helped him through his own struggles. And man, those two are so much in love, none of the rest of us can hardly stand it. They're happy. Mama has a job she loves and three grandbabies she spoils rotten. A little bit crazy doesn't mean nobody's gonna love you."

God, could it be that easy? Just keep on fighting the demons and let Jeremy lend a hand when it looked like the demons might win?

Qay looked up at Elijah. "Can I borrow your phone?"

HE LOOKED up P-Town's number on the Internet and called there. Ptolemy picked up, gasped upon learning it was Qay on the line, and quickly handed the phone to Rhoda.

"Darling! I'm so happy to hear from you! You're not dead!"

"No, just stupid." He could hear conversation and the whir of the espresso machine in the background, and suddenly he was painfully homesick. "Can you give me Jeremy's number? I need to talk to him."

There was a slight pause before she answered. "He's going to be so relieved to hear from you. Where are you, honey?"

He looked around the diner. "Utah?"

"Oh, sweetie. Look, I'm going to give you Jeremy's number, but you need to know something. He's not here. He went to Kansas."

"What? Why?"

"He's looking for you, of course."

Qay was going to tell her that was a stupid idea and Kansas was the last place he'd go. Except… when he thought about his current journey—which he'd thought was directionless—he had to admit that he'd been slowly heading southeast. Directly toward Bailey Springs.

"How long has he been there?"

"He flew out this morning."

"I'm going—I'll get there as soon as I can." He'd have to catch a bus, probably transfer somewhere, hitch a ride to Bailey Springs from the nearest bus stop…. It was going to take a while. "Rhoda? Can you please not tell him I'm coming?"

"Why? He's going nuts, Qay. I can tell him to sit tight and wait for you, and he'll be so—"

"What if I chicken out? I want to go. I think I can do it. But if I lose my shit between here and there, I don't want to break his heart."

"Again," she said, a hint of acid in her tone.

"Again."

He could picture her thinking. No doubt she wore something colorful and interesting, and he heard her tapping her finger against her tooth. "Okay," she finally said. "Here's what we're going to do. It's a compromise. You're going to hightail it to the nearest car rental agency, and—"

"I can't rent a car."

"No license?"

He had a valid Oregon license; getting one had been a step toward becoming a responsible citizen. "No money and no credit card."

"We can deal with that. No arguing, Qay. Just listen." She probably used the same authoritative tone with her son. "Get to the rental agency. Call me from there, and I will authorize you to use my Visa. And—"

"I can't use your money!"

"No arguing, I said! You'll pay me back. Eventually. And knowing you owe me a debt will give you extra incentive to keep on track. You'll rent that car, drive straight to Kansas, and throw yourself into Jeremy's arms. Period, the end, happily ever after. If you promise to do that, I won't call him. I won't need to, because pretty soon he'll see you himself."

Elijah must have been able to hear Rhoda's end of the conversation, because he looked amused. And he nodded emphatic agreement.

Qay took a minute to think about her proposal. He pictured himself doing exactly as she ordered, and although he expected to start sweating and hyperventilating, his breathing stayed slow and easy. He wasn't panicked. He was... relieved.

"Okay. Thanks, Rhoda."

She made a happy little sound. "You're being sensible. Hallelujah. I think this is going to work out just fine."

He wrote down her cell number and Jeremy's on a paper napkin, which he tucked into his pocket. After ending the call, he returned the phone to Elijah.

"I don't know who that lady was," Elijah said. "But I'd pit her against any army on earth."

Qay grinned. "Yeah, I hear you."

Using Elijah's phone, they discovered a car rental agency just a few blocks away. Qay insisted on paying for both dinners, and in the parking lot, he gave Elijah a hug. "I don't know what you intend to do when you get out of the Army, but I sure as hell hope you're considering a career as a counselor."

Elijah's smile stretched from ear to ear. "People used to say I was dumb 'cause I had trouble reading." He shrugged. "Dyslexic. But I'm *not* dumb. I can go to college and do something like that."

"I have the feeling that whatever you decide to do, you're going to impress the hell out of everyone."

"Thanks, man. Now go get your happy ending."

Qay chuckled. "You too. Didn't you say your girlfriend was waiting for you? And Elijah? Stay safe. This world's a better place with you in it."

"I HAVE always depended on the kindness of strangers," Qay said to himself as he crossed the parking lot. And for one of the rare times in his life, fortune continued to smile on him. The car rental agent was agreeable once she spoke with Rhoda, a nearby Starbucks was still open and willing to sell Qay a venti Americano spiked with lots of sugar, and the road was clear. He drove through the night, stopping only a couple of times for a quick stretch, a bladder emptying, and a coffee refill. He kept the speedometer as high as he thought he could get away with.

Traversing the Rockies in the dead of night wasn't exactly fun, but at least the highway had enough interesting curves and slopes to keep him alert. He couldn't find anything decent on the car radio, so he sang loudly—and badly—as he went. And he wasn't scared, not even once. It had been a long time since he'd driven any distance. He'd forgotten how freeing it could feel.

He rolled into Bailey Springs midmorning, feeling cramped, gritty, and exhausted. He yearned for a shower and a bed. But comfort wasn't his priority—Jeremy was. Qay didn't know exactly where his beloved was, but it wasn't a big town. Nobody could stay missing there very long.

Qay stopped at the Burger Hut near the highway. He'd lost his virginity there, in the dark corner between the building and the garbage corral. Now, he walked inside the restaurant, hoping he didn't look too disreputable, and smiled at the girl at the cash register. "We're serving breakfast until eleven," she said, sounding as bored as a nineteen-year-old in rural Kansas could be. He wondered if he'd gone to school with her parents.

"Actually, I was just hoping I could borrow your phone book."

That perked her up slightly, maybe because it was unexpected. "How come?"

"Looking up an old friend."

She gave the universal gesture for *whatever* and reached under the counter. "Here," she said, plopping down the thin book.

There was only one listing for Cox: Frank and Shirley, on Arapaho Drive. He didn't know exactly where that was, but he remembered the section of town with the streets named for Indian tribes, and he figured he could find it. "Thanks," he said after scribbling the address on a napkin. Soon he'd have a whole collection of napkin contacts.

He didn't go there right away. First he went to his old house, and when he saw what condition it was in, a mixture of emotions churned in his belly. He was surprised to discover that grief was among them.

He drove to the cemetery next. It was not far from the center of town, a large flat space surrounded by a low fence that did nothing to keep teenagers out or spirits in. The last time he'd visited had been during the press of full summer, when cicadas buzzed in the elm trees and sprinklers ticked and whirred in the distance. He'd gone home afterward and eaten a silent dinner with his parents. That night he'd snuck out of the house and jumped from the bridge. But today the trees were leafless, the grass dry and brown beneath a light dusting of snow. Shivering in the bitter cold, his hands deep in his pockets and his chin tucked into his coat collar, he crossed to his brother's grave.

It looked exactly as he remembered. A modest headstone of polished granite read KEVIN P. MOORE, 1968-1982. But the stone next to it, that was new to him. It was larger and showier, and it bore two inscriptions. On the left, BARRETT LIONEL MOORE, and next to him, PATRICIA NICKERSON MOORE. They'd both died in 1998, but several months apart.

Qay howled like a banshee. When that didn't assuage his fury and anguish, he kicked the double headstone again and again until his recently injured foot screamed in pain, and then he collapsed to the frozen ground. He sat there until his ass felt like ice and the rest of him was so cold that he couldn't stop shivering. But he didn't cry.

He was calm as he limped to the rental car.

He drove around for ten minutes or so before finding the address on Arapaho Drive. The entire neighborhood looked drab and worn, although it might be a bit cheerier at night, when the Christmas decorations were lit. He parked in front of the Cox house, took several calming breaths, and walked to the door. Silently hoping the gods hadn't abandoned him yet, he rang the bell.

The lady who answered was tall, even though age had stooped her back somewhat, and her eyes—red-rimmed and puffy—had irises the same clear gray as Jeremy's. She held a cigarette in one hand. "Mrs. Cox?" he asked.

She worked her jaw as she stared at him. And then he thought something in her expression softened just a little bit. "You're Keith Moore."

Not any Moore, he almost said, but she wouldn't have gotten the joke. "Yes, ma'am. Is Jeremy here?"

"No," she said shortly.

Fuck. "But he was?"

She gave him a tight, grudging nod.

"Do you know where he is now?"

"No."

"I've come a very long way, and I really need to see him. Please."

She flicked her ashes onto the porch. "I said I don't know where he is."

"If he comes back, will you tell him I'm here, I'm looking for him?"

"He won't be coming back," she said. A flash of regret might have showed, but he wasn't sure.

Oh, damn. Poor Jeremy. What had these people put him through this time? Qay couldn't quite hold his tongue. "Jeremy Cox is easily the best man I have ever met. He knows everything about plants and animals and parks. He's so strong. He's understanding and forgiving. And he would give everything he owned if it would help someone— even a stranger. It's important that you know that about your son."

He turned toward the street, but she grabbed his coat sleeve. "Wait."

Qay stopped and looked back at her. "Yeah?"

"Tell Jeremy…." Her lip wobbled until she took a drag from her cigarette. "Tell him we love him, and it's not just words. Tell him we hope he finds happiness."

"I will," he answered quietly, and she let him go.

As he got in the car, he knew exactly where he would find Jeremy.

LAST TIME he'd walked to the bridge; now he had to think for a few moments about how to get there by car. When he turned the corner, the first thing he saw was a white sedan that, like the one he was driving, screamed rental. The next thing he saw was a big man in a navy blue parka, leaning against the railing in the center of the bridge with his face buried in his arms. A scarf covered his ears and the wind whistled under the bridge, masking the sound of Qay's approaching footsteps.

Qay stopped a few yards away. He wasn't sure he trusted himself too close to the edge.

"I've a feeling we're not in Oregon anymore," he said.

Jeremy whirled around as soon as Qay started speaking, and then he just stood there, gaping. Well, Qay assumed he was gaping. All he could really see of Jeremy's face was a pair of swollen red eyes.

"Q-Qay?"

Qay heaved a small sigh of relief. At the beginning of the stutter, he'd been sure Jeremy was going to call him Keith.

"Yeah."

Jeremy surged forward like a force of nature and enveloped Qay in his big arms, immediately insulating Qay from the worst of the cold. "I was looking for you," Jeremy said.

"I'm not in that river."

"Not what I meant. God, Qay, how…?"

"Can we maybe have this discussion somewhere else? Somewhere warmer?" And without the painful memories.

"Of course."

They drove back to the highway, each in his own rental car. Jeremy followed Qay as if to make sure he'd be able to give chase if Qay suddenly took off. But Qay had no intention of doing that. They pulled into the motel lot and parked side by side.

Only when they were in Jeremy's dingy little room did Qay notice the big, fluffy sock on Jeremy's left hand. It was green with red trim, and the sight of it made Qay laugh until he began to sob. Jeremy held him until he could talk again.

"I wonder which of us looks more like hell ran us over with a dump truck," Jeremy said as they unpeeled their outerwear.

"Me. Greyhounds. Ten straight hours of driving. Finding out my parents are dead. Bawling my eyes out."

Jeremy reached over to chuck his chin. "Me. Frantic about you. Center seat in the airplane. Continued rejection by my parents. Bawling my eyes out."

"You look damn good to me," Qay said honestly.

So Jeremy kissed him. And holy Lord, it was a good kiss, sweet and salty and passionate. Enough to make Qay's cock hard and his knees weak.

They pulled apart eventually and, panting, looked at each other. "How are you feeling about your parents?" Jeremy asked.

"Mixed. I kicked the fuck out of their gravestone. I'm going to need time to process. But not now. It's not what's most important." He moved forward a bit, and Jeremy bent his head so they could lean their brows together. "How about you?"

"Also mixed. Mostly fuck 'em with a side of angst."

"I went to their house looking for you. Your mom had a message for you."

Jeremy snorted. "I bet."

"Not like that. She said they love you—not just words—and they hope you're happy."

"Huh," Jeremy said, considering that. "I need processing time too. I think my dad's dying. But you're right—that's for later. You're here now."

"I'm here for a good long time—well, not in Bailey Springs for a long time. I mean with you. If you want me."

Jeremy made a tiny choked sound and squeezed his eyes shut. "More than anything in the world."

The second kiss was longer and deeper. Qay grabbed Jeremy's ass and held on for dear life, and Jeremy threaded the fingers of his good hand through Qay's hair, tugging just enough to feel like an anchor.

"Wh-what made you decide to come to me?" Jeremy asked after the kiss ended. His lips were delectable—chapped from the cold, slightly swollen, and as delicious as candy.

"Epiphanies and good advice from a stranger. The thing is, I don't want Captain Caffeine. I need to be my own savior."

Jeremy sighed against him. "No plucking you from the hands of the evil arch villain?"

"You're the one who got himself kidnapped, not me," Qay replied, turning his head to nuzzle Jeremy's jawline.

"Ryan Davis was hardly an arch villain. He was just a moron without a conscience."

"Okay. But here's where I *do* need you." Qay shifted a bit to look seriously into Jeremy's eyes. "When I tie myself to the railroad tracks, help me pick those knots free."

"Railroad. Tracks. I see what you've done there." Jeremy rubbed the inside of Qay's left elbow, where his long-sleeved shirt hid the old scars. "And I can do that. You need to know that I love you exactly as you are. Even if you fuck up. Because damn, we all do that."

Qay pulled him close again and rested his head on Jeremy's shoulder. "So we're going to lay Captain Caffeine to rest for good, right?"

"Sure. He's ready for a nice retirement."

"But that little kid, the one everyone picked on? He can come out anytime. He has a good friend now."

The third kiss was the charm. It magically got them out of their clothes and into the bed, and although Qay would have sworn he had no energy left at all, that kiss jump-started him— jump-started *everything*— and he and Jeremy spent the rest of the day making love. And when they fell asleep in each other's arms, it didn't matter whether they were in a Marriott by the river or in a shabby motel with views of the sheep ranch across the highway. It didn't matter if they were in Portland, Oregon, or Bailey Springs, Kansas. They were home.

EPILOGUE

QAY STOOD fidgeting in the middle of the living room, his backpack slung over his shoulder. Despite the late summer heat, he wore a long-sleeved shirt in a shade of green that brought out the color of his eyes. His new jeans were more formfitting than he usually wore. They showed off his long, lean legs.

"Are you sure you don't want a ride?" Jeremy asked. "I'm heading downtown anyway. Meeting with the prosecutor." The DA was considering a plea deal for Davis's minions and, out of courtesy, wanted to discuss it with Jeremy first.

"No, thanks. The bus ride will take longer. I need the time to get my courage up."

"You look great." Jeremy threw in a leer for good measure.

"I feel like a kindergartner on the first day of school. Do you think we'll get cookies at snack time?"

"Sure. The frosted animal ones with sprinkles." Jeremy set his coffee mug on the counter and moved closer to Qay. Although Qay shifted from foot to foot, his color was good and his breathing even. This was simple nervousness, which was understandable when starting at a university. Still, a little boost wouldn't hurt. "Do you want a stabilization hug?"

Qay's smile was a beautiful thing, bringing light to his eyes and making him look years younger. "I'll take a hug from you anytime."

Jeremy embraced him around the backpack, inhaling the scent that had become his own addiction these past nine months: coffee, sugar, the almond soap and woodsy shampoo they both liked, and Qay himself. Intoxicating. Then Jeremy nuzzled Qay's ear. "You blew them away with your scores on all those tests they made you take. You're going to do fine."

When they returned from Kansas in December, Qay had e-mailed Professor Reynolds to apologize for skipping out on class. He hadn't expected Reynolds to do anything about it, but he'd enjoyed the course and wanted the prof to know that. Reynolds had ended up offering to let

Qay make up the work he'd missed. And then not only did he tell Qay he'd earned an A, but he also followed through with his pals at Portland State. Qay got a scholarship and a waiver for several classes, which meant with full-time enrollment and summer courses, he could earn his BA within two more years.

Qay melted slightly against Jeremy. "What if I just stay home and have sex with you instead?"

"Tempting, but I have a meeting, remember? We can wait until tonight and make it first-day-of-school celebratory sex."

Jeremy felt Qay's sigh. "All right. I guess I can be a grown-up about this."

"How about if I promise you a blowjob so spectacular you forget your own name? Will *that* give you incentive to get your ass to school?"

"No. That'll make me miserably hard in these damn jeans. Thanks, Jer." Qay leaned into the embrace a moment longer before pulling away. "Okay. Give me a hike."

This had been Qay's psychiatrist's idea. On mornings that threatened to be stressful, Jeremy reminded him of one of their excursions. Whenever Qay felt panic creeping up on him, he took a few calming breaths and thought about that memory. The exercise didn't dispel all his anxiety, but it helped a lot.

"Hmm," Jeremy said. "How about Cascade Head? Remember that view from the top?"

Qay grinned. "And the rain that started falling when we were only halfway back?"

"It was the Oregon coast in May. What do you expect?"

"That's a good one. Thanks." But he didn't move from his spot in the center of the room, and he had resumed fidgeting.

Jeremy gave him time to get the words out. While he waited, Jeremy looked at the many photos on the walls. Magazine pictures, yes, but also snapshots Qay had taken when he visited Jeremy's parks, or while they were on hikes, or sometimes just when they were sitting at P-Town. Jeremy liked them all, but his favorites were the selfies of the two of them together. Qay said someday when he had an income too, he'd buy some real art to hang in their condo, but Jeremy rather hoped he'd change his mind. The friendly, bright chaos of Qay's collection was better. Jeremy also liked the oversized shelves he'd installed and that

Qay immediately began to fill with books and tchotchkes. All the clutter made their place truly feel like home.

Qay shifted his backpack slightly. "Will you still be downtown at lunch?"

"I can be," Jeremy replied happily. "Perry's? And then you'll hit the gym with me tonight?"

"I'm never going to be buff like you."

"Good. Two of me wouldn't fit on the bed."

"Good point."

Qay reached out and yanked Jeremy close by a belt loop. "I have to cross a bridge to get to school today, you know?"

"Either that or swim."

"So I'm crossing that bridge when I come to it. And... that time I jumped, I thought that was the only freedom I'd ever have." He looked down for a moment, then back up, a hint of a smile curving his lips. "I was so wrong."

Jeremy nodded. He'd always thought he could only be strong if he ran around rescuing others. He'd been wrong about that. "Love and learn," he said.

Qay's laughter was even better than his smile. Then he cradled Jeremy's cheeks in his hands. "You can't conquer everything with love. But it sure makes a hell of an ally." He pressed his lips to Jeremy's, softly at first, then with more urgency, and Jeremy moaned as Qay's tongue swept his mouth. For good measure, Qay moved a hand to Jeremy's crotch and squeezed gently. "Good," Qay said with a chuckle when he broke the kiss. "Now you can be uncomfortable all day too."

He walked to the door confidently, not looking back. And Jeremy smiled as he watched him go.

KIM FIELDING is very pleased every time someone calls her eclectic. Her books have won Rainbow Awards and span a variety of genres. She has migrated back and forth across the western two-thirds of the United States and currently lives in California, where she long ago ran out of bookshelf space. She's a university professor who dreams of being able to travel and write full time. She also dreams of having two perfectly behaved children, a husband who isn't obsessed with football, and a house that cleans itself. Some dreams are more easily obtained than others.

Blogs: kfieldingwrites.com and
www.goodreads.com/author/show/4105707.Kim_Fielding/blog
Facebook: www.facebook.com/KFieldingWrites
E-mail: kim@kfieldingwrites.com Twitter: @KFieldingWrites

Carter Evans is founder and editor-in-chief of *Astounding!*—a formerly popular spec fiction magazine currently in its death throes. Not only can he do nothing to save it, but stuck in a rathole apartment with few interpersonal connections, he can't seem to do much to rescue his future either. And certainly all the booze isn't helping. He snaps when he receives yet another terrible story submission from the mysterious writer J. Harper—and in a drunken haze, Carter sends Harper a rejection letter he soon regrets.

J. Harper turns out to be John Harper, a sweet man who resembles a '50s movie star and claims to be an extraterrestrial. Despite John's delusions, Carter's apology quickly turns into something more as the two lonely men find a powerful connection. Inexplicably drawn to John, Carter invites him along on a road trip. But as they travel, Carter is in for some big surprises, some major heartbreak… and just maybe the promise of a good future after all.

www.dreamspinnerpress.com

MOTEL.

POOL.

KIM FIELDING

In the mid-1950s, Jack Dayton flees his working-class prospects in Omaha and heads to Hollywood, convinced he'll be the next James Dean. But sleazy casting couches don't earn him stardom, and despair leads to a series of poor decisions that ultimately find him at a cheap motel off Route 66, lifeless at the bottom of the pool.

Sixty years later, Tag Manning, feeling hopeless and empty, flees his most recent relationship mistake and takes to the open road. On a roundabout route to Las Vegas, he pulls over to rest at an isolated spot on Route 66. There's no longer a motel or pool, but when Tag resumes his journey to Vegas, he finds he's transporting a hitchhiking ghost. Jack and Tag come to find much-needed friends in each other, but one man is a phantom and the other is strangely cursed. Time is running out for each of them, and they must face the fact that a future together may not only be a gamble... it may not be in the cards.

www.dreamspinnerpress.com

Fiscal analyst Mike Carlson is good with spreadsheets and baseball stats. He doesn't believe in fate, true love, or fantasy. But then a fertility goddess whisks him away to another world. A promise has been broken, and if Mike is ever to return to California—and his comfortable if lonely life—he must complete a pilgrimage to the shrines of a death goddess.

A humiliating event convinces Mike to hire a guard to accompany him, and hunky Goran is handy enough with a sword, if a little too liberal with his ale. A man with no home and no family, Goran is deeper than he first appears. As Mike learns more about Goran, his disbelief wavers and his goals become less clear. Contending with feuding gods, the challenges of the journey, and his growing attraction to Goran, Mike faces a puzzle far harder to solve than simple rows of numbers.

www.dreamspinnerpress.com

RATTLESNAKE

KIM FIELDING

A drifter since his teens, Jimmy Dorsett has no home and no hope. What he does have is a duffel bag, a lot of stories, and a junker car. Then one cold desert night he picks up a hitchhiker and ends up with something more: a letter from a dying man to the son he hasn't seen in years.

On a quest to deliver the letter, Jimmy travels to Rattlesnake, a small town nestled in the foothills of the California Sierras. The centerpiece of the town is the Rattlesnake Inn, where the bartender is handsome former cowboy Shane Little. Sparks fly, and when Jimmy's car gives up the ghost, Shane gets him a job as handyman at the inn.

Both within the community of Rattlesnake and in Shane's arms, Jimmy finds an unaccustomed peace. But it can't be a lasting thing. The open road continues to call, and surely Shane—a strong, proud man with a painful past and a difficult present—deserves better than a lying vagabond who can't stay put for long.

www.dreamspinnerpress.com

CPSIA information can be obtained
at www.ICGtesting.com
Printed in the USA
LVHW03s1813151018
593654LV00012B/1086/P